A MYSTERY READER

STORIES OF DETECTION, ADVENTURE, AND HORROR

A MYSTERY READER

Stories of Detection, Adventure, and Horror

edited by

NANCY ELLEN TALBURT
LYNA LEE MONTGOMERY

University of Arkansas

CHARLES SCRIBNER'S SONS   NEW YORK

ACKNOWLEDGMENTS

W. H. AUDEN, "The Guilty Vicarage," from *The Dyer's Hand* by W. H. Auden. Copyright 1948 by W. H. Auden. Reprinted by permission of Random House, Inc.

ANTHONY BERKELEY, "The Avenging Chance." © The Society of Authors 1974. Reprinted by permission of The Society of Authors.

ROBERT BLOCH, "The Cheaters." Copyright 1947 by Weird Tales. Reprinted by permission of the author and the author's agents, Scott Meredith Literary Agency, Inc., 580 Fifth Avenue, New York, New York 10036.

ELIZABETH BOWEN, "The Demon Lover," from *Ivy Gripped the Steps and Other Stories* by Elizabeth Bowen. Copyright 1946 and renewed 1974 by Elizabeth Bowen. Reprinted by permission of Alfred A. Knopf, Inc. Published in Great Britain in *The Demon Lover*. Reprinted by permission of Jonathan Cape Ltd. and the Estate of Elizabeth Bowen.

THOMAS BURKE, "The Hands of Mr. Ottermole." Copyright by Thomas Burke. Reprinted by permission of Paul R. Reynolds, Inc., 12 East 41 Street, New York, New York 10017.

JOHN DICKSON CARR, "The Gentleman from Paris," from *The Third Bullet* by John Dickson Carr. Copyright 1950 by John Dickson Carr. Reprinted by permission of Harper & Row, Publishers, Inc.

RAYMOND CHANDLER, "I'll Be Waiting" and "The Simple Art of Murder," from *The Simple Art of Murder*. Copyright 1950 by Raymond Chandler. Reprinted by permission of the publisher, Houghton Mifflin Company.

AGATHA CHRISTIE, "Sanctuary," from *Double Sin and Other Stories* by Agatha Christie. Copyright © 1954 by Agatha Christie. Copyright © 1961 by Christie Copyrights Trust. Reprinted by permission of Dodd, Mead & Company, Inc. and Hughes Massie Limited.

EDMUND CRISPIN, "The Crime by the River." Copyright © 1955 by Mercury Publications. Reprinted by permission of Collins-Knowlton-Wing, Inc.

CARTER DICKSON, "Persons or Things Unknown," from *The Department of Queer Complaints* by Carter Dickson, Copyright 1940 by William Morrow & Company, Inc. Renewed 1968 by John Dickson Carr. Reprinted by permission of William Morrow & Company, Inc.

ARTHUR CONAN DOYLE, "The Speckled Band." Reprinted by permission of John Murray (Publishers) Ltd. and Baskervilles Investments Ltd.

LORD DUNSANY (Edward John Moreton Drax Plunkett), "Two Bottles of Relish." First published in Story magazine. Reprinted by permission of Hallie Burnett.

IAN FLEMING, "Risico," from *For Your Eyes Only* by Ian Fleming. Copyright © 1960 by Glidrose Productions Limited. Reprinted by permission of The Viking Press, Inc. and Jonathan Cape Ltd.

DASHIELL HAMMETT, "The Gutting of Couffignal." Copyright 1925 by Pro-Distributors Publishing Company. Renewed 1953 by Popular Publications Inc. Reprinted by permission of The Harold Matson Company, Inc.

ROSS MACDONALD, "Guilt-Edged Blonde." Copyright 1954 by Kenneth Millar. "The Writer as Detective Hero." Copyright © 1964 by Show Magazine, Hartford Publications, Inc. Reprinted by permission of Harold Ober Associates Incorporated.

FRANK D. McSHERRY, JR., "The Shape of Crimes to Come," from *The Mystery Writer's Art*, edited by Francis M. Nevins, Jr., Bowling Green State University Popular Press, 1970. Reprinted by permission of Frank D. McSherry, Jr.

ELLERY QUEEN, "A Lump of Sugar." Copyright, 1950, 1954 by Ellery Queen. Reprinted by permission of the author and the author's agents,

Scott Meredith Literary Agency, Inc., 580 Fifth Avenue, New York, New York 10036.

DOROTHY L. SAYERS, "The Learned Adventure of the Dragon's Head," from *Lord Peter* by Dorothy L. Sayers. Copyright © 1972 by Harper & Row, Publishers, Inc. Reprinted by permission of the publishers, Harper & Row, Publishers, Inc. and Victor Gollancz Ltd.

GEORGES SIMENON, "Journey Backward into Time." Copyright 1944 by Georges Simenon. First published in the United States in Ellery Queen's Mystery Magazine, 1956; translated by Lawrence G. Blochman. Reprinted by permission of the author.

REX STOUT, "Watson Was a Woman." Copyright 1939 by Rex Stout. Copyright renewed © 1967. Reprinted by permission of the author.

T. S. STRIBLING, "A Passage to Benares," from *Clues of the Caribbees*. Copyright 1929 by Doubleday. Copyright renewed © 1958 by T. S. Stribling. Reprinted by permission of Curtis Brown Ltd.

Contents

APPENDIX

Introduction

This anthology brings together under the general classification of "mystery fiction" a number of works that have quite different characteristics. Three types of mystery fiction are included: the detective story, the adventure story, and the horror story.

The majority of selections are examples of the detective story, the most clearly defined and most frequently read of the three types. The outstanding feature of this kind of story is the character of the detective himself. He is usually a strong, memorable figure at the very center of the story. The detective heroes in this collection range in vintage all the way from Edgar Allan Poe's nineteenth-century Auguste Dupin (no longer alive and well in Paris except in the fine imitation Dupin stories still being written by Michael Harrison) to Georges Simenon's Inspector Maigret (still alive and well in Paris); and in personality and social status from Dorothy Sayers' Lord Peter Wimsey—urbane, sophisticated, cultivated, at ease in the smartest and most elegant drawing rooms in London—to Dashiell Hammett's Continental Op—tough and competent in a corrupt world (though not himself corrupt) and having a touch of self-deprecating humor.

Every literary detective is faced with a problem that has baffled other men but that he solves by keen observation, brilliant logical reasoning often accompanied by a flash of dazzling insight, and firm, decisive action. In presenting a heroic figure faced with a seemingly insoluble problem, the detective story is similar to the medieval romance or the fairy tale, in which a strong and resourceful hero is given an apparently impossible task and overcomes great obstacles, often at serious personal risk, in accomplishing it. The most common task of the detective is to discover the identity of a criminal, often by uncovering a hidden motive, or to find a missing object.

Another important feature of the detective story is the planned involvement of the reader in the solution of the problem. At some point in the story, given all (and only) the evidence and information that the detective has, the reader has the same opportunity as the detective to arrive at a solution. Actually, the detective story is written backward in the sense that the motive or cause which initiates the chain of events making up the plot is the last thing to be discovered or revealed. By rereading a well-written detective story, the reader can observe the careful integration of its parts in keeping with underlying relationships that are hidden until the end of the story.

Two separate categories of detective story may be distinguished: the classic and the hardboiled. The classic detective story follows the example set by Poe and Arthur Conan Doyle, abstracting from the early stories of these writers "rules" and conventions that are consciously incorporated into new stories. The hardboiled detective story breaks some of the rules and uses some different conventions, as well as some of the older ones, in order to achieve what is felt, especially by American audiences, to be a more realistic presentation of the facts of crime and sex. Such stories are written in a more informal style, and their detectives occupy a less comfortable place in society and employ different proportions of logic and action than the heroes of classic stories.

The adventure story is the second type of mystery story represented in this collection. As in the detective story, there is a strong hero. But although this hero, like the detective, has a sharp, analytical, and well-trained mind, the reader is likely to be more interested in his actions than in his mental processes. Seldom is the adventure story hero required to perform great feats of reasoning. His main function is to overcome physical obstacles placed in the path of his mission. In the spy adventure story it is usually the spy himself, not a helpless innocent or a beleaguered lady, who is in danger, and often there is a real question of whether he will get out with his life (on occasion he does not, as in John Le Carré's *The Spy Who Came in from the Cold*). Whereas the detective story is usually confined to a small geographic area with interest often focusing on one room, the scene in an adventure story may shift repeatedly as the adventurer travels around the world. And the physical activities of the adventurer are repeated and strenuous. Even the hardboiled detective as a rule fires fewer bullets and engages in fewer chases. Frustrating the intentions of worldwide conspiracies is frequently the adventurer's aim, and he is often supported in his work by a large organization. The detective's adversary, in contrast, is usually a single individual. But like the world of the hardboiled detective, the world of the adventurer is filled with violence and intrigue and temptations and snares. The adventurer may be offered great wealth or relationships with beautiful women, but he would usually have to give up his quest or sell out his friends to accept them.

The horror story is the third type of mystery fiction included in this collection. More often than not, the main character in a horror story is an average man, whose horror, terror, and revulsion the reader can imagine himself feeling. In fact, in the story he represents the reader himself, not a heroic or god-like figure with superior powers. The aim of such a story is to provide an emotional, rather than an intellectual, experience for the reader. The focus, therefore, is on an experience, not on a problem, and the puzzling aspect is the nature of the experience, not the relationship of events. Rather than the known or real world, an unknown world—containing the bizarre, the macabre, the supernatural—may be the setting of the horror story. This kind of story may push the reader to the utmost limits of his capacity for enduring terror. It is almost as if the author were saying to him, "How much can you stand?" Robert Bloch (whose short story "The Cheaters" appears in this collection) wrote such a story in *Psycho*, which, in its film version, frequently caused even the most stout-hearted moviegoers to look away. Curiously enough, such stories may provide a psychological release which is both needed and satisfying. Perhaps in experiencing imaginatively the outermost boundaries of fear, the reader is, at least momentarily, freeing himself from "real" fear.

What we have said above about detective, adventure, and horror stories suggests that every story in this collection can be neatly classified as one of these three types. As a matter of fact, some of the stories combine elements of two of the types. "Two

Bottles of Relish," for example, is a story in which elements of horror and detection are combined, and "I'll Be Waiting" is really an adventure story despite the fact that the hero is a detective. But whether they are detective, adventure, or horror stories, or some combination of these types, all mystery stories share certain basic and significant features: They are concerned with evil in its various manifestations; they are designed to offer colorful and intrinsically interesting subject matter, which is sensational in nature and effect; and they are constructed to involve the reader through suspense and surprise.

Evil is man's oldest problem (it was, after all, the tree of the knowledge of good and evil that was expressly forbidden to the first man in the Garden of Eden); and in its concern with evil, mystery fiction explores a persistent theme in literature. As Ross Macdonald, one of the most talented of the contemporary mystery writers, has put it, "a certain aura of evil hangs around the form." Mystery fiction assumes that some men have an almost infinite capacity for wrongdoing. A character in "The Speckled Band" refers to "the manifold wickedness of the human heart"; in "The Cheaters" even a glimpse of the evil within proves to be more than the mind can endure; and in "The Demon Lover" the suggestion is clearly that evil in this life persists in the afterlife. In the detective story, and often in the adventure story as well, there is a corollary to the insistence upon the real existence of evil. This is the assumption that man has free will and that he possesses the power to make choices and in fact inevitably *must* make choices that determine whether he is essentially good or bad. If the assumption were, on the other hand, that what man is and does are determined by forces beyond his control, then the reader could no more admire the wisdom and courage of the detective or the adventurer than he could condemn the villainy of the criminal. (In some detective and adventure stories, of course, there is a fatalistic tone, and neither side is better than the other.) Similarly, in horror stories the operation of free will can be important. An individual who freely chooses to perform a selfish and destructive act may produce horror for someone else or even, on occasion, for himself.

Evil acts, sometimes by human and sometimes by demonic beings, may produce disorder and even chaos in the fictional world. In Macdonald's novel *The Underground Man*, for example, the detective Lew Archer observes, "The world was changing, as if with one piece missing the whole thing had come loose and was running wild." It is the job of the hero in detective and adventure fiction to find and put back the "one piece missing." In certain horror stories, on the other hand, the original order cannot be restored. At the heart of such stories lies the terrible revelation that evil has produced a basic and irreversible disorder.

Although evil is somewhat differently expressed in the various types of mystery stories, a theme that deals with evil will normally find its expression in a framework of events that are extraordinary and even bizarre. There must be intrinsically interesting subject matter producing maximum effect on the reader. Julian Symons wrote that "Poe's paternity of the detective story is not in dispute, but his fatherhood was unintended. He thought that his mistress was Art, but really she was Sensation." One meaning of "sensation" is "a state of heightened interest or emotion," and clearly it is this state that not only detective fiction but all types of mystery fiction try to produce and sustain in the reader. All of the works in this collection are, in that sense, "sensational." In some of them (notably "The Demon Lover" and "A Passage to Benares") the heightened state results from wonder about the supernatural world, and the pleasure derives from the mystery of questions left unanswered. In many others the heightened state comes from interest in watching an ingenious mind at work, and the pleasure results from the satisfaction of seeing apparently unanswerable questions answered. Literature that is sensational in subject matter and treatment allows the reader to participate vicariously in experiences that he may never encounter in real life; part of the appeal of mystery fiction derives from this participation.

Finally, in addition to an insistence upon the reality of evil and an employment of striking subject matter for sensational effect, all mystery stories are designed to produce suspense by arousing the reader's curiosity and to offer surprising revelations which more than satisfy that curiosity. Mystery fiction raises in the mind of the reader a question central to the outcome of the story. Most often the question is *who* or *how;* occasionally, *where;* and, very rarely, *why?* Sometimes the tone of the story indicates that a certain outcome is inevitable, and then the suspense resides in the reader's fearful anticipation of *when*. The good mystery writer piques the reader's curiosity and sustains it at a high level, balancing suspense with hints concerning the outcome. The hints may be cryptic remarks or things described but not explained. Suspense is likely to be increased if the outcome will affect a character for whom the reader feels affection or sympathy. However, suspense cannot be indefinitely sustained; the reader's curiosity, once aroused, must be satisfied. Generally, in a story of any significant length, suspense is dissipated somewhat by partial revelations and then made to grow again until the climax of the story. It is necessary to insure that the final answer or resolution of the reader's curiosity is equal to the expectations the suspense has aroused—in short, that the reader is satisfied by a resolution that surprises and even astounds him. In every kind of mystery fiction, the reader is surprised because he has been led, along with other characters in the story, into making a wrong assumption. In detective fiction, one of the characters (sometimes, temporarily, the detective himself) may be delayed in finding the right solution to a problem because he has drawn a too-hasty conclusion that leads him to overlook one of the meanings of a word or implications of a situation. This occurs in "The Speckled Band," for example, when Sherlock Holmes assigns the wrong meaning to the word "band." The possibilities for surprise in mystery fiction are almost endlessly varied. In "The Demon Lover" and "The Cheaters," the shock and surprise arise, in the one, when the reader realizes that he has made wrong assumptions concerning the habitat of ghosts and, in the other, when he is forced to question the commonly accepted truism that truth and knowledge, especially self-knowledge, are always desirable goals.

A focus on evil, an emphasis on the sensational, and a creation of suspense and surprise, then, are the hallmarks of mystery fiction and account for much of its appeal. The stories in this collection also offer additional features: provocative themes; engaging, deftly delineated characters; and language memorable for its terseness and economy, its wry and subtle humor, its polished wit, and its apt and vivid figures of speech. These and other aspects of the good mystery writer's art explain why mystery fiction is "the normal recreation of noble minds."

This anthology is divided into two sections, and the arrangement of selections is roughly chronological. Part 1, "The Golden Age of Mystery Fiction," focuses on the classic or traditional mystery story; Part 2, "New Developments: The Hardboiled School and After," focuses on later developments, such as the hardboiled detective story and the mystery adventure story. Among the selections in Part 1 are works by Poe and Doyle, which, with a more recent story by John Dickson Carr, constitute an introduction to the various conventions and practices of the traditional detective story. Besides some additional classic stories, this section contains various other kinds of mysteries: "A Passage to Benares" explores supernatural mysticism, and "The Dragon's Head" combines comedy and treasure-hunting with mystery adventure. In several stories crimes are prevented instead of being solved after the fact. There are two essays in the first part: a humorous "interpretation" of the Sherlock Holmes stories and a study of the classic detective story by a noted poet, W. H. Auden. The last story in this section offers the reader a special "test" in crime solution, with the author's solution provided at the end of the book.

Part 2 contains stories by Dashiell Hammett, Raymond Chandler, and Ross Macdonald; excerpts from an essay by Chandler; and an essay by Macdonald. These, together with the prefaces and comments, provide both illustration and general analysis of the practices of writers in the American hardboiled tradition. In addition, there are examples of other types of mystery fiction: a spy adventure story featuring James Bond ("Risico"); two horror stories with quite different uses of the supernatural ("The Demon Lover" and "The Cheaters"); a police detective story ("Journey Backward into Time"); a traditional adventure story depicting women as investigator and associate ("Sanctuary"); and a historical adventure story posed as a problem in classic deduction ("Persons or Things Unknown"). As in Part 1, the final story, this time by an American writer, Ellery Queen, is a "test" for the reader.

Introductory remarks before each part acquaint the reader with the most distinctive features of the works predominating in that section: Part 1 is prefaced by a discussion of the "rules" of the traditional detective story; Part 2 is introduced by an analysis of the main characteristics of hardboiled fiction and a comparison of that form to the classic story. Introductions to each story or essay provide background information, focus the reader's attention upon significant details, or clarify the intention of the author. Comment and questions at the end of each story draw attention to techniques and design and point out other aspects of the writer's art that a reader might overlook on a first reading. Some of the questions are suitable for development in essays or class discussions. Comments of a more general nature on favorite practices in mystery fiction appear after the stories in which such practices occur. The following appendices will help the reader to locate related materials: (1) a roster of other famous detectives of fiction (most of whom appear in inexpensive and readily available paperback novels), with titles of recommended works; (2) a short list of mystery novels of other kinds; and (3) a brief bibliography of works about detective fiction.

We are grateful to the trustees of the British Museum for permission to use its rich holdings, and to Allen J. Hubin, editor of *The Armchair Detective*, and Jason Rouby, who generously made available to us hard-to-find materials from their own libraries.

Among our colleagues at the University of Arkansas, we wish to thank Ben Kimpel and Larry Guinn, who assisted with translation; Linda Stafstrom, who helped us in our research; Marty Steele, whose knowledgeability about mystery fiction led us to some good stories; and Claude Faulkner, who helped and supported us at every stage of our work.

Favors and kindnesses have been numerous, not a few of which came from the other side of the Atlantic—from the London cabbies who helped us to find out-of-the-way bookshops; the proprietors of those shops, who permitted us to range freely, often by candlelight, among their (sometimes as yet unsorted) collections; and various English friends of mystery fiction who encouraged us by their interest in this book and cheered us with warm and gracious hospitality.

We have been especially fortunate in our editor, Edward J. Cutler, whose congeniality and competence have made our work a pleasure.

1

The Golden Age of Mystery Fiction

Most of the stories in Part 1 are classic detective stories, and all of them illustrate at least some of the techniques of the classic form, which reached its "Golden Age" in the 1920s. By this time many writers whose works were patterned on the example of Poe and Doyle had come to think of their fiction as a highly specialized art form having "rules" and conventions that the serious practitioner would conscientiously follow. If detective fiction was to provide recreation for a reader desiring to match wits with the detective (actually, the author), then reader and author needed to be in agreement about the rules of the game in which both participated. The tradition of "fair play" for the reader resulted in various sets of rules drawn up by detective story authors. At least two writers published complete lists of rules, and many others discussed their favorite rules in more general essays. Among those which were most generally agreed upon and most often followed (although any experienced reader can cite at least one classic story that consciously violates one of these rules) were the following:

1. The story must contain no supernatural happenings and nothing that could not be explained by rational means.

2. The criminal must be a reasonably prominent figure in the work, not a minor figure or one introduced only in the last pages.

3. The criminal must have a personal motive, one intelligible to the reader; he must not kill out of pure malice or psychosis or kill someone chosen at random. Neither can he be a professional killer nor a member of a secret society sworn to overthrow the government or some other group.

4. The crime must not result from accident, nor may the death be a suicide. The lethal agent must actually exist (it cannot be, for example, a nonexistent poison), and it must be one that could really operate as it is supposed to.

5. The reader must share in the detective's discoveries, either "seeing" evidence as it is discovered or being told of its significance as soon as that is established. A popular method of allowing the reader to participate fully is to give the detective a friend and associate who accompanies him and later writes an account of the happenings. The friend sees the evidence but does not share all of the detective's inferences, deductions, and hypotheses.

6. The detective must solve the crime by logical, rational means, using the clues provided in the story. He may make imaginative inferences from limited data, but he must not solve a case entirely by good fortune or intuition. The detective may *call* his knowledge of human psychology "intuition," but the reader sees it to be in fact an analysis of behavior patterns and other psychological evidence.

Some other rules advocated by certain writers but frequently broken by others are:

1. There must be no love interest.

2. The narrator and associate of the detective must conceal none of his thoughts from the audience.

3. Doubles, trap doors, and secret passages must be used rarely, if at all.

4. The crime must be that of murder. (This rule would "rule" out half of the Sherlock Holmes stories.)

5. There must be no undue amount of time and space devoted to characterization or to the exploration of fascinating new places or areas of knowledge.

6. The solution to the crime must not depend upon the detective's (and the reader's) possession of a bit of highly technical or obscure information.

In addition to abiding by many of the rules listed here, classic detective stories commonly share these other features: a clearly superior and almost infallible detective; a closed circle or small group of participants and suspects; a humor consisting mainly of ironic understatements by the detective; and literary or "polite" language that avoids vulgar, shocking, or indecent expressions.

EDGAR ALLAN POE

The Purloined Letter

Edgar Allan Poe originated the detective story, left a lasting mark on other mystery fiction with such works as "Ligeia," "The Gold Bug," and "Thou Art the Man," and was instrumental in defining the short story as a distinct literary form. Poe wrote only three stories about Dupin (the first literary detective), and he called them "stories of ratiocination." Yet these three stories contain all the significant and special characteristics that have come to be associated with detective fiction. "The Purloined Letter" is the last Dupin story, and Poe may have felt that with it he had fully presented Dupin and effectively illustrated the potential of his analytical methods.

No other author immediately wrote fiction patterned on Poe's, but there was one admirer who expressed an intention to reread the Dupin stories every year—Abraham Lincoln. And within a hundred years the influence of Poe and his followers was such that one out of every four new works of fiction would be a detective story.

As you read, pay particular attention to Dupin's methods and the reasons for his success. Notice that his main interest is in the mental operations that are required when a man must figure out not a simple puzzle, but the actual workings of his adversary's mind.

Nil sapientiæ odiosius acumine nimio.[1]—*Seneca.*

At Paris, just after dark one gusty evening in the autumn of 18—, I was enjoying the twofold luxury of meditation and a meerschaum, in company with my friend, C. Auguste Dupin, in his little back library, or bookcloset, *au troisième*,[2] No. 33 *Rue Dunôt, Faubourg St. Germain*. For one hour at least we had maintained a profound silence; while each, to any casual observer, might have seemed intently and exclusively occupied with the curling eddies of smoke that oppressed the atmosphere of the chamber. For myself, however, I was mentally discussing certain topics which had formed matter for conversation between us at an earlier period of the evening; I mean the affair of the Rue Morgue, and the mystery attending the murder of Marie Rogêt. I looked upon it, therefore, as something of a coincidence, when the door of our apartment was thrown open and admitted our old acquaintance, Monsieur G——, the Prefect[3] of the Parisian police.

We gave him a hearty welcome; for there was nearly half as much of the entertaining as of the contemptible about the man, and we had not seen him for several years. We had been sitting in the dark, and Dupin now arose for the purpose of lighting a lamp, but sat down again, without doing so, upon G.'s saying that he had called to consult us, or rather to ask the opinion of my friend, about some official business which had occasioned a great deal of trouble.

"If it is any point requiring reflection," observed Dupin, as he forebore to enkindle the wick, "we shall examine it to better purpose in the dark."

"That is another of your odd notions," said the Prefect, who had the fashion of calling every thing "odd" that was beyond his comprehension, and thus lived amid an absolute legion of "oddities."

"Very true," said Dupin, as he supplied his visitor with a pipe, and rolled toward him a comfortable chair.

"And what is the difficulty now?" I asked. "Nothing more in the assassination way, I hope."

"Oh, no; nothing of that nature. The fact is, the business is *very* simple indeed, and I make no doubt that we can manage it sufficiently well ourselves; but then I thought Dupin would like to hear the details of it, because it is so excessively *odd*."

"Simple and odd," said Dupin.

"Why, yes; and not exactly that either. The fact is, we have all been a good deal puzzled because the affair *is* so simple, and yet baffles us altogether."

"Perhaps it is the very simplicity of the thing which puts you at fault," said my friend.

"What nonsense you *do* talk!" replied the Prefect, laughing heartily.

"Perhaps the mystery is a little *too* plain," said Dupin.

"Oh, good heavens! who ever heard of such an idea?"

"A little *too* self-evident."

"Ha! ha! ha!—ha! ha! ha!—ho! ho! ho!" roared our visitor, profoundly amused, "oh, Dupin, you will be the death of me yet!"

"And what, after all, *is* the matter on hand?" I asked.

"Why, I will tell you," replied the Prefect, as he gave a long, steady, and contemplative puff, and settled himself in his chair. "I will tell you in a few words; but, before I begin, let me caution you that this is an affair demanding the greatest secrecy, and that I should most probably lose the position I now hold, were it known that I confided it to any one."

"Proceed," said I.

"Or not," said Dupin.

"Well, then; I have received personal information, from a very high quarter, that a certain document of the last importance has been purloined from the royal apartments. The individual who purloined it is known; this beyond a doubt; he was seen to take it. It is known, also, that it still remains in his possession."

"How is this known?" asked Dupin.

"It is clearly inferred," replied the Prefect, "from the nature of the document, and from the non-appearance of certain results which would at once arise from its passing *out* of the robber's possession—that is to say, from his employing it as he must design in the end to employ it."

"Be a little more explicit," I said.

"Well, I may venture so far as to say that the paper gives its holder a certain power in a certain quarter where such power is immensely valuable." The Prefect was fond of the cant of diplomacy.

"Still I do not quite understand," said Dupin.

"No? Well; the disclosure of the document to a third person, who shall be nameless, would bring in question the honor of a personage of most exalted station; and this fact gives the holder of the document an ascendancy over the illustrious personage whose honor and peace are so jeopardized."

"But this ascendancy," I interposed, "would depend upon the robber's knowledge of the loser's knowledge of the robber. Who would dare—"

"The thief," said G., "is the Minister D——, who dares all things, those unbecoming as well as those becoming a man. The method of the theft was not less ingenious than bold. The document in question—a letter, to be frank—had been received by the personage robbed while alone in the royal *boudoir*. During its perusal she was suddenly interrupted by the entrance of the other exalted personage from whom especially it was her wish to conceal it. After a hurried and vain endeavor to thrust it in a drawer, she was forced to place it, open as it was, upon a table. The address, however, was uppermost, and, the contents thus unexposed, the letter escaped notice. At this juncture enters the Minister D——. His lynx eye immediately perceives the paper, recognizes the handwriting of the address, observes the confusion of the personage addressed, and fathoms her secret. After some business transactions, hurried through in his ordinary manner, he produces a letter somewhat similar to the one in question, opens it, pretends to read it, and then places it in close juxtaposition to the other. Again he converses, for some fifteen minutes, upon the public affairs. At length, in taking leave, he takes also from the table the letter to which he had no claim. Its rightful owner saw, but of course, dared not call attention to the act, in the presence of the third personage who stood at her elbow. The minister decamped; leaving his own letter—one of no importance—upon the table."

"Here, then," said Dupin to me, "you have precisely what you demand to make the ascendancy complete—the robber's knowledge of the loser's knowledge of the robber."

"Yes," replied the Prefect; "and the power thus attained has, for some months past, been wielded, for political purposes, to a very dangerous extent. The personage robbed is more thoroughly convinced, every day, of the necessity of reclaiming her letter. But this, of course, cannot be done openly. In fine, driven to despair, she has committed the matter to me."

"Than whom," said Dupin, amid a perfect whirlwind of smoke, "no more sagacious agent could, I suppose, be desired, or even imagined."

"You flatter me," replied the Prefect; "but it is possible that some such opinion may have been entertained."

"It is clear," said I, "as you observe, that the letter is still in the possession of the minister; since it is this possession, and not any employment of the letter, which bestows the power. With the employment the power departs."

"True," said G.; "and upon this conviction I proceeded. My first care was to make thorough search of the minister's hotel; and here my chief embarrassment lay in the necessity of searching without his knowledge. Beyond all things, I have been warned of the danger which would result from giving him reason to suspect our design."

"But," said I, "you are quite *au fait*[4] in these investigations. The Parisian police have done this thing often before."

"Oh yes; and for this reason I did not despair. The habits of the minister gave me, too, a great advantage. He is frequently absent from home all night. His servants are by no means numerous. They sleep at a distance from their master's apartment, and, being chiefly Neapolitans, are readily made drunk. I have keys, as you know, with which I can open any chamber or cabinet in Paris. For three months a night has not passed, during the greater part of which I have not been engaged, personally, in ransacking the D—— Hotel. My honor is interested, and, to mention a great secret, the reward is enormous. So I did not abandon the search until I had become fully satisfied that the thief is a more astute man than myself. I fancy that I have investigated every nook and corner of the premises in which it is possible that the paper can be concealed."

"But is it not possible," I suggested, "that although the letter may be in possession of the minister, as it unquestionably is, he may have concealed it elsewhere than upon his own premises?"

"This is barely possible," said Dupin. "The present peculiar condition of affairs at court, and especially of those intrigues in which D—— is known to be involved, would render the instant availability of the document—its susceptibility of being produced at a moment's notice—a point of nearly equal importance with its possession."

"Its susceptibility of being produced?" said I.

"That is to say, of being *destroyed*," said Dupin.

"True," I observed; "the paper is clearly then upon the premises. As for its being upon the person of the minister, we may consider that as out of the question."

"Entirely," said the Prefect. "He has been twice waylaid, as if by footpads, and his person rigidly searched under my own inspection."

"You might have spared yourself this trouble," said Dupin. "D——, I presume, is not altogether a fool, and, if not, must have anticipated these waylayings, as a matter of course."

"Not *altogether* a fool," said G., "but then he is a poet, which I take to be only one remove from a fool."

"True," said Dupin, after a long and thoughtful whiff from his meerschaum, "although I have been guilty of certain doggrel myself."

"Suppose you detail," said I, "the particulars of your search."

"Why, the fact is, we took our time, and we searched *everywhere*. I have had long experience in these affairs. I took the entire building, room by room; devoting the nights of a whole week to each. We examined, first, the furniture of each apartment. We opened every possible drawer; and I presume you know that, to a properly trained police-agent, such a thing as a 'secret' drawer is impossible. Any man is a dolt who permits a 'secret' drawer to escape him in a search of this kind. The thing is *so* plain. There is a certain amount of bulk—of space—to be accounted for in every cabinet. Then we have accurate rules. The fiftieth part of a line could not escape us. After the cabinets we took the chairs. The cushions we probed with the fine long needles you have seen me employ. From the tables we removed the tops."

"Why so?"

"Sometimes the top of a table, or other similarly arranged piece of furniture, is removed by the person wishing to conceal an article; then the leg is excavated, the article deposited within the cavity, and the top replaced. The bottoms and tops of bedposts are employed in the same way."

"But could not the cavity be detected by sounding?" I asked.

"By no means, if, when the article is deposited, a sufficient wadding of cotton be placed around it. Besides, in our case, we were obliged to proceed without noise."

"But you could not have removed—you could not have taken to pieces *all* articles of furniture in which it would have been possible to make a deposit in the manner you mention. A letter may be compressed into a thin spiral roll, not differing much in shape or bulk from a large knitting-needle, and in this form it might be inserted into the rung of a chair, for example. You did not take to pieces all the chairs?"

"Certainly not; but we did better—we examined the rungs of every chair in the hotel, and, indeed, the jointings of every description of furniture, by the aid of a most powerful microscope. Had there been any traces of recent disturbance we should not have failed to detect it instantly. A single grain of gimlet-dust, for example, would have been as obvious as an apple. Any disorder in the gluing—any unusual gaping in the joints—would have sufficed to insure detection."

"I presume you looked to the mirrors, between the boards and the plates, and you probed the beds and the bedclothes, as well as the curtains and carpets."

"That of course; and when we had absolutely completed every particle of the furniture in this way, then we examined the house itself. We divided its entire surface into compartments, which we numbered, so that none might be missed; then we scrutinized each individual square inch throughout the premises, including the two houses immediately adjoining, with the microscope, as before."

"The two houses adjoining!" I exclaimed; "you must have had a great deal of trouble."

"We had; but the reward offered is prodigious."

"You include the *grounds* about the houses?"

"All the grounds are paved with brick. They gave us comparatively little trouble. We examined the moss between the bricks, and found it undisturbed."

"You looked among D——'s papers, of course, and into the books of the library?"

"Certainly; we opened every package and parcel; we not only opened every book, but we turned over every leaf in each volume, not contenting ourselves with a mere shake, according to the fashion of some of our police officers. We also measured the thickness of every book-*cover*, with the most accurate admeasurement, and applied to each the most jealous scrutiny of the microscope. Had any of the bindings been recently meddled with, it would have been utterly impossible that the fact should have escaped observation. Some five or six volumes, just from the hands of the binder, we carefully probed, longitudinally, with the needles."

"You explored the floors beneath the carpets?"

"Beyond doubt. We removed every carpet, and examined the boards with the microscope."

"And the paper on the walls?"

"Yes."

"You looked into the cellars?"

"We did."

"Then," I said, "you have been making a miscalculation, and the letter is *not* upon the premises as you suppose."

"I fear you are right there," said the Prefect. "And now, Dupin, what would you advise me to do?"

"To make a thorough research of the premises."

"That is absolutely needless," replied G——. "I am not more sure that I breathe than I am that the letter is not at the hotel."

"I have no better advice to give you," said Dupin. "You have, of course, an accurate description of the letter?"

"Oh, yes!"—And here the Prefect, producing a memorandum-book, proceeded to read aloud a minute account of the internal, and especially of the external, appearance of the missing document. Soon after finishing the perusal of this description, he took his departure, more entirely depressed in spirits than I had ever known the good gentleman before.

In about a month afterward he paid us another visit, and found us occupied very nearly as before. He took a pipe and a chair and entered into some ordinary conversation. At length I said:

"Well, but G——, what of the purloined letter? I presume you have at last made up your mind that there is no such thing as overreaching the Minister?"

"Confound him, say I—yes; I made the re-examination, however, as Dupin suggested—but it was all labor lost, as I knew it would be."

"How much was the reward offered, did you say?" asked Dupin.

"Why, a very great deal—a *very* liberal reward—I don't like to say how much, precisely; but one thing I *will* say, that I wouldn't mind giving my individual check for fifty thousand francs to any one who could obtain me that letter. The fact is, it is becoming of more and more importance every day; and the reward has been lately doubled. If it were trebled, however, I could do no more than I have done."

"Why, yes," said Dupin, drawlingly, between the whiffs of his meerschaum, "I really—think, G——, you have not exerted yourself—to the utmost in this matter. You might—do a little more, I think, eh?"

"How—in what way?"

"Why—puff, puff—you might—puff, puff—employ counsel in the matter, eh?—puff, puff, puff. Do you remember the story they tell of Abernethy?"

"No; hang Abernethy!"

"To be sure! hang him and welcome. But, once upon a time, a certain rich miser conceived the design of sponging upon this Abernethy for a medical opinion. Getting up, for this purpose, an ordinary conversation in a private company, he insinuated his case to the physician, as that of an imaginary individual.

" 'We will suppose,' said the miser, 'that his symptoms are such and such; now, doctor, what would *you* have directed him to take?'

" 'Take!' said Abernethy, 'why, take *advice*, to be sure.' "

"But," said the Prefect, a little discomposed, "*I* am *perfectly* willing to take advice, and to pay for it. I would *really* give fifty thousand francs to any one who would aid me in the matter."

"In that case," replied Dupin, opening a drawer, and producing a check-book, "you may as well fill me up a check for the amount mentioned. When you have signed it, I will hand you the letter."

I was astounded. The Prefect appeared absolutely thunder-stricken. For some minutes he remained speechless and motion-less, looking incredulously at my friend with open mouth, and eyes that seemed starting from their sockets; then apparently recovering himself in some measure, he seized a pen, and after several pauses and vacant stares, finally filled up and signed a check for fifty thousand francs, and handed it across the table to Dupin. The latter examined it carefully and deposited it in his pocket-book; then, unlocking an *escritoire*, took thence a letter and gave it to the Prefect. This functionary grasped it in a perfect agony of joy, opened it with a trembling hand, cast a rapid glance at its contents, and then, scrambling and struggling to the door rushed at length unceremoniously from the room and from the house, without having uttered a syllable since Dupin had requested him to fill up the check.

When he had gone, my friend entered into some explanations.

"The Parisian police," he said, "are exceedingly able in their way. They are persevering, ingenious, cunning, and thoroughly versed in the knowledge which their duties seem chiefly to demand. Thus, when G—— detailed to us his mode of searching the premises at the Hotel D——, I felt entire confidence in his having made a satisfactory investigation—so far as his labors extended."

"So far as his labors extended?" said I.

"Yes," said Dupin. "The measures adopted were not only the best of their kind, but carried out to absolute perfection. Had the letter been deposited within the range of their search, these fellows would, beyond a question, have found it."

I merely laughed—but he seemed quite serious in all that he said.

"The measures, then," he continued, "were good in their kind, and well executed; their defect lay in their being inapplicable to the case and to the man. A certain set of highly ingenious resources are, with the Prefect, a sort of Procrustean bed,[5] to which he forcibly adapts his designs. But he perpetually errs by being too deep or too shallow for the matter in hand; and many a school-boy is a better reasoner than he. I knew one about eight years of age, whose success at guessing in the game of 'even and odd' attracted universal admiration. This game is simple, and is played with marbles. One player holds in his hand a number of these toys, and demands of another whether that number is even or odd. If the guess is right, the guesser wins one; if wrong he loses one. The boy to whom I allude won all the marbles of the school.

Of course he had some principle of guessing; and this lay in mere observation and admeasurement of the astuteness of his opponents. For example, an arrant simpleton is his opponent, and, holding up his closed hand, asks, 'Are they even or odd?' Our school-boy replies, 'Odd,' and loses; but upon the second trial he wins, for he then says to himself: 'The simpleton had them even upon the first trial, and his amount of cunning is just sufficient to make him have them odd upon the second; I will therefore guess odd';—he guesses odd, and wins. Now, with a simpleton a degree above the first, he would have reasoned thus: 'This fellow finds that in the first instance I guessed odd, and, in the second, he will propose to himself, upon the first impulse, a simple variation from even to odd, as did the first simpleton; but then a second thought will suggest that this is too simple a variation and finally he will decide upon putting it even as before. I will therefore guess even';—he guesses even, and wins. Now this mode of reasoning in the school-boy, whom his fellows termed 'lucky,'—what, in its last analysis, is it?"

"It is merely," I said, "an identification of the reasoner's intellect with that of his opponent."

"It is," said Dupin; "and, upon inquiring of the boy by what means he effected the *thorough* identification in which his success consisted, I received answer as follows: 'When I wish to find out how wise, or how stupid, or how good, or how wicked is any one, or what are his thoughts at the moment, I fashion the expression of my face, as accurately as possible, in accordance with the expression of his, and then wait to see what thoughts or sentiments arise in my mind or heart, as if to match or correspond with the expression.' This response of the school-boy lies at the bottom of all the spurious profundity which has been attributed to Rochefoucault, to La Bougive, to Machiavelli, and to Campanella." [6]

"And the identification," I said, "of the reasoner's intellect with that of his opponent, depends, if I understand you aright, upon the accuracy with which the opponent's intellect is admeasured."

"For its practical value it depends upon this," replied Dupin; "and the Prefect and his cohort fail so frequently, first, by default of this identification, and, secondly, by ill-admeasurement, or rather through non-admeasurement, of the intellect with which they are engaged. They consider only their *own* ideas of ingenuity; and, in searching for any thing hidden, advert only to the modes in which *they* would have hidden it. They are right in this much—that their own ingenuity is a faithful representative of that of *the mass;* but when the cunning of the individual felon is diverse in character from their own, the felon foils them of course. This always happens when it is above their own, and very usually when it is below. They have no variation of principle in their investigations; at best, when urged by some unusual emergency— by some extraordinary reward—they extend or exaggerate their old modes of *practice,* without touching their principles. What, for example, in this case of D——, has been done to vary the principle of action? What is all this boring, and probing, and sounding, and scrutinizing with the microscope, and dividing the surface of the building into registered square inches—what is it all but an exaggeration of *the application* of the one principle or set of principles of search, which are based upon the one set of notions regarding human ingenuity, to which the Prefect, in the long routine of his duty, has been accustomed? Do you not see he has taken it for granted that *all* men proceed to conceal a letter, not exactly in a gimlet-hole bored in a chair-leg, but, at least, in *some* out-of-the-way hole or corner suggested by the same tenor of thought which would urge a man to secrete a letter in a gimlet-hole bored in a chair-leg? And do you not see also, that such *recherchés*[7] nooks for concealment are adapted only for ordinary occasions, and would be adopted only by ordinary intellects; for, in all cases of concealment, a disposal of the article concealed—a disposal of it in this *recherché*[8] manner—is, in the very first instance, presumable and presumed; and thus its discovery depends, not at all upon the acumen, but altogether upon the mere care, patience, and determination of the seekers; and where the case is of importance—or what amounts to the same thing in the political eyes, when the reward is of magnitude —the qualities in question have *never* been known to fail. You will now understand what I meant in suggesting that, had the purloined letter been hidden anywhere within the limits of the Prefect's examination—in other words, had the principle of its concealment been comprehended within the principles of the Prefect—its discovery would have been a matter altogether beyond question. This functionary, however, has been thoroughly mystified; and the remote source of his defeat lies in the supposition that the Minister is a fool, because he has acquired renown as a poet. All fools are poets; this the Prefect *feels;* and he is merely guilty of a *non distributio medii*[9] in thence inferring that all poets are fools."

"But is this really the poet?" I asked. "There are two brothers, I know; and both have attained reputation in letters. The minister I believe has written learnedly on the Differential Calculus. He is a mathematician, and no poet."

"You are mistaken; I know him well; he is both. As poet *and* mathematician, he would reason well; as mere mathematician, he could not have reasoned at all, and thus would have been at the mercy of the Prefect."

"You surprise me," I said, "by these opinions, which have been contradicted by the voice of the world. You do not mean to set at naught the well-digested idea of centuries. The mathematical reason has long been regarded as *the* reason *par excellence*."

" '*Il y a à parier*,' " replied Dupin, quoting from Chamfort,[10] '*que toute idée publique, toute convention reçue, est une sottise, car elle a convenue au plus grand nombre.*' [11] The mathematicians, I grant you, have done their best to promulgate the popular error to which you allude, and which is none the less an error for its promulgation as truth. With an art worthy a better cause, for example, they have insinuated the term 'analysis' into application to algebra. The French are the originators of this particular deception; but if a term is of any importance—if words derive any value from applicability—then 'analysis' conveys 'algebra' about as much as, in Latin, '*ambitus*' implies 'ambition, '*religio*' 'religion,' or '*homines honesti*' a set of *honorable* men."

"You have a quarrel on hand, I see," said I, "with some of the algebraists of Paris; but proceed."

"I dispute the availability, and thus the value, of that reason which is cultivated in any especial form other than the abstractly logical. I dispute, in particular, the reason educed by mathematical study. The mathematics are the science of form and quantity; mathematical reasoning is merely logic applied to observation upon form and quantity. The great error lies in supposing that even the truths of what is called *pure* algebra are abstract or general truths. And this error is so egregious that I am confounded at the universality with which it has been received. Mathematical axioms are *not* axioms of general truth. What is true of *relation*— of form and quantity—is often grossly false in regard to morals, for example. In this latter science it is very usually *un*true that the aggregated parts are equal to the whole. In chemistry also the axiom fails. In the consideration of motive it fails; for two motives, each of a given value, have not, necessarily, a value when united, equal to the sum of their values apart. There are numerous other mathematical truths which are only truths within the limits of *relation*. But the mathematician argues from his *finite truths*, through habit, as if they were of an absolutely general applicability—as the world indeed imagines them to be. Bryant,[12] in his very learned 'Mythology,' mentions an analogous source of error, when he says that 'although the pagan fables are not believed, yet we forget ourselves continually, and make inferences from them as existing realities.' With the algebraists, however, who are pagans themselves, the 'pagan fables' *are* believed, and the inferences are made, not so much through lapse of memory as through an unaccountable addling of the brains. In short, I never yet encountered the mere mathematician who could be trusted out of equal roots, or one who did not clandestinely hold it as a point of his faith that $x^2 + px$ was absolutely and unconditionally equal to q. Say to one of these gentlemen, by way of experiment, if you please, that you believe occasions may occur where $x^2 + px$ is *not* altogether equal to q, and, having made him understand what you mean, get out of his reach as speedily as convenient, for, beyond doubt, he will endeavor to knock you down.

"I mean to say," continued Dupin, while I merely laughed at his last observations, "that if the minister had been no more than a mathematician, the Prefect would have been under no necessity of giving me this check. I knew him, however, as both mathematician and poet, and my measures were adapted to his capacity, with reference to the circumstances by which he was surrounded. I knew him as a courtier, too, and as a bold *intriguant*. Such a man, I considered, could not fail to be aware of the ordinary policial modes of action. He could not have failed to anticipate— and events have proved that he did not fail to anticipate—the waylayings to which he was subjected. He must have foreseen, I reflected, the secret investigations of his premises. His frequent absences from home at night, which were hailed by the Prefect as certain aids to his success, I regarded only as *ruses*, to afford opportunity for thorough search to the police, and thus the sooner to impress them with the conviction to which G——, in fact, did finally arrive—the conviction that the letter was not upon the premises. I felt, also, that the whole train of thought, which I was at some pains in detailing to you just now, concerning the invariable principle of policial action in searches for articles concealed—I felt that this whole train of thought would necessarily pass through the mind of the minister. It would imperatively lead him to despise all the ordinary *nooks* of concealment. *He* could not, I reflected, be so weak as not to see that the most intricate and remote recess of his hotel would be as open as his commonest closets to the eyes, to the probes, to the gimlets, and to the microscopes of the Prefect. I saw, in fine, that he would be driven, as a matter of course, to *simplicity*, if not deliberately induced to it as a matter of choice. You will remember, perhaps, how desperately the Prefect laughed when I suggested, upon our first interview, that it was just possible this mystery troubled him so much on account of its being so *very* self-evident."

"Yes," said I, "I remember his merriment well. I really thought he would have fallen into convulsions."

"The material world," continued Dupin, "abounds with very strict analogies to the immaterial; and thus some color of truth has been given to the rhetorical dogma, that metaphor, or simile, may be made to strengthen an argument as well as to embellish a description. The principle of the *vis inertiæ*,[13] for example, seems to be identical in physics and metaphysics. It is more true in the former, that a large body is with more difficulty set in motion than a smaller one, and that its subsequent *momentum* is commensurate with this difficulty, than it is, in the latter, that intellects of the vaster capacity, while more forcible, more constant, and more eventful in their movements than those of inferior grade, are yet the less readily moved, and more embarrassed, and full of hesitation in the first few steps of their progress. Again: have you ever noticed which of the street signs over the shop doors, are the most attractive of attention?"

"I have never given the matter a thought," I said.

"There is a game of puzzles," he resumed, "which is played upon a map. One party playing requires another to find a given word—the name of town, river, state, or empire—any word, in short, upon the motley and perplexed surface of the chart. A novice in the game generally seeks to embarrass his opponents by giving them the most minutely lettered names; but the adept selects such words as stretch, in large characters, from one end of the chart to the other. These, like the over-largely lettered signs and placards of the street, escape observation by dint of being excessively obvious; and here the physical oversight is precisely analogous with the moral inapprehension by which the intellect suffers to pass unnoticed those considerations which are too obtrusively and too palpably self-evident. But this is a point, it appears, somewhat above or beneath the understanding of the Prefect. He never once thought it probable, or possible, that the minister had deposited the letter immediately beneath the nose of the whole world, by way of best preventing any portion of that world from perceiving it.

"But the more I reflected upon the daring, dashing, and discriminating ingenuity of D——; upon the fact that the document must always have been *at hand*, if he intended to use it to good purpose; and upon the decisive evidence, obtained by the Prefect, that it was not hidden within the limits of that dignitary's ordinary search—the more satisfied I became that, to conceal this letter, the minister had resorted to the comprehensive and sagacious expedient of not attempting to conceal it at all.

"Full of these ideas, I prepared myself with a pair of green spectacles, and called one fine morning, quite by accident, at the Ministerial hotel. I found D—— at home, yawning, lounging, and dawdling, as usual, and pretending to be in the last extremity of *ennui*. He is, perhaps, the most really energetic human being now alive—but that is only when nobody sees him.

"To be even with him, I complained of my weak eyes, and lamented the necessity of the spectacles, under cover of which I cautiously and thoroughly surveyed the whole apartment, while seemingly intent only upon the conversation of my host.

"I paid especial attention to a large writing-table near which he sat, and upon which lay confusedly, some miscellaneous letters and other papers, with one or two musical instruments and a few books. Here, however, after a long and very deliberate scrutiny, I saw nothing to excite particular suspicion.

"At length my eyes, in going the circuit of the room, fell upon a trumpery filigree card-rack of pasteboard, that hung dangling by a dirty blue ribbon, from a little brass knob just beneath the middle of the mantel-piece. In this rack, which had three or four compartments, were five or six visiting cards and a solitary letter. This last was much soiled and crumpled. It was torn nearly in two, across the middle—as if a design, in the first instance, to tear it entirely up as worthless, had been altered, or stayed, in the second. It had a large black seal, bearing the D—— cipher *very* conspicuously, and was addressed, in a diminutive female hand, to D—— the minister, himself. It was thrust carelessly, and even, as it seemed, contemptuously, into one of the uppermost divisions of the rack.

"No sooner had I glanced at this letter than I concluded it to be that of which I was in search. To be sure, it was, to all appearance, radically different from the one of which the Prefect had read us so minute a description. Here the seal was large and black, with the D—— cipher; there it was small and red, with the ducal arms of the S—— family. Here, the address, to the minister, was diminutive and feminine; there, the superscription, to a certain royal personage, was markedly bold and decided; the size alone formed a point of correspondence. But, then, the *radicalness* of these differences, which was excessive; the dirt; the soiled and torn condition of the paper, so inconsistent with the *true* methodical habits of D——, and so suggestive of a design to delude the beholder into an idea of the worthlessness of the document;—these things, together with the hyperobtrusive situation of this document, full in the view of every visitor, and thus exactly in accordance with the conclusions to which I had previously arrived; these things, I say, were strongly corroborative of suspicion, in one who came with the intention to suspect.

"I protracted my visit as long as possible, and, while I maintained a most animated discussion with the minister, upon a topic which I knew well had never failed to interest and excite him, I kept my attention really riveted upon the letter. In this examination, I committed to memory its external appearance and arrangement in the rack; and also fell, at length, upon a discovery which set at rest whatever trivial doubt I might have entertained. In scrutinizing the edges of the paper, I observed them to be more *chafed* than seemed necessary. They presented the *broken* appearance which is manifested when a stiff paper, having been once folded and pressed with a folder, is refolded in a reversed direction, in the same creases or edges which had formed the original fold. This discovery was sufficient. It was clear to me that the letter had been turned, as a glove, inside out, re-directed and re-sealed. I bade the minister good-morning, and took my departure at once, leaving a gold snuff-box upon the table.

"The next morning I called for the snuff-box, when we resumed, quite eagerly, the conversation of the preceding day. While thus engaged, however, a loud report, as if of a pistol, was heard immediately beneath the windows of the hotel, and was succeeded by a series of fearful screams, and the shoutings of a terrified mob. D—— rushed to a casement, threw it open, and looked out. In the meantime I stepped to the card-rack, took the letter, put it in my pocket, and replaced it by a *fac-simile,* (so far as regards externals) which I had carefully prepared at my lodgings—imitating the D—— cipher, very readily, by means of a seal formed of bread.

"The disturbance in the street had been occasioned by the frantic behavior of a man with a musket. He had fired it among a crowd of women and children. It proved, however, to have been without ball, and the fellow was suffered to go his way as a lunatic or a drunkard. When he had gone, D—— came from the window, whither I had followed him immediately upon securing the object in view. Soon afterward I bade him farewell. The pretended lunatic was a man in my own pay."

"But what purpose had you," I asked, "in replacing the letter by a *fac-simile?* Would it not have been better, at the first visit, to have seized it openly, and departed?"

"D——," replied Dupin, "is a desperate man, and a man of nerve. His hotel, too, is not without attendants devoted to his interests. Had I made the wild attempt you suggest, I might never have left the Ministerial presence alive. The good people of Paris might have heard of me no more. But I had an object apart from these considerations. You know my political prepossessions. In this matter, I act as a partisan of the lady concerned. For eighteen months the minister has had her in his power. She has now him in hers—since, being unaware that the letter is not in his possession, he will proceed with his exactions as if it was. Thus will he inevitably commit himself, at once, to his political destruction. His downfall, too, will not be more precipitate than awkward. It is all very well to talk about the *facilis descensus Averni;*[14] but in all kinds of climbing, as Catalani[15] said of singing, it is far more easy to get up than to come down. In the present instance I have no sympathy—at least no pity—for him who descends. He is that *monstrum horrendum,* an unprincipled man of genius. I confess, however, that I should like very well to know the precise character of his thoughts, when, being defied by her whom the Prefect terms 'a certain personage,' he is reduced to opening the letter which I left for him in the card rack."

"How? did you put any thing particular in it?"

"Why—it did not seem altogether right to leave the interior blank—that would have been insulting. D——, at Vienna once, did me an evil turn, which I told him, quite good-humoredly, that I should remember. So, as I knew he would feel some curiosity in regard to the identity of the person who had outwitted him, I thought it a pity not to give him a clew. He is well acquainted with my MS.,[16] and I just copied into the middle of the blank sheet the words—

" '——Un dessein si funeste,
S'il n' est digne d' Atrée, est digne de Thyeste.' [17]

They are to be found in Crébillon's[18] 'Atrée.' "

COMMENT AND QUESTIONS

This story illustrates a number of techniques and conventions that are special characteristics of the traditional, formal detective story:

The gifted but eccentric detective

Dupin is an eccentric in both habit and attitude. For example, he prefers to discuss "points requiring reflection" in the dark, and he says that mathematicians cannot reason at all.

The less clever but admiring friend as narrator

The story is narrated by a close friend and companion of Dupin, one who is intelligent but below Dupin in ability (it would not have occurred to him, for example, to substitute another letter for the one removed from D——'s letter rack). Since the reader knows only what the narrator sees and tells him, both may be jointly mystified, surprised, and appreciative of Dupin's success.

The friendly rivalry with the police

While Dupin is on friendly terms with Monsieur G——, he is contemptuous of G——'s intelligence and of the tendency of the police to apply one means to the solution of every problem.

What evidence is there of the quality of Monsieur G——'s mind? What, for example, is suggested by the fact that G—— rushes off before he learns how Dupin recovered the letter? How does Dupin intend the remark that "no more sagacious agent could, I suppose, be desired, or even imagined" than Monsieur G—— to help the "personage" recover her letter? What does Monsieur G—— think he intends?

The least likely solution

The letter is in the most obvious hiding place—it is, after all, in plain sight.

Dupin explains that one must identify with one's rivals (in a "game") in order to predict what the rival is capable of doing. There are many interesting similarities between the rivals in this story. Both are poets. Both are men of great intelligence and imagination who accurately assess the mental skills of their opponents and outwit them. Both employ substitution as a stratagem in their thefts. The quotation in the substituted letter left for Minister D—— refers to two equally clever and immoral brothers. Are Monsieur Dupin and Minister D—— equally clever? equally immoral?

G——'s statement that Minister D—— "dares all things, those unbecoming as well as those becoming a man," is an allusion to *Macbeth*:

I dare do all that may become a man.
Who dares do more is none.

What does this allusion imply about the character of D——?

How appropriate is the quotation at the beginning of the story? (No wisdom is more hateful than too much sharpness.) To whom does it apply?

After Dupin confirms his hypothesis about where the letter is hidden, why does he not give the facsimile letter to the police, to be substituted secretly for the real letter, and thereby avoid putting himself in a dangerous situation? Why does he choose instead to recover the stolen letter himself?

Does the fact that Edgar Allan Poe was himself a poet affect the story in any significant way?

Does Dupin recover the letter because he wants or needs the large reward? What evidence for your answer do you find in the story?

What crimes or indiscretions are *concealed* by Dupin's restoring the letter?

NOTES

1. *Nil sapientiæ odiosius acumine nimio.* No wisdom is more hateful than too much sharpness.
2. *au troisième.* On the third floor.
3. *Prefect.* The chief of police.
4. *au fait.* Acquainted with the situation.
5. *Procrustean bed.* Procrustes, in Greek mythology, tied his victims to an iron bed and made them fit by stretching those who were too short and cutting off those who were too long.
6. *Rochefoucault, La Bougive, Machiavelli, Campanella.* François La

Rochefoucault was a French moralist and writer, author of *Moral Maxims and Reflections* (1665). Niccolò Machiavelli, an Italian statesman, is best known for *The Prince* (1513), a theoretical study of politics. Tommaso Campanella, an Italian philosopher, wrote *City of the Sun* (1643), an account of a fanciful communist state. Poe sometimes intermingled fictitious names and titles with real ones, and La Bougive may be a name Poe invented. Richard Wilbur, in his edition of "The Purloined Letter," speculates that the name may be an error in transcription for La Bruyère. Jean de La Bruyère wrote *Characters* (1688), brief descriptive sketches of persons who are examples of particular vices or virtues or types. All of these writers are known for their observations on the nature of man.

7. *recherchés*. Out-of-the-way.

8. *recherché*. Carefully contrived.

9. *non distributio medii*. Undistributed middle. In logic, when each and every member of one class or category is completely accounted for with respect to another term, the first term is said to be distributed. Minister G——'s proposition, "All fools are poets," means that within the category of poets we find all the fools in the world. It does not, however, follow that only fools are poets, since all we know is that all the people in the category of fools are included in the category of poets, but not vice versa.

10. *Chamfort*. Sebastian Roch Nicholas Chamfort, an eighteenth-century French writer of maxims and epigrams.

11. *Il y a à parier*, . . . One could bet . . . that every public idea, every received convention, is stupid, because it suited the greatest number.

12. *Bryant*. Jacob Bryant, an Englishman with antiquarian interests, author of *A New System or Analysis of Ancient Mythology* (1774–76).

13. *vis inertiæ*. The force of inertia.

14. *facilis descensus Averni*. Easy is the descent into hell. A quotation from *The Aeneid*.

15. *Catalani*. Angelica Catalani, an Italian singer whose career began in the late eighteenth century.

16. *MS*. Handwriting.

17. ——*Un dessein si funeste*, . . . Such a deadly plan, / If it is not worthy of Atreus, is worthy of Thyestes. (In Greek mythology, Thyestes seduced the wife of his brother Atreus. Atreus tricked Thyestes into eating his own sons in a stew.)

18. *Crébillon*. Pseudonym of Prosper Jolyat, a French dramatist. The quotation is taken from his work *Atreus and Thyestes* (1707).

JOHN DICKSON CARR

The Gentleman from Paris

John Dickson Carr is, like Poe, an American author who is known for his mystery fiction. Since the publication in 1929 of his first novel, *It Walks by Night*, he has continued to write elaborately detailed and plotted novels. In addition, he has written several articles on detective fiction and collaborated with Adrian Conan Doyle (son of Arthur) on "new" Sherlock Holmes stories. He currently reviews mystery fiction and other books in this field for *Ellery Queen's Mystery Magazine*.

Carr is a genius at creating "locked-room" masterpieces (most of his novels are of this type) and recreating the past, but he has rarely surpassed the achievement of "The Gentleman from Paris." In it he employs the locked-room convention first employed in Poe's "The Murders in the Rue Morgue." In this kind of story, the locked room may be the place where something is hidden or the place where a crime is committed. The challenge to the reader is to determine how the murderer, victim, or weapon got into the room or out of it. The room in such stories is, of course, locked, watched by reliable witnesses, and free from secret entrances or hidden panels and so represents a genuine puzzle to both reader and detective.

Historical detective stories—those set in an earlier time than that in which they are written—are comparatively rare. This story is an excellent example of how the appeal of good plot and character may be further increased by an imaginative evocation, full of colorful details, of an earlier era.

Imagine yourself in the New York of 1849 and try to see it through the eyes of an aristocratic Frenchman.

CARLTON HOUSE HOTEL,
BROADWAY, NEW-YORK,
14TH APRIL, 1849

My dear brother:

Were my hand more steady, Maurice, or my soul less agitated, I should have written to you before this. *All is safe:* so much I tell you at once. For the rest, I seek sleep in vain; and this is not merely because I find myself a stranger and a foreigner in New-York. Listen and judge.

We discussed, I think, the humiliation that a Frenchman must go to England ere he could take passage in a reliable ship for America. The *Britannia* steam-packet departed from Liverpool on the second of the month, and arrived here on the seventeenth. Do not smile, I implore you, when I tell you that my first visit on American soil was to Platt's Saloon, under Wallack's Theatre.

Great God, that voyage!

On my stomach I could hold not even champagne. For one of my height and breadth I was as weak as a child.

"Be good enough," I said to a fur-capped coachman, when I had struggled through the horde of Irish immigrants, "to drive me to some fashionable place of refreshment."

The coachman had no difficulty in understanding my English, which pleased me. And how extraordinary are these "saloons"!

The saloon of M. Platt was loud with the thump of hammers cracking ice, which is delivered in large blocks. Though the hand-coloured gas-globes, and the rose-paintings on the front of the bar-counter, were as fine as we could see at the Three Provincial Brothers in Paris, yet I confess that the place did not smell so agreeably. A number of gentlemen, wearing hats perhaps a trifle taller than is fashionable at home, lounged at the bar-counter and shouted. I attracted no attention until I called for a sherry cobbler.

One of the "bartenders," as they are called in New-York, gave me a sharp glance as he prepared the glass.

"Just arrived from the Old Country, I bet?" said he in no unfriendly tone.

Though it seemed strange to hear France mentioned in this way, I smiled and bowed assent.

"Italian, maybe?" said he.

This bartender, of course, could not know how deadly was the insult.

"Sir," I replied, "I am a Frenchman."

And now in truth he was pleased! His fat face opened and smiled like a distorted, gold-toothed flower.

"Is that so, now!" he exclaimed. "And what might your name be? Unless"—and here his face darkened with that sudden defensiveness and suspicion which, for no reason I can discern, will often strike into American hearts—"unless," said he, "you don't want to give it?"

"Not at all," I assured him earnestly. "I am Armand de Lafayette, at your service."

My dear brother, what an extraordinary effect!

It was silence. All sounds, even the faint whistling of the gas-jets, seemed to die away in that stone-flagged room. Every man along the line of the bar was looking at me. I was conscious only of faces, mostly with whiskers under the chin instead of down the cheek-bones, turned on me in basilisk stare.

"Well, well, well!" almost sneered the bartender. "You wouldn't be no relation of the *Marquis* de Lafayette, would you?"

It was my turn to be astonished. Though our father has always forbidden us to mention the name of our late uncle, due to his republican sympathies, yet I knew he occupied small place in the history of France and it puzzled me to comprehend how these people had heard of him.

"The late Marquis de Lafayette," I was obliged to admit, "was my uncle."

"You better be careful, young feller," suddenly yelled a grimy little man with a pistol buckled under his long coat. "We don't like being diddled, we don't."

"Sir," I replied, taking my bundle of papers from my pocket and whacking them down on the bar-counter, "have the goodness to examine my credentials. Should you still doubt my identity, we can then debate the matter in any way which pleases you."

"This is furrin writing," shouted the bartender. "*I* can't read it!"

And then—how sweet was the musical sound on my ear!—I heard a voice addressing me in my own language.

"Perhaps, sir," said the voice, in excellent French and with great stateliness, "I may be able to render you some small service."

The newcomer, a slight man of dark complexion, drawn up under an old shabby cloak of military cut, stood a little way behind me. If I had met him on the boulevards, I might not have found him very prepossessing. He had a wild and wandering eye, with an even wilder shimmer of brandy. He was not very steady on his feet. And yet, Maurice, his manner! It was such that I instinctively raised my hat, and the stranger very gravely did the same.

"And to whom," said I, "have I the honour . . . ?"

"I am Thaddeus Perley, sir, at your service."

"Another furriner!" said the grimy little man, in disgust.

"I am indeed a foreigner," said M. Perley in English, with an accent like a knife. "A foreigner to this dram-shop. A foreigner to this neighbourhood. A foreigner to—" Here he paused, and his eyes acquired an almost frightening blaze of loathing. "Yet I never heard that the reading of French was so *very* singular an accomplishment."

Imperiously—and yet, it seemed to me, with a certain shrinking nervousness—M. Perley came closer and lifted the bundle of papers.

"Doubtless," he said loftily, "I should not be credited were I to translate these. But here," and he scanned several of the papers, "is a letter of introduction in English. It is addressed to President Zachary Taylor from the American minister at Paris."

Again, my brother, what an enormous silence! It was interrupted by a cry from the bartender, who had snatched the documents from M. Perley.

"Boys, this is no diddle," said he. "This gent is the real thing!"

"He ain't!" thundered the little grimy man, with incredulity.

"He is!" said the bartender. "I'll be a son of a roe (*i.e., biche*), if he ain't!"

Well, Maurice, you and I have seen how Paris mobs can change. Americans are even more emotional. In the wink of an eye hostility became frantic affection. My back was slapped, my hand wrung, my person jammed against the bar by a crowd fighting to order me more refreshment.

The name of Lafayette, again and again, rose like a holy diapason. In vain I asked why this should be so. They appeared to think I was joking, and roared with laughter. I thought of M. Thaddeus Perley, as one who could supply an explanation.

But in the first rush towards me M. Perley had been flung backwards. He fell sprawling in some wet stains of tobacco-juice on the floor, and now I could not see him at all. For myself, I was weak from lack of food. A full beaker of whisky, which I was obliged to drink because all eyes were on me, made my head reel. Yet I felt compelled to raise my voice above the clamour.

"Gentlemen," I implored them, "will you hear me?"

"Silence for Lafayette!" said a big but very old man, with faded red whiskers. He had tears in his eyes, and he had been humming a catch called *Yankee Doodle*. "Silence for Lafayette!"

"Believe me," said I, "I am full of gratitude for your hospitality. But I have business in New-York, business of immediate and desperate urgency. If you will allow me to pay my reckoning . . ."

"Your money's no good here, monseer," said the bartender. "You're going to get liquored-up good and proper."

"But I have no wish, believe me, to become liquored-up! It might well endanger my mission! In effect, I wish to go!"

"Wait a minute," said the little grimy man, with a cunning look. "What *is* this here business?"

You, Maurice, have called me quixotic. I deny this. You have also called me imprudent. Perhaps you are right; but what choice was left to me?

"Has any gentleman here," I asked, "heard of Madame Thevenet? Madame Thevenet, who lives at number 23 Thomas Street, near Hudson Street?"

I had not, of course, expected an affirmative reply. Yet, in addition to one or two snickers at mention of the street, several nodded their heads.

"Old miser woman?" asked a sportif character, who wore chequered trousers.

"I regret, sir, that you correctly describe her. Madame Thevenet is very rich. And I have come here," cried I, "to put right a damnable injustice!"

Struggle as I might, I could not free myself.

"How's that?" asked half a dozen.

"Madame Thevenet's daughter, Mademoiselle Claudine, lives in the worst of poverty at Paris. Madame herself has been brought here, under some spell, by a devil of a woman calling herself . . . Gentlemen, I implore you!"

"And I bet you," cried the little grimy man with the pistol, "you're sweet on this daughter what's-her-name?" He seemed delighted. "Ain't you, now?"

How, I ask of all Providence, could these people have surprised my secret? Yet I felt obliged to tell the truth.

"I will not conceal from you," I said, "that I have in truth a high regard for Mlle. Claudine. But this lady, believe me, is engaged to a friend of mine, an officer of artillery."

"Then what do you *get* out of it? Eh?" asked the grimy little man, with another cunning look.

The question puzzled me. I could not reply. But the bartender with the gold teeth leaned over.

"If you want to see the old Frenchie alive, monseer," said he, "you'd better git." (*Sic*, Maurice). "I hearn tell she had a stroke this morning."

But a dozen voices clamoured to keep me there, though this last intelligence sent me into despair. Then up rose the big and very old man with the faded whiskers: indeed, I had never realized how old, because he seemed so hale.

"Which of you was with Washington?" said he, suddenly taking hold of the fierce little man's neckcloth, and speaking with contempt. "Make way for the nephew of Lafayette!"

They cheered me then, Armand. They hurried me to the door, they begged me to return, they promised they would await me. One glance I sought—nor can I say why—for M. Thaddeus Perley. He was sitting at a table by a pillar, under an open gas-jet;

his face whiter than ever, still wiping stains of tobacco-juice from his cloak.

Never have I seen a more mournful prospect than Thomas Street, when my cab set me down there. Perhaps it was my state of mind; for if Mme. Thevenet had died without a sou left to her daughter: you conceive it?

The houses of Thomas Street were faced with dingy yellow brick, and a muddy sky hung over the chimney-pots. It had been warm all day, yet I found my spirit intolerably oppressed. Though heaven knows our Parisian streets are dirty enough, we do not allow pigs in them. Except for these, nothing moved in the forsaken street save a blind street-musician, with his dog and an instrument called a banjo; but even he was silent too.

For some minutes, it seemed to me, I plied the knocker at number 23, with hideous noise. Nothing stirred. Finally, one part of the door swung open a little, as for an eye. Whereupon I heard the shifting of a floor-bolt, and both doors were swung open.

Need I say that facing me stood the woman whom we have agreed to call Mademoiselle Jezebel?

She said to me: "And then, M. Armand?"

"Madame Thevenet!" cried I. "She is still alive?"

"She is alive," replied my companion, looking up at me from under the lids of her greenish eyes. "But she is completely paralyzed."

I have never denied, Maurice, that Mlle. Jezebel has a certain attractiveness. She is not old or even middle-aged. Were it not that her complexion is as muddy as was the sky above us then, she would have been pretty.

"And as for Claudine," I said to her, "the daughter of madame—"

"You have come too late, M. Armand."

And well I remember that at this moment there rose up, in the mournful street outside, the tinkle of the banjo played by the street-musician. It moved closer, playing a popular catch whose words run something thus:

> *Oh, I come from Alabama*
> *With my banjo on my knee;*
> *I depart for Louisiana*
> *My Susannah for to see.*

Across the lips of mademoiselle flashed a smile of peculiar quality, like a razor-cut before the blood comes.

"Gold," she whispered. "Ninety thousand persons, one hears, have gone to seek it. Go to California, M. Armand. It is the only place you will find gold."

This tune, they say, is a merry tune. It did not seem so, as the dreary twanging faded away. Mlle. Jezebel, with her muddy blonde hair parted in the middle and drawn over her ears after the best fashion, faced me implacably. Her greenish eyes were wide open. Her old brown taffeta dress, full at the bust, narrow at the waist, rustled its wide skirts as she glided a step forward.

"Have the kindness," I said, "to stand aside. I wish to enter."

Hitherto in my life I had seen her docile and meek.

"You are no relative," she said. "I will not allow you to enter."

"In that case, I regret, I must."

"If you had ever spoken one kind word to *me*," whispered mademoiselle, looking up from under her eyelids, and with her breast heaving, "one gesture of love—that is to say, of affection—you might have shared five million francs."

"Stand aside, I say!"

"As it is, you prefer a doll-faced consumptive at Paris. So be it!"

I was raging, Maurice; I confess it; yet I drew myself up with coldness.

"You refer, perhaps to Claudine Thevenet?"

"And to whom else?"

"I might remind you, mademoiselle, that the lady is pledged to my good friend Lieutenant Delage. I have forgotten her."

"Have you?" asked our Jezebel, with her eyes on my face and a strange hungry look in them. Mlle. Jezebel added, with more pleasure: "Well, she will die. Unless you can solve a mystery."

"A mystery?"

"I should not have said mystery, M. Armand. Because it is impossible of all solution. It is an Act of God!"

Up to this time the glass-fronted doors of the vestibule had stood open behind her, against a darkness of closed shutters in the house. There breathed out of it an odour of unswept carpets, a sourness of stale living. Someone was approaching, carrying a lighted candle.

"Who speaks?" called a man's voice; shaky, but as French

as Mlle. Jezebel's. "Who speaks concerning an Act of God?"

I stepped across the threshold. Mademoiselle, who never left my side, immediately closed and locked the front doors. As the candle-glimmer moved still closer in gloom, I could have shouted for joy to see the man who (as I correctly guessed) I had come to meet.

"You are M. Duroc, the lawyer!" I said. "You are my brother's friend!"

M. Duroc held the candle higher, to inspect me.

He was a big, heavy man who seemed to sag in all his flesh. In compensation for his bald head, the greyish-brown moustache flowed down and parted into two hairy fans of beard on either side of his chin. He looked at me through oval gold-rimmed spectacles; in a friendly way, but yet frightened. His voice was deep and gruff, clipping the syllables, despite his fright.

"And you—" *clip-clip;* the candleholder trembled—"you are Armand de Lafayette. I had expected you by the steam-packet today. Well! You are here. On a fool's errand, I regret."

"But why?" (And I shouted it at him, Maurice.)

I looked at mademoiselle, who was faintly smiling.

"M. Duroc!" I protested. "You wrote to my brother. You said you had persuaded madame to repent of her harshness towards her daughter!"

"Was that your duty?" asked the Jezebel, looking full at M. Duroc with her greenish eyes. "Was that your right?"

"I am a man of law," said M. Duroc. The deep monosyllables rapped, in ghostly bursts, through his parted beard. He was perspiring. "I am correct. Very correct! And yet—"

"Who nursed her?" asked the Jezebel. "Who soothed her, fed her, wore her filthy clothes, calmed her tempers, endured her interminable abuse? *I* did!"

And yet, all the time she was speaking, this woman kept sidling and sliding against me, brushing my side, as though she would make sure of my presence there.

"Well!" said the lawyer. "It matters little now! This mystery . . ."

You may well believe that all these cryptic remarks, as well as reference to a mystery or an Act of God, had driven me almost frantic. I demanded to know what he meant.

"Last night," said M. Duroc, "a certain article disappeared."

"Well, well?"

"It disappeared," said M. Duroc, drawn up like a grenadier. "But it could not conceivably have disappeared. I myself swear this! Our only suggestions as to how it might have disappeared are a toy rabbit and a barometer."

"Sir," I said, "I do not wish to be discourteous. But—"

"Am I mad, you ask?"

I bowed. If any man can manage at once to look sagging and uncertain, yet stately and dignified, M. Duroc managed it then. And dignity won, I think.

"Sir," he replied, gesturing with the candle towards the rear of the house, "Madame Thevenet lies there in her bed. She is paralyzed. She can move only her eyes or partially the lips, without speech. Do you wish to see her?"

"If I am permitted."

"Yes. That would be correct. Accompany me."

And I saw the poor old woman, Maurice. Call her harridan if you like.

It was a square room of good size, whose shutters had remained closed and locked for years. Can one smell rust? In that room, with faded green wall-paper, I felt I could.

One solitary candle did little more than dispel shadow. It burned atop the mantelpiece well opposite the foot of the bed; and a shaggy man, whom I afterwards learned to be a police-officer, sat in a green-upholstered arm-chair by an unlighted coal fire in the fireplace grate, picking his teeth with a knife.

"If you please, Dr. Harding!" M. Duroc called softly in English.

The long and lean American doctor, who had been bending over the bed so as to conceal from our sight the head and shoulders of Madame Thevenet, turned round. But this cadaverous body—in such fashion were madame's head and shoulders propped up against pillows—his cadaverous body, I say, still concealed her face.

"Has there been any change?" persisted M. Duroc in English.

"There has been no change," replied the dark-complexioned Dr. Harding, "except for the worse."

"Do you want her to be moved?"

"There has never been any necessity," said the physician, picking up his beaver hat from the bed. He spoke dryly. "However, if you want to learn anything more about the toy rabbit or the barometer, I should hurry. The lady will die in a matter of hours, probably less."

And he stood to one side.

It was a heavy bed with four posts and a canopy. The bed-curtains, of some dullish-green material, were closely drawn on every side except the long side by which we saw Madame Thevenet in profile. Lean as a post, rigid, the strings of her cotton nightcap tightly tied under her chin, Madame Thevenet lay propped up there. But one eye rolled towards us, and it rolled horribly.

Up to this time the woman we call the Jezebel had said little. She chose this moment again to come brushing against my side. Her greenish eyes, lids half-closed, shone in the light of M. Duroc's candle. What she whispered was: "You don't really hate me, do you?"

Maurice, I make a pause here.

Since I wrote the sentence, I put down my pen, and pressed my hands over my eyes, and once more I thought. But let me try again.

I spent just two hours in the bedroom of Madame Thevenet. At the end of the time—oh, you shall hear why!—I rushed out of that bedroom, and out of number 23 Thomas Street, like the maniac I was.

The streets were full of people, of carriages, of omnibuses, at early evening. Knowing no place of refuge save the saloon from which I had come, I gave its address to a cabdriver. Since still I had swallowed no food, I may have been light-headed. Yet I wished to pour out my heart to the friends who had bidden me return there. And where were they now?

A new group, all new, lounged against the bar-counter under brighter gaslight and brighter paint. Of all those who smote me on the back and cheered, none remained save the ancient giant who had implied friendship with General Washington. *He*, alas, lay helplessly drunk with his head near a sawdust spitting-box.

Nevertheless I was so moved that I took the liberty of thrusting a handful of bank-notes into his pocket. He alone remained.

Wait, there was another!

I do not believe he had remained there because of me. Yet M. Thaddeus Perley, still sitting alone at the little table by the pillar, with the open gas-jet above, stared vacantly at the empty glass in his hand.

He had named himself a foreigner; he was probably French. That was as well. For, as I lurched against the table, I was befuddled and all English had fled my wits.

"Sir," said I, "will you permit a madman to share your table?"

M. Perley gave a great start, as though roused out of thought. He was now sober: this I saw. Indeed, his shiver and haggard face were due to lack of stimulant rather than too much of it.

"Sir," he stammered, getting to his feet, "I shall be—I shall be honoured by your company." Automatically he opened his mouth to call for a waiter; his hand went to his pocket; he stopped.

"No, no, no!" said I. "If you insist, M. Perley, you may pay for the second bottle. The first is mine. I am sick at heart, and I would speak with a gentleman."

At these last words M. Perley's whole expression changed. He sat down, and gave me a grave courtly nod. His eyes, which were his most expressive feature, studied my face and my disarray.

"You are ill, M. de Lafayette," he said. "Have you so soon come to grief in this—this *civilized* country?"

"I have come to grief, yes. But not through civilization or the lack of it." And I banged my fist on the table. "I have come to grief, M. Perley, through miracles or magic. I have come to grief with a problem which no man's ingenuity can solve!"

M. Perley looked at me in a strange way. But someone had brought a bottle of brandy, with its accessories. M. Perley's trembling hand slopped a generous allowance into my glass, and an even more generous one into his own.

"That is very curious," he remarked, eyeing the glass. "A murder, was it?"

"No. But a valuable document has disappeared. The most thorough search by the police cannot find it."

Touch him anywhere, and he flinched. M. Perley, for some extraordinary reason, appeared to think I was mocking him.

"A document, you say?" His laugh was a trifle unearthly. "Come, now. Was it by any chance—a letter?"

"No, no! It was a will. Three large sheets of parchment, of the size you call foolscap. Listen!"

And as M. Perley added water to his brandy and gulped down about a third of it, I leaned across the table.

"Madame Thevenet, of whom you may have heard me speak in this café, was an invalid. But (until the early hours of this morning) she was not bed-ridden. She could move, and walk about her room, and so on. She had been lured away from Paris and her family by a green-eyed woman named the Jezebel.

"But a kindly lawyer of this city, M. Duroc, believed that madame suffered and had a bad conscience about her own daughter. Last night, despite the Jezebel, he persuaded madame at last to sign a will leaving all her money to this daughter.

"And the daughter, Claudine, is in mortal need of it! From my brother and myself, who have more than enough, she will not accept a sou. Her affiance, Lieutenant Delage, is as poor as she. But, unless she leaves France for Switzerland, she will die. I will not conceal from you that Claudine suffers from that dread disease we politely call consumption."

M. Perley stopped with his glass again half-way to his mouth.

He believed me now; I sensed it. Yet under the dark hair, tumbled on his forehead, his face had gone as white as his neat, mended shirt-frill.

"So very little a thing is money!" he whispered. "So very little a thing!"

And he lifted the glass and drained it.

"You do not think I am mocking you, sir?"

"No, no!" says M. Perley, shading his eyes with one hand. "I knew myself of one such case. She is dead. Pray continue."

"Last night, I repeat, Madame Thevenet changed her mind. When M. Duroc paid his weekly evening visit with the news that I should arrive today, madame fairly chattered with eagerness and a kind of terror. Death was approaching, she said; she had a presentiment."

As I spoke, Maurice, there returned to me the image of that shadowy, arsenic-green bedroom in the shuttered house; and what M. Duroc had told me.

"Madame," I continued, "cried out to M. Duroc that he must bolt the bedroom door. She feared the Jezebel, who lurked but said nothing. M. Duroc drew up to her bedside a portable writing-desk, with two good candles. For a long time madame spoke, pouring out contrition, self-abasement, the story of an unhappy marriage, all of which M. Duroc (sweating with embarrassment) was obliged to write down until it covered three large parchment sheets.

"But it was done, M. Perley!

"The will, in effect, left everything to her daughter, Claudine. It revoked a previous will by which all had been left (and this can be done in French law, as we both know) to Jezebel of the muddy complexion and the muddy yellow hair.

"Well, then! . . .

"M. Duroc sallies out into the street, where he finds two sober fellows who come in. Madame signs the will, M. Duroc sands[1] it, and the two men from the street affix their signatures as witnesses. Then *they* are gone. M. Duroc folds the will lengthways, and prepares to put it into his carpetbag. Now, M. Perley, mark what follows!

" 'No, no, no!' cries madame, with the shadow of her peaked nightcap wagging on the locked shutters beyond. 'I wish to keep it—for this one night!'

" 'For this one night, madame?' asks M. Duroc.

" 'I wish to press it against my heart,' says Madame Thevenet. 'I wish to read it once, twice, a thousand times! M. Duroc, what time is it?'

"Whereupon he takes out his gold repeater,[2] and opens it. To his astonishment it is one o'clock in the morning. Yet he touches the spring of the repeater, and its pulse-beat rings one.

" 'M. Duroc,' pleads Madame Thevenet, 'remain here with me for the rest of the night!'

" 'Madame!' cries M. Duroc, shocked to the very fans of his beard. 'That would not be correct.'

" 'Yes, you are right,' says madame. And never, swears the lawyer, has he seen her less bleary of eye, more alive with wit and cunning, more the great lady of ruin, than there in that green and shadowy and foul-smelling room.

"Yet this very fact puts her in more and more terror of the

Jezebel, who is never seen. She points to M. Duroc's carpetbag.

" 'I think you have much work to do, dear sir?'

"M. Duroc groaned. 'The Good Lord knows that I have!'

" 'Outside the only door of this room,' says madame, 'there is a small dressing-room. Set up your writing-desk beside the door there, so that no one may enter without your knowledge. Do your work there; you shall have a lamp or many candles. Do it,' shrieks madame, 'for the sake of Claudine and for the sake of an old friendship!'

"Very naturally, M. Duroc hesitated.

" '*She* will be hovering,' pleads Madame Thevenet, pressing the will against her breast. '*This* I shall read and read and read, and sanctify with my tears. If I find I am falling asleep,' and here the old lady looked cunning, 'I shall hide it. But no matter! Even *she* cannot penetrate through locked shutters and a guarded door.'

"Well, in fine, the lawyer at length yielded.

"He set up his writing-desk against the very doorpost outside that door. When he last saw madame, before closing the door, he saw her in profile with the green bed-curtains drawn except on that side, propped up with a tall candle burning on a table at her right hand.

"Ah, that night! I think I see M. Duroc at his writing-desk, as he has told me, in an airless dressing-room where no clock ticked. I see him, at times, removing his oval spectacles to press his smarting eyes. I see him returning to his legal papers, while his pen scratched through the wicked hours of the night.

"He heard nothing, or virtually nothing, until five o'clock in the morning. Then, which turned him cold and flabby, he heard a cry which he describes as being like that of a deaf-mute.

"The communicating door had not been bolted on Madame Thevenet's side, in case she needed help. M. Duroc rushed into the other room.

"On the table, at madame's right hand, the tall candle had burnt down to a flattish mass of wax over which still hovered a faint bluish flame. Madame herself lay rigid in her peaked nightcap. That revival of spirit last night, or remorse in her bitter heart, had brought on the last paralysis. Though M. Duroc tried to question her, she could move only her eyes.

"Then M. Duroc noticed that the will, which she had clutched as a doomed religious might clutch a crucifix, was not in her hand or on the bed.

" 'Where is the will?' he shouted at her, as though she were deaf too. 'Where is the will?'

"Madame Thevenet's eyes fixed on him. Then they moved down, and looked steadily at a trumpery toy—a rabbit, perhaps four inches high, made of pink velours or the like—which lay on the bed. Again she looked at M. Duroc, as though to emphasize this. Then her eyes rolled, this time with dreadful effort, towards a large barometer, shaped like a warming-pan, which hung on the wall beside the door. Three times she did this before the bluish candle-flame flickered and went out."

And I, Armand de Lafayette, paused here in my recital to M. Perley.

Again I became aware that I was seated in a garish saloon, swilling brandy, amid loud talk that beat the air. There was a thumping noise from the theatre above our heads, and faint strains of music.

"The will," I said, "was not stolen. Not even the Jezebel could have melted through locked shutters or a guarded door. The will was not hidden, because no inch of the room remains unsearched. *Yet the will is gone!*"

I threw a glance across the table at M. Perley.

To me, I am sure, the brandy had given strength and steadied my nerves. With M. Perley I was not so sure. He was a little flushed. That slightly wild look, which I had observed before, had crept up especially into one eye, giving his whole face a somewhat lop-sided appearance. Yet all his self-confidence had returned. He gave me a little crooked smile.

I struck the table.

"Do you honour me with your attention, M. Perley?"

"What song the Syrens sang," he said to me, "or what name Achilles assumed when he hid himself among women, although puzzling questions, are not beyond *all* conjecture."

"They are beyond *my* conjecture!" I cried. "And so is this!"

M. Perley extended his hand, spread the fingers, and examined them as one who owns the universe.

"It is some little time," he remarked, "since I have concerned myself with these trifles." His eyes retreated into a dream. "Yet I have given some trifling aid, in the past, to the Prefect of the Parisian police."

"You are a Frenchman! I knew it! And the police?" Seeing his lofty look, I added: "As an amateur, understood?"

"Understood!" Then his delicate hand—it would be unjust to call it claw-like—shot across the table and fastened on my arm. The strange eyes burned towards my face. "A little more detail!" he pleaded humbly. "A little more, I beg of you! This woman, for instance, you call the Jezebel?"

"It was she who met me at the house."

"And then?"

I described for him my meeting with the Jezebel, with M. Duroc, and our entrance to the sick-room, where the shaggy police-officer sat in the arm-chair and the saturnine doctor faced us from beside the bed.

"This woman," I exclaimed, with the room vividly before my eyes as I described it, "seems to have conceived for me (forgive me) a kind of passion. No doubt it was due to some idle compliments I once paid her at Paris.

"As I have explained, the Jezebel is *not* unattractive, even if she would only (again forgive me) wash her hair. Nevertheless, when once more she brushed my side and whispered, 'You don't really hate me, do you?' I felt little less than horror. It seemed to me that in some fashion I was responsible for the whole tragedy.

"While we stood beside the bed, M. Duroc the lawyer poured out the story I have recounted. There lay the poor paralytic, and confirmed it with her eyes. The toy rabbit, a detestable pink colour, lay in its same position on the bed. Behind me, hung against the wall by the door, was the large barometer.

"Apparently for my benefit, Madame Thevenet again went through her dumb-show with imploring eyes. She would look at the rabbit; next (as M. Duroc had not mentioned), she would roll her eyes all round her, for some desperate yet impenetrable reason, before fixing her gaze on the barometer.

"It meant . . . what?

"The lawyer spoke then. 'More light!' gulped out M. Duroc. 'If you must have closed shutters and windows, then let us at least have more light!'

"The Jezebel glided out to fetch candles. During M. Duroc's

explanation he had several times mentioned my name. At first mention of it the shaggy police-officer jumped and put away his clasp-knife. He beckoned to the physician, Dr. Harding, who went over for a whispered conference.

"Whereupon the police-officer sprang up.

"'Mr. Lafayette!' And he swung my hand pompously. 'If I'd known it was you, Mr. Lafayette, I wouldn't 'a' sat there like a bump on a log.'

"'You are an officer of police, sir,' said I. 'Can *you* think of no explanation?'

"He shook his head.

"'These people are Frenchies, Mr. Lafayette, and you're an American,' he said, with somewhat conspicuous lack of logic. '*If* they're telling the truth—'

"'Let us assume that!'

"'I can't tell you where the old lady's will is,' he stated positively. 'But I can tell you where it ain't. It ain't hidden in this room!'

"'But surely . . . !' I began in despair.

"At this moment the Jezebel, her brown-taffeta dress rustling, glided back into the room with a handful of candles and a tin box of the new-style Lucifer[3] matches. She lighted several candles, sticking them on any surface in their own grease.

"There were one or two fine pieces of furniture; but the mottled-marble tops were chipped and stained, the gilt sides cracked. There were a few mirrors, creating mimic spectral life. I saw a little more clearly the faded green paper of the walls, and what I perceived to be the partly open door of a cupboard. The floor was of bare boards.

"All this while I was conscious of two pairs of eyes: the imploring gaze of Madame Thevenet, and the amorous gaze of the Jezebel. One or the other I could have endured, but both together seemed to suffocate me.

"'Mr. Duroc here,' said the shaggy police-officer, clapping the distressed advocate on the shoulder, 'sent a messenger in a cab at half-past five this morning. And what time did we get here? I ask you and I tell you! Six o'clock!'

"Then he shook his finger at me, in a kind of pride and fury of efficiency.

" 'Why, Mr. Lafayette, there's been fourteen men at this room from six this morning until just before you got here!'

" 'To search for Madame Thevenet's will, you mean?'

"The shaggy man nodded portentously, and folded his arms.

" 'Floor's solid.' He stamped on the bare boards. 'Walls and ceiling? Nary a inch missed. We reckon we're remarkable smart; and we are.'

" 'But Madame Thevenet,' I persisted, 'was not a complete invalid until this morning. She could move about. If she became afraid of'—the name of the Jezebel choked me—'if she became afraid, and *did* hide the will . . .'

" 'Where'd she hide it? Tell me!'

" 'In the furniture, then?'

" 'Cabinet-makers in, Mr. Lafayette. No secret compartments.'

" 'In one of the mirrors?'

" 'Took the backs of 'em off. No will hid there.'

" 'Up the chimney!' I cried.

" 'Sent a chimney-sweep up there,' replied my companion in a ruminating way. Each time I guessed, he would leer at me in friendly and complacent challenge. 'Ye-es, I reckon we're pretty smart. But we didn't find no will.'

"The pink rabbit also seemed to leer from the bed. I saw madame's eyes. Once again, as a desperate mind will fasten on trifles, I observed the strings of the nightcap beneath her scrawny chin. But I looked again at the toy rabbit.

" 'Has it occurred to you,' I said triumphantly, 'to examine the bed and bedstead of Madame Thevenet herself?'

"My shaggy friend went to her bedside.

" 'Poor old woman,' he said. He spoke as though she were already a corpse. Then he turned round. 'We lifted her out, just as gentle as a new-born babe (didn't we ma'am?). No hollow bedposts! Nothing in the canopy! Nothing in the frame or the feather-beds or the curtains or the bedclothes!'

"Suddenly the shaggy police-officer became angry, as though he wished to be rid of the whole matter.

" 'And it ain't in the toy rabbit,' he said, 'because you can see we slit it up, if you look close. And it ain't in that barometer there. It just—ain't here.'

"There was a silence as heavy as the dusty, hot air of this room.

" 'It is here,' murmured M. Duroc in his gruff voice. 'It must be here!'

"The Jezebel stood there meekly, with downcast eyes.

"And I, in my turn, confess that *I* lost my head. I stalked over to the barometer, and tapped it. Its needle, which already indicated, 'Rain; cold,' moved still further towards that point.

"I was not insane enough to hit it with my fist. But I crawled on the floor, in search of a secret hiding-place. I felt along the wall. The police-officer—who kept repeating that nobody must touch anything and he would take no responsibility until he went off duty at something o'clock—the police-officer I ignored.

"What at length gave me pause was the cupboard, already thoroughly searched. In the cupboard hung a few withered dresses and gowns, as though they had shrivelled with Madame Thevenet's body. But on the shelf of the cupboard . . .

"On the shelf stood a great number of perfume-bottles: even today, I fear, many of our countrymen think perfume a substitute for water and soap; and the state of madame's hands would have confirmed this. *But*, on the shelf, were a few dusty novels. There was a crumpled and begrimed copy of yesterday's New-York *Sun*. This newspaper did not contain a will; but it did contain a black beetle, which ran out across my hand.

"In a disgust past describing, I flung down the beetle and stamped on it. I closed the cupboard door, acknowledging defeat. Madame Thevenet's will was gone. And at the same second, in that dim green room—still badly lighted, with only a few more candles—two voices cried out.

"One was my own voice:

" *'In God's name, where is it?'*

"The other was the deep voice of M. Duroc:

" *'Look at that woman! She knows!'*

"And he meant the Jezebel.

"M. Duroc, with his beard-fans a-tremble, was pointing to a mirror; a little blurred, as these mirrors were. Our Jezebel had been looking into the mirror, her back turned to us. Now she dodged, as at a stone thrown.

"With good poise our Jezebel writhed this movement into a curtsy, turning to face us. But not before I also had seen that smile—like a razor-cut before the blood comes—as well as full knowledge, mocking knowledge, shining out of wide-open eyes in the mirror.

" 'You spoke to me, M. Duroc?' She murmured the reply, also in French.

" 'Listen to me!' the lawyer said formally. 'This will is *not* missing. It is in this room. You were not here last night. Something has made you guess. You know where it is.'

" 'Are you unable to find it?' asked the Jezebel in surprise.

" 'Stand back, young man!' M. Duroc said to me. 'I ask you something, mademoiselle, in the name of justice.'

" 'Ask!' said the Jezebel.

" 'If Claudine Thevenet inherits the money to which she is entitled, you will be well paid; yes, overpaid! You know Claudine. You know that!'

" 'I know it.'

" 'But if the new will be *not* found,' said M. Duroc, again waving me back, 'then you inherit everything. And Claudine will die. For it will be assumed—'

" 'Yes!' said the Jezebel, with one hand pressed against her breast. 'You yourself, M. Duroc, testify that all night a candle was burning at madame's bedside. Well! The poor woman, whom *I* loved and cherished, repented of her ingratitude towards me. She burnt this new will at the candle-flame; she crushed its ashes to powder and blew them away!'

" 'Is that true?' cried M. Duroc.

" 'They will assume it,' smiled the Jezebel, 'as you say.' She looked at me. 'And for you, M. Armand!'

"She glided closer. I can only say that I saw her eyes uncovered; or, if you wish to put it so, her soul and flesh together.

" 'I would give you everything on earth,' she said. 'I will not give you the doll-face in Paris.'

" 'Listen to me!' I said to her, so agitated that I seized her shoulders. 'You are out of your senses! You cannot give Claudine to me! She will marry another man!'

" 'And do you think that matters to me,' asked the Jezebel, with her green eyes full on mine, 'as long as you still love her?'

"There was a small crash as someone dropped a knife on the floor.

"We three, I think, had completely forgotten that we were not alone. There were two spectators, although they did not comprehend our speech.

"The saturnine Dr. Harding now occupied the green armchair. His long thin legs, in tight black trousers with strap under the boot-instep, were crossed and looked spidery; his high beaver hat glimmered on his head. The police-officer, who was picking his teeth with a knife when I first saw him, had now dropped the knife when he tried to trim his nails.

"But both men sensed the atmosphere. Both were alert, feeling out with the tentacles of their nerves. The police-officer shouted at me.

"'What's this gabble?' he said. 'What's a-gitting into your head?'

"Grotesquely, it was that word 'head' which gave me my inspiration.

"'The nightcap!' I exclaimed in English.

"'What nightcap?'

"For the nightcap of Madame Thevenet had a peak; it was large; it was tightly tied under the chin; it might well conceal a flat-pressed document which—but you understand. The police-officer, dull-witted as he appeared, grasped the meaning in a flash. And how I wished I had never spoken! For the fellow meant well, but he was not gentle.

"As I raced round the curtained sides of the bed, the police-officer was holding a candle in one hand and tearing off madame's nightcap with the other. He found no will there, no document at all; only straggly wisps of hair on a skull grown old before its time.

"Madame Thevenet had been a great lady, once. It must have been the last humiliation. Two tears overflowed her eyes and ran down her cheeks. She lay propped up there in a nearly sitting position; but something seemed to wrench inside her.

"And she closed her eyes forever. And the Jezebel laughed.

"That is the end of my story. That is why I rushed out of the house like a madman. The will has vanished as though by magic; or is it still there by magic? In any case, you find me at this table: grubby and dishevelled and much ashamed."

For a little time after I had finished my narrative to M. Perley in the saloon, it seemed to me that the bar-counter was a trifle quieter. But a faint stamping continued from the theatre above our heads. Then all was hushed, until a chorus rose to a tinkle of many banjos.

> *Oh, I come from Alabama*
> *With my banjo on my knee;*
> *I depart for Louisiana. . .*

Enough! The song soon died away, and M. Thaddeus Perley did not even hear it.

M. Perley sat looking downwards into an empty glass, so that I could not see his face.

"Sir," he remarked almost bitterly, "you are a man of good heart. I am glad to be of service in a problem so trifling as this."

"Trifling!"

His voice was a little husky, but not slurred. His hand slowly turned the glass round and round.

"Will you permit two questions?" asked M. Perley.

"Two questions? Ten thousand!"

"More than two will be unnecessary." Still M. Perley did not look up. "This toy rabbit, of which so much was made: I would know its exact position on the bed?"

"It was almost at the foot of the bed, and about the middle in a crossways direction."

"Ah, so I had imagined. Were the three sheets of parchment, forming the will, written upon two sides or upon only one?"

"I had not told you, M. Perley. But M. Duroc said: upon one side only."

M. Perley raised his head.

His face was now flushed and distorted with drink, his eye grown wild. In his cups he was as proud as Satan, and as disdainful of others' intelligence; yet he spoke with dignity, and with careful clearness.

"It is ironic, M. de Lafayette, that I should tell you how to lay your hand on the missing will and the elusive money; since, upon my word, I have never been able to perform a like service for myself." And he smiled, as at some secret joke. "Perhaps," he added, "it is the very simplicity of the thing which puts you at fault."

I could only look at him in bewilderment.

"Perhaps the mystery is a little *too* plain! A little *too* self-evident!"

"You mock me, sir! I will not . . ."

"Take me as I am," said M. Perley, whacking the foot of the glass on the table, "or leave me. Besides," here his wandering eye encountered a list of steam-sailings pasted against the wall, "I—I leave tomorrow by the *Parnassus* for England, and then for France."

"I meant no offence, M. Perley! If you have knowledge, speak!"

"Madame Thevenet," he said, carefully pouring himself more brandy, "hid the will in the middle of the night. Does it puzzle you that she took such precautions to hide the will? But the element of the outré[4] must always betray itself. The Jezebel *must not* find that will! Yet Madame Thevenet trusted nobody—not even the worthy physician who attended her. If madame were to die of a stroke, the police would be there and must soon, she was sure, discover her simple device. Even if she were paralyzed, it would ensure the presence of other persons in the room to act as unwitting guards.

"Your cardinal error," M. Perley continued dispassionately, "was one of ratiocination. You tell me that Madame Thevenet, to give you a hint, looked fixedly at some point near the foot of the bed. Why do you assume that she was looking at the toy rabbit?"

"Because," I replied hotly, "the toy rabbit was the only object she could have looked at!"

"Pardon me; but it was *not*. You several times informed me that the bed-curtains were closely drawn together on three sides. They were drawn on all but the 'long' side towards the door. Therefore the ideal reasoner, without having seen the room, may safely say that the curtains were drawn together at the foot of the bed?"

"Yes, true!"

"After looking fixedly at this point represented by the toy, Madame Thevenet then 'rolls her eyes all round her'—in your phrase. May we assume that she wishes the curtains to be drawn back, so that she may see something *beyond* the bed?"

"It is—possible, yes!"

"It is more than possible, as I shall demonstrate. Let us direct our attention, briefly, to the incongruous phenomenon of the barometer on another wall. The barometer indicates, 'Rain; cold.' "

Here M. Perley's thin shoulders drew together under the old military cloak.

"Well," he said, "the cold is on its way. Yet this day, for April, has been warm outside and indoors, oppressively hot?"

"Yes! Of course!"

"You yourself," continued M. Perley, inspecting his fingernails, "told me what was directly opposite the foot of the bed. Let us suppose that the bed-curtains are drawn open. Madame Thevenet, in her nearly seated position, is looking *downwards*. What would she have seen?"

"The fireplace!" I cried. "The grate of the fireplace!"

"Already we have a link with the weather. And what, as you have specifically informed me, was in the grate of the fireplace?"

"An unlighted coal fire!"

"Exactly. And what is essential for the composition of such a fire? We need coal; we need wood; but primarily and above all, we need . . ."

"*Paper!*" I cried.

"In the cupboard of that room," said M. Perley, with his disdainful little smile, "was a very crumpled and begrimed (mark that; not dusty) copy of *yesterday's* New-York *Sun*. To light fires is the most common, and indeed the best, use for our daily press. That copy had been used to build yesterday's fire. But something else, during the night, was substituted for it. You yourself remarked the extraordinarily dirty state of Madame Thevenet's hands."

M. Perley swallowed the brandy, and his flush deepened.

"Sir," he said loudly, "you will find the will crumpled up, with ends most obviously protruding, under the coal and wood in the fireplace grate. Even had anyone taken the fire to pieces, he would have found only what appeared to be dirty blank paper, written side undermost, which could never be a valuable will. It was too self-evident to be seen.—Now go!"

"Go?" I echoed stupidly.

M. Perley rose from his chair.

"Go, I say!" he shouted, with an even wilder eye. "The Jezebel could not light that fire. It was too warm, for one thing; and all day there were police-officers with instructions that an outsider must touch nothing. But now? *Madame Thevenet kept warning you that the fire must not be lighted, or the will would be destroyed!"*

"Will you await me here?" I called over my shoulder.

"Yes, yes! And perhaps there will be peace for the wretched girl with—with the lung-trouble."

Even as I ran out of the door I saw him, grotesque and pitiful, slump across the table. Hope, rising and surging, seemed to sweep me along like a crack of the cabman's whip. But when I reached my destination, hope receded.

The shaggy police-officer was just descending the front steps.

"None of us coming back here, Mr. Lafayette!" he called cheerily. "Old Mrs. What's-her-name went and burnt that will at a candle last night.—Here, what's o'clock?"

The front door was unlocked. I raced through that dark house, and burst into the rear bedroom.

The corpse still lay in the big, gloomy bed. Every candle had flickered almost down to its socket. The police-officer's clasp-knife, forgotten since he had dropped it, still lay on bare boards. But the Jezebel was there.

She knelt on the hearth, with the tin box of Lucifer matches she had brought there earlier. The match spurted, a bluish fire; I saw her eagerness; she held the match to the grate.

"A Lucifer," I said, "in the hand of a Jezebel!"

And I struck her away from the grate, so that she reeled against a chair and fell. Large coals, small coals rattled down in puffs of dust as I plunged my hands into the unlighted fire. Little sticks, sawed sticks; and I found it there: crumpled parchment-sheets, but incontestably madame's will.

"M. Duroc!" I called. "M. Duroc!"

You and I, my brother Maurice, have fought the Citizen-King[5] with bayonets as we now fight the upstart Bonapartist; we need not be ashamed of tears. I confess, then, that the tears overran my eyes and blinded me. I scarcely saw M. Duroc as he hurried into the room.

Certainly I did not see the Jezebel stealthily pick up the police-officer's knife. I noticed nothing at all until she flew at me, and stabbed me in the back.

Peace, my brother: I have assured you all is well. At that time, faith, I was not much conscious of any hurt. I bade M. Duroc, who was trembling, to wrench out the knife; I borrowed his roomy greatcoat to hide the blood; I must hurry, hurry, hurry back to that little table under the gas-jet.

I planned it all on my way back. M. Perley, apparently a stranger in this country, disliked it and was evidently very poor even in France. But *we* are not precisely paupers. Even with his intense pride, he could not refuse (for such a service) a sum which would comfort him for the rest of his life.

Back I plunged into the saloon, and hurried down it. Then I stopped. The little round table by the pillar, under the flaring gas-jet, was empty.

How long I stood there I cannot tell. The back of my shirt, which at first had seemed full of blood, now stuck to the borrowed greatcoat. All of a sudden I caught sight of the fat-faced bartender with the gold teeth, who had been on service that afternoon and had returned now. As a mark of respect, he came out from behind the bar-counter to greet me.

"Where is the gentleman who was sitting at that table?"

I pointed to it. My voice, in truth, must have sounded so hoarse and strange that he mistook it for anger.

"Don't you worry about that, monseer!" said he reassuringly. "*That's* been tended to! We threw the drunken tramp out of here!"

"You threw . . ."

"Right bang in the gutter. Had to crawl along in it before he could stand up." My bartender's face was pleased and vicious. "Ordered a bottle of best brandy, and couldn't pay for it." The face changed again. "Goddelmighty, monseer, what's wrong?"

"*I* ordered that brandy."

"*He* didn't say so, when the waiter brought me over. Just looked me up and down, crazy-like, and said a gentleman would give his I.O.U. Gentleman!"

"M. Perley," I said, restraining an impulse to kill that bartender, "is a friend of mine. He departs for France early tomorrow morning. Where is his hotel? Where can I find him?"

"Perley!" sneered my companion. "That ain't even his real

name, I hearn tell. Gits high-and-mighty ideas from upper Broadway. But his real name's on the I.O.U."

A surge of hope, once more, almost blinded me. "Did you keep that I.O.U.?"

"Yes, I kepp it," growled the bartender, fishing in his pocket. "God knows why, but I kepp it."

And at last, Maurice, I triumphed!

True, I collapsed from my wound; and the fever would not let me remember that I must be at the dock when the *Parnassus* steam-packet departed from New-York next morning. I must remain here, shut up in a hotel-room and unable to sleep at night, until I can take ship for home. But where I failed, you can succeed. He was to leave on the morrow by the *Parnassus* for England, and then for France—so he told me. You can find him—in six months at the most. In six months, I give you my word, he will be out of misery forever!

"I.O.U.," reads the little slip, *"for one bottle of your best brandy, forty-five cents. Signed: Edgar A. Poe."*

> I remain, Maurice,
> Your affectionate brother,
> Armand

COMMENT AND QUESTIONS

The student of Poe will recognize a number of correspondences between Thaddeus Perley and Edgar A. Poe. For one thing, Perley has a special interest in the consumptive girl whose life Lafayette seeks to save, and Poe's own young wife, Virginia Clemm, died of tuberculosis (consumption). Ironically, he could not save her but could save Lafayette's friend. For another, Thaddeus Perley was a name actually used by Poe on at least one occasion. Perley also uses the quotation that prefaces "The Murders in the Rue Morgue" ("What song the Syrens sang, or what name Achilles assumed when he hid himself among women, although puzzling questions, are not beyond *all* conjecture"), and his continued presence in the saloon is a reminder of Poe's reputation for excessive drinking.

Parallels with "The Purloined Letter" are numerous. There are words spoken by Perley that are direct quotations from the story ("Perhaps it is the very simplicity of the thing which puts you at fault." "Perhaps the mystery is a little *too* plain! A little *too* self-evident!") The American policemen are distinctly reminiscent of Monsieur G—— and his associates, and their search procedures are remarkably similar. In each case the object of the search is a document that must be recovered to prevent disaster.

In addition to the locked room, this story provides an example of two other conventions in detective fiction: armchair detection and fair play for the reader. Carr makes it quite clear that the will cannot have been removed from the room. The man who determines the will's hiding place never visits the scene of the crime and does no active investigating at all. The description of the room given to him is included in the story, so the reader theoretically has the chance to solve the crime from *his* armchair. The inclusion of all necessary clues (the assurance that the will is in the room and the description of the room) is considered "playing fair" with the reader.

This story imparts two distinct varieties of pleasurable experience to a reader. One derives from the simple satisfaction of seeing a well-constructed puzzle solved. But the other is more complex. In order to participate fully in the experience of "The Gentleman from Paris," one must know Poe and "The Purloined Letter." No footnote can serve as an adequate substitute for a previous reading of Poe's story. Can you think of additional stories or novels that you enjoy more because of your familiarity with other works of literature?

What is the advantage of having the story told in a letter?

Does the assurance made in the opening lines that "all is safe" destroy the suspense? Does the author assume a greater burden in giving this assurance? Explain.

What difference is there between Armand's attitude toward his uncle and that of the saloon crowd?

Read the biblical account of an incident in the life of Jezebel in I Kings 21. Is "the Jezebel" an appropriate name for the companion of Madame Thevenet? Notice the verbs used to describe her movements. Do they help to characterize her?

Compare the style of this story with that of "The Purloined Letter." Has the author imitated Poe? If so, in what way?

Aside from his extraordinary intelligence, the detective hero often seems to be different from ordinary men in manner, habit, and appearance. What details are given to suggest Perley's strangeness?

Poe's writings have had even more influence on French literature, especially poetry, than on American literature, and M. Armand thought that Thaddeus Perley was a Frenchman because he said he was a "foreigner." In what ways might Perley have felt a foreigner in his own country?

Which hiding place has more dramatic potential—that of Poe or that of Carr? Why?

NOTES

1. *sands.* Sprinkles with sand for the purpose of blotting.
2. *repeater.* A watch that can be made to strike the hour or quarter hour just past.
3. *Lucifer.* The rebellious archangel, who fell from heaven. He is usually identified with Satan.
4. *outré.* Bizarre, strange, unconventional.
5. *Citizen-King.* Louis Philippe, ruler of France from 1830 to 1849.

ARTHUR CONAN DOYLE

The Speckled Band

Sherlock Holmes made his first appearance in 1887 with the publication of Arthur Conan Doyle's *A Study in Scarlet*, but the great public interest in the character dates from 1891 and the publication of "A Scandal in Bohemia." Very soon editors were bargaining for sets of a dozen stories, and Doyle was supplying them. Soon, however, he tired of the restraints of this kind of writing and decided to have an adventure end with Holmes' death. Thus, the Great Detective plunged to his death over the Reichenbach Falls (in Switzerland), locked in deadly embrace with his rival, the arch-villain Professor Moriarty. Public outrage was great, and sorrowful and angry letters flooded Doyle's desk. But it was not until eight years later that Doyle consented to bring Holmes back to life.

Reportedly, more commentary has been written on Sherlock Holmes than on any other literary character except Hamlet. This is just one mark of the popularity that the character has enjoyed since the 1890s. Even today mail is addressed to Holmes at the famous residence, 221B Baker Street, and is answered by a secretary at one of the businesses occupying the space where Holmes' flat would have stood. Indeed, Sherlock Holmes' exploits have become a modern myth, and nearly every detective created in the twentieth century owes some aspect of his being to this striking and original figure.

Doyle once spoke in detail of his great debt to Poe, and he quite successfully used the special conventions originated by Poe to create one of the most memorable fictional characters ever presented to a reader. Like Dupin, Holmes has rather odd living habits. He loves doing experiments in his rooms and keeps his pipe tobacco in his slippers, preferring comfortable untidiness to order. In addition, he is subject to fits of depression, sitting or lying for days in melancholy gloom, and on other occasions taking three injections of cocaine a day. Many films and plays have reinterpreted him, and the Royal Shakespeare Company in 1974 brought Holmes back to a joyful welcome on the London stage.

"The Speckled Band" appeared in the first series of Sherlock Holmes adventures, and Doyle declared it to be his favorite of all the stories about his famous sleuth. In it there is a deliberate and successful building up of an atmosphere of terror that apparently can be neither dispelled nor explained by rational means. It is the terror of an eerie nighttime whistle and of a speckled band whose power goes beyond barred windows and doors and seems to produce death from sheer terror. This story shows Holmes and Watson at their finest, putting things right in the world, protecting the innocent, and tracing fear and evil to their source.

I t was early in April in the year '83 that I woke one morning to find Sherlock Holmes standing, fully dressed, by the side of my bed. He was a late riser, as a rule, and as the clock on the mantelpiece showed me that it was only a quarter-past seven, I blinked up at him in some surprise, and perhaps just a little resentment, for I was myself regular in my habits.

"Very sorry to wake you up, Watson," said he, "but it's the common lot this morning. Mrs. Hudson has been awakened, she retorted upon me, and I on you."

"What is it, then—a fire?"

"No; a client. It seems that a young lady has arrived in a considerable state of excitement, who insists upon seeing me. She is waiting now in the sitting room."

I had no keener pleasure than in following Holmes in his professional investigations, and in admiring the rapid deductions, as swift as intuitions, and yet always founded on a logical basis, with which he unraveled the problems which were submitted to him. I rapidly threw on my clothes and was ready in a few minutes to accompany my friend down to the sitting room. A lady dressed in black and heavily veiled, who had been sitting in the window, rose as we entered.

"Good morning, madam," said Holmes cheerily. "My name is Sherlock Holmes. This is my intimate friend and associate, Dr. Watson, before whom you can speak as freely as before myself. Ha! I am glad to see that Mrs. Hudson has had the good sense to light the fire. Pray draw up to it, and I shall order you a cup of hot coffee, for I observe that you are shivering."

"It is not cold which makes me shiver," said the woman in a low voice, changing her seat as requested.

"What, then?"

"It is fear, Mr. Holmes. It is terror." She raised her veil as she spoke, and we could see that she was indeed in a pitiable state of agitation, her face all drawn and gray, with restless, frightened eyes, like those of some hunted animal.

"You must not fear," said he soothingly, bending forward and patting her forearm. "We shall soon set matters right, I have no doubt. You have come in by train this morning, I see."

"You know me, then?"

"No, but I observe the second half of a return ticket in the palm of your left glove. You must have started early, and yet you had a good drive in a dog cart, along heavy roads, before you reached the station."

The lady gave a violent start and stared in bewilderment at my companion.

"There is no mystery, my dear madam," said he, smiling. "The left arm of your jacket is spattered with mud in no less than seven places. The marks are perfectly fresh. There is no vehicle save a dog cart which throws up mud in that way, and then only when you sit on the left-hand side of the driver."

"Whatever your reasons may be, you are perfectly correct," said she. "I started from home before six, reached Leatherhead at twenty past, and came in by the first train to Waterloo. Sir, I can stand this strain no longer; I shall go mad if it continues. I have no one to turn to—none, save only one, who cares for me, and he, poor fellow, can be of little aid.

"I have heard of you, Mr. Holmes; I have heard of you from Mrs. Farintosh, whom you helped in the hour of her sore need."

"Farintosh," said he. "Ah yes, I recall the case; it was concerned with an opal tiara. I think it was before your time, Watson. I can only say, madam, that I shall be happy to devote the same care to your case as I did to that of your friend. As to reward, my profession is its own reward; but you are at liberty to defray whatever expenses I may be put to, at the time which suits you best. And now I beg that you will lay before us everything that may help us in forming an opinion upon the matter."

"My name is Helen Stoner, and I am living with my stepfather, who is the last survivor of one of the oldest Saxon families in England, the Roylotts of Stoke Moran, on the western border of Surrey."

Holmes nodded his head. "The name is familiar to me," said he.

"The family was at one time among the richest in England. In the last century, however, four successive heirs were of a dissolute and wasteful disposition, and the family ruin was eventually completed by a gambler in the days of the Regency. Nothing was left save a few acres of ground, and the two-hundred-year-old house, which is itself crushed under a heavy mortgage.

"The last squire dragged out his existence there, living the horrible life of an aristocratic pauper; but his only son, my stepfather, seeing that he must adapt himself to the new conditions, obtained an advance from a relative, which enabled him to take a medical degree, and went out to Calcutta, where, by his professional skill and his force of character, he established a large practice. In a fit of anger, however, caused by some robberies which had been perpetrated in the house, he beat his native butler to death and narrowly escaped a capital sentence. As it was, he suffered a long term of imprisonment and afterwards returned to England a morose and disappointed man.

"When Dr. Roylott was in India he married my mother, Mrs. Stoner, the young widow of Major-General Stoner, of the Bengal Artillery. My sister Julia and I were twins, and we were only two years old at the time of my mother's re-marriage. She had a considerable sum of money—and this she bequeathed to Dr. Roylott entirely while we resided with him, with a provision that a certain annual sum should be allowed to each of us in the event of our marriage. Shortly after our return to England my mother died—she was killed eight years ago in a railway accident near Crewe. Dr. Roylott then took us to live with him in the old ancestral house at Stoke Moran. The money which my mother had left was enough for all our wants, and there seemed to be no obstacle to our happiness.

"But a terrible change came over our stepfather about this time. Instead of making friends and exchanging visits with our neighbors, who had at first been overjoyed to see a Roylott of Stoke Moran back in the old family seat, he shut himself up in his house and seldom came out save to indulge in ferocious quarrels with whoever might cross his path.

"Violence of temper approaching to mania has been hereditary in the men of the family, and in my stepfather's case it had, I believe, been intensified by his long residence in the tropics. A series of disgraceful brawls took place, two of which ended in the police court, until at last he became the terror of the village, and the folks would fly at his approach, for he is a man of immense strength, and absolutely uncontrollable in his anger.

"He had no friends at all save the wandering gypsies, and he would give these vagabonds leave to encamp upon the few acres of bramble-covered land which represent the family estate. He has a passion also for Indian animals, which are sent over to him by a correspondent, and he has at this moment a cheetah and a baboon, which wander freely over his grounds and are feared by the villagers almost as much as is their master.

"You can imagine from what I say that my poor sister Julia and I had no great pleasure in our lives. No servant would stay with us, and for a long time we did all the work of the house. She was but thirty at the time of her death, and yet her hair had already begun to whiten, even as mine has."

"Your sister is dead, then?"

"She died just two years ago, and it is of her death that I wish to speak to you. You can understand that, living the life which I have described, we were little likely to see anyone of our own age and position. We had, however, an aunt who lives near Harrow. Julia went there at Christmas two years ago, and met there a major in the Marines, to whom she became engaged. My stepfather learned of the engagement when my sister returned and offered no objection to the marriage; but within a fortnight of the day which had been fixed for the wedding, the terrible event occurred which has deprived me of my only companion."

Sherlock Holmes had been leaning back in his chair with his eyes closed and his head sunk in a cushion, but he half opened his lids now and glanced across at his visitor. He wanted to hear everything.

"Pray be precise as to details," said he.

"It is easy for me to be so, for every event of that dreadful time is seared into my memory. The manor house is, as I have already said, very old, and only one wing is now inhabited. The bedrooms in this wing are on the ground floor, the sitting rooms being in the central block of the buildings. Of these bedrooms the first is Dr. Roylott's, the second my sister's, and the third my own. There is no communication between them, but they all open out into the same corridor. Do I make myself plain?"

"Perfectly so."

"The windows of the three rooms open out upon the lawn. That fatal night my sister came into my room because she was troubled by the smell of Dr. Roylott's cigar. She sat for some time, chatting about her approaching wedding. At eleven o'clock she rose to leave me, but she paused at the door and looked back.

" 'Tell me, Helen,' said she, 'have you ever heard anyone whistle in the dead of the night?'

" 'Never,' said I.

" 'I suppose that you could not possibly whistle, yourself, in your sleep?'

" 'Certainly not. But why?'

" 'Because during the last few nights I have always, about three in the morning, heard a low, clear whistle. I thought that I would just ask you whether you had heard it.'

" 'No, I have not. It must be those wretched gypsies.'

" 'Well, it is of no great consequence, at any rate.' She smiled back at me, closed my door, and a few moments later I heard her key turn in the lock."

"Indeed," said Holmes. "Was it your custom always to lock yourselves in at night?"

"Always."

"And why?"

"I think that I mentioned to you that the doctor kept a cheetah and a baboon. We had no feeling of security unless our doors were locked."

"Quite so. Pray proceed with your statement."

"I could not sleep that night. A vague feeling of impending misfortune impressed me. My sister and I, you will recollect, were twins, and you know how subtle are the links which bind two souls which are so closely allied. It was a wild night. The wind was howling outside, and the rain was beating and splashing against the windows. Suddenly, amid all the hubbub of the gale, there burst forth the wild scream of a terrified woman. I knew that it was my sister's voice. I sprang from my bed, wrapped a shawl round me, and rushed to the door.

"As I entered the corridor, I seemed to hear a low whistle, such as my sister had described, and a few moments later a clanging sound, as if a mass of metal had fallen. As I ran down the passage, I saw that my sister's door was unlocked, and revolved slowly upon its hinges. I stared at it horror-stricken, not knowing what was about to issue from it. By the light of the corridor lamp I saw my sister appear at the opening, her face blanched with terror, her hands groping for help, her whole figure swaying to and fro like that of a drunkard.

"I ran to her and threw my arms around her, but at that moment her knees seemed to give way and she fell to the ground. She writhed as one who is in terrible pain, and her limbs were dreadfully convulsed. At first I thought that she had not recognized me, but as I bent over her she suddenly shrieked out in a voice which I shall never forget, 'Oh, my God! Helen! It was the band! The speckled band!'

"There was something else which she would fain have said, and she stabbed with her finger into the air in the direction of the doctor's room, but a fresh convulsion seized her and choked her words. I rushed out, calling loudly for my stepfather, and I met him hastening from his room in his dressing gown. When he reached my sister's side she was unconscious, and though he poured brandy down her throat and sent for medical aid from the village, all efforts were in vain, for she slowly sank and died without having recovered her consciousness. Such was the dreadful end of my beloved sister."

"One moment," said Holmes, "are you sure about this whistle and metallic sound? Could you swear to it?"

"That was what the county coroner asked me at the inquiry. It is my strong impression that I heard it, and yet, among the crash of the gale and the creaking of an old house, I may possibly have been deceived."

"Was your sister dressed?"

"No, she was in her nightdress. In her right hand was found the charred stump of a match, and in her left a match box."

"Showing that she had struck a light and looked about her when the alarm took place. That is important. And what conclusions did the coroner come to?"

"He investigated the case with great care, for Dr. Roylott's conduct had long been notorious in the county, but he was unable to find any satisfactory cause of death. My evidence showed that the door had been fastened upon the inner side, and the windows were blocked by old-fashioned shutters with broad iron bars, which were secured every night.

"The walls were carefully sounded and were shown to be quite solid all round, and the flooring was also thoroughly examined, with the same result. The chimney is wide, but is barred up by four large staples. It is certain, therefore, that my sister was quite alone when she met her end. Besides, there were no marks of any violence upon her."

"How about poison?"

"The doctors examined her for it, but without success."

"Were there gypsies on the plantation at the time?"

"Yes, there are nearly always some there."

"Ah, and what did you gather from this allusion to a band—a speckled band?"

"Sometimes I have thought that it was merely the wild talk of delirium; sometimes that it may have referred to some band of people, perhaps to these very gypsies on the plantation. I do not know whether the spotted handkerchiefs which so many of them wear over their heads might have suggested the strange adjective which she used."

Holmes shook his head like a man who is far from being satisfied.

"These are very deep waters," said he; "pray go on with your narrative."

"Two years have passed since then, and my life has been until lately lonelier than ever. A month ago, however, a dear friend, whom I have known for many years, did me the honor to ask my hand in marriage and we are to be married in the spring.

"Two days ago some repairs were started in the west wing of the building, and my bedroom wall was pierced, so that I have had to move into the chamber in which my sister died, and to sleep in the very bed in which she slept. Imagine, then, my thrill of terror when last night, as I lay awake, thinking over her terrible fate, I suddenly heard in the silence of the night the low whistle which had been the herald of her own death. I sprang up and lit the lamp, but nothing was to be seen in the room.

"I was too shaken to go to bed again, however, so I dressed, and as soon as it was daylight I slipped out, got a dog-cart at the Crown Inn, which is opposite, and drove to Leatherhead, from whence I have come on this morning with the one object of seeing you and asking your advice."

"You have done wisely," said my friend. "But have you told me all?"

"Why, what do you mean? What is it?"

For answer Holmes pushed back the frill of black lace which fringed the hand that lay upon our visitor's knee. Five little livid spots, the marks of four fingers and a thumb, were printed upon the white wrist.

"You have been cruelly used," said Holmes.

The lady colored deeply and covered over her injured wrist. "He is a hard man," she said, "and perhaps he hardly knows his own strength."

There was a long silence, during which Holmes leaned his chin upon his hands and stared into the crackling fire.

"This is a very deep business," he said at last. "There are a thousand details which I should desire to know before I decide upon our course of action. Yet we have not a moment to lose. If we were to come to Stoke Moran today, would it be possible for us to look over these rooms without the knowledge of your stepfather?"

"As it happens, he spoke of coming into town today upon some most important business. It is probable that he will be away all day."

"Excellent. You are not averse to this trip, Watson?"

"By no means."

"Then we shall both come. What are you going to do yourself?"

"I have one or two things which I would wish to do now that I am in town. But I shall return by the twelve o'clock train, so as to be there in time for your coming."

"And you may expect us early in the afternoon. I have myself some small business matters to attend to. Will you not wait and breakfast?"

"No, I must go. My heart is lightened already since I have confided my trouble to you. I shall look forward to seeing you again this afternoon." She dropped her thick black veil over her face and softly glided from the room.

"And what do you think of it all, Watson?" asked Sherlock Holmes, leaning back in his chair.

"It seems to me to be a most dark and sinister business."

"Dark enough and sinister enough."

"Yet if the lady is correct in saying that the flooring and walls are sound, and that the door, window, and chimney are impassable, then her sister must undoubtedly have been alone when she met her mysterious end."

"What becomes, then, of these nocturnal whistles, and what of the very peculiar words of the dying woman?" mused Holmes.

"I cannot think."

"When you combine the ideas of whistles at night, the presence of a band of gypsies who are on intimate terms with this old doctor, the fact that we have every reason to believe that the doctor has an interest in preventing his stepdaughter's marriage, the dying allusion to a band, and, finally, the fact that Miss Helen Stoner heard a metallic clang, which might have been caused by one of those metal bars that secured the shutters falling back into its place, I think that these factors all point to a theory that may help clear the mystery."

"But what, then, did the gypsies do?" I asked quickly.

"I cannot imagine," Holmes responded thoughtfully. "It is precisely for that reason that we are going to Stoke Moran this day. I want to see for myself whether there are any fatal objections to my theory. Only a spot investigation will tell me what I want to know.—But what in the name of the devil!"

The ejaculation had been drawn from my companion by the fact that our door had been suddenly dashed open, and that a huge man had framed himself in the aperture. His costume was a peculiar mixture of the professional and of the agricultural, having a black top-hat, a long frock-coat, and a pair of high gaiters, with a hunting crop swinging in his hand. So tall was he that his hat actually brushed the cross bar of the doorway, and his breadth seemed to span it across from side to side. A large face, seared with a thousand wrinkles, burned yellow with the sun, and marked with every evil passion, was turned from one to the other of us, while his deep-set, bile-shot eyes, and his high, thin, fleshless nose, gave him somewhat the resemblance to a fierce old bird of prey.

"Which of you is Holmes?" asked this apparition.

"My name, sir; but you have the advantage of me," said my companion quietly.

"I am Dr. Grimesby Roylott, of Stoke Moran."

"Indeed, Doctor," said Holmes blandly. "Pray take a seat."

"I will do nothing of the kind. My stepdaughter has been here. I have traced her. What has she been saying to you?"

"It is a little cold for this time of year," said Holmes.

"What has she been saying to you?" screamed the old man furiously.

"But I have heard that the crocuses promise well," continued my companion imperturbably.

"Ha! You put me off, do you?" said our new visitor, taking a step forward and shaking his hunting crop. "I know you, you scoundrel! I have heard of you before. You are Holmes, the meddler."

My friend smiled.

"Holmes, the busybody!"

His smile broadened.

"Holmes, the Scotland Yard Jack-in-office!"

Holmes chuckled heartily. "Your conversation is most entertaining," said he. "When you go out close the door, for there is a decided draught."

"I will go when I have said my say. Don't you dare to meddle with my affairs. I know that Miss Stoner has been here. I traced her! I am a dangerous man to fall foul of! See here." He stepped swiftly forward, seized the poker, and bent it into a curve with his huge brown hands.

"See that you keep yourself out of my grip," he snarled, and hurling the twisted poker into the fireplace he strode out of the room.

"He seems a very amiable person," said Holmes, laughing. "I am not quite so bulky, but if he had remained I might have shown him that my grip was not much more feeble than his own." As he spoke he picked up the steel poker and, with a sudden effort, straightened it out again.

"Fancy his having the insolence to confound me with the official detective force! This incident gives zest to our investigation, however, and I only trust that our little friend will not suffer from her imprudence in allowing this brute to trace her. And now, Watson, we shall order breakfast, and afterwards I shall walk down to Doctors' Commons,[1] where I hope to get some data which may help us in this matter."

It was nearly one o'clock when Sherlock Holmes returned from his excursion. He held in his hand a sheet of blue paper, scrawled over with notes and figures.

"I have seen the will of the deceased wife," said he. "Each daughter can claim an income in case of marriage. It is evident, therefore, that if both girls had married, this beauty would have had a mere pittance, while even one of them would cripple him to a very serious extent. My morning's work has not been wasted, since it has proved that he has the very strongest motives for standing in the way of anything of the sort.

"And now, Watson, this is too serious for dawdling, especially as the old man is aware that we are interesting ourselves in his affairs; so if you are ready, we shall call a cab and drive to Waterloo. I should be very much obliged if you would slip your revolver into your pocket. An Eley's No. 2 is an excellent argument with gentlemen who can twist steel pokers into knots. That and a toothbrush are, I think, all that we need."

At Waterloo we were fortunate in catching a train for

Leatherhead, where we hired a trap at the station inn and drove for four or five miles through the lovely Surrey lanes. It was a perfect day, with a bright sun and a few fleecy clouds in the heavens. The trees and wayside hedges were just throwing out their first green shoots, and the air was full of the pleasant smell of the moist earth. To me at least there was a strange contrast between the sweet promise of the spring and this sinister quest upon which we were engaged. My companion sat in the front of the trap, his arms folded, his hat pulled down over his eyes, and his chin sunk upon his breast, buried in the deepest thought. Suddenly, however, he started, tapped me on the shoulder, and pointed over the meadows.

"Look there!" said he.

A heavily timbered park stretched up in a gentle slope, thickening into a grove at the highest point. From amid the branches there jutted out the gray gables and high rooftops of a very old mansion.

"Stoke Moran?" Holmes asked the driver.

"Yes, sir, that be the house of Dr. Grimesby Roylott," remarked the driver.

"There is some building going on there," said Holmes; "that is where we are going."

"There's the village," said the driver, pointing to a cluster of roofs some distance to the left; "but if you want to get to the house, you'll find it shorter to get over this stile, and go by the footpath over the fields. There it is, where the lady is walking."

"And the lady, I fancy, is Miss Stoner," observed Holmes, shading his eyes. "Yes, I think we had better do as you suggest."

We got off, paid our fare, and the trap rattled back on its way to Leatherhead.

"I thought it as well," said Holmes as we climbed the stile, "that this fellow should think we had come here as architects, or on some definite business. It may stop his gossip. Good afternoon, Miss Stoner. You see that we have been as good as our word."

Our client of the morning had hurried forward to meet us with a face which spoke her joy. "I have been waiting so eagerly for you," she cried, shaking hands with us warmly. "All has turned out splendidly. Dr. Roylott has gone to town, and it is unlikely that he will be back before evening."

"We have had the pleasure of making the doctor's acquaintance," said Holmes, and in a few words he sketched out what had occurred. Miss Stoner turned white to the lips as she listened.

"Good heavens!" she cried, "he has followed me, then."

"So it appears."

"He is so cunning that I never know when I am safe from him. What will he say when he returns?"

"He must guard himself, for he may find that there is someone more cunning than himself upon his track. You must lock yourself up from him tonight. If he is violent, we shall take you away to your aunt's at Harrow. Now, we must make the best use of our time, so kindly take us at once to the rooms which we are to examine."

The building was of gray, lichen-blotched stone, with a high central portion and two curving wings, like the claws of a crab, thrown out on each side. In one of these wings the windows were broken and blocked with wooden boards, while the roof was partly caved in, a picture of ruin. The central portion was in little better repair, but the right-hand block was comparatively modern, and the blinds in the windows, with the blue smoke curling up from the chimneys, showed that this was where the family resided. Some scaffolding had been erected against the end wall, and the stone work had been broken into, but there were no signs of any workmen at the moment of our visit. Holmes walked slowly up and down the ill-trimmed lawn and examined with deep attention the outsides of the windows.

"This, I take it, belongs to the room in which you used to sleep, the center one to your sister's, and the one next to the main building to Dr. Roylott's chamber?"

"Exactly so. But I am now sleeping in the middle one."

"Pending the alterations, as I understand. By the way, there does not seem to be any very pressing need for repairs at that end wall."

"There were none. I believe that it was an excuse to move me from my room."

"Ah! that is suggestive. Now, on the other side of this narrow wing runs the corridor from which these three rooms open. There are windows in it, of course?"

"Yes, but very small ones. Too narrow for anyone to pass through."

"As you both locked your doors at night, your rooms were unapproachable from that side. Now, would you have the kindness to go into your room and bar your shutters?"

Miss Stoner did so, and Holmes, after a careful examination through the open window, endeavoured in every way to force the shutter open, but without success. There was no slit through which a knife could be passed to raise the bar. Then with his lens he tested the hinges, but they were of solid iron, built firmly into the massive masonry. "Hum!" said he, scratching his chin in some perplexity, "my theory certainly presents some difficulties. No one could pass through these shutters if they were bolted. Well, we shall see if the inside throws any light upon the matter."

A small side door led into the whitewashed corridor from which the three bedrooms opened. Holmes refused to examine the third chamber, so we passed at once to the second, that in which Miss Stoner was now sleeping, and in which her sister had met with her fate. It was a homely little room, with a low ceiling and a gaping fireplace, after the fashion of old country houses. A brown chest of drawers stood in one corner, a narrow white-counterpaned bed in another, and a dressing table on the left-hand side of the window. These articles, with two small wickerwork chairs, made up all the furniture in the room save for a square of Wilton carpet in the center. The boards round and the panelling of the walls were of brown, worm-eaten oak, so old and discoloured that it may have dated from the original building of the house. Holmes drew one of the chairs into a corner and sat silent, while his eyes travelled round and round and up and down, taking in every detail of the room.

"Where does that bell communicate with?" he asked at last, pointing to a thick bell-rope which hung down beside the bed, the tassel actually lying upon the pillow.

"It goes to the housekeeper's room."

"It looks newer than the other things?"

"Yes, it was only put there a couple of years ago."

"Your sister asked for it, I suppose?"

"No, I never heard of her using it. We used always to get what we wanted for ourselves."

"Indeed, it seemed unnecessary to put so nice a bell-pull there. You will excuse me for a few minutes while I satisfy myself as to this floor." He threw himself down upon his face with his lens in his hand and crawled swiftly backward and forward, examining minutely the cracks between the boards. Then he did the same with the woodwork with which the chamber was panelled. Finally he walked over to the bed and spent some time in staring at it and in running his eye up and down the wall. Finally he took the bell-rope in his hand and gave it a brisk tug.

"Why, it's a dummy," said he.

"Won't it ring?"

"No, it is not even attached to a wire. This is very interesting. You can see now that it is fastened to a hook just above where the little opening for the ventilator is."

"How very absurd! I never noticed that before."

"Very strange!" muttered Holmes, pulling at the rope. "There are one or two very singular points about this room. For example, what a fool a builder must be to open a ventilator into another room, when, with the same trouble, he might have placed the ventilator so as to communicate with the outside air!"

"That is also quite modern," said the lady.

"Done about the same time as the bell-rope?" remarked Holmes.

"Yes, there were several little changes carried out about that time."

"They seem to have been of a most interesting character— dummy bell-ropes, and ventilators which do not ventilate. With your permission, Miss Stoner, we shall now carry our researches into the inner apartment."

Dr. Grimesby Roylott's chamber was larger than that of his stepdaughter, but was as plainly furnished. A camp bed, a small wooden shelf full of books, mostly of a technical character, an armchair beside the bed, a plain wooden chair against the wall, a round table, and a large iron safe were the principal things which met the eye. Holmes walked slowly round and examined each of them with the keenest interest.

"What's in here?" he asked, tapping the safe.

"My stepfather's business papers."

"There isn't a cat in it, for example?"

"No. What a strange idea!"

"Well, look at this!" He took up a small saucer of milk which stood on the top of it.

"No; we don't keep a cat. But there is a cheetah and a baboon."

"Ah, yes, of course! Well, a cheetah is just a big cat, and yet a saucer of milk does not go very far in satisfying its wants, I daresay. There is one point which I should wish to determine." He squatted down in front of the wooden chair and examined the seat of it with the greatest attention.

"Thank you. That is quite settled," said he, rising and putting his lens in his pocket. "Hello! Here is something interesting!"

The object which had caught his eye was a small dog lash hung on one corner of the bed. The lash, however, was curled upon itself and tied so as to make a loop of whipcord.

"What do you make of that, Watson?"

"It's a common enough lash. But I don't know why it should be tied."

"That is not quite so common, is it? Ah, me! It's a wicked world, and when a clever man turns his brains to crime it is the worst of all. I think that I have seen enough now, Miss Stoner, and with your permission we shall walk out upon the lawn."

I had never seen my friend's face so grim or his brow so dark as it was when we turned from the scene of this investigation. We had walked several times up and down the lawn, neither Miss Stoner nor myself liking to break in upon his thoughts before he roused himself from his reverie.

"It is very essential, Miss Stoner," said he, "that you should absolutely follow my advice in every respect."

"I shall most certainly do so."

"The matter is too serious for any hesitation. Your life may depend upon your compliance."

"I assure you that I am in your hands."

"In the first place, both my friend and I must spend the night in your room."

Both Miss Stoner and I gazed at him in astonishment.

"Yes, it must be so. Let me explain. I believe that that is the village inn over there?"

"Yes, that is the 'Crown'," answered Miss Stoner.

"Very good. Your windows would be visible from there?"

"Certainly."

"You must confine yourself to your room, on pretense of a headache when your stepfather comes back. Then when you hear him retire for the night, you must open the shutters of your window, undo the hasp, put your lamp there as a signal to us, and then withdraw quietly with everything which you are likely to want into the room which you used to occupy."

"But what will you do?"

"We shall spend the night in your room, and we shall investigate the cause of this noise which has disturbed you."

"I believe, Mr. Holmes, that you have already made up your mind," said Miss Stoner, laying her hand upon my companion's sleeve.

"Perhaps I have."

"Then, for pity's sake, tell me what was the cause of my sister's death."

"I should prefer to have clearer proofs before I speak."

"You can at least tell me whether my own thought is correct, and if she died from some sudden fright."

"No, I do not think so. I think that there was probably some more tangible cause. And now, Miss Stoner, we must leave you, for if Dr. Roylott returned and saw us our journey would be in vain. Good-bye, and be brave; for if you will do what I have told you, you may rest assured that we shall soon drive away the dangers that threaten you."

Sherlock Holmes and I had no difficulty in engaging a bedroom and sitting room at the Crown Inn. They were on the upper floor, and from our window we could command a view of the avenue gate, and of the inhabited wing of Stoke Moran Manor House. At dusk we saw Dr. Grimesby Roylott drive past, his huge form looming up beside the little figure of the lad who drove him. The boy had some slight difficulty in undoing the heavy iron gates, and we heard the hoarse roar of the doctor's voice and saw the fury with which he shook his clenched fists at him. The trap drove on, and a few minutes later we saw a sudden light spring up among the trees as the lamp was lit in one of the sitting rooms.

"Do you know, Watson," said Holmes as we sat together in the gathering darkness, "I have really some scruples as to taking you tonight. There is a distinct element of danger."

"Can I be of assistance?"

"Your presence might be invaluable."

"Then I shall certainly come."

"It is very kind of you."

"You speak of danger. You have evidently seen more in these rooms than was visible to me."

"No, but I fancy that I may have deduced a little more. I imagine that you saw all that I did."

"I saw nothing remarkable save the bell-rope, and what purpose that could answer I confess is more than I can imagine."

"You saw the ventilator, too?"

"Yes, but I do not think that it is such a very unusual thing to have a small opening between two rooms. It was so small that a rat could hardly pass through."

"I knew that we should find a ventilator before ever we came to Stoke Moran."

"My dear Holmes!"

"Oh, yes, I did. You remember in her statement she said that her sister could smell Dr. Roylott's cigar. Now, of course that suggested at once that there must be a communication between the two rooms. It could only be a small one, or it would have been remarked upon at the coroner's inquiry. I deduced a ventilator."

"But what harm can there be in that?"

"Well, there is at least a curious coincidence of dates. A ventilator is made, a cord is hung, and a lady who sleeps in the bed dies. Does not that strike you?"

"I cannot as yet see any connection."

"Did you observe anything very peculiar about that bed?"

"No."

"It was clamped to the floor. Did you ever see a bed fastened like that before?"

"I cannot say that I have," I acknowledged.

"The lady could not move her bed. It must always be in the same relative position to the ventilator and to the rope—for so we may call it, since it was clearly never meant for a bell-pull."

"Holmes," I cried, "I seem to see dimly what you are hinting at. We are only just in time to prevent some subtle and horrible crime."

"Subtle enough and horrible enough. When a doctor does go

wrong he is the first of criminals. He has nerve and he has knowledge. Palmer and Pritchard[2] were among the heads of their profession. This man strikes even deeper, but I think, Watson, that we shall be able to strike deeper still. But we shall have horrors enough before the night is over; for goodness' sake let us have a quiet pipe and turn our minds for a few hours to something more cheerful."

About nine o'clock the light among the trees was extinguished, and all was dark in the direction of the Manor House. Two hours passed slowly away, and then, suddenly, just at the stroke of eleven, a single bright light shone out right in front of us.

"That is our signal," said Holmes, springing to his feet; "it comes from the middle window."

As we passed out he exchanged a few words with the landlord, explaining that we were going on a late visit to an acquaintance, and that it was possible that we might spend the night there. A moment later we were out on the dark road, a chill wind blowing in our faces, and one yellow light twinkling in front of us through the gloom to guide us on our somber errand.

There was little difficulty in entering the grounds, for unrepaired breaches gaped in the old park wall. Making our way among the trees, we reached the lawn, crossed it, and were about to enter through the window when out from a clump of laurel bushes there darted what seemed to be a hideous and distorted child, who threw itself upon the grass with writhing limbs and then ran swiftly across the lawn into the darkness.

"My God!" I whispered; "did you see it?"

Holmes was for the moment as startled as I. His hand closed like a vise upon my wrist in his agitation. Then he broke into a low laugh and put his lips to my ear.

"It is a nice household," he murmured. "That is the baboon."

I had forgotten the strange pets which the doctor affected. There was a cheetah, too; perhaps we might find it upon our shoulders at any moment. I confess that I felt easier in my mind when, after following Holmes's example and slipping off my shoes, I found myself inside the bedroom. My companion noiselessly closed the shutters, moved the lamp onto the table, and cast his eyes round the room. All was as we had seen it in the daytime. Then creeping up to me and making a trumpet of his hand, he whispered into my ear so gently that it was all that I could do to distinguish the words, "The least sound would be fatal to our plans."

I nodded to show that I had heard.

"We must sit without light. He would see it through the ventilator."

I nodded again.

"Do not go asleep; your very life may depend upon it. Have your pistol ready in case we should need it. I will sit on the side of the bed, and you in that chair."

I took out my revolver and laid it on the table.

Holmes had brought up a long thin cane, and this he placed upon the bed beside him. By it he laid the box of matches and the stump of a candle. Then he turned down the lamp, and we were left in darkness.

How shall I ever forget that dreadful vigil? I could not hear a sound, not even the drawing of a breath, and yet I knew that my companion sat open-eyed, within a few feet of me, in the same state of nervous tension in which I was myself. The shutters cut off the least ray of light, and we waited in absolute darkness. From outside came the occasional cry of a night bird, and once at our very window a long-drawn catlike whine, which told us that the cheetah was indeed at liberty. Far away we could hear the deep tones of the parish clock, which boomed out every quarter of an hour. How long they seemed, those quarters! Twelve struck, and one and two and three, and still we sat waiting silently for whatever might befall.

Suddenly there was the momentary gleam of a light up in the direction of the ventilator, which vanished immediately, but was succeeded by a strong smell of burning oil and heated metal. Someone in the next room had lit a dark-lantern. I heard a gentle sound of movement, and then all was silent once more, though the smell grew stronger. For half an hour I sat with straining ears. Then suddenly another sound became audible—a very gentle, soothing sound, like that of a small jet of steam escaping continually from a kettle. The instant that we heard it, Holmes sprang from the bed, struck a match, and lashed furiously with his cane at the bell-pull.

"You see it, Watson?" he yelled. "You see it?"

But I saw nothing. At the moment when Holmes struck the light I heard a low, clear whistle, but the sudden glare flashing into my weary eyes made it impossible for me to tell what it was at which my friend lashed so savagely. I could, however, see that his face was deadly pale and filled with horror and loathing.

He had ceased to strike and was gazing up at the ventilator when suddenly there broke from the silence of the night the most horrible cry to which I have ever listened. It swelled up louder and louder, a hoarse yell of pain and fear and anger all mingled in the one dreadful shriek. They say that way down in the village, and even in the distant parsonage, that cry raised the sleepers from their beds. It struck cold to our hearts, and I stood gazing at Holmes, and he at me, until the last echoes of it had died away into the silence from which it rose.

"What can it mean?" I gasped.

"It means that it is all over," Holmes answered. "And perhaps, after all, it is for the best. Take your pistol, and we will enter Dr. Roylott's room."

With a grave face he lit the lamp and led the way down the corridor. Twice he struck at the chamber door without any reply from within. Then he turned the handle and entered, I at his heels, with the cocked pistol in my hand.

It was a singular sight which met my eyes. On the table stood a dark-lantern with the shutter half open, throwing a brilliant beam of light upon the iron safe, the door of which was ajar. Beside this table, on the wooden chair, sat Dr. Grimesby Roylott, clad in a long gray dressing gown, his bare ankles protruding beneath, and his feet thrust into red heelless Turkish slippers. Across his lap lay the short stock with the long lash which we had noticed during the day. His chin was cocked upward and his eyes were fixed in a dreadful, rigid stare at the corner of the ceiling. Round his brow he had a peculiar yellow band, with brownish speckles, which seemed to be bound tightly round his head. As we entered he made neither sound nor motion.

"The band! The speckled band!" whispered Holmes.

I took a step forward. In an instant his strange headgear began to move, and there reared itself from among his hair the squat diamond-shaped head and puffed neck of a loathsome serpent.

"It is a swamp adder!" cried Holmes, "the deadliest snake in

India. He has died within ten seconds of being bitten. Violence does, in truth, recoil upon the violent, and the schemer falls into the pit which he digs for another. Let us thrust this creature back into its den, and we can then remove Miss Stoner to some place of shelter and let the county police know what has happened."

As he spoke he drew the dog whip swiftly from the dead man's lap, and throwing the noose round the reptile's neck he drew it from its horrid perch and, carrying it at arm's length, threw it into the iron safe, which he closed upon it.

Such are the true facts of the death of Dr. Grimesby Roylott, of Stoke Moran. It is not necessary that I should prolong a narrative which has already run to too great a length by telling how we broke the sad news to the terrified girl, how we conveyed her by the morning train to the care of her good aunt at Harrow, of how the slow process of official inquiry came to the conclusion that the doctor met his fate while indiscreetly playing with a dangerous pet. The little which I had yet to learn of the case was told me by Sherlock Holmes as we travelled back next day.

"I had," said he, "come to an entirely erroneous conclusion; which shows, my dear Watson, how dangerous it always is to reason from insufficient data. The presence of the gypsies, and the word 'band,' used by the poor girl, no doubt to explain that which she had caught a hurried glimpse of by the light of her match, were sufficient to put me upon an entirely wrong scent. I can only claim the merit that I instantly reconsidered my position when it became clear to me that whatever danger threatened an occupant of the room, could not come in from either the door or the window. I then sought other evidence.

"My attention was speedily drawn, as I have already remarked to you, to this ventilator, and to the bell-rope which hung down to the bed. The discovery that this was a dummy, and that the bed was clamped to the floor, instantly gave rise to the suspicion that the rope was there as a bridge for something passing through the hole and coming to the bed. The idea of a snake instantly occurred to me, and when I coupled it with my knowledge that the doctor was furnished with a supply of creatures from India, I felt that I was probably on the right track.

"The idea of using a form of poison which could not possibly be discovered by any chemical test was just such a one as would occur to a clever and ruthless man who had had an Eastern training. The rapidity with which such a poison would take effect would also, from his point of view, be an advantage. It would be a sharp-eyed coroner, indeed, who could distinguish the two little dark punctures which would show where the poison fangs had done their work.

"Then I thought of the whistle. Of course he must recall the snake before the morning light revealed it to the victim. He had trained it, probably by the use of the milk which we saw, to return to him when summoned. He would put it through this ventilator at the hour that he thought best, with the certainty that it would crawl down the rope and land on the bed. It might or might not bite the occupant, perhaps she might escape every night for a week, but sooner or later she must fall a victim.

"I had come to these conclusions before ever I had entered his room. An inspection of his chair showed me that he had been in the habit of standing on it, which of course would be necessary in order that he should reach the ventilator. The sight of the safe, the saucer of milk, and the loop of whipcord were enough to finally dispel any doubts which may have remained. The metallic clang heard by Miss Stoner was obviously caused by her stepfather hastily closing the door of his safe upon its terrible occupant. Having once made up my mind, you know the steps which I took in order to put the matter to the proof. I heard the creature hiss, as I have no doubt that you did also, and I instantly lit the light and attacked it."

"With the result of driving it through the ventilator."

"And also with the result of causing it to turn upon its master at the other side. Some of the blows of my cane came home and roused its snakish temper, so that it flew upon the first person it saw. In this way, I am no doubt indirectly responsible for Dr. Grimesby Roylott's death, and I cannot say that it is likely to weigh very heavily upon my conscience."

COMMENT AND QUESTIONS

Sherlock Holmes is *the* Great Detective. The reader shares with Watson an awed astonishment at his intellect and an almost reverential belief in his powers. Clients come to him near despair over impossible situations yet heartened by what they have heard of his exploits. His secure and cozily disordered room becomes a sanctuary because of his presence. Brilliant, courageous, and assured—he is the dispenser of a higher justice.

In "The Speckled Band" and other cases, Holmes employs a method that consists of the following steps: He listens to the client's account of the problem, summarizes the facts, and forms a hypothesis; then he visits the scene of the crime to gain further evidence and perhaps test his hypothesis; finally he sets a trap to test his theory and incriminate or ensnare the suspect.

In following this procedure, Holmes demonstrates marvelous powers of deduction, often dazzling his client at the very first meeting. Holmes' remarks to Miss Stoner about her journey are an example of his virtuosity.

Throughout the case Holmes displays a grim sense of humor, which expresses itself in ironic comments such as "He seems a very amiable person" (of Dr. Roylott) and "It is a nice household" (after meeting the baboon).

Often Holmes is required to rely upon physical strength and courage—for example, bending the bar and ambushing the snake—and it is not uncommon for Holmes and Watson to be seriously endangered as they bring their quarry to bay.

At some point in the adventure, Holmes will usually make a statement similar to the one in this story, "You may rest assured that we shall soon drive away the dangers that threaten you." And he always lives up to his promise.

In this story the death of Julia appears at first to have come about in some supernatural way, or at least to have resulted from a shock greater than the mind can endure. Normally, when fears of the supernatural are dispelled, the reader feels a sense of relief at his return to the "real" world. However, one of the fine achievements of this story is that the horror is, if anything, intensified by the revelation of the means of the murder. How do you account for this intensification? Does it have anything to do with what Helen refers to as "the manifold wickedness of the human heart" in her first interview with Watson and Holmes?

Although Watson obviously lacks Holmes' penetrating intellect and logical powers, he serves a number of useful functions. What personal qualities make him an appropriate companion to Holmes, an effective narrator of the story, and an admirable person in his own right?

Our readiness to believe that the menace of the situation is real is strengthened not only by the inescapable fact of Julia's death but also by the belief that her sister Helen is clearly a credible witness. What details about Helen's character make us feel that her account can be trusted?

What role do "exotic" things play in the story? Is it significant, for example, that Dr. Roylott lived in India, collected strange pets like a baboon and a cheetah, and spent much time with gypsies?

What clues does Holmes successfully interpret to prevent a second violent death?

Holmes says that "when a doctor does go wrong he is the first of criminals." What reasons can you give to support this statement?

Many detective stories are based on the underlying assumption that "right will out." Does Holmes' statement that "the schemer falls into the pit which he digs for another" apply in this story? In "The Purloined Letter"?

NOTES

1. *Doctors' Commons.* The repository for wills in England until 1874. Holmes doubtless uses the term simply to mean a place where one may consult a will to determine its provisions.

2. *Palmer and Pritchard.* William Palmer, executed in 1856 for poisoning a friend, and Edward William Pritchard, a Glasgow practitioner who was hanged in 1865 for poisoning his wife and mother-in-law.

REX STOUT

Watson Was a Woman

Rex Stout is himself a master of the art of mystifying readers. His Nero Wolfe, a gargantuan gourmet and orchid fancier, is the American detective most like Sherlock Holmes in his eccentricities and force of personality. He appears in a long series of very popular novels and novelettes narrated by Archie Goodwin, an associate more independent and observant than Watson, whose complete recall of people and places permits Wolfe to sit in a big yellow armchair and solve most of his mysteries in the comfort of his study.

"Watson Was a Woman" was originally delivered as an address to a meeting of the Baker Street Irregulars, a club formed for study and discussion of Holmes lore. In this "study," Stout delights us with his sharp wit and outrageous use of much information actually in the Sherlock Holmes stories.

You will forgive me for refusing to join your commemorative toast, "The Second Mrs. Watson," when you learn it was a matter of conscience. I could not bring myself to connive at the perpetuation of a hoax. Not only was there never a second Mrs. Watson; there was not even a first Mrs. Watson. Furthermore, there was no Doctor Watson.

Please keep your chairs.

Like all true disciples, I have always recurrently dipped into the Sacred Writings (called by the vulgar the Sherlock Holmes stories) for refreshment; but not long ago I reread them from beginning to end, and I was struck by a singular fact that reminded me of the dog in the night. The singular fact about the dog in the night, as we all know, was that it didn't bark; and the singular fact about Holmes in the night is that he is never seen going to bed. The writer of the tales, the Watson person, describes over and over again, in detail, all the other minutiæ of that famous household— suppers, breakfasts, arrangement of furniture, rainy evenings at home—but not once are we shown either Holmes or Watson going to bed. I wondered, why not? Why such unnatural and obdurate restraint, nay, concealment, regarding one of the pleasantest episodes of the daily routine?

I got suspicious.

The uglier possibilities that occurred to me, as that Holmes had false teeth or that Watson wore a toupee, I rejected as preposterous. They were much too obvious, and shall I say unsinister. But the game was afoot, and I sought the trail, in the only field available to me, the Sacred Writings themselves. And right at the very start, on page 9 of *A Study in Scarlet*, I found this:

. . . It was rare for him to be up after ten at night, and he had invariably breakfasted and gone out before I rose in the morning.

I was indescribably shocked. How had so patent a clue escaped so many millions of readers through the years? That was, that could only be, a woman speaking of a man. Read it over. The true authentic speech of a wife telling of her husband's—but wait. I was not indulging in idle speculation, but seeking evidence to establish a fact. It was unquestionably a woman speaking of a man, yes, but whether a wife of a husband, or a mistress of a lover, . . . I admit I blushed. I blushed for Sherlock Holmes, and I closed the book. But the fire of curiosity was raging in me, and soon I opened again to the same page, and there in the second paragraph I saw:

The reader may set me down as a hopeless busybody, when I confess how much this man stimulated my curiosity, and how often I endeavored to break through the reticence which he showed on all that concerned himself.

You bet she did. She would. Poor Holmes! She doesn't even bother to employ one of the stock euphemisms, such as, "I wanted to understand him better," or, "I wanted to share things with him." She proclaims it with brutal directness, "I endeavored to break through the reticence." I shuddered, and for the first time in my life felt that Sherlock Holmes was not a god, but human—human by his suffering. Also, from that one page I regarded the question of the Watson person's sex as settled for good. Indubitably she was a female, but wife or mistress? I went on. Two pages later I found:

. . . his powers upon the violin . . . at my request he has played me some of Mendelssohn's *Lieder* . . ."

Imagine a man asking another man to play him some of Mendelssohn's *Lieder* on a violin!

And on the next page:

. . . I rose somewhat earlier than usual, and found that Sherlock Holmes had not yet finished his breakfast . . . my place had not been laid nor my coffee prepared. With . . . petulance . . . I rang the bell and gave a curt intimation that I was ready. Then I picked up a magazine from the table and attempted to while away the time with it, while my companion munched silently at his toast.

That is a terrible picture, and you know and I know how bitterly realistic it is. Change the diction, and it is practically a love story by Ring Lardner. That Sherlock Holmes, like other men, had breakfasts like that is a hard pill for a true disciple to swallow, but we must face the facts. The chief thing to note of this excerpt is that it not only reinforces the conviction that Watson was a lady—that is to say, a woman—but also it bolsters our hope that Holmes did not through all those years live in sin. A man does not munch silently at his toast when breakfasting with his mistress; or, if he does, it won't be long until he gets a new one. But Holmes stuck to her—or she to him—for over a quarter of a century. Here are a few quotations from the later years:

. . . Sherlock Holmes was standing smiling at me. . . . I rose to my feet, stared at him for some seconds in utter amazement, and then it appears that I must have fainted. . . ."

—"The Adventure of the Empty House," page 4.

I believe that I am one of the most long-suffering of mortals.
—"The Tragedy of Birlstone," page 1.

The relations between us in those latter days were peculiar. He was a man of habits, narrow and concentrated habits, and I had become one of them. As an institution I was like the violin, the shag tobacco, the old black pipe, the index books, and others perhaps less excusable.
—"The Adventure of the Creeping Man," page 1.

And we have been expected to believe that a man wrote those things! The frank and unconcerned admission that she fainted at sight of Holmes after an absence! "I am one of the most long-suffering of mortals"—the oldest uxorial cliché in the world; Aeschylus used it; no doubt cave-men gnashed their teeth at it! And the familiar pathetic plaint, "As an institution I was like the old black pipe!"

Yes, uxorial, for surely she was wife. And the old black pipe itself provides us with a clincher on that point. This comes from page 16 of *The Hound of the Baskervilles:*

. . . did not return to Baker Street until evening. It was nearly nine o'clock when I found myself in the sitting-room once more.

My first impression as I opened the door was that a fire had broken out, for the room was so filled with smoke that the light of the lamp upon the table was blurred by it. As I entered, however, my fears were set to rest, for it was the acrid fumes of strong coarse tobacco which took me by the throat and set me coughing. Through the haze I had a vague vision of Holmes in his dressing-gown coiled up in an armchair with his black clay pipe between his lips. Several rolls of paper lay around him.

"Caught cold, Watson?" said he.

"No, it's this poisonous atmosphere."

"I suppose it *is* pretty thick, now that you mention it."

"Thick! It is intolerable!"

"Open the window, then!"

I say husband and wife. Could anyone alive doubt it after reading that painful banal scene? Is there any need to pile on the evidence?

For a last-ditch skeptic there is more evidence, much more. The efforts to break Holmes of the cocaine habit, mentioned in various places in the Sacred Writings, display a typical reformist wife in action, especially the final gloating over her success. A more complicated, but no less conclusive, piece of evidence is the strange, the astounding recital of Holmes's famous disappearance, in "The Final Problem," and the reasons given therefore in a later tale, "The Adventure of the Empty House." It is incredible that this monstrous deception was not long ago exposed.

Holmes and Watson had together wandered up the valley of the Rhone, branched off at Leuk, made their way over the Gemmi Pass, and gone on, by way of Interlaken, to Meiringen. Near that village, as they were walking along a narrow trail high above a tremendous abyss, Watson was maneuvered back to the hotel by a fake message. Learning that the message was a fake, she (he) flew back to their trail, and found that Holmes was gone. No Holmes. All that was left of him was a polite and regretful note of farewell, there on a rock with his cigarette case for a paperweight, saying that Professor Moriarty had arrived and was about to push him into the abyss.

That in itself was rather corny. But go on to "The Adventure of the Empty House." Three years have passed. Sherlock Holmes has suddenly and unexpectedly reappeared in London, causing the Watson person to collapse in a faint. His explanation of his long absence is fantastic. He says that he had grappled with Professor Moriarty on the narrow trail and tossed him into the chasm; that, in order to deal at better advantage with the dangerous Sebastian Moran, he had decided to make it appear that he too had toppled over the cliff; that, so as to leave no returning footprints on the narrow trail, he had attempted to scale the upper cliff, and, while he was doing so, Sebastian Moran himself had appeared up above and thrown rocks at him; that by herculean efforts he had eluded Moran and escaped over the mountains; that for three years he had wandered around Persia and Tibet and France, communicating with no one but his brother Mycroft, so that Sebastian Moran would think he was dead. *Though by his own account Moran knew, must have known, that he had got away!*

That is what Watson says that Holmes told her (him). It is simply gibberish, below the level even of a village half-wit. It is impossible to suppose that Sherlock Holmes ever dreamed of imposing on any sane person with an explanation like that; it is impossible to believe that he would insult his own intelligence by offering such an explanation even to an idiot. I deny that he ever did. I believe that all he said, after Watson recovered from the faint, was this, "My dear, I am willing to try it again," for he was a courteous man. And it was Watson, who, attempting to cook up an explanation, made such a terrible hash of it.

Then who was this person whose nom de plume was "Doctor Watson"? Where did she come from? What was she like? What was her name before she snared Holmes?

Let us see what we can do about the name, by methods that Holmes himself might have used. It was Watson who wrote the immortal tales; therefore, if she left a record of her name anywhere it must have been in the tales themselves. But what we are looking for is not her characteristics or the facts of her life, but her *name*, that is to say, her *title;* so obviously the place to look is in the *titles* of the tales.

There are sixty of the tales all told. The first step is to set them down in chronological order, and number them from 1 to 60. Now, which shall we take first? Evidently the reason why Watson was at such pains to conceal her name in this clutter of titles was to *mystify* us, so the number to start with should be the most *mystical* number, namely seven. And to make it doubly sure, we shall make it seven times seven, which is 49. Very well. The 49th tale is "The Adventure of the Illustrious Client." We of course discard the first four words, "The Adventure of the," which are repeated in most of the titles. Result: "ILLUSTRIOUS CLIENT."

The next most significant thing about Watson is her (his) constant effort to convince us that those things happened exactly as she (he) tells them; that they are on the *square*. Good. The first square of an integer is the integer 4. We take the title of the 4th tale and get "RED-HEADED LEAGUE."

We proceed to elimination. Of all the factors that contribute to an ordinary man's success, which one did Holmes invariably exclude, or eliminate? Luck. In crap-shooting, what are the lucky numbers? Seven and eleven. But we have already used 7, which eliminates it, so there is nothing left but 11. The 11th tale is about the "ENGINEER'S THUMB."

Next, what was Holmes's age at the time he moved to Baker

Street? Twenty-seven. The 27th tale is the adventure of the "NORWOOD BUILDER." And what was Watson's age? Twenty-six. The 26th tale is the adventure of the "EMPTY HOUSE." But there is no need to belabor the obvious. Just as it is a simple matter to decipher the code of the Dancing Men when Holmes has once put you on the right track, so can you, for yourself, make the additional required selections now that I have explained the method. And you will inevitably get what I got:

Illustrious Client
Red-Headed League
Engineer's Thumb
Norwood Builder
Empty House

Wisteria Lodge
Abbey Grange
Twisted Lip
Study in Scarlet
Orange Pips
Noble Bachelor

And, acrostically simple, the initial letters read down, the carefully hidden secret is ours. Her name was Irene Watson.

But not so fast. Is there any way of checking that? Of discovering her name by any other method, say *a priori*? We can try and see. A woman wrote the stories about Sherlock Holmes, that has been demonstrated; and that woman was his wife. Does there appear, anywhere in the stories, a woman whom Holmes fell for? Whom he really cottoned to? Indeed there does. "A Scandal in Bohemia" opens like this:

To Sherlock Holmes she is always *the* woman. . . . In his eyes she eclipses and predominates the whole of her sex.

And what was the name of *the* woman? Irene!

But, you say, not Irene Watson, but Irene Adler. Certainly. Watson's whole purpose, from beginning to end, was to confuse and bewilder us regarding her identity. So note that name well. Adler. What is an adler, or, as it is commonly spelled, addler? An addler is one who, or that which, addles. Befuddles. Confuses. I admit I admire that stroke; it is worthy of Holmes himself. In the very act of deceiving and confusing us, she has the audacity to employ a name that brazenly announces her purpose!

An amusing corroborative detail about this Irene of "Scandal in Bohemia"—*the* woman to Holmes according to the narrator of the tales—is that Holmes was present at her wedding at the Church of St. Monica in the Edgeware Road. It is related that he was there as a witness, but that is pure poppycock. Holmes himself says, "I was half-dragged up to the altar, and before I knew where I was I found myself mumbling responses. . . ." Those are not the words of an indifferent witness, but of a reluctant, ensnared, bulldozed man—in short, a bridegroom. And in all the 1323 pages of the Sacred Writings, that is the only wedding we ever see—the only one, so far as we are told, that Holmes ever graced with his presence.

All this is very sketchy. I admit it. I am now collecting material for a fuller treatment of the subject, a complete demonstration of the evidence and the inevitable conclusion. It will fill two volumes, the second of which will consist of certain speculations regarding various concrete results of that long-continued and—I fear, alas—none-too-happy union. For instance, what of the parentage of Lord Peter Wimsey, who was born, I believe, around the turn of the century—about the time of the publication of "The Adventure of the Second Stain"? That will bear looking into.

COMMENT AND QUESTIONS

The reader's enjoyment of "Watson Was a Woman" depends upon his having read at least one of the Sherlock Holmes stories and will be enhanced if he is quite familiar with these adventures. In this respect the essay is like the story "The Gentleman from Paris," except that it is possible to enjoy that story at least in one way without knowing Poe. In Stout's essay, however, the humor derives chiefly from the contrast of the Watson presented by Doyle with the Irene Watson described in the essay and characterized by actual words taken from Doyle. This humor would not be present if only one half of the contrasted pair were known to the reader. Part of his pleasure in reading such an essay is this use of familiar materials in a new way; part is the contrast between the absurdity of the thesis—Watson was a woman—and the seriousness with which the evidence seems to be presented.

Does Stout ridicule the Sherlock Holmes stories? The readers of the stories?

Does the author poke some fun at "scholarly" studies of literary works?

What effect does this reinterpretation of Watson have on our attitude toward the character of Holmes?

THOMAS BURKE

The Hands of Mr. Ottermole

Thomas Burke considered "The Hands of Mr. Ottermole" his best story, and most readers have agreed with his assessment. This story is set in the East End of London, not far from the Limehouse district popularized by Burke in other of his stories. Its thoughtful and suggestive examination of human behavior and its use of an all-knowing narrator to tell the story (with a resultant deemphasizing of the individual human characters) contribute to its unusual effect. "The Hands of Mr. Ottermole" is a timeless story, free from the "period piece" atmosphere that characterizes many stories written in the twenties and thirties. Because of its plot and narrative technique, the story has the power to grip and hold the reader's attention, and its extraordinary and startling suggestions about criminals and their motivations will linger in his mind for a long time.

At six o'clock of a January evening Mr. Whybrow was walking home through the cobweb alleys of London's East End. He had left the golden clamour of the great High Street to which the tram had brought him from the river and his daily work, and was now in the chess-board of byways that is called Mallon End. None of the rush and gleam of the High Street trickled into these byways. A few paces south—a flood-tide of life, foaming and beating. Here—only slow shuffling figures and muffled pulses. He was in the sink of London, the last refuge of European vagrants.

As though in tune with the street's spirit, he too walked slowly, with head down. It seemed that he was pondering some pressing trouble, but he was not. He had no trouble. He was walking slowly because he had been on his feet all day, and he was bent in abstraction because he was wondering whether the Missis would have herrings for his tea, or haddock; and he was trying to decide which would be the more tasty on a night like this. A wretched night it was, of damp and mist, and the mist wandered into his throat and his eyes, and the damp had settled on pavement and roadway, and where the sparse lamplight fell it sent up a greasy sparkle that chilled one to look at. By contrast it made his speculation more agreeable, and made him ready for that tea—whether herring or haddock. His eye turned from the glum bricks that made his horizon, and went forward half a mile. He saw a gas-lit kitchen, a flamy fire and a spread tea-table. There was toast in the hearth and a singing kettle on the side and a piquant effusion of herrings, or maybe of haddock, or perhaps sausages. The vision gave his aching feet a throb of energy. He shook imperceptible damp from his shoulders, and hastened towards its reality.

But Mr. Whybrow wasn't going to get any tea that evening—or any other evening. Mr. Whybrow was going to die. Somewhere within a hundred yards of him another man was walking: a man much like Mr. Whybrow and much like any other man, but without the only quality that enables mankind to live peaceably together and not as madmen in a jungle. A man with a dead heart eating into itself and bringing forth the foul organisms that arise from death and corruption. And that thing in man's shape, on a whim or a settled idea—one cannot know—had said within himself that Mr. Whybrow should never taste another herring. Not that Mr. Whybrow had injured him. Not that he had any dislike of Mr. Whybrow. Indeed, he knew nothing of him save as a familiar figure about the streets. But, moved by a force that had taken possession of his empty cells, he had picked on Mr. Whybrow with that blind choice that makes us pick one restaurant table that has nothing to mark it from four or five other tables, or one apple from a dish of half a dozen equal apples; or that drives Nature to send a cyclone upon one corner of this planet, and destroy five hundred lives in that corner, and leave another five hundred in the same corner unharmed. So this man had picked on Mr. Whybrow, as he might have picked on you or me, had we been within his daily observation; and even now he was creeping through the blue-toned streets, nursing his large white hands, moving ever closer to Mr. Whybrow's tea-table, and so closer to Mr. Whybrow himself.

He wasn't, this man, a bad man. Indeed, he had many of the social and amiable qualities, and passed as a respectable man, as most successful criminals do. But the thought had come into his mouldering mind that he would like to murder somebody, and, as he held no fear of God or man, he was going to do it, and would then go home to *his* tea. I don't say that flippantly, but as a statement of fact. Strange as it may seem to the humane, murderers must and do sit down to meals after a murder. There is no reason why they shouldn't, and many reasons why they should. For one thing, they need to keep their physical and mental vitality at full beat for the business of covering their crime. For another, the strain of their effort makes them hungry, and satisfaction at the accomplishment of a desired thing brings a feeling of relaxation towards human pleasures. It is accepted among non-murderers that the murderer is always overcome by fear for his safety and horror at his act; but this type is rare. His own safety is, of course, his immediate concern, but vanity is a marked quality of most murderers, and that, together with the thrill of conquest, makes him confident that he can secure it, and when he has restored his strength with food he goes about securing it as a young hostess goes about the arranging of her first big dinner—a little anxious, but no more. Criminologists and detectives tell us that *every* murderer, however intelligent or cunning, always makes one slip in his tactics—one little slip that brings the affair home to him. But that is only half true. It is true only of the murderers who are caught. Scores of murderers are not caught: therefore scores of murderers do not make any mistake at all. This man didn't.

As for horror or remorse, prison chaplains, doctors, and lawyers have told us that of murderers they have interviewed under condemnation and the shadow of death, only one here and there has expressed any contrition for his act, or shown any sign of mental misery. Most of them display only exasperation at having been caught when so many have gone undiscovered, or indignation at being condemned for a perfectly reasonable act. However normal and humane they may have been before the murder, they are utterly without conscience after it. For what is conscience? Simply a polite nickname for superstition, which is a polite nickname for fear. Those who associate remorse with murder are, no doubt, basing their ideas on the world-legend of the remorse of Cain, or are projecting their own frail minds into the mind of the murderer, and getting false reactions. Peaceable folk cannot hope to make contact with this mind, for they are not merely different in mental type from the murderer: they are different in their personal chemistry and construction. Some men can and do kill, not one man, but two or three, and go calmly about their daily affairs. Other men could not, under the most agonizing provocation, bring themselves even to wound. It is men of this sort who imagine the murderer in torments of remorse and fear of the law, whereas he is actually sitting down to his tea.

The man with the large white hands was as ready for his tea as Mr. Whybrow was, but he had something to do before he went to it. When he had done that something, and made no mistake about it, he would be even more ready for it, and would go to it as comfortably as he went to it the day before, when his hands were stainless.

Walk on, then, Mr. Whybrow, walk on; and as you walk, look your last upon the familiar features of your nightly journey. Follow your jack-o'-lantern tea-table. Look well upon its warmth and colour and kindness; feed your eyes with it, and tease your nose with its gentle domestic odours; for you will never sit down to it. Within ten minutes' pacing of you a pursuing phantom has spoken in his heart, and you are doomed. There you go—you and phantom—two nebulous dabs of mortality, moving through green air along pavements of powder-blue, the one to kill, the other to be killed. Walk on. Don't annoy your burning feet by hurrying, for the more slowly you walk, the longer you will breathe the green air of this January dusk, and see the dreamy lamplight and the little shops, and hear the agreeable commerce of the London crowd and the haunting pathos of the street-organ. These things are dear to you, Mr. Whybrow. You don't know it now, but in fifteen minutes you will have two seconds in which to realize how inexpressibly dear they are.

Walk on, then, across this crazy chess-board. You are in Lagos Street now, among the tents of the wanderers of Eastern Europe. A minute or so, and you are in Loyal Lane, among the lodging-houses that shelter the useless and the beaten of London's camp-followers. The lane holds the smell of them, and its soft darkness seems heavy with the wail of the futile. But you are not sensitive to impalpable things, and you plod through it, unseeing, as you do every evening, and come to Blean Street, and plod through that. From basement to sky rise the tenements of an alien colony. Their windows slit the ebony of their walls with lemon. Behind those windows strange life is moving, dressed with forms that are not of London or of England, yet, in essence, the same agreeable life that you have been living, and tonight will live no more. From high above you comes a voice crooning *The Song of Katta*. Through a window you see a family keeping a religious rite. Through another you see a woman pouring out tea for her husband. You see a man mending a pair of boots; a mother bathing her baby. You have seen all these things before, and never noticed them. You do not notice them now, but if you knew that you were never going to see them again, you would notice them. You never *will* see them again, not because your life has run its natural course, but because a man whom you have often passed in the street has at his own solitary pleasure decided to usurp the awful authority of nature, and destroy you. So perhaps it's as well that you don't notice them, for your part in them is ended. No more for you these pretty moments of our earthly travail: only one moment of terror, and then a plunging darkness.

Closer to you this shadow of massacre moves, and now he is twenty yards behind you. You can hear his footfalls, but you do not turn your head. You are familiar with footfalls. You are in London, in the easy security of your daily territory, and footfalls behind you, your instinct tells you, are no more than a message of human company.

But can't you hear something in those footfalls—something that goes with a widdershins beat? Something that says: *Look out, look out. Beware, beware.* Can't you hear the very syllables of *murd-er-er, murd-er-er?* No; there is nothing in footfalls. They are neutral. The foot of villainy falls with the same quiet note as the foot of honesty. But those footfalls, Mr. Whybrow, are bearing on to you a pair of hands, and there *is* something in hands. Behind you that pair of hands is even now stretching its muscles in preparation for your end. Every minute of your days you have been seeing human hands. Have you ever realized the sheer horror of hands—those appendages that are a symbol for our moments of trust and affection and salutation? Have you thought of the sickening potentialities that lie within the scope of that five-tentacled member? No, you never have; for all the human hands that you have seen have been stretched to you in kindness or fellowship. Yet, though the eyes can hate, and the lips can sting, it is only that dangling member that can gather the accumulated essence of evil, and electrify it into currents of destruction. Satan may enter into man by many doors, but in the hands alone can he find the servants of his will.

Another minute, Mr. Whybrow, and you will know all about the horror of human hands.

You are nearly home now. You have turned into your street— Caspar Street—and you are in the centre of the chess-board. You can see the front window of your little four-roomed house. The street is dark, and its three lamps give only a smut of light that is more confusing than darkness. It is dark—empty, too. Nobody about; no lights in the front parlours of the houses, for the families are at tea in their kitchens; and only a random glow in a few upper rooms occupied by lodgers. Nobody about but you and your following companion, and you don't notice him. You see him so often that he is never seen. Even if you turned your head and saw him, you would only say 'Good evening' to him, and walk on. A suggestion that he was a possible murderer would not even make you laugh. It would be too silly.

And now you are at your gate. And now you have found your door key. And now you are in, and hanging up your hat and coat. The Missis has just called a greeting from the kitchen, whose smell is an echo of that greeting (herring!) and you have answered it, when the door shakes under a sharp knock.

Go away, Mr. Whybrow. Go away from that door. Don't touch

it. Get right away from it. Get out of the house. Run with the Missis to the back garden, and over the fence. Or call the neighbours. But don't touch that door. Don't, Mr. Whybrow, don't open . . .

Mr. Whybrow opened the door.

That was the beginning of what became known as London's Strangling Horrors. Horrors they were called because they were something more than murders: they were motiveless, and there was an air of black magic about them. Each murder was committed at a time when the street where the bodies were found was empty of any perceptible or possible murderer. There would be an empty alley. There would be a policeman at its end. He would turn his back on the empty alley for less than a minute. Then he would look round and run into the night with news of another strangling. And in any direction he looked nobody to be seen and no report to be had of anybody being seen. Or he would be on duty in a long quiet street, and suddenly be called to a house of dead people whom a few seconds earlier he had seen alive. And, again, whichever way he looked nobody to be seen; and although police whistles put an immediate cordon around the area, and all houses were searched, no possible murderer to be found.

The first news of the murder of Mr. and Mrs. Whybrow was brought by the station sergeant. He had been walking through Caspar Street on his way to the station for duty, when he noticed the open door of No. 98. Glancing in, he saw by the gaslight of the passage a motionless body on the floor. After a second look he blew his whistle, and when the constables answered him he took one to join him in a search of the house, and sent others to watch all neighbouring streets, and make inquiries at adjoining houses. But neither in the house nor in the streets was anything found to indicate the murderer. Neighbours on either side, and opposite, were questioned, but they had seen nobody about, and had heard nothing. One had heard Mr. Whybrow come home—the scrape of his latchkey in the door was so regular an evening sound, he said, that you could set your watch by it for half-past six—but he had heard nothing more than the sound of the opening door until the sergeant's whistle. Nobody had been seen to enter the house or leave it, by front or back, and the necks of the dead people carried no finger-prints or other traces. A nephew was called in to go over the house, but he could find nothing missing; and anyway his uncle possessed nothing worth stealing. The little money in the house was untouched, and there were no signs of any disturbance of the property, or even of struggle. No signs of anything but brutal and wanton murder.

Mr. Whybrow was known to neighbours and work-mates as a quiet, likeable, home-loving man; such a man as could not have any enemies. But, then, murdered men seldom have. A relentless enemy who hates a man to the point of wanting to hurt him seldom wants to murder him, since to do that puts him beyond suffering. So the police were left with an impossible situation: no clue to the murderer and no motive for the murders; only the fact that they had been done.

The first news of the affair sent a tremor through London generally, and an electric thrill through all Mallon End. Here was murder of two inoffensive people, not for gain and not for revenge; and the murderer, to whom, apparently, killing was a casual impulse, was at large. He had left no traces, and, provided he had no companions, there seemed no reason why he should not remain at large. Any clear-headed man who stands alone, and has no fear of God or man, can, if he chooses, hold a city, even a nation, in subjection; but your everyday criminal is seldom clear-headed, and dislikes being lonely. He needs, if not the support of confederates, at least somebody to talk to; his vanity needs the satisfaction of perceiving at first hand the effect of his work. For this he will frequent bars and coffee-shops and other public places. Then, sooner or later, in a glow of comradeship, he will utter the one word too much; and the nark, who is everywhere, has an easy job.

But though the doss-houses and saloons and other places were "combed" and set with watches, and it was made known by whispers that good money and protection were assured to those with information, nothing attaching to the Whybrow case could be found. The murderer clearly had no friends and kept no company. Known men of this type were called up and questioned, but each was able to give a good account of himself; and in a few days the police were at a dead end. Against the constant public gibe that the thing had been done almost under their noses, they became restive, and for four days each man of the force was working his daily beat under a strain. On the fifth day they became still more restive.

It was the season of annual teas and entertainments for the children of the Sunday Schools, and on an evening of fog, when London was a world of groping phantoms, a small girl, in the bravery of best Sunday frock and shoes, shining face and new-washed hair, set out from Logan Passage for St. Michael's Parish Hall. She never got there. She was not actually dead until half-past six, but she was as good as dead from the moment she left her mother's door. Somebody like a man, pacing the street from which the Passage led, saw her come out; and from that moment she was dead. Through the fog somebody's large white hands reached after her, and in fifteen minutes they were about her.

At half-past six a whistle screamed trouble, and those answering it found the body of little Nellie Vrinoff in a warehouse entry in Minnow Street. The sergeant was first among them, and he posted his men to useful points, ordering them here and there in the tart tones of repressed rage, and berating the officer whose beat the street was. "I saw you, Magson, at the end of the lane. What were you up to there? You were there ten minutes before you turned." Magson began an explanation about keeping an eye on a suspicious-looking character at that end, but the sergeant cut him short: "Suspicious characters be damned. You don't want to look for suspicious characters. You want to look for *murderers*. Messing about . . . and then this happens right where you ought to be. Now think what they'll say."

With the speed of ill news came the crowd, pale and perturbed; and on the story that the unknown monster had appeared again, and this time to a child, their faces streaked the fog with spots of hate and horror. But then came the ambulance and more police, and swiftly they broke up the crowd; and as it broke the sergeant's thought was thickened into words, and from all sides came low murmurs of "Right under their noses." Later inquiries showed that four people of the district, above suspicion, had passed that entry at intervals of seconds before the murder, and seen nothing and heard nothing. None of them had passed the child alive or seen her dead. None of them had seen anybody in the street except themselves. Again the police were left with no motive and with no clue.

And now the district, as you will remember, was given over, not to panic, for the London public never yields to that, but to apprehension and dismay. If these things were happening in their familiar streets, then anything might happen. Wherever people met—in the streets, the markets and the shops—they debated the one topic. Women took to bolting their windows and doors at the first fall of dusk. They kept their children closely under their eye. They did their shopping before dark, and watched anxiously, while pretending they weren't watching, for the return of their husbands from work. Under the Cockney's semi-humorous resignation to disaster, they hid an hourly foreboding. By the whim of one man with a pair of hands the structure and tenor of their daily life were shaken, as they always can be shaken by any man contemptuous of humanity and fearless of its laws. They began to realize that the pillars that supported the peaceable society in which they lived were mere straws that anybody could snap; that laws were powerful only so long as they were obeyed; that the police were potent only so long as they were feared. By the power of his hands this one man had made a whole community do something new: he had made it think, and left it gasping at the obvious.

And then, while it was yet gasping under his first two strokes, he made his third. Conscious of the horror that his hands had created, and hungry as an actor who has once tasted the thrill of the multitude, he made fresh advertisement of his presence; and on Wednesday morning, three days after the murder of the child, the papers carried to the breakfast-tables of England the story of a still more shocking outrage.

At 9:32 on Tuesday night a constable was on duty in Jarnigan Road, and at that time spoke to a fellow-officer named Peterson at the top of Clemming Street. He had seen this officer walk down that street. He could swear that the street was empty at that time, except for a lame boot-black whom he knew by sight, and who passed him and entered a tenement on the side opposite that on which his fellow-officer was walking. He had the habit, as all constables had just then, of looking constantly behind him and around him, whichever way he was walking, and he was certain that the street was empty. He passed his sergeant at 9:33, saluted him, and answered his inquiry for anything seen. He reported that he had seen nothing, and passed on. His beat ended at a short distance from Clemming Street, and, having paced it, he turned and came again at 9:34 to the top of the street. He had scarcely reached it before he heard the hoarse voice of the sergeant: "Gregory! You there? Quick. Here's another. My God, it's Peterson! Garrotted. Quick, call 'em up!"

That was the third of the Strangling Horrors, of which there were to be a fourth and a fifth; and the five horrors were to pass into the unknown and unknowable. That is, unknown as far as authority and the public were concerned. The identity of the murderer *was* known, but to two men only. One was the murderer himself; the other was a young journalist.

This young man, who was covering the affairs for his paper, the *Daily Torch*, was no smarter than the other zealous newspaper men who were hanging about these byways in the hope of a sudden story. But he was patient, and he hung a little closer to the case than the other fellows, and by continually staring at it he at last raised the figure of the murderer like a genie from the stones on which he had stood to do his murders.

After the first few days the men had given up any attempt at exclusive stories, for there was none to be had. They met regularly at the police station, and what little information there was they shared. The officials were agreeable to them, but no more. The sergeant discussed with them the details of each murder; suggested possible explanations of the man's methods; recalled from the past those cases that had some similarity; and on the matter of motive reminded them of the motiveless Neil Cream and the wanton John Williams, and hinted that work was being done which would soon bring the business to an end; but about that work he would not say a word. The inspector, too, was gracefully garrulous on the theme of murder, but whenever one of the party edged the talk towards what was being done in this immediate matter, he glided past it. Whatever the officials knew, they were not giving it to newspaper men. The business had fallen heavily upon them, and only by a capture made by their own efforts could they rehabilitate themselves in official and public esteem. Scotland Yard, of course, was at work, and had all the station's material; but the station's hope was that they themselves would have the honour of settling the affair; and however useful the co-operation of the Press might be in other cases they did not want to risk a defeat by a premature disclosure of their theories and plans.

So the sergeant talked at large, and propounded one interesting theory after another, all of which the newspaper men had thought of themselves.

The young man soon gave up these morning lectures on the Philosophy of Crime, and took to wandering about the streets and making bright stories out of the effect of the murders on the normal life of the people. A melancholy job made more melancholy by the district. The littered roadways, the crestfallen houses, the bleared windows—all held the acid misery that evokes no sympathy: the misery of the frustrated poet. The misery was the creation of the aliens, who were living in this makeshift fashion because they had no settled homes, and would neither take the trouble to make a home where they *could* settle, nor get on with their wandering.

There was little to be picked up. All he saw and heard were indignant faces and wild conjectures of the murderer's identity and of the secret of his trick of appearing and disappearing unseen. Since a policeman himself had fallen a victim, denunciations of the force had ceased, and the unknown was now invested with a cloak of legend. Men eyed other men, as though thinking: It might be *him*. It might be *him*. They were no longer looking for a man who had the air of a Madame Tussaud murderer; they were looking for a man, or perhaps some harridan woman, who had done these particular murders. Their thoughts ran mainly on the foreign set. Such ruffianism could scarcely belong to England, nor could the bewildering cleverness of the thing. So they turned to Rumanian gipsies and Turkish carpet-sellers. There, clearly, would be found the "warm" spot. These Eastern fellows—they knew all sorts of tricks, and they had no real religion—nothing to hold them within bounds. Sailors returning from those parts had told tales of conjurors who made themselves invisible; and there were tales of Egyptian and Arab potions that were used for abysmally queer purposes. Perhaps it *was* possible to them; you never knew. They were so slick and cunning, and they had such gliding movements; no Englishman could melt away as they could. Almost certainly the murderer would be found to be one of that sort—with some dark trick of his own—and just because they were sure that he *was* a magician, they felt that it was useless to look for him. He was a power, able to hold them in subjection and to hold himself untouchable. Superstition, which so easily cracks the frail shell of reason, had got into them. He could do anything he chose; he would never be discovered. These two points they settled, and they went about the streets in a mood of resentful fatalism.

They talked of their ideas to the journalist in half-tones, looking right and left, as though *HE* might overhear them and visit them. And though all the district was thinking of him and ready to pounce upon him, yet, so strongly had he worked upon them, that if any man in the street—say, a small man of commonplace features and form—had cried "*I* am the monster!" would their stifled fury have broken into flood and have borne him down and engulfed him? Or would they not suddenly have seen something unearthly in that everyday face and figure, something unearthly in his everyday boots, something unearthly about his hat, something that marked him as one whom none of their weapons could alarm or pierce? And would they not momentarily have fallen back from this devil, as the devil fell back from the cross made by the sword of Faust, and so have given him time to escape? I do not know; but so fixed was their belief in his invincibility that it is at least likely that they would have made this hesitation, had such an occasion arisen. But it never did. To-day this commonplace fellow, his murder-lust glutted, is still seen and observed among them as he was seen and observed all the time; but because nobody then dreamt, or now dreams, that he was what he was, they observed him then, and observe him now, as people observe a lamp-post.

Almost was their belief in his invincibility justified; for five days after the murder of the policeman Peterson, when the experience and inspiration of the whole detective force of London were turned towards his identification and capture, he made his fourth and fifth strokes.

At nine o'clock that evening, the young newspaper man, who

hung about every night until his paper was away, was strolling along Richards Lane. Richards Lane is a narrow street, partly a stall-market, and partly residential. The young man was in the residential section, which carries on one side small working-class cottages, and on the other the wall of a railway goods yard. The great wall hung a blanket of shadow over the lane, and the shadow and the cadaverous outline of the now deserted market stalls gave it the appearance of a living lane that had been turned to frost in the moment between breath and death. The very lamps, that elsewhere were nimbuses of gold, had here the rigidity of gems. The journalist, feeling this message of frozen eternity, was telling himself that he was tired of the whole thing, when in one stroke the frost was broken. In the moment between one pace and another silence and darkness were racked by a high scream and through the scream a voice: "Help! help! *He's here!*"

Before he could think what movement to make, the lane came to life. As though its invisible populace had been waiting on that cry, the door of every cottage was flung open, and from them and from the alleys poured shadowy figures bent in question-mark form. For a second or so they stood as rigid as the lamps; then a police whistle gave them direction, and the flock of shadows sloped up the street. The journalist followed them, and others followed him. From the main street and from surrounding streets they came, some risen from unfinished suppers, some disturbed in their ease of slippers and shirt-sleeves, some stumbling on infirm limbs, and some upright, and armed with pokers or the tools of their trade. Here and there above the wavering cloud of heads moved the bold helmets of policemen. In one dim mass they surged upon a cottage whose doorway was marked by the sergeant and two constables; and voices of those behind urged them on with "Get in! Find him! Run round the back! Over the wall!" and those in front cried: "Keep back! Keep back!"

And now the fury of a mob held in thrall by unknown peril broke loose. He was here—on the spot. Surely this time he *could not* escape. All minds were bent upon the cottage; all energies thrust towards its doors and windows and roof; all thought was turned upon one unknown man and his extermination. So that no one man saw any other man. No man saw the narrow, packed lane and the mass of struggling shadows, and all forgot to look among themselves for the monster who never lingered upon his victims. All forgot, indeed, that they, by their mass crusade of vengeance, were affording him the perfect hiding-place. They saw only the house, and they heard only the rending of woodwork and the smash of glass at back and front, and the police giving orders or crying with the chase; and they pressed on.

But they found no murderer. All they found was news of murder and a glimpse of the ambulance, and for their fury there was no other object than the police themselves, who fought against this hampering of their work.

The journalist managed to struggle through to the cottage door, and to get the story from the constable stationed there. The cottage was the home of a pensioned sailor and his wife and daughter. They had been at supper, and at first it appeared that some noxious gas had smitten all three in mid-action. The daughter lay dead on the hearthrug, with a piece of bread and butter in her hand. The father had fallen sideways from his chair, leaving on his plate a filled spoon of rice-pudding. The mother lay half under the table, her lap filled with the pieces of a broken cup and splashes of cocoa. But in three seconds the idea of gas was dismissed. One glance at their necks showed that this was the Strangler again; and the police stood and looked at the room and momentarily shared the fatalism of the public. They were helpless.

This was his fourth visit, making seven murders in all. He was to do, as you know, one more—and to do it that night; and then he was to pass into history as the unknown London horror, and return to the decent life that he had always led, remembering little of what he had done, and worried not at all by the memory. Why did he stop? Impossible to say. Why did he begin? Impossible again. It just happened like that; and if he thinks at all of those days and nights, I surmise that he thinks of them as we think of foolish or dirty little sins that we committed in childhood. We say that they were not really sins, because we were not then consciously ourselves: we had not come to realization; and we look back at that foolish little creature that we once were, and forgive him because he didn't know. So, I think, with this man.

There are plenty like him. Eugene Aram, after the murder of Daniel Clark, lived a quiet, contented life for fourteen years, unhaunted by his crime and unshaken in his self-esteem. Dr. Crippen murdered his wife, and then lived pleasantly with his mistress in the house under whose floor he had buried his wife. Constance Kent, found Not Guilty of the murder of her young brother, led a peaceful life for five years before she confessed. George Joseph Smith and William Palmer lived amiably among their fellows untroubled by fear or by remorse for their poisonings and drownings. Charles Peace, at the time he made his one unfortunate essay, had settled down into a respectable citizen with an interest in antiques. It happened that, after a lapse of time, these men were discovered, but more murderers than we guess are living decent lives to-day, and will die in decency, undiscovered and unsuspected. As this man will.

But he had a narrow escape, and it was perhaps this narrow escape that brought him to a stop. The escape was due to an error of judgment on the part of the journalist.

As soon as he had the full story of the affair, which took some time, he spent fifteen minutes on the telephone, sending the story through, and at the end of the fifteen minutes, when the stimulus of the business had left him, he felt physically tired and mentally dishevelled. He was not yet free to go home; the paper would not go away for another hour; so he turned into a bar for a drink and some sandwiches.

It was then, when he had dismissed the whole business from his mind, and was looking about the bar and admiring the landlord's taste in watch-chains and his air of domination, and was thinking that the landlord of a well-conducted tavern had a more comfortable life than a newspaper man, that his mind received from nowhere a spark of light. He was not thinking about the Strangling Horrors; his mind was on his sandwich. As a public-house sandwich, it was a curiosity. The bread had been thinly cut, it was buttered, and the ham was not two months stale; it was ham as it should be. His mind turned to the inventor of this refreshment, the Earl of Sandwich, and then to George the Fourth, and then to the Georges, and to the legend of that George who was worried to know how the apple got into the apple-dump-ling. He wondered whether George would have been equally puzzled to know how the ham got into the ham sandwich, and how long it would have been before it occurred to him that the ham could not have got there unless somebody had put it there. He got up to order another sandwich, and in that moment a little active corner of his mind settled the affair. If there was ham in his sandwich, somebody must have put it there. If seven people had been murdered, somebody must have been there to murder them. There was no aeroplane or automobile that would go into a man's pocket; therefore that somebody must have escaped either by running away or standing still; and again therefore——

He was visualizing the front page story that his paper would carry if his theory were correct, and if—a matter of conjecture— his editor had the necessary nerve to make a bold stroke, when a cry of "Time, gentlemen, please! All out!" reminded him of the hour. He got up and went out into a world of mist, broken by the ragged disks of roadside puddles and the streaming lightning of motor buses. He was certain that he had *the* story, but, even if it were proved, he was doubtful whether the policy of his paper would permit him to print it. It had one great fault. It was truth, but it was impossible truth. It rocked the foundations of everything that newspaper readers believed and that newspaper editors helped them to believe. They might believe that Turkish carpet-sellers had the gift of making themselves invisible. They would not believe this.

As it happened, they were not asked to, for the story was never written. As his paper had by now gone away, and as he was nourished by his refreshment and stimulated by his theory, he thought he might put in an extra half-hour by testing that theory. So he began to look about for the man he had in mind—a man with white hair, and large white hands; otherwise an everyday figure whom nobody would look twice at. He wanted to spring his idea on this man without warning, and he was going to place himself within reach of a man armoured in legends of dreadfulness and grue. This might appear to be an act of supreme courage— that one man, with no hope of immediate outside support, should place himself at the mercy of one who was holding a whole parish in terror. But it wasn't. He didn't think about the risk. He didn't think about his duty to his employers or loyalty to his paper. He was moved simply by an instinct to follow a story to its end.

He walked slowly from the tavern and crossed into Fingal Street, making for Deever Market, where he had hope of finding his man. But his journey was shortened. At the corner of Lotus Street he saw him—or a man who looked like him. This street was poorly lit, and he could see little of the man: but he *could* see white hands. For some twenty paces he stalked him; then drew level with him; and at a point where the arch of a railway crossed the street, he was sure that this was his man. He approached him with the current conversational phrase of the district: "Well, seen anything of the murderer?" The man stopped to look sharply at him; then, satisfied that the journalist was not the murderer, said:

"Eh? No, nor's anybody else, curse it. Doubt if they ever will."

"I don't know. I've been thinking about them, and I've got an idea."

"So?"

"Yes. Came to me all of a sudden. Quarter of an hour ago. And I'd felt that we'd all been blind. It's been staring us in the face."

The man turned again to look at him, and the look and the movement held suspicion of this man who seemed to know so much. "Oh? Has it? Well, if you're so sure, why not give us the benefit of it?"

"I'm going to." They walked level, and were nearly at the end of the little street where it meets Deever Market, when the journalist turned casually to the man. He put a finger on his arm. "Yes, it seems to me quite simple now. But there's still one point I don't understand. One little thing I'd like to clear up. I mean the motive. Now, as man to man, tell me, Sergeant Ottermole, just *why* did you kill those inoffensive people?"

The sergeant stopped, and the journalist stopped. There was just enough light from the sky, which held the reflected light of the continent of London, to give him a sight of the sergeant's face, and the sergeant's face was turned to him with a wide smile of such urbanity and charm that the journalist's eyes were frozen as they met it. The smile stayed for some seconds. Then said the sergeant: "Well, to tell you the truth, Mister Newspaper Man, I don't know. I really don't know. In fact, I've been worried about it myself. But I've got an idea—just like you. Everybody knows that we can't control the workings of our minds. Don't they? Ideas come into our minds without asking. But everybody's supposed to be able to control his body. Why? Eh? We get our minds from lord-knows-where—from people who were dead hundreds of years before we were born. Mayn't we get our bodies in the same way? Our faces—our legs—our heads—they aren't completely ours. We don't make 'em. They come to us. And couldn't ideas come into our bodies like ideas come into our minds? Eh? Can't ideas live in nerve and muscle as well as in brain? Couldn't it be that parts of our bodies aren't really us, and couldn't ideas come into those parts all of a sudden, like ideas come into—into"—he shot his arms out, showing the great white-gloved hands and hairy wrists; shot them out so swiftly to the journalist's throat that his eyes never saw them—"into *my hands.*"

COMMENT AND QUESTIONS

In this story the detective who solves the crime is a newspaper reporter, known to the reader only as the journalist. In what ways is he similar to the classic detective? In what ways is he different?

Among other elements unusual in a detective story (the policeman as murderer and the death of the individual who solves the crime), this story includes an analysis of the criminal that suggests a psychology quite different from that of the usual murderer. Is this analysis convincing? Why or why not?

The author refers to the instinct of Mr. Whybrow, the instinct of the journalist, and the instinctive behavior of Mr. Ottermole's hands. How is motivation for the crimes linked to the manner of solution of the crime? Do any of the characters seem to exercise choice? When and in what ways?

Which rules of the classic detective story are broken in this story?

The author "speaks" to characters in the story, warning them of their fate. He also tells the reader other things that will happen in the story (the murderer will go unpunished, for example) before they occur. Does this practice lessen the suspense? Why or why not?

Is the fictional world of the story logical? orderly? predictable? Explain.

Is this story primarily a detective story or a horror story? Explain.

What techniques has the author used to intensify the horror of the crimes?

DOROTHY L. SAYERS

The Dragon's Head

Dorothy Sayers was the first woman to graduate with a "first"
(high honors) in medieval literature from Somerset College,
Oxford. She worked as a copywriter in an advertising firm;
wrote poetry, drama, and essays; and made translations of the
Song of Roland and Dante's *Inferno* that are widely used in
schools and colleges. Book collecting was her hobby, and she
once said that she wrote detective fiction so that she could
afford to buy rare books.

Speculating on the reason man takes pleasure in puzzles
of the kind offered in detective stories—"the art of self-
tormenting is an ancient one, with a long and honourable
literary tradition"—she observed that

it may be that in them he finds a sort of catharsis or purging of his
fears and self-questionings. These mysteries made only to be solved,
these horrors which he knows to be mere figments of the creative
brain, comfort him by subtly persuading that life is a mystery which
death will solve, and whose horrors will pass away as a tale that is
told.

It is of some interest that the psychoanalyst Sigmund Freud
enjoyed Miss Sayers' detective stories.

While some humor is found in the best mystery fiction, in
"The Dragon's Head" it is of primary importance. Even the
criminals afford us a smile. The story is sound evidence that
adventure can coexist with a spirit of lighthearted comedy.

115

"Uncle Peter!"

"Half a jiff, Gherkins. No, I don't think I'll take the Catullus, Mr. Ffolliott. After all, thirteen guineas is a bit steep without either the title or the last folio, what? But you might send me round the Vitruvius and the Satyricon when they come in; I'd like to have a look at them, anyhow. Well, old man, what is it?"

"Do come and look at these pictures, Uncle Peter. I'm sure it's an awfully old book."

Lord Peter Wimsey sighed as he picked his way out of Mr. Ffolliott's dark back shop, strewn with the flotsam and jetsam of many libraries. An unexpected outbreak of measles at Mr. Bultridge's excellent preparatory school, coinciding with the absence of the Duke and Duchess of Denver on the Continent, had saddled his lordship with his ten-year-old nephew, Viscount St. George, more commonly known as Young Jerry, Jerrykins, or Pickled Gherkins. Lord Peter was not one of those born uncles who delight old nurses by their fascinating "way with" children. He succeeded, however, in earning tolerance on honourable terms by treating the young with the same scrupulous politeness which he extended to their elders. He therefore prepared to receive Gherkins' discovery with respect, though a child's taste was not to be trusted, and the book might quite well be some horror of woolly mezzotints or an inferior modern reprint adorned with leprous electros.[1] Nothing much better was really to be expected from the "cheap shelf" exposed to the dust of the street.

"Uncle! There's such a funny man here, with a great long nose and ears and a tail and dogs' heads all over his body. *Monstrum hoc Cracoviæ*—that's a monster, isn't it? I should jolly well think it was. What's *Cracoviæ*, Uncle Peter?"

"Oh," said Lord Peter, greatly relieved, "the Cracow monster?" A portrait of that distressing infant certainly argued a respectable antiquity. "Let's have a look. Quite right, it's a very old book—Münster's[2] *Cosmographia universalis*. I'm glad you know good stuff when you see it, Gherkins. What's the *Cosmographia* doing out here, Mr. Ffolliott, at five bob?"

"Well, my lord," said the bookseller, who had followed his customers to the door, "it's in a very bad state, you see; covers loose and nearly all the double-page maps missing. It came in a few weeks ago—dumped in with a collection we bought from a gentleman in Norfolk—you'll find his name in it—Dr. Conyers of Yelsall Manor. Of course, we might keep it and try to make up a complete copy when we get another example. But it's rather out of our line, as you know, classical authors being our speciality. So we just put it out to go for what it would fetch in the *status quo,* as you might say."

"Oh, look!" broke in Gherkins. "Here's a picture of a man being chopped up in little bits. What does it say about it?"

"I thought you could read Latin."

"Well, but it's all full of sort of pothooks. What do they mean?"

"They're just contractions," said Lord Peter patiently. " '*Solent quoque hujus insulæ cultores*'—It is the custom of the dwellers in this island, when they see their parents stricken in years and of no further use, to take them down into the market-place and sell them to the cannibals, who kill them and eat them for food. This they do also with younger persons when they fall into any desperate sickness."

"Ha, ha!" said Mr. Ffolliott. "Rather sharp practice on the poor cannibals. They never got anything but tough old joints or diseased meat, eh?"

"The inhabitants seem to have had thoroughly advanced notions of business," agreed his lordship.

The viscount was enthralled.

"I *do* like this book," he said; "could I buy it out of my pocket-money, please?"

"Another problem for uncles," thought Lord Peter, rapidly ransacking his recollections of the *Cosmographia* to determine whether any of its illustrations were indelicate; for he knew the duchess to be strait-laced. On consideration, he could only remember one that was dubious, and there was a sporting chance that the duchess might fail to light upon it.

"Well," he said judicially, "in your place, Gherkins, I should be inclined to buy it. It's in a bad state, as Mr. Ffolliott has honourably told you—otherwise, of course, it would be exceedingly valuable; but, apart from the lost pages, it's a very nice clean copy, and certainly worth five shillings to you, if you think of starting a collection."

Till that moment, the viscount had obviously been more impressed by the cannibals than by the state of the margins, but the idea of figuring next term at Mr. Bultridge's as a collector of rare editions had undeniable charm.

"None of the other fellows collect books," he said; "they collect stamps, mostly. I think stamps are rather ordinary, don't you, Uncle Peter? I was rather thinking of giving up stamps. Mr. Porter, who takes us for history, has got a lot of books like yours, and he is a splendid man at footer."

Rightly interpreting this reference to Mr. Porter, Lord Peter gave it as his opinion that book collecting could be a perfectly manly pursuit. Girls, he said, practically never took it up, because it meant so much learning about dates and type faces and other technicalities which called for a masculine brain.

"Besides," he added, "it's a very interesting book in itself, you know. Well worth dipping into."

"I'll take it, please," said the viscount, blushing a little at transacting so important and expensive a piece of business; for the duchess did not encourage lavish spending by little boys, and was strict in the matter of allowances.

Mr. Ffolliott bowed, and took the *Cosmographia* away to wrap it up.

"Are you all right for cash?" enquired Lord Peter discreetly. "Or can I be of temporary assistance?"

"No, thank you, Uncle; I've got Aunt Mary's half-crown and four shillings of my pocket-money, because, you see, with the measles happening, we didn't have our dormitory spread, and I was saving up for that."

The business being settled in this gentlemanly manner, and the budding bibliophile taking personal and immediate charge of the stout, square volume, a taxi was chartered which, in due course of traffic delays, brought the *Cosmographia* to 110A Piccadilly.

"And who, Bunter, is Mr. Wilberforce Pope?"

"I do not think we know the gentleman, my lord. He is asking to see your lordship for a few minutes on business."

"He probably wants me to find a lost dog for his maiden aunt. What it is to have acquired a reputation as a sleuth! Show him in. Gherkins, if this good gentleman's business turns out to be private, you'd better retire into the dining-room."

"Yes, Uncle Peter," said the viscount dutifully. He was extended on his stomach on the library hearthrug, laboriously picking his way through the more exciting-looking bits of the *Cosmographia*, with the aid of Messrs. Lewis & Short,[3] whose monumental compilation he had hitherto looked upon as a barbarous invention for the annoyance of upper forms.

Mr. Wilberforce Pope turned out to be a rather plump, fair gentleman in the late thirties, with a prematurely bald forehead, horn-rimmed spectacles, and an engaging manner.

"You will excuse my intrusion, won't you?" he began. "I'm sure you must think me a terrible nuisance. But I wormed your name and address out of Mr. Ffolliott. Not his fault, really. You won't blame him, will you? I positively badgered the poor man. Sat down on his doorstep and refused to go, though the boy was putting up the shutters. I'm afraid you will think me very silly when you know what it's all about. But you really mustn't hold poor Mr. Ffolliott responsible, now, will you?"

"Not at all," said his lordship. "I mean, I'm charmed and all that sort of thing. Something I can do for you about books? You're a collector, perhaps? Will you have a drink or anything?"

"Well, no," said Mr. Pope, with a faint giggle. "No, not exactly a collector. Thank you very much, just a spot—no, no, literally a spot. Thank you; no"—he glanced round the bookshelves, with their rows of rich old leather bindings—"certainly not a collector. But I happen to be—er, interested—sentimentally interested—in a purchase you made yesterday. Really, such a very small matter. You will think it foolish. But I am told you are the present owner of a copy of Münster's *Cosmographia*, which used to belong to my uncle, Dr. Conyers."

Gherkins looked up suddenly, seeing that the conversation had a personal interest for him.

"Well, that's not quite correct," said Wimsey. "I was there at the time, but the actual purchaser is my nephew. Gerald, Mr.

Pope is interested in your *Cosmographia*. My nephew, Lord St. George."

"How do you do, young man," said Mr. Pope affably. "I see that the collecting spirit runs in the family. A great Latin scholar, too, I expect, eh? Ready to decline *jusjurandum*[4] with the best of us? Ha, ha! And what are you going to do when you grow up? Be Lord Chancellor, eh? Now, I bet you think you'd rather be an engine-driver, what, what?"

"No, thank you," said the viscount, with aloofness.

"What, not an engine-driver? Well, now, I want you to be a real business man this time. Put through a book deal, you know. Your uncle will see I offer you a fair price, what? Ha, ha! Now, you see, that picture-book of yours has a great value for me that it wouldn't have for anybody else. When *I* was a little boy of your age it was one of my very greatest joys. I used to have it to look at on Sundays. Ah, dear! the happy hours I used to spend with those quaint old engravings, and the funny old maps with the ships and salamanders and '*Hic dracones*'—you know what *that* means, I dare say. What does it mean?"

"Here are dragons," said the viscount, unwillingly but still politely.

"Quite right. I *knew* you were a scholar."

"It's a very attractive book," said Lord Peter. "My nephew was quite entranced by the famous Cracow monster."

"Ah yes—a glorious monster, isn't it?" agreed Mr. Pope, with enthusiasm. "Many's the time I've fancied myself as Sir Lancelot or somebody on a white war horse, charging that monster, lance in rest, with the captive princess cheering me on. Ah! Childhood! You're living the happiest days of your life, young man. You won't believe me, but you are."

"Now what is it exactly you want my nephew to do?" enquired Lord Peter a little sharply.

"Quite right, quite right. Well now, you know, my uncle, Dr. Conyers, sold his library a few months ago. I was abroad at the time, and it was only yesterday, when I went down to Yelsall on a visit, that I learnt the dear old book had gone with the rest. I can't tell you how distressed I was. I know it's not valuable—a great many pages missing and all that—but I can't bear to think of its being gone. So, purely from sentimental reasons, as I said, I hurried off to Ffolliott's to see if I could get it back. I was quite upset to find I was too late, and gave poor Mr. Ffolliott no peace till he told me the name of the purchaser. Now, you see, Lord St. George, I'm here to make you an offer for the book. Come, now, double what you gave for it. That's a good offer, isn't it, Lord Peter? Ha, ha! And you will be doing me a very great kindness as well."

Viscount St. George looked rather distressed, and turned appealingly to his uncle.

"Well, Gerald," said Lord Peter, "it's your affair, you know. What do you say?"

The viscount stood first on one leg and then on the other. The career of a book collector evidently had its problems, like other careers.

"If you please, Uncle Peter," he said, with embarrassment, "may I whisper?"

"It's not usually considered the thing to whisper, Gherkins, but you could ask Mr. Pope for time to consider his offer. Or you could say you would prefer to consult me first. That would be quite in order."

"Then, if you don't mind, Mr. Pope, I should like to consult my uncle first."

"Certainly, certainly; ha, ha!" said Mr. Pope. "Very prudent to consult a collector of greater experience, what? Ah! The younger generation, eh, Lord Peter? Regular little business men already."

"Excuse us, then, for one moment," said Lord Peter, and drew his nephew into the dining-room.

"I say, Uncle Peter," said the collector breathlessly, when the door was shut, "*need* I give him my book? I don't think he's a very nice man. I *hate* people who ask you to decline nouns for them."

"Certainly you needn't, Gherkins, if you don't want to. The book is yours, and you've a right to it."

"What would *you* do, Uncle?"

Before replying, Lord Peter, in the most surprising manner, tiptoed gently to the door which communicated with the library and flung it suddenly open, in time to catch Mr. Pope kneeling on the hearthrug intently turning over the pages of the coveted volume, which lay as the owner had left it. He started to his feet in a flurried manner as the door opened.

"Do help yourself, Mr. Pope, won't you?" cried Lord Peter hospitably, and closed the door again.

"What is it, Uncle Peter?"

"If you want my advice, Gherkins, I should be rather careful how you had any dealings with Mr. Pope. I don't think he's telling the truth. He called those woodcuts engravings—though, of course, that may be just his ignorance. But I can't believe that he spent all his childhood's Sunday afternoons studying those maps and picking out the dragons in them, because, as you may have noticed for yourself, old Münster put very few dragons into his maps. They're mostly just plain maps—a bit queer to our ideas of geography, but perfectly straightforward. That was why I brought in the Cracow monster, and, you see, he thought it was some sort of dragon."

"Oh, I say, Uncle! So you said that on purpose!"

"If Mr. Pope wants the *Cosmographia*, it's for some reason he doesn't want to tell us about. And, that being so, I wouldn't be in too big a hurry to sell, if the book were mine. See?"

"Do you mean there's something frightfully valuable about the book, which we don't know?"

"Possibly."

"How exciting! It's just like a story in the 'Boys' Friend Library.' What am I to say to him, Uncle?"

"Well, in your place I wouldn't be dramatic or anything. I'd just say you've considered the matter, and you've taken a fancy to the book and have decided not to sell. You thank him for his offer, of course."

"Yes—er, won't you say it for me, Uncle?"

"I think it would look better if you did it yourself."

"Yes, perhaps it would. Will he be very cross?"

"Possibly," said Lord Peter, "but, if he is, he won't let on. Ready?"

The consulting committee accordingly returned to the library. Mr. Pope had prudently retired from the hearthrug and was examining a distant bookcase.

"Thank you very much for your offer, Mr. Pope," said the viscount, striding stoutly up to him, "but I have considered it, and I have taken a—a—a fancy for the book and decided not to sell."

"Sorry and all that," put in Lord Peter, "but my nephew's

adamant about it. No, it isn't the price; he wants the book. Wish I could oblige you, but it isn't in my hands. Won't you take something else before you go? Really? Ring the bell, Gherkins. My man will see you to the lift. *Good* evening."

When the visitor had gone, Lord Peter returned and thoughtfully picked up the book.

"We were awful idiots to leave him with it, Gherkins, even for a moment. Luckily, there's no harm done."

"You don't think he found out anything while we were away, do you, Uncle?" gasped Gherkins, open-eyed.

"I'm sure he didn't."

"Why?"

"He offered me fifty pounds for it on the way to the door. Gave the game away. H'm! Bunter."

"My lord?"

"Put this book in the safe and bring me back the keys. And you'd better set all the burglar alarms when you lock up."

"Oo—er!" said Viscount St. George.

On the third morning after the visit of Mr. Wilberforce Pope, the viscount was seated at a very late breakfast in his uncle's flat, after the most glorious and soul-satisfying night that ever boy experienced. He was almost too excited to eat the kidneys and bacon placed before him by Bunter, whose usual impeccable manner was not in the least impaired by a rapidly swelling and blackening eye.

It was about two in the morning that Gherkins—who had not slept very well, owing to too lavish and grown-up a dinner and theatre the evening before—became aware of a stealthy sound somewhere in the direction of the fire-escape. He had got out of bed and crept very softly into Lord Peter's room and woken him up. He had said: "Uncle Peter, I'm sure there's burglars on the fire-escape." And Uncle Peter, instead of saying, "Nonsense, Gherkins, hurry up and get back to bed," had sat up and listened and said: "By Jove, Gherkins, I believe you're right." And had sent Gherkins to call Bunter. And on his return, Gherkins, who had always regarded his uncle as a very top-hatted sort of person, actually saw him take from his handkerchief drawer an undeniable automatic pistol.

It was at this point that Lord Peter was apotheosed from the state of Quite Decent Uncle to that of Glorified Uncle. He said:—

"Look here, Gherkins, we don't know how many of these blighters there'll be, so you must be jolly smart and do anything I say sharp, on the word of command—even if I have to say 'Scoot.' Promise?"

Gherkins promised, with his heart thumping, and they sat waiting in the dark, till suddenly a little electric bell rang sharply just over the head of Lord Peter's bed and a green light shone out.

"The library window," said his lordship, promptly silencing the bell by turning a switch. "If they heard, they may think better of it. We'll give them a few minutes."

They gave them five minutes, and then crept very quietly down the passage.

"Go round by the dining-room, Bunter," said his lordship. "They may bolt that way."

With infinite precaution, he unlocked and opened the library door, and Gherkins noticed how silently the locks moved.

A circle of light from an electric torch was moving slowly along the bookshelves. The burglars had obviously heard nothing of the counter attack. Indeed, they seemed to have troubles enough of their own to keep their attention occupied. As his eyes grew accustomed to the dim light, Gherkins made out that one man was standing holding the torch, while the other took down and examined the books. It was fascinating to watch his apparently disembodied hands move along the shelves in the torch-light.

The men muttered discontentedly. Obviously the job was proving a harder one than they had bargained for. The habit of ancient authors of abbreviating the titles on the backs of their volumes, or leaving them completely untitled, made things extremely awkward. From time to time the man with the torch extended his hand into the light. It held a piece of paper, which they anxiously compared with the title-page of a book. Then the volume was replaced and the tedious search went on.

Suddenly some slight noise—Gherkins was sure *he* did not make it; it may have been Bunter in the dining-room—seemed to catch the ear of the kneeling man.

"Wot's that?" he gasped, and his startled face swung round into view.

"Hands up!" said Lord Peter, and switched the light on.

The second man made one leap for the dining-room door, where a smash and an oath proclaimed that he had encountered Bunter. The kneeling man shot his hands up like a marionette.

"Gherkins," said Lord Peter, "do you think you can go across to that gentleman by the bookcase and relieve him of the article which is so inelegantly distending the right-hand pocket of his coat? Wait a minute. Don't on any account get between him and my pistol, and mind you take the thing out *very* carefully. There's no hurry. That's splendid. Just point it at the floor while you bring it across, would you? Thanks. Bunter has managed for himself, I see. Now run into my bedroom, and in the bottom of my wardrobe you will find a bundle of stout cord. Oh! I beg your pardon; yes, put your hands down by all means. It must be very tiring exercise."

The arms of the intruders being secured behind their backs with a neatness which Gherkins felt to be worthy of the best traditions of Sexton Blake,[5] Lord Peter motioned his captives to sit down and despatched Bunter for whiskey-and-soda.

"Before we send for the police," said Lord Peter, "you would do me a great personal favour by telling me what you were looking for, and who sent you. Ah! thanks, Bunter. As our guests are not at liberty to use their hands, perhaps you would be kind enough to assist them to a drink. Now then, say when."

"Well, you're a gentleman, guv'nor," said the First Burglar, wiping his mouth politely on his shoulder, the back of his hand not being available. "If we'd a known wot a job this wos goin' ter be, blow me if we'd a touched it. The bloke said, ses 'e, 'It's takin' candy from a baby,' 'e ses. 'The gentleman's a reg'lar softie,' 'e ses, 'one o' these 'ere sersiety toffs wiv a maggot fer old books,' that's wot 'e ses, 'an' ef yer can find this 'ere old book fer me,' 'e ses, 'ther's a pony[6] fer yer.' Well! Sech a job! 'E didn't mention as 'ow there'd be five 'undred fousand bleedin' ole books all as alike as a regiment o' bleedin' dragoons. Nor as 'ow yer kept a nice little machine-gun like that 'andy by the bedside, *nor* yet as 'ow yer was so bleedin' good at tyin' knots in a bit o' string. No—'e didn't think ter mention them things."

"Deuced unsporting of him," said his lordship. "Do you happen to know the gentleman's name?"

"No—that was another o' them things wot 'e didn't mention. 'E's a stout, fair party, wiv 'orn rims to 'is goggles and a bald 'ead. One o' these 'ere philanthropists, I reckon. A friend o' mine, wot got inter trouble onct, got work froo 'im, and the gentleman comes round and ses to 'im, 'e ses, 'Could yer find me a couple o' lads ter do a little job?' 'e ses, an' my friend, finkin' no 'arm, you see, guv'nor, but wot it might be a bit of a joke like, 'e gets 'old of my pal an' me, an' we meets the gentleman in a pub dahn Whitechapel way. W'ich we was ter meet 'im there again Friday night, us 'avin' allowed that time fer ter git 'old of the book."

"The book being, if I may hazard a guess, the *Cosmographia universalis*?"

"Sumfink like that, guv'nor. I got its jaw-breakin' name wrote down on a bit o' paper, wot my pal 'ad in 'is 'and. Wot did yer do wiv that 'ere bit o' paper, Bill?"

"Well, look here," said Lord Peter, "I'm afraid I must send for the police, but I think it likely, if you give us your assistance to get hold of your gentleman, whose name I strongly suspect to be Wilberforce Pope, that you will get off pretty easily. Telephone the police, Bunter, and then go and put something on that eye of yours. Gherkins, we'll give these gentlemen another drink, and then I think perhaps you'd better hop back to bed; the fun's over. No? Well, put a good thick coat on, there's a good fellow, because what your mother will say to me if you catch a cold I don't like to think."

So the police had come and taken the burglars away, and now Detective-Inspector Parker, of Scotland Yard, a great personal friend of Lord Peter's, sat toying with a cup of coffee and listening to the story.

"But what's the matter with the jolly old book, anyhow, to make it so popular?" he demanded.

"I don't know," replied Wimsey, "but after Mr. Pope's little visit the other day I got kind of intrigued about it and had a look through it. I've got a hunch it may turn out rather valuable, after all. Unsuspected beauties and all that sort of thing. If only Mr. Pope had been a trifle more accurate in his facts, he might have got away with something to which I feel pretty sure he isn't entitled. Anyway, when I'd seen—what I saw, I wrote off to Dr. Conyers of Yelsall Manor, the late owner—"

"Conyers, the cancer man?"

"Yes. He's done some pretty important research in his time, I fancy. Getting on now, though; about seventy-eight, I fancy. I hope he's more honest than his nephew, with one foot in the grave like that. Anyway, I wrote (with Gherkins' permission, naturally) to say we had the book and had been specially interested by something we found there, and would he be so obliging as to tell us something of its history. I also—"

"But what did you find in it?"

"I don't think we'll tell him yet, Gherkins, shall we? I like to keep policemen guessing. As I was saying, when you so rudely interrupted me, I also asked him whether he knew anything about his good nephew's offer to buy it back. His answer has just arrived. He says he knows of nothing specially interesting about the book. It has been in the library untold years, and the tearing out of the maps must have been done a long time ago by some family vandal. He can't think why his nephew should be so keen on it, as he certainly never pored over it as a boy. In fact, the old man declares the engaging Wilberforce has never even set foot in Yelsall Manor to his knowledge. So much for the fire-breathing monsters and the pleasant Sunday afternoons."

"Naughty Wilberforce!"

"M'm. Yes. So, after last night's little dust-up, I wired the old boy we were tooling down to Yelsall to have a heart-to-heart talk with him about his picture-book and his nephew."

"Are you taking the book down with you?" asked Parker. "I can give you a police escort for it if you like."

"That's not a bad idea," said Wimsey. "We don't know where the insinuating Mr. Pope may be hanging out, and I wouldn't put it past him to make another attempt."

"Better be on the safe side," said Parker. "I can't come myself, but I'll send down a couple of men with you."

"Good egg," said Lord Peter. "Call up your myrmidons. We'll get a car round at once. You're coming, Gherkins, I suppose? God knows what your mother would say. Don't ever be an uncle, Charles; it's frightfully difficult to be fair to all parties."

Yelsall Manor was one of those large, decaying country mansions which speak eloquently of times more spacious than our own. The original late Tudor construction had been masked by the addition of a wide frontage in the Italian manner, with a kind of classical portico surmounted by a pediment and approached by a semicircular flight of steps. The grounds had originally been laid out in that formal manner in which grove nods to grove and each half duly reflects the other. A late owner, however, had burst out into the more eccentric sort of landscape gardening which is associated with the name of Capability Brown.[7] A Chinese pagoda, somewhat resembling Sir William Chambers'[8] erection in Kew Gardens, but smaller, rose out of a grove of laurustinus towards the eastern extremity of the house, while at the rear appeared a large artificial lake, dotted with numerous islands, on which odd little temples, grottos, tea-houses, and bridges peeped out from among clumps of shrubs, once ornamental, but now sadly overgrown. A boat-house, with wide eaves like the designs on a willow-pattern plate, stood at one corner, its landing-stage fallen into decay and wreathed with melancholy weeds.

"My disreputable old ancestor, Cuthbert Conyers, settled down here when he retired from the sea in 1732," said Dr. Conyers, smiling faintly. "His elder brother died childless, so the black sheep returned to the fold with the determination to become respectable and found a family. I fear he did not succeed altogether. There were very queer tales as to where his money came from. He is said to have been a pirate, and to have sailed with the notorious Captain Blackbeard. In the village, to this day, he is remembered and spoken of as Cut-throat Conyers. It used to make the old man very angry, and there is an unpleasant story of his slicing the ears off a groom who had been heard to call him 'Old Cut-throat.' He was not an uncultivated person, though. It was he who did the landscape-gardening round at the back, and he built the pagoda for his telescope. He was reputed to study the Black Art, and there were certainly a number of astrological works in the library with his name on the fly-leaf, but probably the telescope was only a remembrance of his seafaring days.

"Anyhow, towards the end of his life he became more and more odd and morose. He quarrelled with his family, and turned his younger son out of doors with his wife and children. An unpleasant old fellow.

"On his deathbed he was attended by the parson—a good,

earnest, God-fearing sort of man, who must have put up with a deal of insult in carrying out what he firmly believed to be the sacred duty of reconciling the old man to this shamefully treated son. Eventually, 'Old Cut-throat' relented so far as to make a will, leaving to the younger son 'My treasure which I have buried in Munster.' The parson represented to him that it was useless to bequeath a treasure unless he also bequeathed the information where to find it, but the horrid old pirate only chuckled spitefully, and said that, as he had been at the pains to collect the treasure, his son might well be at the pains of looking for it. Further than that he would not go, and so he died, and I dare say went to a very bad place.

"Since then the family has died out, and I am the sole representative of the Conyerses, and heir to the treasure, whatever and wherever it is, for it was never discovered. I do not suppose it was very honestly come by, but, since it would be useless now to try and find the original owners, I imagine I have a better right to it than anybody living.

"You may think it very unseemly, Lord Peter, that an old, lonely man like myself should be greedy for a hoard of pirate's gold. But my whole life has been devoted to studying the disease of cancer, and I believe myself to be very close to a solution of one part at least of the terrible problem. Research costs money, and my limited means are very nearly exhausted. The property is mortgaged up to the hilt, and I do most urgently desire to complete my experiments before I die, and to leave a sufficient sum to found a clinic where the work can be carried on.

"During the last year I have made very great efforts to solve the mystery of 'Old Cut-throat's' treasure. I have been able to leave much of my experimental work in the most capable hands of my assistant, Dr. Forbes, while I pursued my researches with the very slender clue I had to go upon. It was the more expensive and difficult that Cuthbert had left no indication in his will whether Münster in Germany or Munster in Ireland was the hiding-place of the treasure. My journeys and my search in both places cost money and brought me no further on my quest. I returned, disheartened, in August, and found myself obliged to sell my library, in order to defray my expenses and obtain a little money with which to struggle on with my sadly delayed experiments."

"Ah!" said Lord Peter. "I begin to see light."

The old physician looked at him enquiringly. They had finished tea, and were seated around the great fireplace in the study. Lord Peter's interested questions about the beautiful, dilapidated old house and estate had led the conversation naturally to Dr. Conyers' family, shelving for the time the problem of the *Cosmographia*, which lay on a table beside them.

"Everything you say fits into the puzzle," went on Wimsey, "and I think there's not the smallest doubt what Mr. Wilberforce Pope was after, though how he knew that you had the *Cosmographia* here I couldn't say."

"When I disposed of the library, I sent him a catalogue," said Dr. Conyers. "As a relative, I thought he ought to have the right to buy anything he fancied. I can't think why he didn't secure the book then, instead of behaving in this most shocking fashion."

Lord Peter hooted with laughter.

"Why, because he never tumbled to it till afterwards," he said. "And oh, dear, how wild he must have been! I forgive him everything. Although," he added, "I don't want to raise your hopes too high, sir, for, even when we've solved old Cuthbert's riddle, I don't know that we're very much nearer to the treasure."

"To the *treasure?*"

"Well, now, sir. I want you first to look at this page, where there's a name scrawled in the margin. Our ancestors had an untidy way of signing their possessions higgledy-piggledy in margins instead of in a decent, Christian way in the fly-leaf. This is a handwriting of somewhere about Charles I's reign: *Jac: Coniers*. I take it that goes to prove that the book was in the possession of your family at any rate as early as the first half of the seventeenth century, and has remained there ever since. Right. Now we turn to page 1099, where we find a description of the discoveries of Christopher Columbus. It's headed, you see, by a kind of map, with some of Mr. Pope's monsters swimming about in it, and apparently representing the Canaries, or, as they used to be called, the Fortunate Isles. It doesn't look much more accurate than old maps usually are, but I take it the big island on the right is meant for Lanzarote, and the two nearest to it may be Teneriffe and Gran Canaria."

"But what's that writing in the middle?"

"That's just the point. The writing is later than *Jac: Coniers'* signature; I should put it about 1700—but, of course, it may have been written a good deal later still. I mean, a man who was elderly in 1730 would still use the style of writing he adopted as a young man, especially if, like your ancestor the pirate, he had spent the early part of his life in outdoor pursuits and hadn't done much writing."

"Do you mean to say, Uncle Peter," broke in the viscount excitedly, "that that's 'Old Cut-throat's' writing?"

"I'd be ready to lay a sporting bet it is. Look here, sir, you've been scouring round Münster in Germany and Munster in Ireland—but how about good old Sebastian Münster here in the library at home?"

"God bless my soul! Is it possible?"

"It's pretty nearly certain, sir. Here's what he says, written, you see, round the head of that sort of sea-dragon:—

> *Hic in capite draconis ardet perpetuo Sol.*
> [Here the sun shines perpetually upon the Dragon's head.]

Rather doggy Latin—sea-dog Latin, you might say, in fact."

"I'm afraid," said Dr. Conyers, "I must be very stupid, but I can't see where that leads us."

"No; 'Old Cut-throat' was rather clever. No doubt he thought that, if anybody read it, they'd think it was just an allusion to where it says, further down, that 'the islands were called *Fortunatæ* because of the wonderful temperature of the air and the clemency of the skies.' But the cunning old astrologer up in his pagoda had a meaning of his own. Here's a little book published in 1678—Middleton's *Practical Astrology*—just the sort of popular handbook an amateur like 'Old Cut-throat' would use. Here you are: 'If in your figure you find Jupiter or Venus or *Dragon's head,* you may be confident there is Treasure in the place supposed. . . . If you find *Sol* to be the Significator of the hidden Treasure, you may conclude there is Gold, or some jewels.' You know, sir, I think we may conclude it."

"Dear me!" said Dr. Conyers. "I believe, indeed, you must be right. And I am ashamed to think that if anybody had suggested to me that it could ever be profitable to me to learn the terms of astrology, I should have replied in my vanity that my time was too valuable to waste on such foolishness. I am deeply indebted to you."

"Yes," said Gherkins, "but where *is* the treasure, Uncle?"

"That's just it," said Lord Peter. "The map is very vague; there is no latitude or longitude given; and the directions, such as they are, seem not even to refer to any spot on the islands, but to some place in the middle of the sea. Besides, it is nearly two hundred years since the treasure was hidden, and it may already have been found by somebody or other."

Dr. Conyers stood up.

"I am an old man," he said, "but I still have some strength. If I can by any means get together the money for an expedition, I will not rest till I have made every possible effort to find the treasure and to endow my clinic."

"Then, sir, I hope you'll let me give a hand to the good work," said Lord Peter.

Dr. Conyers had invited his guests to stay the night, and, after the excited viscount had been packed off to bed, Wimsey and the old man sat late, consulting maps and diligently reading Münster's chapter *"De Novis Insulis,"* in the hope of discovering some further clue. At length, however, they separated, and Lord Peter went upstairs, the book under his arm. He was restless, however, and, instead of going to bed, sat for a long time at his window, which looked out upon the lake. The moon, a few days past the full, was riding high among small, windy clouds, and picked out the sharp eaves of the Chinese tea-houses and the straggling tops of the unpruned shrubs. "Old Cut-throat" and his landscape-gardening! Wimsey could have fancied that the old pirate was sitting now beside his telescope in the preposterous pagoda, chuckling over his riddling testament and counting the craters of the moon. "If *Luna*, there is silver." The water of the lake was silver enough; there was a great smooth path across it, broken by the sinister wedge of the boat-house, the black shadows of the islands, and, almost in the middle of the lake, a decayed fountain, a writhing celestial dragon-shape, spiny-backed and ridiculous.

Wimsey rubbed his eyes. There was something strangely familiar about the lake; from moment to moment it assumed the queer unreality of a place which one recognizes without having ever known it. It was like one's first sight of the Leaning Tower of Pisa—too like its picture to be quite believable. Surely, thought Wimsey, he knew that elongated island on the right, shaped rather like a winged monster, with its two little clumps of buildings. And the island to the left of it, like the British Isles, but warped out of shape. And the third island, between the others, and nearer. The three formed a triangle, with the Chinese fountain in the centre, the moon shining steadily upon its dragon head. *"Hic in capite draconis ardet perpetuo—"*

Lord Peter sprang up with a loud exclamation, and flung open the door into the dressing-room. A small figure wrapped in an eiderdown hurriedly uncoiled itself from the window-seat.

"I'm sorry, Uncle Peter," said Gherkins. "I was so *dreadfully* wide awake, it wasn't any good staying in bed."

"Come here," said Lord Peter, "and tell me if I'm mad or dreaming. Look out of the window and compare it with the map—'Old Cut-throat's' 'New Islands.' He made 'em, Gherkins; he put 'em here. Aren't they laid out just like the Canaries? Those three islands in a triangle, and the fourth down here in the corner? And the boat-house where the big ship is in the picture? And the dragon fountain where the dragon's head is? Well, my son, that's where your hidden treasure's gone to. Get your things on, Gherkins, and damn the time when all good little boys should be in bed! We're going for a row on the lake, if there's a tub in that boat-house that'll float."

"Oh, Uncle Peter! This is a *real* adventure!"

"All right," said Wimsey. "Fifteen men on the dead man's chest, and all that! Yo-ho-ho, and a bottle of Johnny Walker! Pirate expedition fitted out in dead of night to seek hidden treasure and explore the Fortunate Isles! Come on, crew!"

Lord Peter hitched the leaky dinghy to the dragon's knobbly tail and climbed out carefully, for the base of the fountain was green and weedy.

"I'm afraid it's your job to sit there and bail, Gherkins," he said. "All the best captains bag the really interesting jobs for themselves. We'd better start with the head. If the old blighter said head, he probably meant it." He passed an arm affectionately round the creature's neck for support, while he methodically pressed and pulled the various knobs and bumps of its anatomy. "It seems beastly solid, but I'm sure there's a spring somewhere. You won't forget to bail, will you? I'd simply hate to turn round and find the boat gone. Pirate chief marooned on island and all that. Well, it isn't its back hair, anyhow. We'll try its eyes. I say, Gherkins, I'm sure I felt something move, only it's frightfully stiff. We might have thought to bring some oil. Never mind; it's dogged as does it. It's coming. It's coming. Booh! Pah!"

A fierce effort thrust the rusted knob inwards, releasing a huge spout of water into his face from the dragon's gaping throat. The fountain, dry for many years, soared rejoicingly heavenwards, drenching the treasure-hunters, and making rainbows in the moonlight.

"I suppose this is 'Old Cut-throat's' idea of humour," grumbled Wimsey, retreating cautiously round the dragon's neck. "And now I can't turn it off again. Well, dash it all, let's try the other eye."

He pressed for a few moments in vain. Then, with a grinding clang, the bronze wings of the monster clapped down to its sides, revealing a deep square hole, and the fountain ceased to play.

"Gherkins!" said Lord Peter. "We've done it. (But don't neglect bailing on that account!) There's a box here. And it's beastly heavy. No; all right, I can manage. Gimme the boat-hook. Now I do hope the old sinner really did have a treasure. What a bore if it's only one of his little jokes. Never mind—hold the boat steady. There. Always remember, Gherkins, that you can make quite an effective crane with a boat-hook and a stout pair of braces. Got it? That's right. Now for home and beauty. . . . Hullo! What's all that?"

As he paddled the boat round, it was evident that something was happening down by the boat-house. Lights were moving about, and a sound of voices came across the lake.

"They think we're burglars, Gherkins. Always misunderstood. Give way, my hearties—

> *"A-roving, a-roving, since roving's been my ru-i-in,*
> *I'll go no more a-roving with you, fair maid."*

"Is that you, my lord?" said a man's voice as they drew in to the boat-house.

"Why, it's our faithful sleuths!" cried his lordship. "What's the excitement?"

"We found this fellow sneaking round the boat-house," said the man from Scotland Yard. "He says he's the old gentleman's nephew. Do you know him, my lord?"

"I rather fancy I do," said Wimsey. "Mr. Pope, I think. Good evening. Were you looking for anything? Not a treasure, by any chance? Because we've just found one. Oh! Don't say that. *Maxima reverentia,*[9] you know. Lord St. George is of tender years. And, by the way, thank you so much for sending your delightful friends to call on me last night. Oh, yes, Thompson, I'll charge him all right. You there, Doctor? Splendid. Now, if anybody's got a spanner or anything handy, we'll have a look at Great-grand-papa Cuthbert. And if he turns out to be old iron, Mr. Pope, you'll have had an uncommonly good joke for your money."

An iron bar was produced from the boat-house and thrust under the hasp of the chest. It creaked and burst. Dr. Conyers knelt down tremulously and threw open the lid.

There was a little pause.

"The drinks are on you, Mr. Pope," said Lord Peter. "I think, Doctor, it ought to be a jolly good hospital when it's finished."

COMMENT AND QUESTIONS

Lord Peter appears in numerous stories and novels, and from them we have a great deal of information about him. Millions of television viewers have come to know him through the plays which were presented on "Masterpiece Theatre." Like his creator, he is an Oxford graduate; and without his special knowledge, the solution to the puzzle of the enigmatic will would not have been possible. He is one of the most consistently developed of the detective heroes who appear in a series of works. Although he is not a trivial or frivolous person—he has serious scholarly interests; he is a humanitarian; he has searing memories of being buried alive in the trench warfare of World War I—he never takes himself or life too seriously, and he never loses his cheerful, bantering tone, both amused and amusing. (He shares his creator's pleasant sense of humor. Consider his remark to young Jerry that girls never took up book collecting "because it meant so much learning about dates and type faces and other technicalities which called for a masculine brain" in the light of Miss Sayers' own interest in rare books.) He and others in his tradition are sometimes called "gentleman" detectives. What evidence in this story qualifies him for the title of "gentleman"? Has the idea of "gentleman" gone out of fashion?

Portraying child characters who are both believable and engaging is not easy. Has Miss Sayers succeeded in this story? What does the stay with his uncle provide Gherkins with, besides a good adventure?

Lord Peter and Mr. Pope treat Jerry in quite different ways. Compare the two ways and notice how they help to characterize each adult.

Why might a reader be sympathetic to the two burglars instead of seeing them primarily as criminals?

What do you think of Old Cut-throat's making his heirs work to find his treasure?

NOTES

1. *mezzotints . . . electros.* Mezzotint, a sort of reverse engraving process, was widely used in the eighteenth and nineteenth centuries to reproduce paintings. Mezzotints had a characteristic fuzzy quality, hence the adjective "woolly" used here. Electros were illustrations produced by the electrotype process.

2. *Münster.* Sebastian Münster, a German scholar and geographer. His geography, *Cosmographia universalis* (1544), was standard for over a century.

3. *Lewis and Short.* Charlton T. Lewis (1834–1904) and Charles Short (1821–1886), authors of *Harper's Latin Dictionary.*

4. *jusjurandum.* The law of swearing.

5. *Sexton Blake.* A writer of sensational pulp fiction (penny-dreadfuls).

6. *pony.* Twenty-five pounds.

7. *Capability Brown.* An eighteenth-century English landscape gardener and architect.

8. *Sir William Chambers.* One of the foremost English architects of the eighteenth century.

9. *Maxima reverentia.* With greatest reverence.

LORD DUNSANY

Two Bottles of Relish

Humor, detection, and horror are successfully blended in this
superb story, told by a narrator who is surely one of the most
deftly individualized in mystery fiction. The armchair detective and his "Watson" are a most oddly paired team, but a
good combination, nevertheless.

Edward John Moreton Drax Plunkett, Lord Dunsany, was
an Irish poet, playwright, novelist, and writer of tales. He
served in the Coldstream Guards in the Boer War and World
War I and later was Byron Professor of English Literature at
Athens University in Greece.

Smithers is my name. I'm what you might call a small man,
and in a small way of business. I travel for Num-numo, a
relish for meats and savories; the world famous relish I
ought to say. It's really quite good, no deleterious acids in it, and
does not affect the heart; so it is quite easy to push. I wouldn't
have got the job if it weren't. But I hope some day to get
something that's harder to push, as of course the harder they are
to push, the better the pay. At present I can just make my way,
with nothing at all over; but then I live in a very expensive flat. It
happened like this, and that brings me to my story. And it isn't the
story you'd expect from a small man like me, yet there's nobody
else to tell it. Those that know anything of it besides me, are all for
hushing it up. They won't speak a word of it.

Well, I was looking for a room to live in in London when first I got my job; it had to be in London, to be central; and I went to a block of buildings, very gloomy they looked, and saw the man that ran them and asked him for what I wanted; flats they called them; just a bedroom and a sort of a cupboard. Well he was showing a man 'round at the time who was a gent, in fact more than that, so he didn't take much notice of me, the man that ran all those flats didn't, I mean. So I just ran behind for a bit, seeing all sorts of rooms, and waiting till I could be shown my class of thing. We came to a very nice flat, a sitting room, bedroom and bathroom, and a sort of little place that they called a hall. And that's how I came to know Linley. He was the bloke that was being shown 'round.

"Bit expensive," he said.

And the man that ran the flats turned away to the window and picked his teeth. It's funny how much you can show by a simple thing like that. What he meant to say was that he'd hundreds of flats like that, and thousands of people looking for them, and he didn't care who had them or whether they all went on looking. There was no mistaking him, somehow. And yet he never said a word, only looked away out of the window and picked his teeth. And I ventured to speak to Mr. Linley then; and I said, "How about it, sir, if I paid half, and shared it? I wouldn't be in the way, and I'm out all day, and whatever you said would go, and really I wouldn't be no more in your way than a cat."

You may be surprised at my doing it; and you'll be much more surprised at him accepting it; at least, you would if you knew me, just a small man in a small way of business; and yet I could see at once that he was taking to me more than he was taking to the man at the window.

"But there's only one bedroom," he said.

"I could make up my bed easy in that little room there," I said.

"The hall," said the man looking 'round from the window, without taking his toothpick out.

"And I'd have the bed out of the way and hid in the cupboard by any hour you like," I said.

He looked thoughtful, and the other man looked out over London; and in the end, do you know, he accepted.

"Friend of yours?" said the flat man.

"Yes," answered Mr. Linley.

It was really very nice of him.

I'll tell you why I did it. Able to afford it? Of course not. But I heard him tell the flat man that he had just come down from Oxford and wanted to live for a few months in London. It turned out he wanted just to be comfortable and do nothing for a bit while he looked things over and chose a job, or probably just as long as he could afford it. Well I said to myself, what's the Oxford manner worth in business, especially a business like mine? Why, simply everything you've got. If I picked up only a quarter of it from this Mr. Linley I'd be able to double my sales, and that would soon mean I'd be given something a lot harder to push, with perhaps treble the pay. Worth it every time. And you can make a quarter of an education go twice as far again, if you're careful with it. I mean you don't have to quote the whole of the Inferno to show that you've read Milton; half a line may do it.

Well, about that story I have to tell. And you mightn't think that a little man like me could make you shudder. Well, I soon forgot about the Oxford manner when we settled down in our flat. I forgot it in the sheer wonder of the man himself. He had a mind like an acrobat's body, like a bird's body. It didn't want education. You didn't notice whether he was educated or not. Ideas were always leaping up in him, things you'd never have thought of. And not only that, but if any ideas were about, he'd sort of catch them. Time and again I've found him knowing just what I was going to say. Not thought-reading, but what they call intuition. I used to try to learn a bit about chess, just to take my thoughts off Num-numo in the evening, when I'd done with it. But problems I never could do. Yet he'd come along and glance at my problem and say, "You probably move that piece first," and I'd say, "But where?" and he'd say, "Oh, one of those three squares." And I'd say, "But it will be taken on all of them." And the piece a queen all the time, mind you. And he'd say, "Yes, it's doing no good there: you're probably meant to lose it."

And, do you know, he'd be right.

You see he'd been following out what the other man had been thinking. That's what he'd been doing.

Well one day there was that ghastly murder at Unge. I don't know if you remember it. But Seeger had gone down to live with a girl in a bungalow on the North Downs, and that was the first we had heard of him.

The girl had £200, and he got every penny of it and she utterly disappeared. And Scotland Yard couldn't find her.

Well I'd happened to read that Seeger had bought two bottles of Num-numo; for the Otherthorpe police had found out everything about him, except what he did with the girl; and that of course attracted my attention or I should have never thought again about the case or said a word of it to Linley. Num-numo was always on my mind, as I always spent every day pushing it, and that kept me from forgetting the other thing. And so one day I said to Linley, "I wonder with all that knack you have for seeing through a chess problem, and thinking of one thing and another, that you don't have a go at the Otherthorpe mystery. It's a problem as much as chess," I said.

"There's not the mystery in ten murders that there is in one game of chess," he answered.

"It's beaten Scotland Yard," I said.

"Has it?" he asked.

"Knocked them end-wise," I said.

"It shouldn't have done that," he said. And almost immediately after he said, "What are the facts?"

We were both sitting at supper and I told him the facts, as I had them straight from the papers. She was a pretty blonde, she was small, she was called Nancy Elth, she had £200, they lived at the bungalow for five days. After that he stayed there for another fortnight, but nobody ever saw her alive again. Seeger said she had gone to South America, but later said he had never said South America, but South Africa. None of her money remained in the bank where she had kept it, and Seeger was shown to have come by at least £150 just at that time. Then Seeger turned out to be a vegetarian, getting all his food from the greengrocer, and that made the constable in the village of Unge suspicious of him, for a vegetarian was something new to the constable. He watched Seeger after that, and it's well he did, for there was nothing that Scotland Yard asked him that he couldn't tell them about him, except of course the one thing. And he told the police at Otherthorpe five or six miles away, and they came and took a hand at it too.

They were able to say, for one thing, that he never went outside the bungalow and its tidy garden ever since she disappeared. You see, the more they watched him the more suspicious they got, as you naturally do if you're watching a man; so that very soon they were watching every move he made, but if it hadn't been for his being a vegetarian they'd never have started to suspect him, and there wouldn't have been enough evidence even for Linley. Not that they found out anything much against him, except that £150 dropping in from nowhere, and it was Scotland Yard that found that, not the police of Otherthorpe.

No, what the constable of Unge found out was about the larch trees, and that beat Scotland Yard utterly, and beat Linley up to the very last, and of course it beat me. There were ten larch trees in the bit of a garden, and he'd made some sort of an arrangement with the landlord, Seeger had, before he took the bungalow, by which he could do what he liked with the larch trees. And then from about the time that little Nancy Elth must have died he cut every one of them down. Three times a day he went at it for nearly a week, and when they were all down he cut them all up into logs of no more than two feet long and laid them all in neat heaps. You never saw such work. And what for? To give an excuse for the axe was one theory. But the excuse was bigger than the axe: it took him a fortnight, hard work every day. And he could have killed a little thing like Nancy Elth without an axe, and cut her up, too. Another theory was that he wanted firewood, to make away with the body. But he never used it. He left it all standing there in those neat stacks. It fairly beat everybody.

Well, those are the facts I told Linley. Oh yes, and he bought a big butcher's knife. Funny thing, they all do. And yet it isn't so funny after all; if you've got to cut a woman up, you've got to cut her up; and you can't do that without a knife. Then, there were some negative facts. He hadn't burned her. Only had a fire in the small stove now and then, and only used it for cooking. They got on to that pretty smartly, the Unge constable did, and the men that were lending him a hand from Otherthorpe. There were some little woody places lying 'round, shaws they call them in that part of the country, the country people do, and they could climb a tree handy and unobserved and get a sniff at the smoke in almost any direction it might be blowing. They did now and then and there was no smell of flesh burning, just ordinary cooking. Pretty smart of the Otherthorpe police that was, though of course it didn't help to hang Seeger. Then later on the Scotland Yard men went down and got another fact, negative but narrowing things down all the while. And that was that the chalk under the bungalow and under the little garden had none of it been disturbed. And he'd never been outside it since Nancy disappeared. Oh yes, and he had a big file besides the knife. But there was no sign of any ground bones found on the file, or any blood on the knife. He'd washed them of course. I told all that to Linley.

Now I ought to warn you before I go any further; I am a small man myself and you probably don't expect anything horrible from me. But I ought to warn you this man was a murderer, or at any rate somebody was; the woman had been made away with, a nice pretty little girl, too, and the man that had done that wasn't necessarily going to stop at things you might think he'd stop at. With the mind to do a thing like that, and with the shadow of the rope to drive him further, you can't say what he'll stop at. Murder tales seem nice things sometimes for a lady to sit and read all by herself by the fire. But murder isn't a nice thing, and when a murderer's desperate and trying to hide his tracks he isn't even as nice as he was before. I'll ask you to bear that in mind. Well, I've warned you.

So I says to Linley, "And what do you make of it?"

"Drains?" said Linley.

"No," I says, "you're wrong there. Scotland Yard has been into that. And the Otherthorpe people before them. They've had a look in the drains, such as they are, a little thing running into a cesspool beyond the garden; and nothing has gone down it, nothing that oughtn't to have, I mean."

He made one or two other suggestions, but Scotland Yard had been before him in every case. That's really the crab of my story, if you'll excuse the expression. You want a man who sets out to be a detective to take his magnifying glass and go down to the spot; to go to the spot before everything; and then to measure the footmarks and pick up the clues and find the knife that the police have overlooked. But Linley never went near the place, and he hadn't got a magnifying glass, not as I ever saw, and Scotland Yard was before him every time.

In fact they had more clues than anybody could make head or tail of. Every kind of clue to show that he'd murdered the poor little girl; every kind of clue to show that he hadn't disposed of the body; and yet the body wasn't there. It wasn't in South America, either, and not much more likely in South Africa. And all the time, mind you, that enormous bunch of chopped larch wood, a clue that was staring everyone in the face and leading nowhere. No we didn't seem to want any more clues, and Linley never went near the place. The trouble was to deal with the clues we'd got. I was completely mystified; so was Scotland Yard; and Linley seemed to be getting no forwarder; and all the while the mystery was hanging on me. I mean if it were not for the trifle I'd chanced to remember, and if it were not for one chance word I said to Linley, that mystery would have gone the way of all the other mysteries that men have made nothing of, a darkness, a little patch of night in history.

Well, the fact was Linley didn't take much interest in it at first, but I was so absolutely sure that he could do it, that I kept him to the idea. "You can do chess problems," I said.

"That's ten times harder," he said, sticking to his point.

"Then why don't you do this?" I said.

"Then go and take a look at the board for me," said Linley.

That was his way of talking. We'd been a fortnight together, and I knew it by now. He meant go down to the bungalow at Unge. I know you'll say why didn't he go himself, but the plain truth of it is that if he'd been tearing about the countryside he'd never have been thinking, whereas sitting there in his chair by the fire in our flat there was no limit to the ground he could cover, if you follow my meaning. So down I went by train next day, and got out at Unge station. And there were the North Downs rising up before me.

"It's up there, isn't it?" I said to the porter.

"That's right," he said. "Up there by the lane; and mind to turn to your right when you get to the old yew tree, a very big tree, you can't mistake it, and then . . ." and he told me the way so that I couldn't go wrong. I found them all like that, very nice and helpful. You see it was Unge's day at last; everyone had heard of Unge now; you could have got a letter there any time just then without putting the county or post town; and that was what Unge had to show. I dare say if you tried to find Unge now . . . ; well, anyway, they were making hay while the sun shone.

Well, there the hill was, going up into sunlight, going up like a song. You don't want to hear about the spring, and all the May colors that came down over everything later on in the day, and all those birds; but I thought, "What a nice place to bring a girl to." And then when I thought that he'd killed her there, well I'm only a small man, as I said, but when I thought of her on that hill with all the birds singing I said to myself, "Wouldn't it be odd if it turned out to be me after all that got that man killed, if he did murder her."

So I soon found my way up to the bungalow and began prying about, looking over the hedge into the garden. And I didn't find much, and I found nothing at all that the police hadn't found already, but there were those heaps of larch logs staring me in the face and looking very queer.

I did a lot of thinking, leaning against the hedge, breathing the smell of the May, and looking over the top of it at the larch logs, and the neat little bungalow the other side of the garden. Lots of theories I thought of; till I came to the best thought of all; and that was that if I left the thinking to Linley, with his Oxford-and-Cambridge education, and only brought him the facts, as he had told me, I should be doing more good in my way than if I tried to do any big thinking. I forgot to say that I had gone to Scotland Yard in the morning. Well, there wasn't really much to tell. What they asked me was, what I wanted. And, not having an answer exactly ready, I didn't find out very much from them.

But it was quite different at Unge; everyone was most obliging; it was their day there, as I said. The constable let me go indoors, so long as I didn't touch anything, and he gave me a look at the garden from the inside. And I saw the stumps of the ten larch trees, and I noticed one thing that Linley said was very observant of me, not that it turned out to be any use, but anyway I was doing my best; I noticed that the stumps had been all chopped anyhow. And from that I thought that the man that did it didn't know much about chopping. The constable said this was a deduction. So then I said that the axe was blunt when he used it; and that certainly made the constable think, though he didn't actually say I was right this time.

Did I tell you that Seeger never went outdoors, except to the little garden to chop wood, ever since Nancy disappeared? I think I did. Well it was perfectly true. They'd watched him night and day, one or another of them, and the Unge constable told me that himself. That limited things a good deal. The only thing I didn't like about it was that I felt Linley ought to have found all that out instead of ordinary policemen, and I felt that he could have too. There'd have been romance in a story like that. And they'd never have done it if the news hadn't gone 'round that the man was a vegetarian and only dealt at the greengrocers. Likely as not even that was only started out of pique by the butcher. It's queer what little things may trip a man up. Best to keep straight is my motto. But perhaps I'm straying a bit away from my story. I should like to do that forever; forget that it ever was; but I can't.

Well I picked up all sorts of information; clues I suppose I should call it in a story like this; though they none of them seemed to lead anywhere. For instance, I found out everything he ever bought at the village; I could even tell you the kind of salt he bought, quite plain with no phosphates in it, that they sometimes put in to make it tidy. And then he got ice from the fishmongers, and plenty of vegetables, as I said, from the greengrocer, Mergin and Sons. And I had a bit of talk over it all with the constable. Slugger he said his name was. I wondered why he hadn't come in and searched the place as soon as the girl was missing. "Well, you can't do that," he said. "And besides, we didn't suspect at once, not about the girl, that is. We only suspected there was something wrong about him on account of him being a vegetarian. He stayed a good fortnight after the last was seen of her. And then we slipped in like a knife. But, you see, no one had been inquiring about her, there was no warrant out."

"And what did you find," I asked Slugger, "when you went in?"

"Just a big file," he said, "and the knife and the axe that he must have got to chop her up with."

"But he got the axe to chop trees with," I said.

"Well, yes," he said, but rather grudgingly.

"And what did he chop them for?" I asked.

"Well of course my superiors have theories about that," he said, "that they mightn't tell to everybody."

You see, it was those logs that were beating them.

"But did he cut her up at all?" I asked.

"Well, he said that she was going to South America," he answered. Which was really very fair-minded of him.

I don't remember now much else that he told me. Seeger left the plates and dishes all washed up and very neat, he said.

Well, I brought all this back to Linley, going up by the train that started just about sunset. I'd like to tell you about the late spring evening, so calm over that grim bungalow; but you'll want to hear of the murder. Well, I told Linley everything, though much of it didn't seem to me to be worth the telling. The trouble was that the moment I began to leave anything out, he'd know it, and make me drag it in. "You can't tell what may be vital," he'd say. "A tin tack swept away by a housemaid might hang a man," he'd say.

All very well, but be consistent even if you are educated at Eton and Harrow; and whenever I mentioned Num-numo, which after all was the beginning of the whole story, because he wouldn't have heard of it if it hadn't been for me, and my noticing that Seeger had bought two bottles of it, why then he said that things like that were trivial and we should keep to the main issues. I naturally talked a bit about Num-numo, because only that day I had pushed close on fifty bottles of it in Unge. A murder certainly stimulates people's minds, and Seeger's two bottles gave me an opportunity that only a fool could have failed to make something of. But of course all that was nothing at all to Linley.

You can't see a man's thoughts and you can't look into his mind, so that all the most exciting things in the world can never be told of. But what I think happened all that evening with Linley, while I talked to him before supper, and all through supper, and sitting smoking afterwards in front of our fire, was that his thoughts were stuck at a barrier there was no getting over. And the barrier wasn't the difficulty of finding ways and means by which Seeger might have made away with the body, but the impossibility of finding why he chopped those masses of wood every day for a fortnight, and paid as I'd just found out, £25 to his landlord to be allowed to do it. That's what was beating Linley. As for the ways by which Seeger might have hidden the body, it seemed to me that every way was blocked by the police. If you said he buried it they said the chalk was undisturbed, if you said he carried it away

they said he never left the place, if you said he burned it they said
no smell of burning was ever noticed when the smoke blew low,
and when it didn't they climbed trees after it. I'd taken to Linley
wonderfully, and I didn't have to be educated to see there was
something big in a mind like his, and I thought that he could have
done it. When I saw the police getting in before him like that, and
no way that I could see of getting past them, I felt real sorry.

Did anyone come to the house, he asked me once or twice? Did
anyone take anything away from it? But we couldn't account for it
that way. Then perhaps I made some suggestion that was no good,
or perhaps I started talking of Num-numo again, and he interrupted me rather sharply.

"But what would you do, Smithers?" he said. "What would you
do yourself?"

"If I'd murdered poor Nancy Elth?" I asked.

"Yes," he said.

"I can't ever imagine doing such a thing," I told him.

He sighed at that, as though it were something against me.

"I suppose I should never be a detective," I said. And he just
shook his head.

Then he looked broodingly into the fire for what seemed an
hour. And then he shook his head again. We both went to bed
after that.

I shall remember the next day all my life. I was till evening, as
usual, pushing Num-numo. And we sat down to supper about
nine. You couldn't get things cooked at those flats, so of course we
had it cold. And Linley began with a salad. I can see it now, every
bit of it. Well, I was still a bit full of what I'd done in Unge,
pushing Num-numo. Only a fool, I know, would have been unable
to push it there; but still, I *had* pushed it; and about fifty bottles,
forty-eight to be exact, are something in a small village, whatever
the circumstances. So I was talking about it a bit; and then all of a
sudden I realized that Num-numo was nothing to Linley, and I
pulled myself up with a jerk. It was really very kind of him; do
you know what he did? He must have known at once why I
stopped talking, and he just stretched out a hand and said:
"Would you give me a little of your Num-numo for my salad?"

I was so touched I nearly gave it him. But of course you don't take Num-numo with salad. Only for meats and savories. That's on the bottle.

So I just said to him, "Only for meats and savories." Though I don't know what savories are. Never had any.

I never saw a man's face go like that before.

He seemed still for a whole minute. And nothing speaking about him but that expression. Like a man that's seen a ghost, one is tempted to say. But it wasn't really at all. I'll tell you what he looked like. Like a man that's seen something that no one has ever looked at before, something he thought couldn't be.

And then he said in a voice that was all quite changed, more low and gentle and quiet it seemed, "No good for vegetables, eh?"

"Not a bit," I said.

And at that he gave a kind of sob in his throat. I hadn't thought he could feel things like that. Of course I didn't know what it was all about; but, whatever it was, I thought all that sort of thing would have been knocked out of him at Eton and Harrow, an educated man like that. There were no tears in his eyes but he was feeling something horribly.

And then he began to speak with big spaces between his words, saying, "A man might make a mistake perhaps, and use Num-numo with vegetables."

"Not twice," I said. What else could I say?

And he repeated that after me as though I had told of the end of the world, and adding an awful emphasis to my words, till they seemed all clammy with some frightful significance, and shaking his head as he said it.

Then he was quite silent.

"What is it?" I asked.

"Smithers," he said.

And I said, "Well?"

"Look here Smithers," he said, "you must phone down to the grocer at Unge and find out from him this."

"Yes?"

"Whether Seeger bought those two bottles, as I expect he did, on the same day, and not a few days apart. He couldn't have done that."

I waited to see if any more was coming, and then I ran out and did what I was told. It took me some time, being after nine o'clock, and only then with the help of the police. About six days apart they said; and so I came back and told Linley. He looked up at me so hopefully when I came in, but I saw that it was the wrong answer by his eyes.

You can't take things to heart like that without being ill, and when he didn't speak I said, "What you want is a good brandy, and go to bed early."

And he said, "No. I must see someone from Scotland Yard. Phone 'round to them. Say here at once."

But I said, "I can't get an inspector from Scotland Yard to call on us at this hour."

His eyes were all lit up. He was all there all right.

"Then tell them," he said, "they'll never find Nancy Elth. Tell one of them to come here and I'll tell him why." And he added, I think only for me, "They must watch Seeger, till one day they get him over something else."

And, do you know, he came. Inspector Ulton; he came himself.

While we were waiting I tried to talk to Linley. Partly curiosity, I admit. But I didn't want to leave him to those thoughts of his, brooding away by the fire. I tried to ask him what it was all about. But he wouldn't tell me. "Murder is horrible," is all he would say. "And as a man covers his tracks up it only gets worse."

He wouldn't tell me. "There are tales," he said, "that one never wants to hear."

That's true enough. I wish I'd never heard this one. I never did actually. But I guessed it from Linley's last words to Inspector Ulton, the only ones that I overheard. And perhaps this is the point at which to stop reading my story, so that you don't guess it too; even if you think you want murder stories. For don't you rather want a murder story with a bit of romantic twist, and not a story about real foul murder? Well, just as you like.

In came Inspector Ulton, and Linley shook hands in silence, and pointed the way to his bedroom; and they went in there and talked in low voices, and I never heard a word.

A fairly hearty-looking man was the inspector when they went into that room.

They walked through our sitting room in silence when they came out, and together they went into the hall, and there I heard the only words they said to each other. It was the inspector that first broke that silence.

"But why," he said, "did he cut down the trees?"

"Solely," said Linley, "in order to get an appetite."

COMMENT AND QUESTIONS

Although this is certainly not an ordinary detective story, there are points of similarity between it and earlier stories in this collection. For example, Linley responds to the challenge of the murder mystery only after he is told that it has "knocked" Scotland Yard "end-wise." How is this attitude similar to that which produces rivalry between detective and police in earlier stories? Does Linley act out of duty? Moral resentment of the crime? Pride? In traditional detective stories, physical clues are often crucial to the solution of a crime. Notice what Smithers first expects of a detective; the description sounds like Sherlock Holmes. Linley never leaves the flat, but Smithers comes to realize that "there was no limit to the ground he could cover." This application of intellectual power pays off, and the crime is solved. One question is left, however. What happened to the bones? How would you answer this question? (Does it mean anything that there is a chalk soil for the garden and the bungalow? That the trees are chopped with a dull axe, even though Seeger has a large file?)

The crime is solved as the result of the unlikely association of a simple relish salesman with a man of extraordinary mental powers just down from Oxford. Several incidents or clues that at first seem insignificant turn out to be important. (Smithers observes, in fact, that it is "queer what little things may trip a man up.") Would you say that chance is an important element in the outcome of the story? Or does the solution come about naturally from the particular qualities of mind and character of Smithers and Linley? Explain your answer.

Point out aspects of the narrator's conversational and informal style. What instances are there of particularly effective dialogue involving the two main characters?

What effect does the notoriety surrounding the disappearance of Nancy Elth have on the village of Unge? Have you seen or heard of similar reactions to tragedy in small towns (or large ones)? What view of human psychology might account for such behavior?

What is Smithers' biggest "sale"? More than one interpretation of "pushing" or selling is, of course, quite possible.

Because of his seemingly unselfconscious and artless manner of narration, we learn a great deal about the attitudes and nature of the narrator. What are some of the things we learn?

T. S. STRIBLING

A Passage to Benares

Elements of the exotic East find their way into this absorbing story. Dr. Henry Poggioli, a psychologist at The Ohio State University, is visiting the Caribbean on a sabbatical leave, and the complex and heterogeneous culture he finds there offers him the opportunity to satisfy at first hand his curiosity concerning customs and attitudes different from his own. This psychological and philosophical inquiry is of particular interest to a present-day reader.

T. S. Stribling, an American author, wrote this story as the last in a collection entitled *Clues of the Caribbees*. He is one of the few writers of detective fiction to have been awarded a Pulitzer prize.

In Port of Spain, Trinidad, at half past five in the morning, Mr. Henry Poggioli, the American psychologist, stirred uneasily, became conscious of a splitting headache, opened his eyes in bewilderment, and then slowly reconstructed his surroundings. He recognized the dome of the Hindu temple seen dimly above him, the jute rug on which he lay; the blur of the image of Krishna[1] sitting cross-legged on the altar. The American had a dim impression that the figure had not sat thus on the altar all night long—a dream, no doubt; he had a faint memory of lurid nightmares. The psychologist allowed the thought to lose itself as he got up slowly from the sleeping rug which the cicerone[2] had spread for him the preceding evening.

153

In the circular temple everything was still in deep shadow, but the gray light of dawn filled the arched entrance. The white man moved carefully to the door so as not to jar his aching head. A little distance from him he saw another sleeper, a coolie beggar stretched out on a rug, and he thought he saw still another farther away. As he passed out of the entrance the cool freshness of the tropical morning caressed his face like the cool fingers of a woman. Kiskadee birds were calling from palms and saman trees, and there was a wide sound of dripping dew. Not far from the temple a coolie woman stood on a seesaw with a great stone attached to the other end of the plank, and by stepping to and fro she swung the stone up and down and pounded some rice in a mortar.

Poggioli stood looking at her a moment, then felt in his pocket for the key to his friend Lowe's garden gate. He found it and moved off up Tragarette Road to where the squalid East Indian village gave way to the high garden walls and ornamental shrubbery of the English suburb of Port of Spain. He walked on more briskly as the fresh air eased his head, and presently he stopped and unlocked a gate in one of the bordering walls. He began to smile as he let himself in; his good humor increased as he walked across a green lawn to a stone cottage which had a lower window still standing open. This was his own room. He reached up to the sill and drew himself inside, which gave his head one last pang. He shook this away, however, and began undressing for his morning shower.

Mr. Poggioli was rather pleased with his exploit, although he had not forwarded the experiment which had induced him to sleep in the temple. It had come about in this way: On the foregoing evening the American and his host in Port of Spain, a Mr. Lowe, a bank clerk, had watched a Hindu wedding procession enter the same temple in which Poggioli had just spent the night. They had watched the dark-skinned white-robed musicians smiting their drums and skirling their pipes with bouffant cheeks. Behind them marched a procession of coolies. The bride was a little cream-colored girl who wore a breast-plate of linked gold coins over her childish bosom, while anklets and bracelets almost covered her arms and legs. The groom, a tall, dark coolie, was the only man in the procession who wore European clothes, and he, oddly enough, was attired in a full evening dress suit. At the incongruous sight Poggioli burst out laughing, but Lowe touched his arm and said in an undertone:

"Don't take offense, old man, but if you didn't laugh it might help me somewhat."

Poggioli straightened his face.

"Certainly, but how's that?"

"The groom, Boodman Lal, owns one of the best curio shops in town and carries an account at my bank. That fifth man in the procession, the skeleton wearing the yellow *kapra*,[3] is old Hira Dass. He is worth something near a million in pounds sterling."

The psychologist became sober enough, out of his American respect for money.

"Hira Dass," went on Lowe, "built this temple and rest house. He gives rice and tea to any traveler who comes in for the night. It's an Indian custom to help mendicant pilgrims to the different shrines. A rich Indian will build a temple and a rest house just as your American millionaires erect libraries."

The American nodded again, watching now the old man with the length of yellow silk wrapped around him. And just at this point Poggioli received the very queer impression which led to his night's adventure.

When the wedding procession entered the temple the harsh music stopped abruptly. Then, as the line of robed coolies disappeared into the dark interior the psychologist had a strange feeling that the procession had been swallowed up and had ceased to exist. The bizarre red-and-gold building stood in the glare of sunshine, a solid reality, while its devotees had been dissipated into nothingness.

So peculiar, so startling was the impression, that Poggioli blinked and wondered how he ever came by it. The temple had somehow suggested the Hindu theory of Nirvana.[4] Was it possible that the Hindu architect had caught some association of ideas between the doctrine of obliteration and these curves and planes and colors glowing before him? Had he done it by contrast or simile? The fact that Poggioli was a psychologist made the problem all the more intriguing to him—the psychologic influence of architecture. There must be some rationale behind it. An idea how he might pursue this problem came into his head. He turned to his friend and exclaimed:

"Lowe, how about staying all night in old Hira Dass's temple?"

"Doing what?" with a stare of amazement.

"Staying a night in the temple. I had an impression just then, a—"

"Why, my dear fellow!" ejaculated Lowe, "no white man ever stayed all night in a coolie temple. It simply isn't done!"

The American argued his case a moment:

"You and I had a wonderful night aboard the *Trevemore* when we became acquainted."

"That was a matter of necessity," said the bank clerk. "There were no first-class cabin accommodations left on the *Trevemore*, so we had to make the voyage on deck."

Here the psychologist gave up his bid for companionship. Late that night he slipped out of Lowe's cottage, walked back to the grotesque temple, was given a cup of tea, a plate of rice, and a sleeping rug. The only further impression the investigator obtained was a series of fantastic and highly colored dreams, of which he could not recall a detail. Then he waked with a miserable headache and came home.

Mr. Poggioli finished his dressing and in a few minutes the breakfast bell rang. He went to the dining room to find the bank clerk unfolding the damp pages of the Port of Spain *Inquirer*. This was a typical English sheet using small, solidly set columns without flaming headlines. Poggioli glanced at it and wondered mildly if nothing worth featuring ever happened in Trinidad.

Ram Jon, Lowe's Hindu servant, slipped in and out of the breakfast room with peeled oranges, tea, toast, and a custard fruit flanked by a half lemon to squeeze over it.

"Pound sterling advanced a point," droned Lowe from his paper.

"It'll reach par," said the American, smiling faintly and wondering what Lowe would say if he knew of his escapade.

"Our new governor general will arrive in Trinidad on the twelfth."

"Surely that deserved a headline," said the psychologist.

"Don't try to debauch me with your American yellow journalism," smiled the bank clerk.

"Go your own way if you prefer doing research work every morning for breakfast."

The bank clerk laughed again at this, continued his perusal, then said:

"Hello, another coolie kills his wife. Tell me, Poggioli, as a psychologist, why do coolies kill their wives?"

"For various reasons, I fancy, or perhaps this one didn't kill her at all. Surely now and then some other person—"

"Positively no! It's always the husband, and instead of having various reasons, they have none at all. They say their heads are hot, and so to cool their own they cut off their wives'!"

The psychologist was amused in a dull sort of way.

"Lowe, you Englishmen are a nation with fixed ideas. You genuinely believe that every coolie woman who is murdered is killed by her husband without any motive whatever."

"Sure, that's right," nodded Lowe, looking up from his paper.

"That simply shows me you English have no actual sympathy with your subordinate races. And that may be the reason your empire is great. Your aloofness, your unsympathy—by becoming automatic you become absolutely dependable. The idea, that every coolie woman is murdered by her husband without a motive!"

"That's correct," repeated Lowe with English imperturbability.

The conversation was interrupted by a ring at the garden-gate bell. A few moments later the two men saw through the shadow Ram Jon unlock the wall door, open it a few inches, parley a moment, and receive a letter. Then he came back with his limber, gliding gait.

Lowe received the note through the open window, broke the envelope, and fished out two notes instead of one. The clerk looked at the inclosures and began to read with a growing bewilderment in his face.

"What is it?" asked Poggioli at last.

"This is from Hira Dass to Jeffries, the vice-president of our bank. He says his nephew Boodman Lal has been arrested and he wants Jeffries to help get him out."

"What's he arrested for?"

"Er—for murdering his wife," said Lowe with a long face. Poggioli stared.

"Wasn't he the man we saw in the procession yesterday?"

"Damn it, yes!" cried Lowe in sudden disturbance, "and he's a sensible fellow, too, one of our best patrons." He sat staring at the American over the letter, and then suddenly recalling a point, drove it home English fashion.

"That proves my contention, Poggioli—a groom of only six or eight hours' standing killing his wife. They simply commit uxoricide without any reason at all, the damned irrational rotters!"

"What's the other letter?" probed the American, leaning across the table.

"It's from Jeffries. He says he wants me to take this case and get the best talent in Trinidad to clear Mr. Hira Dass's house and consult with him." The clerk replaced the letters in the envelope. "Say, you've had some experience in this sort of thing. Won't you come with me?"

"Glad to."

The two men arose promptly from the table, got their hats, and went out into Tragarette Road once more. As they stood in the increasing heat waiting for a car, it occurred to Poggioli that the details of the murder ought to be in the morning's paper. He took the *Inquirer* from his friend and began a search through its closely printed columns. Presently he found a paragraph without any heading at all:

"Boodman Lal, nephew of Mr. Hira Dass, was arrested early this morning at his home in Peru, the East Indian suburb, for the alleged murder of his wife, whom he married yesterday at the Hindu temple in Peru. The body was found at six o'clock this morning in the temple. The attendant gave the alarm. Mrs. Boodman Lal's head was severed completely from her body and she lay in front of the Buddhist altar in her bridal dress. All of her jewelry was gone. Five coolie beggars who were asleep in the temple when the body was discovered were arrested. They claimed to know nothing of the crime, but a search of their persons revealed that each beggar had a piece of the young bride's jewelry and a coin from her necklace.

"Mr. Boodman Lal and his wife were seen to enter the temple

at about eleven o'clock last night for the Krishnian rite of purification. Mr. Boodman, who is a prominent curio dealer in this city, declines to say anything further than that he thought his wife had gone back to her mother's home for the night after her prayers in the temple. The young bride, formerly a Miss Maila Ran, was thirteen years old. Mr. Boodman is the nephew of Mr. Hira Dass, one of the wealthiest men in Trinidad."

The paragraph following this contained a notice of a tea given at Queen's Park Hotel by Lady Henley-Hoads, and the names of her guests.

The psychologist spent a painful moment pondering the kind of editor who would run a millionaire murder mystery, without any caption whatever, in between a legal notice and a society note. Then he turned his attention to the gruesome and mysterious details the paragraph contained.

"Lowe, what do you make of those beggars, each with a coin and a piece of jewelry?"

"Simple enough. The rotters laid in wait in the temple till the husband went out and left his wife, then they murdered her and divided the spoil."

"But that child had enough bangles to give a dozen to each man."

"Ye-es, that's a fact," admitted Lowe.

"And why should they continue sleeping in the temple?"

"Why shouldn't they? They knew they would be suspected, and they couldn't get off the island without capture, so they thought they might as well lie back down and go to sleep."

Here the street car approached and Mr. Poggioli nodded, apparently in agreement.

"Yes, I am satisfied that is how it occurred."

"You mean the beggars killed her?"

"No, I fancy the actual murderer took the girl's jewelry and went about the temple thrusting a bangle and a coin in the pockets of each of the sleeping beggars to lay a false scent."

"Aw, come now!" cried the bank clerk, "that's laying it on a bit too thick, Poggioli!"

"My dear fellow, that's the only possible explanation for the coins in the beggars' pockets."

By this time the men were on the tramcar and were clattering off down Tragarette Road. As they dashed along toward the Hindu village Poggioli remembered suddenly that he had walked this same distance the preceding night and had slept in this same temple. A certain sharp impulse caused the American to run a hand swiftly into his own pockets. In one side he felt the keys of his trunk and of Lowe's cottage; in the other he touched several coins and a round hard ring. With a little thrill he drew these to the edge of his pocket and took a covert glance at them. One showed the curve of a gold bangle; the other the face of an old English gold coin which evidently had been soldered to something.

With a little sinking sensation Poggioli eased them back into his pocket and stared ahead at the coolie village which they were approaching. He moistened his lips and thought what he would better do. The only notion that came into his head was to pack his trunk and take passage on the first steamer out of Trinidad, no matter to what port it was bound.

In his flurry of uneasiness the psychologist was tempted to drop the gold pieces then and there, but as the street car rattled into Peru he reflected that no other person in Trinidad knew that he had these things, except indeed the person who slipped them into his pocket, but that person was not likely to mention the matter. Then, too, it was such an odd occurrence, so piquing to his analytic instinct, that he decided he would go on with the inquiry.

Two minutes later Lowe rang down the motorman and the two companions got off in the Hindu settlement. By this time the street was full of coolies, greasy men and women gliding about with bundles on their heads or coiled down in the sunshine in pairs where they took turns in examining each other's head for vermin. Lowe glanced about, oriented himself, then started walking briskly past the temple, when Poggioli stopped him and asked him where he was going.

"To report to old Hira Dass, according to my instructions from Jeffries," said the Englishman.

"Suppose we stop in the temple a moment. We ought not to go to the old fellow without at least a working knowledge of the scene of the murder."

The clerk slowed up uncertainly, but at that moment they glanced through the temple door and saw five coolies sitting inside. A policeman at the entrance was evidently guarding these men as prisoners. Lowe approached the guard, made his mission known, and a little later he and his guest were admitted into the temple.

The coolie prisoners were as repulsive as are all of their kind. Four were as thin as cadavers, the fifth one greasily fat. All five wore cheesecloth around their bodies, which left them as exposed as if they had worn nothing at all. One of the emaciated men held his mouth open all the time with an expression of suffering caused by a chronic lack of food. The five squatted on their rugs and looked at the white men with their beadlike eyes. The fat one said in a low tone to his companions:

"The sahib."

This whispered ejaculation disquieted Poggioli somewhat, and he reflected again that it would have been discretion to withdraw from the murder of little Maila Ran as quietly as possible. Still he could explain his presence in the temple simply enough. And besides, the veiled face of the mystery seduced him. He stood studying the five beggars: the greasy one, the lean ones, the one with the suffering face.

"Boys," he said to the group, for all coolies are boys, "did any of you hear any noises in this temple last night?"

"Much sleep, sahib, no noise. Police-y-man punch us 'wake this morning make sit still here."

"What's your name?" asked the American of the loquacious fat mendicant.

"Chuder Chand, sahib."

"When did you go to sleep last night?"

"When I ate rice and tea, sahib."

"Do you remember seeing Boodman Lal and his wife enter this building last night?"

Here their evidence became divided. The fat man remembered; two of the cadavers remembered only the wife, one only Boodman Lal, and one nothing at all.

Poggioli confined himself to the fat man.

"Did you see them go out?"

All five shook their heads.

"You were all asleep then?"

A general nodding.

"Did you have any impressions during your sleep, any disturbance, any half rousing, any noises?"

The horror-struck man said in a ghastly tone:

"I dream bad dream, sahib. When police-y-man punch me awake this morning I think my dream is come to me."

"And me, sahib."

"Me, sahib."

"Me."

"Did you all have bad dreams?"

A general nodding.

"What did you dream, Chuder Chand?" inquired the psychologist with a certain growth of interest.

"Dream me a big fat pig, but still I starved, sahib."

"And you?" at a lean man.

"That I be mashed under a great bowl of rice, sahib, but hungry."

"And you?" asked Poggioli of the horror-struck coolie.

The coolie wet his dry lips and whispered in his ghastly tones:

"Sahib, I dreamed I was Siva,[5] and I held the world in my hands and bit it and it tasted bitter, like the rind of a mammy apple. And I said to Vishnu, 'Let me be a dog in the streets, rather than taste the bitterness of this world,' and then the policeman punched me, sahib, and asked if I had murdered Maila Ran."

The psychologist stood staring at the sunken temples and withered chaps of the beggar, amazed at the enormous vision of godhood which had visited the old mendicant's head. No doubt this grandiloquent dream was a sort of compensation for the starved and wretched existence the beggar led.

Here the bank clerk intervened to say that they would better go on around to old Hira Dass's house according to instructions.

Poggioli turned and followed his friend out of the temple.

"Lowe, I think we can now entirely discard the theory that the beggars murdered the girl."

"On what grounds?" asked the clerk in surprise. "They told you nothing but their dreams."

"That is the reason. All five had wild, fantastic dreams. That suggests they were given some sort of opiate in their rice or tea last night. It is very improbable that five ignorant coolies would have wit enough to concoct such a piece of evidence as that."

"That's a fact," admitted the Englishman, a trifle surprised, "but I don't believe a Trinidad court would admit such evidence."

"We are not looking for legal evidence; we are after some indication of the real criminal."

By this time the two men were walking down a hot, malodorous alley which emptied into the square a little east of the temple. Lowe jerked a bell-pull in a high adobe wall, and Poggioli was surprised that this could be the home of a millionaire Hindu. Presently the shutter opened and Mr. Hira Dass himself stood in the opening. The old Hindu was still draped in yellow silk which revealed his emaciated form almost as completely as if he had been naked. But his face was alert with hooked nose and brilliant black eyes, and his wrinkles did not so much suggest great age as they did shrewdness and acumen.

The old coolie immediately led his callers into an open court surrounded by marble columns with a fountain in its center and white doves fluttering up to the frieze or floating back down again.

The Hindu began talking immediately of the murder and his anxiety to clear his unhappy nephew. The old man's English was very good, no doubt owing to the business association of his latter years.

"A most mysterious murder," he deplored, shaking his head, "and the life of my poor nephew will depend upon your exertions, gentlemen. What do you think of those beggars that were found in the temple with the bangles and coins?"

Mr. Hira Dass seated his guests on a white marble bench, and now walked nervously in front of them, like some fantastic old scarecrow draped in yellow silk.

"I am afraid my judgment of the beggars will disappoint you, Mr. Hira Dass," answered Poggioli. "My theory is they are innocent of the crime."

"Why do you say that?" queried Hira Dass, looking sharply at the American.

The psychologist explained his deduction from their dreams.

"You are not English, sir," exclaimed the old man. "No Englishman would have thought of that."

"No, I'm half Italian and half American."

The old Indian nodded.

"Your Latin blood has subtlety, Mr. Poggioli, but you base your proof on the mechanical cause of the dreams, not upon the dreams themselves."

The psychologist looked at the old man's cunning face and gnomelike figure and smiled.

"I could hardly use the dreams themselves, although they were fantastic enough."

"Oh, you did inquire into the actual dreams?"

"Yes, by the way of professional interest."

"What is your profession? Aren't you a detective?"

"No, I'm a psychologist."

Old Hira Dass paused in his rickety walking up and down the marble pavement to stare at the American and then burst into the most wrinkled cachinnation Poggioli had ever seen.

"A psychologist, and inquired into a suspected criminal's dreams out of mere curiosity!" the old gnome cackled again, then became serious. He held up a thin finger at the American. "I must not laugh. Your oversoul, your *atman*, is at least groping after knowledge as the blindworm gropes. But enough of that, Mr. Poggioli. Our problem is to find the criminal who committed this crime and restore my nephew Boodman Lal to liberty. You can imagine what a blow this is to me. I arranged this marriage for my nephew."

The American looked at the old man with new ground for deduction.

"You did—arranged a marriage for a nephew who is in the thirties?"

"Yes, I wanted him to avoid the pitfalls into which I fell," replied old Hira Dass seriously. "He was unmarried, and had already begun to add dollars to dollars. I did the same thing, Mr. Poggioli, and now look at me—an empty old man in a foreign land. What good is this marble court where men of my own kind cannot come and sit with me, and when I have no grandchildren to feed the doves? No, I have piled up dollars and pounds. I have eaten the world, Mr. Poggioli, and found it bitter; now here I am, an outcast."

There was a passion in this outburst which moved the American, and at the same time the old Hindu's phraseology was sharply reminiscent of the dreams told him by the beggars in the temple. The psychologist noted the point hurriedly and curiously in the flow of the conversation, and at the same moment some other part of his brain was inquiring tritely:

"Then why don't you go back to India, Mr. Hira Dass?"

"With this worn-out body," the old Hindu made a contemptuous gesture toward himself, "and with this face, wrinkled with pence! Why, Mr. Poggioli, my mind is half English. If I should return to Benares I would walk about thinking what the temples cost, what was the value of the stones set in the eyes of Krishna's image. That is why we Hindus lose our caste if we travel abroad and settle in a foreign land, because we do indeed lose caste. We become neither Hindus nor English. Our minds are divided, so if I would ever be one with my own people again, Mr. Poggioli, I must leave this Western mind and body here in Trinidad."

Old Hira Dass's speech brought to the American that fleeting credulity in transmigration of the soul which an ardent believer always inspires. The old Hindu made the theory of palingenesis appear almost matter-of-fact. A man died here and reappeared as a babe in India. There was nothing so unbelievable in that. A man's basic energy, which has loved, hated, aspired, and grieved here, must go somewhere, while matter itself was a mere dance of atoms. Which was the most permanent, Hira Dass's passion or his marble court? Both were mere forms of force. The psychologist drew himself out of his reverie.

"That is very interesting, or I should say moving, Hira Dass. You have strange griefs. But we were discussing your nephew, Boodman Lal. I think I have a theory which may liberate him."

"And what is that?"

"As I have explained to you, I believe the beggars in the temple were given a sleeping potion. I suspect the temple attendant doped the rice and later murdered your nephew's wife."

The millionaire became thoughtful.

"That is good Gooka. I employ him. He is a miserably poor man, Mr. Poggioli, so I cannot believe he committed this murder."

"Pardon me, but I don't follow your reasoning. If he is poor he would have a strong motive for the robbery."

"That's true, but a very poor man would never have dropped the ten pieces of gold into the pockets of the beggars to lay a false scent. The man who did this deed must have been a well-to-do person accustomed to using money to forward his purposes. Therefore, in searching for the criminal I would look for a moneyed man."

"But, Mr. Hira Dass," protested the psychologist, "that swings suspicion back to your nephew."

"My nephew!" cried the old man, growing excited again. "What motive would my nephew have to slay his bride of a few hours!"

"But what motive," retorted Poggioli with academic curtness, "would a well-to-do man have to murder a child? And what chance would he have to place an opiate in the rice?"

The old Hindu lifted a finger and came closer.

"I'll tell you my suspicions," he said in a lowered voice, "and you can work out the details."

"Yes, what are they?" asked Poggioli, becoming attentive again.

"I went down to the temple this morning to have the body of my poor murdered niece brought here to my villa for burial. I talked to the five beggars and they told me that there was a sixth sleeper in the temple last night." The old coolie shook his finger, lifted his eyebrows, and assumed a very gnomish appearance indeed.

A certain trickle of dismay went through the American. He tried to keep from moistening his lips and perhaps he did, but all he could think to do was to lift his eyebrows and say:

"Was there, indeed?"

"Yes—and a white man!"

Lowe, the bank clerk, who had been sitting silent through all this, interrupted. "Surely not, Mr. Hira Dass, not a white man!"

"All five of the coolies and my man Gooka told me it was true," reiterated the old man, "and I have always found Gooka a truthful man. And besides, such a man would fill the rôle of assailant exactly. He would be well-to-do, accustomed to using money to forward his purposes."

The psychologist made a sort of mental lunge to refute this rapid array of evidence old Hira Dass was piling up against him.

"But, Mr. Hira Dass, decapitation is not an American mode of murder."

"American!"

"I—I was speaking generally," stammered the psychologist, "I mean a white man's method of murder."

"That is indicative in itself," returned the Hindu promptly. "I meant to call your attention to that point. It shows the white man was a highly educated man, who had studied the mental habit of other peoples than his own, so he was enabled to give the crime an extraordinary resemblance to a Hindu crime. I would suggest, gentlemen, that you begin your search for an intellectual white man."

"What motive could such a man have?" cried the American.

"Robbery, possibly, or if he were a very intellectual man indeed he might have murdered the poor child by way of experiment. I read not long ago in an American paper of two youths who committed such a crime." [6]

"A murder for experiment!" cried Lowe, aghast.

"Yes, to record the psychological reaction."

Poggioli suddenly got to his feet.

"I can't agree with such a theory as that, Mr. Hira Dass," he said in a shaken voice.

"No, it's too far-fetched," declared the clerk at once.

"However, it is worth while investigating," persisted the Hindu.

"Yes, yes," agreed the American, evidently about to depart, "but I shall begin my investigations, gentlemen, with the man Gooka."

"As you will," agreed Hira Dass, "and in your investigations, gentlemen, hire any assistants you need, draw on me for any amount. I want my nephew exonerated, and above all things, I want the real criminal apprehended and brought to the gallows."

Lowe nodded.

"We'll do our best, sir," he answered in his thorough-going English manner.

The old man followed his guests to the gate and bowed them out into the malodorous alleyway again.

As the two friends set off through the hot sunshine once more the bank clerk laughed.

"A white man in that temple! That sounds like pure fiction to me to shield Boodman Lal. You know these coolies hang together like thieves."

He walked on a little way pondering, then added, "Jolly good thing we didn't decide to sleep in the temple last night, isn't it, Poggioli?"

A sickish feeling went over the American. For a moment he was tempted to tell his host frankly what he had done and ask his advice in the matter, but finally he said:

"In my opinion the actual criminal is Boodman Lal."

Lowe glanced around sidewise at his guest and nodded faintly.

"Same here. I thought it ever since I first saw the account in the *Inquirer*. Somehow these coolies will chop their wives to pieces for no reason at all."

"I know a very good reason in this instance," retorted the American warmly, taking out his uneasiness in this manner. "It's these damned child marriages! When a man marries some child he doesn't care a tuppence for——What do you know about Boodman Lal anyway?"

"All there is to know. He was born here and has always been a figure here in Port of Spain because of his rich uncle."

"Lived here all his life?"

"Except when he was in Oxford for six years."

"Oh, he's an Oxford man!"

"Yes."

"There you are, there's the trouble."

"What do you mean?"

"No doubt he fell in love with some English girl. But when his wealthy uncle, Hira Dass, chose a Hindu child for his wife, Boodman could not refuse the marriage. No man is going to quarrel with a million-pound legacy, but he chose this ghastly method of getting rid of the child."

"I venture you are right," declared the bank clerk. "I felt sure Boodman Lal had killed the girl."

"Likely as not he was engaged to some English girl and was waiting for his uncle's death to make him wealthy."

"Quite possible, in fact probable."

Here a cab came angling across the square toward the two men as they stood in front of the grotesque temple. The Negro driver waved his whip interrogatively. The clerk beckoned him in. The cab drew up at the curb. Lowe climbed in but Poggioli remained on the pavement.

"Aren't you coming?"

"You know, Lowe," said Poggioli seriously, "I don't feel that I can conscientiously continue this investigation trying to clear a person whom I have every reason to believe guilty."

The bank clerk was disturbed.

"But, man, don't leave me like this! At least come on to the police headquarters and explain your theory about the temple keeper, Gooka, and the rice. That seems to hang together pretty well. It is possible Boodman Lal didn't do this thing after all. We owe it to him to do all we can."

As Poggioli still hung back on the curb, Lowe asked:

"What do you want to do?"

"Well, I—er—thought I would go back to the cottage and pack my things."

The bank clerk was amazed.

"Pack your things—your boat doesn't sail until Friday!"

"Yes, I know, but there is a daily service to Curaçao. It struck me to go—"

"Aw, come!" cried Lowe in hospitable astonishment, "you can't run off like that, just when I've stirred up an interesting murder mystery for you to unravel. You ought to appreciate my efforts as a host more than that."

"Well, I do," hesitated Poggioli seriously. At that moment his excess of caution took one of those odd, instantaneous shifts that come so unaccountably to men, and he thought to himself, "Well, damn it, this is an interesting situation. It's a shame to leave it, and nothing will happen to me."

So he swung into the cab with decision and ordered briskly: "All right, to the police station, Sambo!"

"Sounds more like it," declared the clerk, as the cab horses set out a brisk trot through the sunshine.

Mr. Lowe, the bank clerk, was not without a certain flair for making the most of a house guest, and when he reached the police station he introduced his companion to the chief of police as "Mr. Poggioli, a professor in an American university and a research student in criminal psychology."

The chief of police, a Mr. Vickers, was a short, thick man with a tropic-browned face and eyes habitually squinted against the sun. He seemed not greatly impressed with the titles Lowe gave his friend but merely remarked that if Mr. Poggioli was hunting crimes, Trinidad was a good place to find them.

The bank clerk proceeded with a certain importance in his manner.

"I have asked his counsel in the Boodman Lal murder case. He has developed a theory, Mr. Vickers, as to who is the actual murderer of Mrs. Boodman Lal."

"So have I," replied Vickers with a dry smile.

"Of course you think Boodman Lal did it," said Lowe in a more commonplace manner.

Vickers did not answer this but continued looking at the two taller men in a listening attitude which caused Lowe to go on.

"Now in this matter, Mr. Vickers, I want to be perfectly frank with you. I'll admit we are in this case in the employ of Mr. Hira Dass, and are making an effort to clear Boodman Lal. We felt confident you would use the well-known skill of the police department of Port of Spain to work out a theory to clear Boodman Lal just as readily as you would to convict him."

"Our department usually devotes its time to conviction and not to clearing criminals."

"Yes, I know that, but if our theory will point out the actual murderer—"

"What is your theory?" inquired Vickers without enthusiasm.

The bank clerk began explaining the dream of the five beggars and the probability that they had been given sleeping potions.

The short man smiled faintly.

"So Mr. Poggioli's theory is based on the dreams of these men?"

Poggioli had a pedagogue's brevity of temper when his theories were questioned.

"It would be a remarkable coincidence, Mr. Vickers, if five men had lurid dreams simultaneously without some physical cause. It suggests strongly that their tea or rice was doped."

As Vickers continued looking at Poggioli the American continued with less acerbity:

"I should say that Gooka, the temple keeper, either doped the rice himself or he knows who did it."

"Possibly he does."

"My idea is that you send a man for the ricepot and teapot, have their contents analyzed, find out what soporific was used, then have your men search the sales records of the drug stores in the city to see who has lately bought such a drug."

Mr. Vickers grunted a noncommittal uh-huh, and then began in the livelier tones of a man who meets a stranger socially:

"How do you like Trinidad, Mr. Poggioli?"

"Remarkably luxuriant country—oranges and grapefruit growing wild."

"You've just arrived?"

"Yes."

"In what university do you teach?"

"Ohio State."

Mr. Vickers's eyes took on a humorous twinkle.

"A chair of criminal psychology in an ordinary state university —is that the result of your American prohibition laws, Professor?"

Poggioli smiled at this thrust.

"Mr. Lowe misstated my work a little. I am not a professor, I am simply a docent. And I have not specialized on criminal psychology. I quiz on general psychology."

"You are not teaching now?"

"No; this is my sabbatical year."

Mr. Vickers glanced up and down the American.

"You look young to have taught in a university six years."

There was something not altogether agreeable in this observation, but the officer rectified it a moment later by saying, "But you Americans start young—land of specialists. Now you, Mr. Poggioli—I suppose you are wrapped up heart and soul in your psychology?"

"I am," agreed the American positively.

"Do anything in the world to advance yourself in the science?"

"I rather think so," asserted Poggioli, with his enthusiasm mounting in his voice.

"Especially keen on original research work—"

Lowe interrupted, laughing.

"That's what he is, Chief. Do you know what he asked me to do yesterday afternoon?"

"No, what?"

The American turned abruptly on his friend.

"Now, Lowe, don't let's burden Mr. Vickers with household anecdotes."

"But I am really curious," declared the police chief. "Just what did Professor Poggioli ask you to do yesterday afternoon, Mr. Lowe?"

The bank clerk looked from one to the other, hardly knowing whether to go on or not. Mr. Vickers was smiling; Poggioli was very serious as he prohibited anecdotes about himself. The bank clerk thought: "This is real modesty." He said aloud: "It was just a little psychological experiment he wanted to do."

"Did he do it?" smiled the chief.

"Oh, no, I wouldn't hear of it."

"As unconventional as that!" cried Mr. Vickers, lifting sandy brows.

"It was really nothing," said Lowe, looking at his guest's rigid face and then at the police captain.

Suddenly Mr. Vickers dropped his quizzical attitude.

"I think I could guess your anecdote if I tried, Lowe. About a half hour ago I received a telephone message from my man stationed at the Hindu temple to keep a lookout for you and Mr. Poggioli."

The American felt a tautening of his muscles at this frontal attack. He had suspected something of the sort from the policeman's manner. The bank clerk stared at the officer in amazement.

"What was your bobby telephoning about us for?"

"Because one of the coolies under arrest told him that Mr. Poggioli slept in the temple last night."

"My word, that's not true!" cried the bank clerk. "That is exactly what he did not do. He suggested it to me but I said No. You remember, Poggioli—"

Mr. Lowe turned for corroboration, but the look on his friend's face amazed him.

"You didn't do it, did you Poggioli?" he gasped.

"You see he did," said Vickers dryly.

"But, Poggioli—in God's name—"

The American braced himself for an attempt to explain. He lifted his hand with a certain pedagogic mannerism.

"Gentlemen, I—I had a perfectly valid, an important reason for sleeping in the temple last night."

"I told you," nodded Vickers.

"In coolie town, in a coolie temple!" ejaculated Lowe.

"Gentlemen, I—can only ask your—your sympathetic attention to what I am about to say."

"Go on," said Vickers.

"You remember, Lowe, you and I were down there watching a wedding procession. Well, just as the music stopped and the line of coolies entered the building, suddenly it seemed to me as if—as if—they had—" Poggioli swallowed at nothing and then added the odd word, "vanished."

Vickers looked at him.

"Naturally, they had gone into the building."

"I don't mean that. I'm afraid you won't understand what I do mean—that the whole procession had ceased to exist, melted into nothingness."

Even Mr. Vickers blinked. Then he drew out a memorandum book and stolidly made a note.

"Is that all?"

"No, then I began speculating on what had given me such a strange impression. You see that is really the idea on which the Hindus base their notion of heaven—oblivion, nothingness."

"Yes, I've heard that before."

"Well, our medieval Gothic architecture was a conception of our Western heaven; and I thought perhaps the Indian architecture had somehow caught the motif of the Indian religion; you know, suggested Nirvana. That was what amazed and intrigued me. That was why I wanted to sleep in the place. I wanted to see if I could further my shred of impression. Does this make any sense to you, Mr. Vickers?"

"I dare say it will, sir, to the criminal judge," opined the police chief cheerfully.

The psychologist felt a sinking of heart.

Mr. Vickers proceeded in the same matter-of-fact tone: "But no matter why you went in, what you did afterward is what counts. Here in Trinidad nobody is allowed to go around chopping off heads to see how it feels."

Poggioli looked at the officer with a ghastly sensation in his midriff.

"You don't think I did such a horrible thing as an experiment?"

Mr. Vickers drew out the makings of a cigarette.

"You Americans, especially you intellectual Americans, do some pretty stiff things, Mr. Poggioli. I was reading about two young intellectuals—"

"Good Lord!" quivered the psychologist with this particular reference beginning to grate on his nerves.

"These fellows I read about also tried to turn an honest penny by their murder—I don't suppose you happened to notice yesterday that the little girl, Maila Ran, was almost covered over with gold bangles and coins?"

"Of course I noticed it!" cried the psychologist, growing white, "but I had nothing whatever to do with the child. Your insinuations are brutal and repulsive. I did sleep in the temple—"

"By the way," interrupted Vickers suddenly, "you say you slept on a rug just as the coolies did?"

"Yes, I did."

"You didn't wake up either?"

"No."

"Then did the murderer of the child happen to put a coin and a bangle in your pockets, just as he did the other sleepers in the temple?"

"That's exactly what he did!" cried Poggioli, with the first ray of hope breaking upon him. "When I found them in my pocket on the tram this morning I came pretty near throwing them away, but fortunately I didn't. Here they are."

And gladly enough now he drew the trinkets out and showed them to the chief of police.

Mr. Vickers looked at the gold pieces, then at the psychologist.

"You don't happen to have any more, do you?"

The American said No, but it was with a certain thrill of anxiety that he began turning out his other pockets. If the mysterious criminal had placed more than two gold pieces in his pockets he would be in a very difficult position. However, the remainder of his belongings were quite legitimate.

"Well, that's something," admitted Vickers slowly. "Of course, you might have expected just such a questioning as this and provided yourself with these two pieces of gold, but I doubt it. Somehow, I don't believe you are a bright enough man to think of such a thing." He paused, pondering, and finally said, "I suppose you have no objection to my sending a man to search your baggage in Mr. Lowe's cottage?"

"Instead of objecting, I invite it, I request it."

Mr. Vickers nodded agreeably.

"Who can I telegraph to in America to learn something about your standing as a university man?"

"Dean Ingram, Ohio State, Columbus, Ohio, U.S.A."

Vickers made this note, then turned to Lowe.

"I suppose you've known Mr. Poggioli for a long time, Mr. Lowe?"

"Why n-no, I haven't," admitted the clerk.

"Where did you meet him?"

"Sailing from Barbuda to Antigua. On the *Trevemore*."

"Did he seem to have respectable American friends aboard?"

Lowe hesitated and flushed faintly.

"I—can hardly say."

"Why?"

"If I tell you Mr. Poggioli's mode of travel I am afraid you would hold it to his disadvantage."

"How did he travel?" queried the officer in surprise.

"The fact is he traveled as a deck passenger."

"You mean he had no cabin, shipped along on deck with the Negroes!"

"I did it myself!" cried Lowe, growing ruddy. "We couldn't get a cabin—they were all occupied."

The American reflected rapidly, and realized that Vickers could easily find out the real state of things from the ship's agents up the islands.

"Chief," said the psychologist with a tongue that felt thick, "I boarded the *Trevemore* at St. Kitts. There were cabins available. I chose deck passage deliberately. I wanted to study the natives."

"Then you are broke, just as I thought," ejaculated Mr. Vickers, "and I'll bet pounds to pence we'll find the jewelry around your place somewhere."

The chief hailed a passing cab, called a plain-clothes man, put the three in the vehicle and started them briskly back up Prince Edward's Street, toward Tragarette Road, and thence to Lowe's cottage beyond the Indian village and its ill-starred temple.

The three men and the Negro driver trotted back up Tragarette, each lost in his own thoughts. The plain-clothes man rode on the front seat with the cabman, but occasionally he glanced back to look at his prisoner. Lowe evidently was reflecting how this contretemps would affect his social and business standing in the city. The Negro also kept peering back under the hood of his cab, and finally he ejaculated:

"Killum jess to see 'em die. I declah, dese 'Mericans—" and he shook his kinky head.

A hot resentment rose up in the psychologist at this continued recurrence of that detestable crime. He realized with deep resentment that the crimes of particular Americans were held tentatively against all American citizens, while their great national charities and humanities were forgotten with the breath that told them. In the midst of these angry thoughts the cab drew up before the clerk's garden gate.

All got out. Lowe let them in with a key and then the three walked in a kind of grave haste across the lawn. The door was opened by Ram Jon, who took their hats and then followed them into the room Lowe had set apart for his guest.

This room, like all Trinidad chambers, was furnished in the sparest and coolest manner possible; a table, three chairs, a bed with sheets, and Poggioli's trunk. It was so open to inspection nothing could have been concealed in it. The plain-clothes man opened the table drawer.

"Would you mind opening your trunk, Mr. Poggioli?"

The American got out his keys, knelt and undid the hasp of his wardrobe trunk, then swung the two halves apart. One side held containers, the other suits. Poggioli opened the drawers casually; collar and handkerchief box at the top, hat box, shirt box. As he did this came a faint clinking sound. The detective stepped forward and lifted out the shirts. Beneath them lay a mass of coins and bangles flung into the tray helter-skelter.

The American stared with an open mouth, unable to say a word.

The plain-clothes man snapped with a certain indignant admiration in his voice: "Your nerve almost got you by!"

The thing seemed unreal to the American. He had the same uncanny feeling that he had experienced when the procession entered the temple. Materiality seemed to have slipped a cog. A wild thought came to him that somehow the Hindus had dematerialized the gold and caused it to reappear in his trunk. Then there came a terrifying fancy that he had committed the crime in his sleep. This last clung to his mind. After all, he had murdered the little girl bride, Maila Ran!

The plain-clothes man spoke to Lowe:

"Have your man bring me a sack to take this stuff back to headquarters."

Ram Jon slithered from the room and presently returned with a sack. The inspector took his handkerchief, lifted the pieces out with it, one by one, and placed them in the sack.

"Lowe," said Poggioli pitifully, "you don't believe I did this, do you?"

The bank clerk wiped his face with his handkerchief.

"In your trunk, Poggioli—"

"If I did it I was sleepwalking!" cried the unhappy man. "My God, to think it is possible—but right here in my own trunk—" he stood staring at the bag, at the shirt box.

The plain-clothes man said dryly: "We might as well start back, I suppose. This is all."

Lowe suddenly cast in his lot with his guest.

"I'll go back with you, Poggioli. I'll see you through this pinch. Somehow I can't, I won't believe you did it!"

"Thanks! Thanks!"

The bank clerk masked his emotion under a certain grim facetiousness.

"You know, Poggioli, you set out to clear Boodman Lal—it looks as if you've done it."

"No, he didn't," denied the plain-clothes man. "Boodman Lal was out of jail at least an hour before you fellows drove up a while ago."

"Out—had you turned him out?"

"Yes."

"How was that?"

"Because he didn't go to the temple at all last night with his wife. He went down to Queen's Park Hotel and played billiards till one o'clock. He called up some friends and proved that easily enough."

Lowe stared at his friend, aghast.

"My word, Poggioli, that leaves nobody but—you." The psychologist lost all semblance of resistance.

"I don't know anything about it. If I did it I was asleep. That's all I can say. The coolies—" He had a dim notion of accusing them again, but he recalled that he had proved to himself clearly and logically that they were innocent. "I don't know anything about it," he repeated helplessly.

Half an hour later the three men were at police headquarters once more, and the plain-clothes man and the turnkey, a humble, gray sort of man, took the American back to a cell. The turnkey unlocked one in a long row of cells and swung it open for Poggioli.

The bank clerk gave him what encouragement he could.

"Don't be too downhearted. I'll do everything I can. Somehow I believe you are innocent. I'll hire your lawyers, cable your friends—"

Poggioli was repeating a stunned "Thanks! Thanks!" as the cell door shut between them. The bolt clashed home and was locked. And the men were tramping down the iron corridor. Poggioli was alone.

There was a chair and a bunk in the cell. The psychologist looked at these with an irrational feeling that he would not stay in the prison long enough to warrant his sitting down. Presently he did sit down on the bunk.

He sat perfectly still and tried to assemble his thoughts against the mountain of adverse evidence which suddenly had been piled against him. His sleep in the temple, the murder, the coins in his shirt box—after all he must have committed the crime in his sleep.

As he sat with his head in his hands pondering this theory, it grew more and more incredible. To commit the murder in his sleep, to put the coins in the pockets of the beggars in a clever effort to divert suspicion, to bring the gold to Lowe's cottage, and then to go back and lie down on the mat, all while he was asleep—that was impossible. He could not believe any human being could perform so fantastic, so complicated a feat.

On the other hand, no other criminal would place the whole booty in Poggioli's trunk and so lose it. That too was irrational. He was forced back to his dream theory.

When he accepted this hypothesis he wondered just what he had dreamed. If he had really murdered the girl in a nightmare, then the murder was stamped somewhere in his subconscious, divided from his day memories by the nebulous associations of sleep. He wondered if he could reproduce them.

To recall a lost dream is perhaps one of the nicest tasks that ever a human brain was driven to. Poggioli, being a psychologist, had had a certain amount of experience with such attempts. Now he lay down on his bunk and began the effort in a mechanical way.

He recalled as vividly as possible his covert exit from Lowe's cottage, his walk down Tragarette Road between perfumed gardens, the lights of Peru, and finally his entrance into the temple. He imagined again the temple attendant, Gooka, looking curiously at him, but giving him tea and rice and pointing out his rug. Poggioli remembered that he lay down on the rug on his back with his hands under his head exactly as he was now lying on his cell bunk. For a while he had stared at the illuminated image of Krishna, then at the dark spring of the dome over his head.

And as he lay there, gazing thus, his thoughts had begun to waver, to lose beat with his senses, to make misinterpretations. He had thought that the Krishna moved slightly, then settled back and became a statue again—here some tenuous connection in his thoughts snapped, and he lost his whole picture in the hard bars of his cell again.

Poggioli lay relaxed a while, then began once more. He reached the point where the Krishna moved, seemed about to speak, and then—there he was back in his cell.

It was nerve-racking, tantalizing, this fishing for the gossamers of a dream which continually broke; this pursuing the grotesqueries of a nightmare and trying to connect it with his solid everyday life of thought and action. What had he dreamed?

Minutes dragged out as Poggioli pursued the vanished visions of his head. Yes, it had seemed to him that the image of the Buddha moved, that it had even risen from its attitude of meditation, and suddenly, with a little thrill, Poggioli remembered that the dome of the Hindu temple was opened and this left him staring upward into a vast abyss. It seemed to the psychologist that he stared upward, and the Krishna stared upward, both gazing into an unending space, and presently he realized that he and the great upward-staring Krishna were one; that they had always been one; and that their oneness filled all space with enormous, with infinite power. But this oneness which was Poggioli was alone in an endless, featureless space. No other thing existed, because nothing had ever been created; there was only a creator. All the creatures and matter which had ever been or ever would be were wrapped up in him, Poggioli, or Buddha. And then Poggioli saw that space and time had ceased to be, for space and time are the offspring of division. And at last Krishna or Poggioli was losing all entity or being in this tranced immobility.

And Poggioli began struggling desperately against nothingness. He writhed at his deadened muscles, he willed in torture to retain some vestige of being, and at last after what seemed millenniums of effort he formed the thought:

"I would rather lose my oneness with Krishna and become the vilest and poorest of creatures—to mate, fight, love, lust, kill, and be killed than to be lost in this terrible trance of the universal!"

And when he had formed this tortured thought Poggioli remembered that he had awakened and it was five o'clock in the morning. He had arisen with a throbbing headache and had gone home.

That was his dream.

The American arose from his bunk filled with the deepest satisfaction from his accomplishment. Then he recalled with surprise that all five of the coolies had much the same dream; grandiloquence and power accompanied by great unhappiness.

"That was an odd thing," thought the psychologist, "six men dreaming the same dream in different terms. There must have been some physical cause for such a phenomenon."

Then he remembered that he had heard the same story from another source. Old Hira Dass in his marble court had expressed the same sentiment, complaining of the emptiness of his riches and power. However—and this was crucial—Hira Dass's grief was not a mere passing nightmare, it was his settled condition.

With this a queer idea popped into Poggioli's mind. Could not these six dreams have been a transference of an idea? While he and the coolies lay sleeping with passive minds, suppose old Hira

Dass had entered the temple with his great unhappiness in his mind, and suppose he had committed some terrible deed which wrought his emotions to a monsoon of passion. Would not his horrid thoughts have registered themselves in different forms on the minds of the sleeping men!

Here Poggioli's ideas danced about like the molecules of a crystal in solution, each one rushing of its own accord to take its appointed place in a complicated crystalline design. And so a complete understanding of the murder of little Maila Ran rushed in upon him.

Poggioli leaped to his feet and hallooed his triumph.

"Here, Vickers! Lowe! Turnkey! I have it! I've solved it! Turn me out! I know who killed the girl!"

After he had shouted for several minutes Poggioli saw the form of a man coming up the dark aisle with a lamp. He was surprised at the lamp but passed over it.

"Turnkey!" he cried, "I know who murdered the child—old Hira Dass! Now listen—" He was about to relate his dream, but realized that would avail nothing in an English court, so he leaped to the physical end of the crime, matter with which the English juggle so expertly. His thoughts danced into shape.

"Listen, turnkey, go tell Vickers to take that gold and develop all the finger prints on it—he'll find Hira Dass's prints! Also, tell him to follow out that opiate clue I gave him—he'll find Hira Dass's servant bought the opiate. Also, Hira Dass sent a man to put the gold in my trunk. See if you can't find brass or steel filings in my room where the scoundrel sat and filed a new key. Also, give Ram Jon the third degree; he knows who brought the gold."

The one with the lamp made a gesture.

"They've done all that, sir, long ago."

"They did!"

"Certainly, sir, and old Hira Dass confessed everything, though why a rich old man like him should have murdered a pretty child is more than I can see. These Hindus are unaccountable, sir, even the millionaires."

Poggioli passed over so simple a query.

"But why did the old devil pick on me for a scapegoat?" he cried, puzzled.

"Oh, he explained that to the police, sir. He said he picked on a white man so the police would make a thorough investigation and be sure to catch him. In fact, he said, sir, that he had willed that you should come and sleep in the temple that night."

Poggioli stared with a little prickling sensation at this touch of the occult world.

"What I can't see, sir," went on the man with the lamp, "was why the old coolie wanted to be caught and hanged—why didn't he commit suicide?"

"Because then his soul would have returned in the form of some beast. He wanted to be slain. He expects to be reborn instantly in Benares with little Maila Ran. He hopes to be a great man with wife and children."

"Nutty idea!" cried the fellow.

But the psychologist sat staring at the lamp with a queer feeling that possibly such a fantastic idea might be true after all. For what goes with this passionate, uneasy force in man when he dies? May not the dead struggle to reanimate themselves as he had done in his dream? Perhaps the numberless dead still will to live and be divided; and perhaps living things are a result of the struggles of the dead, and not the dead of the living.

His thoughts suddenly shifted back to the present.

"Turnkey," he snapped with academic sharpness, "why didn't you come and tell me of old Hira Dass's confession the moment it occurred? What did you mean, keeping me locked up here when you knew I was an innocent man?"

"Because I couldn't," said the form with the lamp sorrowfully, "Old Hira Dass didn't confess until a month and ten days after you were hanged, sir."

And the lamp went out.

COMMENT AND QUESTIONS

The story raises questions about the possible transmigration of souls, about the possibility of extrasensory perception, and about the desirability of Nirvana. That is, the story concerns itself on a basic level with the nature of reality and the nature of dreams. We do not even know for sure what occurs and what is dreamed. Discuss what the story says and implies about the relationship between consciousness or reality and dreams or visions. Does Poggioli die or dream that he is dead? Does he return briefly from death to hear the final result of the murder investigation? Does he actually unite himself with a cosmic being or simply dream this vision? How can we know what is real?

Henry Poggioli spends the night in the Hindu temple despite the horrified opposition of his friend to such an act. He is motivated, he says, by his observation that the wedding procession entering the temple door seems to vanish. Does Poggioli eliminate himself by entering the temple and spending the night? Explain.

Compare the attitude of Lowe toward coolies who murder their wives with that of the Negro cabman toward " 'mericans" who "killum jess to see 'um die." Are there other expressions of such attitudes in the story?

Trinidad is a place where representatives of several very different cultures come together. What effect does this setting have on the story?

Reinterpret Henry Poggioli's dream as he relives or reconstructs it on his jail-cell bunk in light of the story's conclusion.

What are possible interpretations of the last line of the story?

What examples of particularly vivid or colorful words and expressions do you find in the story?

NOTES

1. *Krishna.* A deity of later Hinduism worshiped as an incarnation of Vishnu, the preserver god of the Hindu sacred triad; one of the more joyful expressions of deity.
2. *cicerone.* A guide who conducts sightseers.

3. *kapra.* Clothing.

4. *Nirvana.* A concept of both Hinduism and Buddhism denoting a state of mind in which pain and mental anguish have ceased.

5. *Siva.* The god of destruction and regeneration in the Hindu sacred triad.

6. . . . *two youths who committed such a crime.* Nathan Leopold and Richard Loeb, the defendants in a celebrated murder trial in 1924. They were convicted of kidnapping and murdering a thirteen-year-old boy.

ANTHONY BERKELEY

The Avenging Chance

In the first paragraph of this story, Anthony Berkeley challenges the reader to penetrate the illusion and solve the crime. Berkeley's challenge contains real clues to the solution of the murder. Notice the fine economy of the narrative. The content of the story has been pared down into an almost perfect summary; what is presented is nothing more than this condensed puzzle. This economy, however, results in conciseness, not simplicity. Many aspects of scene and character are provided by a single suitable phrase that needs no elaboration. The movement of the story is admirable, too. There is no waiting for something to happen; the story is consistently moving forward toward its inevitable conclusion.

Roger Sheringham has a most unusual personality for a traditional detective hero—he is ordinary and normal to the last degree. He was originally intended to be offensive, Mr. Berkeley said, for the purposes of amusement, but readers took him so seriously that he had to be toned down.

Roger Sheringham was inclined to think afterwards that the Poisoned Chocolates Case, as the papers called it, was perhaps the most perfectly planned murder he had ever encountered. The motive was so obvious, when you knew where to look for it—but you didn't know; the method was so significant when you had grasped its real essentials—but you didn't grasp them; the traces were so thinly covered, when you had realised what was covering them—but you didn't realise. But for a piece of the merest bad luck, which the murderer could not possibly have foreseen, the crime must have been added to the classical list of great mysteries.

This is the gist of the case, as Chief-Inspector Moresby told it one evening to Roger in the latter's rooms in the Albany a week or so after it happened:

On Friday morning, the fifteenth of November, at half-past ten in the morning, in accordance with his invariable custom, Sir William Anstruther walked into his club in Piccadilly, the very exclusive Rainbow Club, and asked for his letters. The porter handed him three and a small parcel. Sir William walked over to the fireplace in the big lounge hall to open them.

A few minutes later another member entered the club, a Mr. Graham Beresford. There were a letter and a couple of circulars for him, and he also strolled over to the fireplace, nodding to Sir William, but not speaking to him. The two men only knew each other very slightly, and had probably never exchanged more than a dozen words in all.

Having glanced through his letters, Sir William opened the parcel and, after a moment, snorted with disgust. Beresford looked at him, and with a grunt Sir William thrust out a letter which had been enclosed in the parcel. Concealing a smile (Sir William's ways were a matter of some amusement to his fellow-members), Beresford read the letter. It was from a big firm of chocolate manufacturers, Mason & Sons, and set forth that they were putting on the market a new brand of liqueur-chocolates designed especially to appeal to men; would Sir William do them the honour of accepting the enclosed two-pound box and letting the firm have his candid opinion on them?

"Do they think I'm a blank chorus-girl?" fumed Sir William. "Write 'em testimonials about their blank chocolates, indeed! Blank 'em! I'll complain to the blank committee. That sort of blank thing can't blank well be allowed here."

"Well, it's an ill wind so far as I'm concerned," Beresford soothed him. "It's reminded me of something. My wife and I had a box at the Imperial last night. I bet her a box of chocolates to a hundred cigarettes that she wouldn't spot the villain by the end of the second act. She won. I must remember to get them. Have you seen it—*The Creaking Skull*? Not a bad show."

Sir William had not seen it, and said so with force.

"Want a box of chocolates, did you say?" he added, more mildly. "Well, take this blank one. I don't want it."

For a moment Beresford demurred politely and then, most unfortunately for himself, accepted. The money so saved meant nothing to him for he was a wealthy man; but trouble was always worth saving.

By an extraordinarily lucky chance neither the outer wrapper of the box nor its covering letter were thrown into the fire, and this was the more fortunate in that both men had tossed the envelopes of their letters into the flames. Sir William did, indeed, make a bundle of the wrapper, letter and string, but he handed it over to Beresford, and the latter simply dropped it inside the fender. This bundle the porter subsequently extracted and, being a man of orderly habits, put it tidily away in the wastepaper basket, whence it was retrieved later by the police.

Of the three unconscious protagonists in the impending tragedy, Sir William was without doubt the most remarkable. Still a year or two under fifty, he looked, with his flaming red face and thickset figure, a typical country squire of the old school, and both his manners and his language were in accordance with tradition. His habits, especially as regards women, were also in accordance with tradition—the tradition of the bold, bad baronet which he undoubtedly was.

In comparison with him, Beresford was rather an ordinary man, a tall, dark, not unhandsome fellow of two-and-thirty, quiet and reserved. His father had left him a rich man, but idleness did not appeal to him, and he had a finger in a good many business pies.

Money attracts money. Graham Beresford had inherited it, he made it, and, inevitably, he had married it, too. The daughter of a late shipowner in Liverpool, with not far off half a million in her own right. But the money was incidental, for he needed her and would have married her just as inevitably (said his friends) if she had not had a farthing. A tall, rather serious-minded, highly cultured girl, not so young that her character had not had time to form (she was twenty-five when Beresford married her, three years ago), she was the ideal wife for him. A bit of a Puritan perhaps in some ways, but Beresford, whose wild oats, though duly sown, had been a sparse crop, was ready enough to be a Puritan himself by that time if she was. To make no bones about it, the Beresfords succeeded in achieving that eighth wonder of the modern world, a happy marriage.

And into the middle of it there dropped with irretrievable tragedy, the box of chocolates.

Beresford gave them to her after lunch as they sat over their coffee, with some jesting remark about paying his honourable debts, and she opened the box at once. The top layer, she noticed, seemed to consist only of kirsch and maraschino. Beresford, who did not believe in spoiling good coffee, refused when she offered him the box, and his wife ate the first one alone. As she did so she exclaimed in surprise that the filling seemed exceedingly strong and positively burnt her mouth.

Beresford explained that they were samples of a new brand and then, made curious by what his wife had said, took one too. A burning taste, not intolerable but much too strong to be pleasant, followed the release of the liquid, and the almond flavouring seemed quite excessive.

"By jove," he said, "they are strong. They must be filled with neat alcohol."

"Oh, they wouldn't do that, surely," said his wife, taking another. "But they are very strong. I think I rather like them, though."

Beresford ate another, and disliked it still more. "I don't," he said with decision. "They make my tongue feel quite numb. I shouldn't eat any more of them if I were you. I think there's something wrong with them."

"Well, they're only an experiment, I suppose," she said. "But they do burn. I'm not sure whether I like them or not."

A few minutes later Beresford went out to keep a business appointment in the City. He left her still trying to make up her mind whether she liked them, and still eating them to decide. Beresford remembered that scrap of conversation afterwards very vividly, because it was the last time he saw his wife alive.

That was roughly half-past two. At a quarter to four Beresford arrived at his club from the City in a taxi, in a state of collapse. He was helped into the building by the driver and the porter, and both described him subsequently as pale to the point of ghastliness, with staring eyes and livid lips, and his skin damp and clammy. His mind seemed unaffected, however, and when they had got him up the steps he was able to walk, with the porter's help, into the lounge.

The porter, thoroughly alarmed, wanted to send for a doctor at once, but Beresford, who was the last man in the world to make a fuss, refused to let him, saying that it must be indigestion and he would be all right in a few minutes. To Sir William Anstruther, however, who was in the lounge at the time, he added after the porter had gone:

"Yes, and I believe it was those infernal chocolates you gave me, now I come to think of it. I thought there was something funny about them at the time. I'd better go and find out if my wife——" He broke off abruptly. His body, which had been leaning back limply in his chair, suddenly heaved rigidly upright; his jaws locked together, the livid lips drawn back in a horrible grin, and his hands clenched on the arms of his chair. At the same time Sir William became aware of an unmistakable smell of bitter almonds.

Thoroughly alarmed, believing indeed that the man was dying under his eyes, Sir William raised a shout for the porter and a doctor. The other occupants of the lounge hurried up, and between them they got the convulsed body of the unconscious man into a more comfortable position. Before the doctor could arrive a telephone message was received at the club from an agitated butler asking if Mr. Beresford was there, and if so would he come home at once as Mrs. Beresford had been taken seriously ill. As a matter of fact she was already dead.

Beresford did not die. He had taken less of the poison than his wife, who after his departure must have eaten at least three more of the chocolates, so that its action was less rapid and the doctor had time to save him. As a matter of fact it turned out afterwards that he had not had a fatal dose. By about eight o'clock that night he was conscious; the next day he was practically convalescent.

As for the unfortunate Mrs. Beresford, the doctor had arrived too late to save her, and she passed away very rapidly in a deep coma.

The police had taken the matter in hand as soon as Mrs.

Beresford's death was reported to them and the fact of poison established, and it was only a very short time before things had become narrowed down to the chocolates as the active agent.

Sir William was interrogated, the letter and wrapper were recovered from the waste-paper basket, and, even before the sick man was out of danger, a detective-inspector was asking for an interview with the managing-director of Mason & Sons. Scotland Yard moves quickly.

It was the police theory at this stage, based on what Sir William and the two doctors had been able to tell them, that by an act of criminal carelessness on the part of one of Mason's employees, an excessive amount of oil of bitter almonds had been included in the filling mixture of the chocolates, for that was what the doctor had decided must be the poisoning ingredient. However, the managing-director quashed this idea at once: oil of bitter almonds, he asserted, was never used by Mason's.

He had more interesting news still. Having read with undisguised astonishment the covering letter, he at once declared that it was a forgery. No such letter, no such samples had been sent out by the firm at all; a new variety of liqueur-chocolates had never even been mooted.[1] The fatal chocolates were their ordinary brand.

Unwrapping and examining one more closely, he called the Inspector's attention to a mark on the underside, which he suggested was the remains of a small hole drilled in the case, through which the liquid could have been extracted and the fatal filling inserted, the hole afterwards being stopped up with softened chocolate, a perfectly simple operation.

He examined it under a magnifying-glass and the Inspector agreed. It was now clear to him that somebody had been trying deliberately to murder Sir William Anstruther.

Scotland Yard doubled its activities. The chocolates were sent for analysis, Sir William was interviewed again, and so was the now conscious Beresford. From the latter the doctor insisted that the news of his wife's death must be kept till the next day, as in his weakened condition the shock might be fatal, so that nothing very helpful was obtained from him.

Nor could Sir William throw any light on the mystery or produce a single person who might have any grounds for trying to

kill him. He was living apart from his wife, who was the principal
beneficiary in his will, but she was in the South of France, as the
French police subsequently confirmed. His estate in Worcester-
shire, heavily mortgaged, was entailed and went to a nephew; but
as the rent he got for it barely covered the interest on the
mortgage, and the nephew was considerably better off than Sir
William himself, there was no motive there. The police were at a
dead end.

The analysis brought one or two interesting facts to light. Not
oil of bitter almonds but nitrobenzine, a kindred substance, chiefly
used in the manufacture of aniline dyes, was the somewhat
surprising poison employed. Each chocolate in the upper layer
contained exactly six minims of it, in a mixture of kirsch and
maraschino. The chocolates in the other layers were harmless.

As to the other clues, they seemed equally useless. The sheet of
Mason's note paper was identified by Merton's, the printers, as of
their work, but there was nothing to show how it had got into the
murderer's possession. All that could be said was that, the edges
being distinctly yellowed, it must be an old piece. The machine on
which the letter had been typed, of course, could not be traced.
From the wrapper, a piece of ordinary brown paper with Sir
William's address hand-printed on it in large capitals, there was
nothing to be learnt at all beyond that the parcel had been posted
at the office in Southampton Street between the hours of 8:30 and
9:30 on the previous evening.

Only one thing was quite clear. Whoever had coveted Sir
William's life had no intention of paying for it with his or her own.

"And now you know as much as we do, Mr. Sheringham,"
concluded Chief-Inspector Moresby; "and if you can say who sent
those chocolates to Sir William, you'll know a good deal more."

Roger nodded thoughtfully.

"It's a brute of a case. I met a man only yesterday who was at
school with Beresford. He didn't know him very well because
Beresford was on the modern side and my friend was a classical
bird, but they were in the same house. He says Beresford's
absolutely knocked over by his wife's death. I wish you could find
out who sent those chocolates, Moresby."

"So do I, Mr. Sheringham," said Moresby gloomily.

"It might have been anyone in the whole world," Roger mused.

"What about feminine jealousy, for instance? Sir William's private life doesn't seem to be immaculate. I dare say there's a good deal of off with the old light-o'-love and on with the new."

"Why, that's just what I've been looking into, Mr. Sheringham, sir," retorted Chief-Inspector Moresby reproachfully. "That was the first thing that came to me. Because if anything does stand out about this business it is that it's a woman's crime. Nobody but a woman would send poisoned chocolates to a man. Another man would send a poisoned sample of whisky, or something like that."

"That's a very sound point, Moresby," Roger meditated. "Very sound indeed. And Sir William couldn't help you?"

"Couldn't," said Moresby, not without a trace of resentment, "or wouldn't. I was inclined to believe at first that he might have his suspicions and was shielding some woman. But I don't think so now."

"Humph!" Roger did not seem quite so sure. "It's reminiscent, this case, isn't it? Didn't some lunatic once send poisoned chocolates to the Commissioner of Police himself? A good crime always gets imitated, as you know."

Moresby brightened.

"It's funny you should say that, Mr. Sheringham, because that's the very conclusion I've come to. I've tested every other theory, and so far as I know there's not a soul with an interest in Sir William's death, whether from motives of gain, revenge, or what you like, whom I haven't had to rule quite out of it. In fact, I've pretty well made up my mind that the person who sent those chocolates was some irresponsible lunatic of a woman, a social or religious fanatic who's probably never even seen him. And if that's the case," Moresby sighed, "a fat chance I have of ever laying hands on her."

"Unless Chance steps in, as it so often does," said Roger brightly, "and helps you. A tremendous lot of cases get solved by a stroke of sheer luck, don't they? *Chance the Avenger.* It would make an excellent film-title. But there's a lot of truth in it. If I were superstitious, which I'm not, I should say it wasn't chance at all, but Providence avenging the victim."

"Well, Mr. Sheringham," said Moresby, who was not superstitious either, "to tell the truth, I don't mind what it is, so long as it lets me get my hands on the right person."

If Moresby had paid his visit to Roger Sheringham with any hope of tapping that gentleman's brains, he went away disappointed.

To tell the truth, Roger was inclined to agree with the Chief Inspector's conclusion, that the attempt on the life of Sir William Anstruther and the actual murder of the unfortunate Mrs. Beresford must be the work of some unknown criminal lunatic. For this reason, although he thought about it a good deal during the next few days, he made no attempt to take the case in hand. It was the sort of affair, necessitating endless inquiries that a private person would have neither the time nor the authority to carry out, which can be handled only by the official police. Roger's interest in it was purely academic.

It was hazard, a chance encounter nearly a week later, which translated this interest from the academic into the personal.

Roger was in Bond Street, about to go through the distressing ordeal of buying a new hat. Along the pavement he suddenly saw bearing down on him Mrs. Verreker-le-Flemming. Mrs. Verreker-le-Flemming was small, exquisite, rich, and a widow, and she sat at Roger's feet whenever he gave her the opportunity. But she talked. She talked, in fact, and talked, and talked. And Roger, who rather liked talking himself, could not bear it. He tried to dart across the road, but there was no opening in the traffic stream. He was cornered.

Mrs. Verreker-le-Flemming fastened on him gladly.

"Oh, Mr. Sheringham! *Just* the person I wanted to see. Mr. Sheringham, *do* tell me. In confidence. *Are* you taking up this dreadful business of poor Joan Beresford's death?"

Roger, the frozen and imbecile grin of civilised intercourse on his face, tried to get a word in; without result.

"I was horrified when I heard of it—simply horrified. You see, Joan and I were such *very* close friends. Quite intimate. And the awful thing, the truly *terrible* thing is that Joan brought the whole business on herself. Isn't that *appalling?*"

Roger no longer wanted to escape.

"What did you say?" he managed to insert incredulously.

"I suppose it's what they call tragic irony," Mrs. Verreker-le-Flemming chattered on. "Certainly it was tragic enough, and I've never heard anything so terribly ironical. You know about that bet she made with her husband, of course, so that he had to get her a box of chocolates, and if he hadn't Sir William would never have given him the poisoned ones and he'd have eaten them and died himself and good riddance? Well, Mr. Sheringham——" Mrs. Verreker-le-Flemming lowered her voice to a conspirator's whisper and glanced about her in the approved manner. "I've never told anybody else this, but I'm telling you because I know you'll appreciate it. *Joan wasn't playing fair!*"

"How do you mean?" Roger asked, bewildered.

Mrs. Verreker-le-Flemming was artlessly pleased with her sensation.

"Why, she'd seen the play before. We went together, the very first week it was on. She *knew* who the villain was all the time."

"By Jove!" Roger was as impressed as Mrs. Verreker-le-Flemming could have wished. "Chance the Avenger! We're none of us immune from it."

"Poetic justice, you mean?" twittered Mrs. Verreker-le-Flemming, to whom these remarks had been somewhat obscure. "Yes, but Joan Beresford of all people! That's the extraordinary thing. I should never had thought Joan *would* do a thing like that. She was such a *nice* girl. A little close with money, of course, considering how well-off they are, but that isn't anything. Of course it was only fun, and pulling her husband's leg, but I always used to think Joan was such a *serious girl*, Mr. Sheringham. I mean, ordinary people don't talk about honour, and truth, and playing the game, and all those things one takes for granted. But Joan did. She was always saying that this wasn't honourable, or that wouldn't be playing the game. Well, she paid herself for not playing the game, poor girl, didn't she? Still, it all goes to show the truth of the old saying, doesn't it?"

"What old saying?" said Roger, hypnotised by this flow.

"Why, that still waters run deep. Joan must have been deep, I'm afraid." Mrs. Verreker-le-Flemming sighed. It was evidently a social error to be deep. "I mean, she certainly took me in. She can't have been quite so honourable and truthful as she was always pretending, can she? And I can't help wondering whether a girl who'd deceive her husband in a little thing like that might not—oh, well, I don't want to say anything against poor Joan now she's dead, poor darling, but she can't have been *quite* such a plaster saint after all, can she? I mean," said Mrs. Verreker-le-Flemming, in hasty extenuation of these suggestions, "I do think psychology is so very interesting, don't you, Mr. Sheringham?"

"Sometimes, very," Roger agreed gravely. "But you mentioned Sir William Anstruther just now. Do you know him, too?"

"I used to," Mrs. Verreker-le-Flemming replied, without particular interest. "Horrible man! Always running after some woman or other. And when he's tired of her, just drops her—biff!—like that. At least," added Mrs. Verreker-le-Flemming somewhat hastily, "so I've heard."

"And what happens if she refuses to be dropped?"

"Oh dear, I'm sure I don't know. I suppose you've heard the latest?"

Mrs. Verreker-le-Flemming hurried on, perhaps a trifle more pink than the delicate aids to nature on her cheeks would have warranted.

"He's taken up with that Bryce woman now. You know, the wife of the oil man, or petrol, or whatever he made his money in. It began about three weeks ago. You'd have thought that dreadful business of being responsible, in a way, for poor Joan Beresford's death would have sobered him up a little, wouldn't you? But not a bit of it; he——"

Roger was following another line of thought.

"What a pity you weren't at the Imperial with the Beresfords that evening. She'd never have made that bet if you had been." Roger looked extremely innocent. "You weren't, I suppose?"

"I?" queried Mrs. Verreker-le-Flemming in surprise. "Good gracious, no. I was at the new revue at the Pavilion. Lady Gavelstoke had a box and asked me to join her party."

"Oh, yes. Good show, isn't it? I thought that sketch *The Sempiternal Triangle* very clever. Didn't you?"

"*The Sempiternal Triangle?*" wavered Mrs. Verreker-le-Flemming.

"Yes, in the first half."

"Oh! Then I didn't see it. I got there disgracefully late, I'm afraid. But then," said Mrs. Verreker-le-Flemming with pathos, "I always do seem to be late for simply everything."

Roger kept the rest of the conversation resolutely upon theatres. But before he left her he had ascertained that she had photographs of both Mrs. Beresford and Sir William Anstruther, and had obtained permission to borrow them some time. As soon as she was out of view he hailed a taxi and gave Mrs. Verreker-le-Flemming's address. He thought it better to take advantage of her permission at a time when he would not have to pay for it a second time over.

The parlourmaid seemed to think there was nothing odd in his mission, and took him up to the drawing-room at once. A corner of the room was devoted to the silver-framed photographs of Mrs. Verreker-le-Flemming's friends, and there were many of them. Roger examined them with interest, and finally took away with him not two photographs but six, those of Sir William, Mrs. Beresford, Beresford, two strange males who appeared to belong to the Sir William period, and, lastly, a likeness of Mrs. Verreker-le-Flemming herself. Roger liked confusing his trail.

For the rest of the day he was very busy.

His activities would have no doubt seemed to Mrs. Verreker-le-Flemming not merely baffling but pointless. He paid a visit to a public library, for instance, and consulted a work of reference, after which he took a taxi and drove to the offices of the Anglo-Eastern Perfumery Company, where he inquired for a certain Mr. Joseph Lea Hardwick and seemed much put out on hearing that no such gentleman was known to the firm and was certainly not employed in any of their branches. Many questions had to be put about the firm and its branches before he consented to abandon the quest.

After that he drove to Messrs. Weall and Wilson, the well-known institution which protects the trade interests of individuals and advises its subscribers regarding investments. Here he entered his name as a subscriber, and explaining that he had a large sum of money to invest, filled in one of the special enquiry-forms which are headed Strictly Confidential.

Then he went to the Rainbow Club, in Piccadilly.

Introducing himself to the porter without a blush as connected with Scotland Yard, he asked the man a number of questions, more or less trivial, concerning the tragedy.

"Sir William, I understand," he said finally, as if by the way, "did not dine here the evening before?"

There it appeared that Roger was wrong. Sir William had dined in the club, as he did about three times a week.

"But I quite understood he wasn't here that evening?" Roger said plaintively.

The porter was emphatic. He remembered quite well. So did a waiter, whom the porter summoned to corroborate him. Sir William had dined, rather late, and had not left the dining-room till about nine o'clock. He spent the evening there, too, the waiter knew, or at least some of it, for he himself had taken him a whisky-and-soda in the lounge not less than half an hour later.

Roger retired.

He retired to Merton's, in a taxi.

It seemed that he wanted some new notepaper printed, of a very special kind, and to the young woman behind the counter he specified at great length and in wearisome detail exactly what he did want. The young woman handed him the books of specimen pieces and asked him to see if there was any style there which would suit him. Roger glanced through them, remarking garrulously to the young woman that he had been recommended to Merton's by a very dear friend, whose photograph he happened to have on him at that moment. Wasn't that a curious coincidence? The young woman agreed that it was.

"About a fortnight ago, I think, my friend was in here last," said Roger, producing the photograph. "Recognise this?"

The young woman took the photograph, without apparent interest.

"Oh, yes. I remember. About some notepaper, too, wasn't it? So that's your friend. Well, it's a small world. Now this is a line we're selling a good deal of just now."

Roger went back to his rooms to dine. Afterwards, feeling restless, he wandered out of the Albany and turned up Piccadilly. He wandered round the Circus, thinking hard, and paused for a moment out of habit to inspect the photographs of the new revue hung outside the Pavilion. The next thing he realised was that he had got as far as Jermyn Street and was standing outside the Imperial Theatre. Glancing at the advertisements of *The Creaking Skull*, he saw that it began at half-past eight. Glancing at his watch, he saw that the time was twenty-nine minutes past the hour. He had an evening to get through somehow. He went inside.

The next morning, very early for Roger, he called on Moresby at Scotland Yard.

"Moresby," he said without preamble, "I want you to do something for me. Can you find me a taximan who took a fare from Piccadilly Circus or its neighbourhood at about ten past nine on the evening before the Beresford crime, to the Strand somewhere near the bottom of Southampton Street, and another who took a fare back between those points. I'm not sure about the first. Or one taxi might have been used for the double journey, but I doubt that. Anyhow, try to find out for me, will you?"

"What are you up to now, Mr. Sheringham?" Moresby asked suspiciously.

"Breaking down an interesting alibi," replied Roger serenely. "By the way, I know who sent those chocolates to Sir William. I'm just building up a nice structure of evidence for you. Ring up my rooms when you've got those taximen."

He strolled out, leaving Moresby positively gaping after him.

The rest of the day he spent apparently trying to buy a second-hand typewriter. He was very particular that it should be a Hamilton No. 4. When the shop-people tried to induce him to consider other makes he refused to look at them, saying that he had had the Hamilton No. 4 so strongly recommended to him by a friend who had bought one about three weeks ago. Perhaps it was at this very shop? No? They hadn't sold a Hamilton No. 4 for the last three months? How odd.

But at one shop they had sold a Hamilton No. 4 within the last month, and that was odder still.

At half-past four Roger got back to his rooms to await the telephone message from Moresby. At half-past five it came.

"There are fourteen taxi-drivers here, littering up my office," said Moresby offensively. "What do you want me to do with 'em?"

"Keep them till I come, Chief Inspector," returned Roger with dignity.

The interview with the fourteen was brief enough, however. To each man in turn Roger showed a photograph, holding it so that Moresby could not see it, and asked if he could recognise his fare. The ninth man did so, without hesitation.

At a nod from Roger, Moresby dismissed them, then sat at his table and tried to look official. Roger seated himself on the table, looking most unofficial, and swung his legs. As he did so, a photograph fell unnoticed out of his pocket and fluttered, face downwards, under the table. Moresby eyed it but did not pick it up.

"And now, Mr. Sheringham, sir," he said, "perhaps you'll tell me what you've been doing?"

"Certainly, Moresby," said Roger blandly. "Your work for you. I really have solved the thing, you know. Here's your evidence." He took from his note-case an old letter and handed it to the Chief Inspector. "Was that typed on the same machine as the forged letter from Mason's, or was it not?"

Moresby studied it for a moment, then drew the forged letter from a drawer of his table and compared the two minutely.

"Mr. Sheringham," he said soberly, "where did you get hold of this?"

"In a second-hand typewriter shop in St. Martin's Lane. The machine was sold to an unknown customer about a month ago. They identified the customer from that same photograph. As it happened, this machine had been used for a time in the office after it was repaired, to see that it was O.K., and I easily got hold of that specimen of its work."

"And where is the machine now?"

"Oh, at the bottom of the Thames, I expect," Roger smiled. "I tell you, this criminal takes no unnecessary chances. But that doesn't matter. There's your evidence."

"Humph! It's all right so far as it goes," conceded Moresby. "But what about Mason's paper?"

"That," said Roger calmly, "was extracted from Merton's book of sample notepapers, as I'd guessed from the very yellowed edges might be the case. I can prove contact of the criminal with the book, and there is a gap which will certainly turn out to have been filled by that piece of paper."

"That's fine," Moresby said more heartily.

"As for the taximan, the criminal had an alibi. You've heard it broken down. Between ten past nine and twenty-five past, in fact during the time when the parcel must have been posted, the murderer took a hurried journey to that neighbourhood, going probably by 'bus or Underground, but returning, as I expected, by taxi, because time would be getting short."

"And the murderer, Mr. Sheringham?"

"The person whose photograph is in my pocket," Roger said unkindly. "By the way, do you remember what I was saying the other day about Chance the Avenger, my excellent film-title? Well, it's worked again. By a chance meeting in Bond Street with a silly woman I was put, by the merest accident, in possession of a piece of information which showed me then and there who had sent those chocolates addressed to Sir William. There were other possibilities, of course, and I tested them, but then and there on the pavement I saw the whole thing, from first to last."

"Who was the murderer, then, Mr. Sheringham?" repeated Moresby.

"It was so beautifully planned," Roger went on dreamily. "We never grasped for one moment that we were making the fundamental mistake that the murderer all along intended us to make."

"And what was that?" asked Moresby.

"Why, that the plan had miscarried. That the wrong person had been killed. That was just the beauty of it. The plan had *not* miscarried. It had been brilliantly successful. The wrong person was *not* killed. Very much the right person was."

Moresby gasped.

"Why, how on earth do you make that out, sir?"

"Mrs. Beresford was the objective all the time. That's why the plot was so ingenious. Everything was anticipated. It was perfectly natural that Sir William should hand the chocolates over to Beresford. It was foreseen that we should look for the criminal among Sir William's associates and not the dead woman's. It was probably even foreseen that the crime would be considered the work of a woman!"

Moresby, unable to wait any longer, snatched up the photograph.

"Good heavens! But Mr. Sheringham, you don't mean to tell me that . . . Sir William himself!"

"He wanted to get rid of Mrs. Beresford," Roger continued.

"He had liked her well enough at the beginning, no doubt, though it was her money he was after all the time.

"But the real trouble was that she was too close with her money. He wanted it, or some of it, pretty badly; and she wouldn't part. There's no doubt about the motive. I made a list of the firms he's interested in and got a report on them. They're all rocky, every one. He'd got through all his own money, and he had to get more.

"As for the nitrobenzine which puzzled us so much, that was simple enough. I looked it up and found that beside the uses you told me, it's used largely in perfumery. And he's got a perfumery business. The Anglo-Eastern Perfumery Company. That's how he'd know about it being poisonous, of course. But I shouldn't think he got his supply from there. He'd be cleverer than that. He probably made the stuff himself. Any schoolboy knows how to treat benzol with nitric acid to get nitrobenzine."

"But," stammered Moresby, "But Sir William . . . He was at Eton."

"Sir William?" said Roger sharply. "Who's talking about Sir William? I told you the photograph of the murderer was in my pocket." He whipped out the photograph in question and confronted the astounded Chief Inspector with it. "Beresford, man! Beresford's the murderer of his own wife.

"Beresford, who still had hankerings after a gay life," he went on more mildly, "didn't want his wife but did want her money. He contrived this plot, providing as he thought against every contingency that could possibly arise. He established a mild alibi, if suspicion ever should arise, by taking his wife to the Imperial, and slipped out of the theatre at the first interval. (I sat through the first act of the dreadful thing myself last night to see when the interval came.) Then he hurried down to the Strand, posted his parcel, and took a taxi back. He had ten minutes, but nobody would notice if he got back to the box a minute late.

"And the rest simply followed. He knew Sir William came to the club every morning at ten-thirty, as regularly as clockwork; he knew that for a psychological certainty he could get the chocolates handed over to him if he hinted for them; he knew that the police would go chasing after all sorts of false trails starting from

Sir William. And as for the wrapper and the forged letter, he carefully didn't destroy them because they were calculated not only to divert suspicion but actually to point away from him to some anonymous lunatic."

"Well, it's very smart of you, Mr. Sheringham," Moresby said, with a little sigh, but quite ungrudgingly. "Very smart indeed. What was it the lady told you that showed you the whole thing in a flash?"

"Why, it wasn't so much what she actually told me as what I heard between her words, so to speak. What she told me was that Mrs. Beresford knew the answer to that bet; what I deduced was that, being the sort of person she was, it was quite incredible that she should have made a bet to which she knew the answer. *Ergo*, she didn't. *Ergo*, there never was such a bet. *Ergo*, Beresford was lying. *Ergo*, Beresford wanted to get hold of those chocolates for some reason other than he stated. After all, we only had Beresford's word for the bet, hadn't we?

"Of course he wouldn't have left her that afternoon till he'd seen her take, or somehow made her take, at least six of the chocolates, more than a lethal dose. That's why the stuff was in those meticulous six-minim doses. And so that he could take a couple himself, of course. A clever stroke, that."

Moresby rose to his feet.

"Well, Mr. Sheringham, I'm much obliged to you, sir. And now I shall have to get busy myself." He scratched his head. "Chance the Avenger, eh? Well, I can tell you one pretty big thing Beresford left to Chance the Avenger, Mr. Sheringham. Suppose Sir William hadn't handed over the chocolates after all? Supposing he'd kept 'em, to give to one of his own ladies?"

Roger positively snorted. He felt a personal pride in Beresford by this time.

"Really, Moresby! It wouldn't have had any serious results if Sir William had. Do give my man credit for being what he is. You don't imagine he sent the poisoned ones to Sir William, do you? Of course not! He'd send harmless ones, and exchange them for the others on his way home. Dash it all, he wouldn't go right out of his way to present opportunities to Chance.

"If," added Roger, "Chance really is the right word."

COMMENT AND QUESTIONS

Crime fiction writers have the difficulty, if they are conscientious, of dealing with the fact that the most likely murderer suspects are those closest to the victims. An imaginative method of murder misdirects the reader's attention from the obvious suspect in "The Avenging Chance," but the story does suggest that, if familiarity breeds contempt, union (in marriage, business, or family) may breed hatred and, finally, murder. It may be that Graham Beresford does not murder his wife simply out of greed but rather from a sense of desperation at being mismatched with a person by whom he is constantly being misunderstood or frustrated. Consider whether Joan Beresford was in any way the "perfect" wife for Graham Beresford. What sort of attitudes on the part of their acquaintances might have led to this assumption?

What does the title of the story mean? What does the title suggest about the attitude of the author?

As is often the case in detective fiction, the reader must imaginatively supply or *infer* from the clues the motive for the crime, and he must correctly reinterpret the information that is given. Are there enough clues in this story to allow the reader to arrive at the right solution?

Does the potential murderer make a correct assessment of Sir William Anstruther? Compare this "psychology" to that practiced by Dupin.

NOTES

1. *mooted.* Dug up, unearthed.

EDMUND CRISPIN

The Crime by the River

Now it's your turn! Here is a short and concise murder mystery that plays fair with the reader. The conclusion of the story is omitted to give you a chance to match wits with the author. Read the story carefully and try to identify the murderer if you can. You will find the final portion of the story, containing the solution, on page 447.

N o, the housekeeper said, she was sorry, but the Chief Constable still wasn't back from London. He ought to be arriving any time now, though, so if the Superintendent would care to wait . . . The Superintendent said that he would wait in the garden.

But it was the farmhouse across the river, rather than the gentle air of the October evening, which made him decide to stay out of doors.

At first he was resolute in ignoring its summons. Then, as time wore on, his determination weakened. And presently (as in his heart of hearts he had known must happen in the end) he found himself crossing the leaf-strewn front lawn, found himself halted by the bedraggled hedge at the far side and staring over the stream at the out-building where Elsie the servant girl had kept her last assignation—death by strangling.

Across the river, a figure, unidentifiable in the failing light, emerged from the stables, then trudged through the yard. It was Wregson, obviously: Wregson the retired Indian Civil Servant,

Wregson the tenant of the farmhouse, Wregson the widower, Wregson the pathetic, Wregson the bore; Wregson who had no doubt been fussing in the stables over the horse he had bought that morning . . .

Glumly the Superintendent watched him until he disappeared from view. In a few weeks' time the Superintendent, too, would be retiring.

I'll be glad to be done with it, he said to himself now; *my God, yes, I'll be glad to get away from it all.*

The sound of a car roused him, and he returned to the house. "Here we are, sir," he said with a cheerfulness he was far from feeling, as he helped the Chief Constable out of the driver's seat. "Conference go off all right?"

"Hello, Tom." The Chief Constable was thin and old, and his complexion looked bleached. "The conference? Oh, the usual thing, you know: too many speeches and too few resolutions. Ruddy awful hotel, too."

"What time did you leave town?"

"Two o'clock."

"Well, that's not bad going . . . I've had a packet this afternoon, sir. Do you want a bath or a meal or something first, or shall I—"

"No, I'd rather stretch my legs. Let's stroll down to the river."

At first they walked in silence—the companionable silence of men who have worked together amicably for many years. Then, as they came in sight of the farmhouse on the opposite bank, the Superintendent nodded toward it and spoke.

"That's where it happened, sir—almost on your own doorstep, really. It's the servant girl, Elsie. Throttled in an out-building some time this afternoon."

The Chief Constable took his time about assimilating this. Presently he nodded. "Yes, I've only visited Wregson twice," he said. "Mostly it's been the other way about. But I think I remember seeing the girl."

"I daresay she was striking enough." But the Superintendent spoke from inference only: it was a stiff and staring thing, a purple-tongued horror, that he had actually seen. "It wasn't a premeditated job, sir, as far as I can make out. Just someone in a sudden passion. And I had it from Dr. Hands that the girl came to him a couple of weeks ago for a pregnancy test: result positive. You can see what that points to."

"Yes." The Chief Constable's head was hunched down between his shoulders as he stared in front of him into the gathering dusk. "A very well-worn track, that one . . . Has Wregson still got his nephew staying with him?"

"Yes, he's still there." A flabby, fluttering young man, the Superintendent had thought, like the furry, overblown kind of moth. "He and Wregson are the prime suspects, obviously." For a moment his voice trailed away; then, with something of an effort: "Seeing that they were neighbors of yours, sir, I didn't—"

"My dear chap, they may be neighbors, but they certainly aren't friends. No, you mustn't let that worry you. But of course, I'm interested to know how things stand."

"Well, sir," said the Superintendent, perceptibly relieved, "briefly, it's like this. Dr. Hands says the thing happened between one and three P.M., approximately. The body was found by Wregson at about five. They'd had an early lunch, which the girl served, and after that neither of the men set eyes on her—so they say. From lunch onward the nephew says he was alone in his room, working. About two o'clock Wregson rode over here to look you up, hoping you'd be back—"

"So he's bought himself a horse at last, has he? He's been talking about it for long enough . . . Yes, sorry, Tom. Go on."

"Well, he didn't find you, of course, so he rode back again and arrived home about a quarter to three. From then on he didn't see the nephew, and the nephew didn't see him—so they say."

The Chief Constable took his time about this, too. It was a trait, the Superintendent reflected, which had been increasingly in evidence since his wife's sudden and tragic death two years before. And God knows, living alone in this great barn of a house with no one but an aging servant for company—

But by the time the Superintendent reached this stage in his meditations the Chief Constable was functioning again. "Any fingerprints?" he asked.

"Only Wregson's and the girl's and the nephew's so far—what you'd expect. But then, if it was an outsider who did it, he wouldn't have needed to leave any prints. All he'd have to do, if the girl was waiting for him in the out-building, would be to go through an open gate and an open door, and there he'd be. As to footmarks—well, the ground's as hard as brass."

They had reached the river bank and were standing beside a tree half of whose roots had been laid bare by the water's steady erosion. Midges hovered above their heads. On the far bank the dinghy in which Wregson had been accustomed to scull himself across on his visits to the Chief Constable bumped lazily against its mooring post, and in the kitchen window of the farmhouse a light went on . . .

"Not an easy one, no," the Chief Constable was saying. "You'll be finding out about Elsie's boy friends, of course, and I suppose that until you've done that you won't be wanting to commit yourself."

He looked up sharply when there was no reply and saw that the Superintendent was staring out over the water with eyes that had gone suddenly blank. "Tom! I was saying that I imagined . . ."

But it was a long while before he was answered. And when at last the answer came, it was in the voice of a stranger.

"But you're wrong, sir," said the Superintendent dully. "I know who did it, all right."

Fractionally he hesitated; then: "I tell you frankly," he went on with more vigor, "that I haven't got anything that would stand up in court. It's like the Rogers case, as far as that goes . . . It's like the Rogers case in more ways than one."

The Chief Constable nodded. "I remember . . ."

W. H. AUDEN

The Guilty Vicarage

W. H. Auden was one of the most distinguished poets of the twentieth century, and he also wrote occasional critical essays. It was his fondness for detective fiction that moved him to analyze this popular literary form. The following excerpt from his essay "The Guilty Vicarage" preserves his provocative comments on the construction and components of the detective story and his thoughtful comparison of detective fiction with Greek tragedy.

Definition

The vulgar definition, "a Whodunit," is correct. The basic formula is this: a murder occurs; many are suspected; all but one suspect, who is the murderer, are eliminated; the murderer is arrested or dies. . . .

As in the Aristotelian description of tragedy, there is Concealment (the innocent seem guilty and the guilty seem innocent) and Manifestation (the real guilt is brought to consciousness). There is also peripeteia, in this case not a reversal of fortune but a double reversal from apparent guilt to innocence and from apparent innocence to guilt. The formula may be diagrammed as follows.

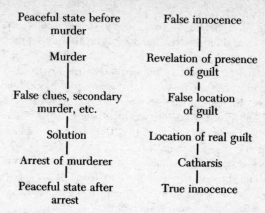

Peaceful state before murder
|
Murder
|
False clues, secondary murder, etc.
|
Solution
|
Arrest of murderer
|
Peaceful state after arrest

False innocence
|
Revelation of presence of guilt
|
False location of guilt
|
Location of real guilt
|
Catharsis
|
True innocence

In Greek tragedy the audience knows the truth; the actors do not, but discover or bring to pass the inevitable. In modern, *e.g.*, Elizabethan, tragedy the audience knows neither less nor more than the most knowing of the actors. In the detective story the audience does not know the truth at all; one of the actors—the murderer—does; and the detective, of his own free will, discovers and reveals what the murderer, of his own free will, tries to conceal.

Greek tragedy and the detective story have one characteristic in common, in which they both differ from modern tragedy, namely, the characters are not changed in or by their actions: in Greek tragedy because their actions are fated, in the detective story because the decisive event, the murder, has already occurred. Time and space therefore are simply the when and where of revealing either what has to happen or what has actually happened. In consequence, the detective story probably should, and usually does, obey the classical unities, whereas modern tragedy in which the characters develop with time can only do so by a technical tour de force; and the thriller, like the picaresque novel, even demands frequent changes of time and place. . . . The detective story has five elements—the milieu, the victim, the murderer, the suspects, the detectives.

The Milieu (Human)

The detective story requires:

(1) A closed society so that the possibility of an outside

murderer (and hence of the society being totally innocent) is excluded; and a closely related society so that all its members are potentially suspect (*cf.* the thriller, which requires an open society in which any stranger may be a friend or enemy in disguise).

Such conditions are met by: (a) the group of blood relatives (the Christmas dinner in the country house); (b) the closely knit geographical group (the old world village); (c) the occupational group (the theatrical company); (d) the group isolated by the neutral place (the Pullman car).

In this last type the concealment-manifestation formula applies not only to the murder but also to the relations between the members of the group who first appear to be strangers to each other, but are later found to be related.

(2) It must appear to be an innocent society in a state of grace, *i.e.*, a society where there is no need of the law, no contradiction between the aesthetic individual and the ethical universal, and where murder, therefore, is the unheard-of act which precipitates a crisis (for it reveals that some member has fallen and is no longer in a state of grace). The law becomes a reality and for a time all must live in its shadow, till the fallen one is identified. With his arrest, innocence is restored, and the law retires forever.

The characters in a detective story should, therefore, be eccentric (aesthetically interesting individuals) and good (instinctively ethical)—good, that is, either in appearance, later shown to be false, or in reality, first concealed by an appearance of bad. . . .

The Milieu (Natural)

In the detective story, as in its mirror image, the Quest for the Grail, maps (the ritual of space) and timetables (the ritual of time) are desirable. Nature should reflect its human inhabitants, *i.e.*, it should be the Great Good Place; for the more Eden-like it is, the greater the contradiction of murder. The country is preferable to the town, a well-to-do neighborhood (but not too well-to-do—or there will be a suspicion of ill-gotten gains) better than a slum. The corpse must shock not only because it is a corpse but also because, even for a corpse, it is shockingly out of place, as when a dog makes a mess on a drawing room carpet.

Mr. Raymond Chandler has written that he intends to take the body out of the vicarage garden and give murder back to those who are good at it. If he wishes to write detective stories, *i.e.*, stories where the reader's principal interest is to learn who did it, he could not be more mistaken; for in a society of professional criminals, the only possible motives for desiring to identify the murderer are blackmail or revenge, which both apply to individuals, not to the group as a whole, and can equally well inspire murder. Actually, whatever he may say, I think Mr. Chandler is interested in writing, not detective stories, but serious studies of a criminal milieu, the Great Wrong Place, and his powerful but extremely depressing books should be read and judged, not as escape literature, but as works of art.

The Victim

The victim has to try to satisfy two contradictory requirements. He has to involve everyone in suspicion, which requires that he be a bad character; and he has to make everyone feel guilty, which requires that he be a good character. . . .

The Murderer

Murder is negative creation, and every murderer is therefore the rebel who claims the right to be omnipotent. His pathos is his refusal to suffer. The problem for the writer is to conceal his demonic pride from the other characters and from the reader, since, if a person has this pride, it tends to appear in everything he does and says. To surprise the reader when the identity of the murderer is revealed, yet at the same time to convince him that everything that has previously been said about the murderer is consistent with his being a murderer, is the test of a good detective story. . . .

The Suspects

The detective-story society is a society consisting of apparently innocent individuals. . . .
. . . The suspects must be guilty of something, because, now that the aesthetic and the ethical are in opposition, if they are

completely innocent (obedient to the ethical) they lose their aesthetic interest and the reader will ignore them.

For suspects, the principal causes of guilt are:

(1) the wish or even the intention to murder;

(2) crimes of Class A or vices of Class C (e.g., illicit amours) which the suspect is afraid or ashamed to reveal;

(3) a *hubris* of intellect which tries to solve the crime itself and despises the official police (assertion of the supremacy of the aesthetic over the ethical). If great enough, this *hubris* leads to its subject getting murdered;

(4) a *hubris* of innocence which refuses to co-operate with the investigation;

(5) a lack of faith in another loved suspect, which leads its subject to hide or confuse clues.

The Detective

Completely satisfactory detectives are extremely rare. Indeed, I only know of three: Sherlock Holmes (Conan Doyle), Inspector French (Freeman Wills Crofts), and Father Brown (Chesterton).

The job of the detective is to restore the state of grace in which the aesthetic and the ethical are as one. . . .

Sherlock Holmes

Holmes is the exceptional individual who is in a state of grace because he is a genius in whom scientific curiosity is raised to the status of a heroic passion. He is erudite but his knowledge is absolutely specialized (e.g., his ignorance of the Copernican system); he is in all matters outside his field as helpless as a child (e.g., his untidiness), and he pays the price for his scientific detachment (his neglect of feeling) by being the victim of melancholia which attacks him whenever he is unoccupied with a case (e.g., his violin playing and cocaine taking).

His motive for being a detective is, positively, a love of the neutral truth (he has no interest in the feelings of the guilty or the innocent), and, negatively, a need to escape from his own feelings of melancholy. His attitude toward people and his technique of observation and deduction are those of the chemist or physicist. If he chooses human beings rather than inanimate matter as his material, it is because investigating the inanimate is unheroically easy since it cannot tell lies, which human beings can and do, so that in dealing with them, observation must be twice as sharp and logic twice as rigorous. . . .

[The comments on Inspector French and Father Brown are omitted.]

The Reader

The most curious fact about the detective story is that it makes its greatest appeal precisely to those classes of people who are most immune to other forms of daydream literature. The typical detective story addict is a doctor or clergyman or scientist or artist, *i.e.*, a fairly successful professional man with intellectual interests and well-read in his own field, who could never stomach the *Saturday Evening Post* or *True Confessions* or movie magazines or comics. . . .

The phantasy, then, which the detective story addict indulges is the phantasy of being restored to the Garden of Eden, to a state of innocence, where he may know love as love and not as the law. The driving force behind this daydream is the feeling of guilt, the cause of which is unknown to the dreamer. The phantasy of escape is the same, whether one explains the guilt in Christian, Freudian, or any other terms. One's way of trying to face the reality, on the other hand, will, of course, depend very much on one's creed. . . .

COMMENT AND QUESTIONS

While Greek tragedies were popular art forms in the culture that produced them, it has usually been the view in the twentieth century that what we call "art" is not popular and that what is "popular" cannot be art. Mr. Auden might agree with such a view, for (in a part of the essay that has been omitted) he comments that he is convinced that "detective stories have nothing to do with works of art." Yet he proceeds to compare the structure of the detective story to that of Greek tragedy. This would indicate to some readers that if the structure of a work is an aspect of its art, then there is "art" in detective fiction. Auden also states in the essay that Holmes "is a genius in whom scientific curiosity is raised to the status of a heroic passion," and he describes the reader of detective fiction as "a fairly successful professional man with intellectual interests and well-read in his own field." Thus, even if the detective story is not "art" to Auden, it is the product of skilled craftsmen capable of creating heroes and appealing to educated men.

According to Auden, what human needs does the reading of detective stories seem to satisfy? In what sense does a traditional detective story restore the reader to the Garden of Eden?

Auden states that the Quest for the Grail is the mirror image of the detective story. What is the Grail he speaks of? In what ways could it be compared with the objects of a detective's search?

What effect is produced by Auden's referring to himself and other readers of detective fiction as addicts?

2

New Developments: The Hardboiled School and After

The stories in the second section of this book illustrate the diversity of mystery stories written since the Golden Age of mystery fiction. The classic detective story, although it continued to be written, was soon rivaled in popularity by the hardboiled detective story—a form related to its predecessor but which had its own distinctive characteristics. In addition, variations and combinations of both forms flourished.

Even writers of classic detective stories, as can be observed from the readings in Part 1, rarely followed the "rules" completely and scrupulously. Some of the best stories by the best writers violated one, if not more, of the rules. Near the close of the Golden Age, Dorothy Sayers astutely predicted that the detective story "has probably many years to go yet, and in the meantime a new and less rigid formula will probably have developed. . . ." And that is what actually happened. This new form, like the classic one, originated in America. Even as one author in New York (S. S. Van Dine) was formulating "rules," another author in California (Dashiell Hammett) was breaking just enough of them to produce a new kind of detective story and thereby helping to inaugurate and establish what has come to be known as hardboiled detective fiction.

The new detective hero (sometimes called the private eye), though strong, shrewd, and competent, and a superior being in the world in which he moves, is not quite so transcendent and infallible as his counterpart in the classic story. The violence of the criminal world may be directed against him, and he may suffer personally in his attempt to discover the truth. Often in the hardboiled story the detective must seek his quarry in a large group of suspects rather than in a small closed circle. The wisecracks of the characters in hardboiled detective fiction are typically more irreverent, more spontaneous, and often more self-deprecatory than the humorous observations of characters in the classic detective story. There is a tough but mirthful cynicism in the best hardboiled detective stories, deriving partly from the slangy, colloquial language and partly from the detective's cool, brisk movement through a landscape littered with bodies and blondes.

Modern variations on the classic form of detective story are still being successfully written by both American and English authors. "A Lump of Sugar," which is included in this section, is such a one. This story meticulously observes the tradition of playing fair with the reader; the emphasis is on the logical analysis of a problem, with a maximum of intellectual activity, a minimum of physical exertion, and no violence beyond that of the initial criminal act. A half-serious comment made by Ellery Queen, the author, illustrates his view of the kind of story he writes as compared to the modern hardboiled detective story: "The so-called tough writers are all for love: they combine sex and sleuthery until you usually can't tell one from the other; or where one leaves off and the other begins. The more sedate school—call us soft-boiled, if you wish—are not prudes; nevertheless, we are forced to skirt the problem with almost puritanical delicacy."

Another modern variation of the detective story has a policeman as its central figure. The records, data, and scientific equipment available to him, plus his official status, make his method different from that of the private investigator. The vast organization of information-gatherers who aid the policeman gives him an advantage over the criminal that the private detective does not enjoy; but his identification with an official body robs him of some of his freedom and may reduce him to a man who hunts down lawbreakers simply because that is his job. "Journey Backward into Time," in which Inspector Maigret of the Paris police is the detective, is consistent with most of the conventions of the classic detective story. In addition, it includes a sordid setting, a particularly cruel crime, and a detective who faces this rather bleak scene with grim humor and determination, qualities that are shared with hardboiled detective fiction.

Clearly, the richness of the present age in mystery fiction derives largely from the development of the hardboiled detective story, its many variations, and the combination of this new form with the classic detective story.

DASHIELL HAMMETT

The Gutting of Couffignal

Dashiell Hammett attained popularity just before 1930, the same time that Ernest Hemingway was beginning to be widely read. Both men wrote with a style remarkable for its direct statement and its spare use of adjectives. But Hammett seems to have perfected his style with no other influence than the editorial demands of *Black Mask*, the pulp magazine in which most of his early stories were published. He combined his simple, fast-moving narrative style with an ironic, irreverent wit and subject matter consisting of a detective's adventures with gangsters, confidence men, and their victims in a violent, post-depression society. The novels and stories that resulted are classified today as hardboiled detective fiction. While Hammett was not the sole founder of the hardboiled school of detection, he gave it its most meaningful attributes and a wider and continuing popularity.

Since Hammett was a Pinkerton detective for eight years before he turned to writing, his accounts of the adventures of a private eye might be expected to have the ring of authenticity. However, a reader familiar with his writing will recognize that only a small part of its appeal ultimately derives from that actual experience. He was a careful writer, perhaps as fond of the humor in his "tough" characters' views of life as of their daring deeds. His most famous detectives are Sam Spade of *The Maltese Falcon* and Nick and Nora Charles of *The Thin Man*, but the Continental Op of this selection is an even greater favorite of many readers.

Wedge-shaped Couffignal is not a large island, and not far from the mainland, to which it is linked by a wooden bridge. Its western shore is a high, straight cliff that jumps abruptly up out of San Pablo Bay. From the top of this cliff the island slopes eastward, down to a smooth pebble beach that runs into the water again, where there are piers and a clubhouse and moored pleasure boats.

Couffignal's main street, paralleling the beach, has the usual bank, hotel, moving-picture theater, and stores. But it differs from most main streets of its size in that it is more carefully arranged and preserved. There are trees and hedges and strips of lawn on it, and no glaring signs. The buildings seem to belong beside one another, as if they had been designed by the same architect, and in the stores you will find goods of a quality to match the best city stores.

The intersecting streets—running between rows of neat cottages near the foot of the slope—become winding hedged roads as they climb toward the cliff. The higher these roads get, the farther apart and larger are the houses they lead to. The occupants of these higher houses are the owners and rulers of the island. Most of them are well-fed old gentlemen who, the profits they took from the world with both hands in their younger days now stowed away at safe percentages, have bought into the island colony so they may spend what is left of their lives nursing their livers and improving their golf among their kind. They admit to the island only as many storekeepers, working people, and similar riffraff as are needed to keep them comfortably served.

That is Couffignal.

It was some time after midnight. I was sitting in a second-story room in Couffignal's largest house, surrounded by wedding presents whose value would add up to something between fifty and a hundred thousand dollars.

Of all the work that comes to a private detective (except divorce work, which the Continental Detective Agency doesn't handle) I like weddings as little as any. Usually I manage to avoid them, but this time I hadn't been able to. Dick Foley, who had been slated for the job, had been handed a black eye by an unfriendly pickpocket the day before. That let Dick out and me in. I had come up to Couffignal—a two-hour ride from San Francisco by ferry and auto stage—that morning, and would return the next.

This had been neither better nor worse than the usual wedding detail. The ceremony had been performed in a little stone church down the hill. Then the house had begun to fill with reception guests. They had kept it filled to overflowing until some time after the bride and groom had sneaked off to their eastern train.

The world had been well represented. There had been an admiral and an earl or two from England; an ex-president of a South American country; a Danish baron; a tall young Russian princess surrounded by lesser titles, including a fat, bald, jovial and black-bearded Russian general, who had talked to me for a solid hour about prize fights, in which he had a lot of interest, but not so much knowledge as was possible; an ambassador from one of the Central European countries; a justice of the Supreme Court; and a mob of people whose prominence and near-prominence didn't carry labels.

In theory, a detective guarding wedding presents is supposed to make himself indistinguishable from the other guests. In practice, it never works out that way. He has to spend most of his time within sight of the booty, so he's easily spotted. Besides that, eight or ten people I recognized among the guests were clients or former clients of the Agency, and so knew me. However, being known doesn't make so much difference as you might think, and everything had gone off smoothly.

A couple of the groom's friends, warmed by wine and the necessity of maintaining their reputations as cutups, had tried to smuggle some of the gifts out of the room where they were displayed and hide them in the piano. But I had been expecting that familiar trick, and blocked it before it had gone far enough to embarrass anybody.

Shortly after dark a wind smelling of rain began to pile storm clouds up over the bay. Those guests who lived at a distance, especially those who had water to cross, hurried off for their homes. Those who lived on the island stayed until the first raindrops began to patter down. Then they left.

The Hendrixson house quieted down. Musicians and extra servants left. The weary house servants began to disappear in the direction of their bedrooms. I found some sandwiches, a couple of books and a comfortable armchair, and took them up to the room where the presents were now hidden under gray-white sheeting.

Keith Hendrixson, the bride's grandfather—she was an orphan —put his head in at the door. "Have you everything you need for your comfort?" he asked.

"Yes, thanks."

He said good night and went off to bed—a tall old man, slim as a boy.

The wind and the rain were hard at it when I went downstairs to give the lower windows and doors the up-and-down. Everything on the first floor was tight and secure, everything in the cellar. I went upstairs again.

Pulling my chair over by a floor lamp, I put sandwiches, books, ashtray, gun and flashlight on a small table beside it. Then I switched off the other lights, set fire to a Fatima, sat down, wriggled my spine comfortably into the chair's padding, picked up one of the books, and prepared to make a night of it.

The book was called *The Lord of the Sea*, and had to do with a strong, tough and violent fellow named Hogarth, whose modest plan was to hold the world in one hand. There were plots and counterplots, kidnapings, murders, prisonbreakings, forgeries and burglaries, diamonds large as hats and floating forts larger than Couffignal. It sounds dizzy here, but in the book it was as real as a dime.

Hogarth was still going strong when the lights went out.

In the dark, I got rid of the glowing end of my cigarette by grinding it in one of the sandwiches. Putting the book down, I picked up gun and flashlight, and moved away from the chair.

Listening for noises was no good. The storm was making hundreds of them. What I needed to know was why the lights had gone off. All the other lights in the house had been turned off some time ago. So the darkness of the hall told me nothing.

I waited. My job was to watch the presents. Nobody had touched them yet. There was nothing to get excited about.

Minutes went by, perhaps ten of them.

The floor swayed under my feet. The windows rattled with a violence beyond the strength of the storm. The dull boom of a heavy explosion blotted out the sounds of wind and falling water. The blast was not close at hand, but not far enough away to be off the island.

Crossing to the window, peering through the wet glass, I could see nothing. I should have seen a few misty lights far down the hill. Not being able to see them settled one point. The lights had gone out all over Couffignal, not only in the Hendrixson house.

That was better. The storm could have put the lighting system out of whack, could have been responsible for the explosion—maybe.

Staring through the black window, I had an impression of great excitement down the hill, of movement in the night. But all was too far away for me to have seen or heard even had there been lights, and all too vague to say what was moving. The impression was strong but worthless. It didn't lead anywhere. I told myself I was getting feebleminded, and turned away from the window.

Another blast spun me back to it. This explosion sounded nearer than the first, maybe because it was stronger. Peering through the glass again, I still saw nothing. And still had the impression of things that were big moving down there.

Bare feet pattered in the hall. A voice was anxiously calling my name. Turning from the window again, I pocketed my gun and snapped on the flashlight. Keith Hendrixson, in pajamas and bathrobe, looking thinner and older than anybody could be, came into the room.

"Is it—"

"I don't think it's an earthquake," I said, since that is the first calamity your Californian thinks of. "The lights went off a little while ago. There have been a couple of explosions down the hill since the—"

I stopped. Three shots, close together, had sounded. Rifle-shots, but of the sort that only the heaviest of rifles could make. Then, sharp and small in the storm, came the report of a far-away pistol.

"What is it?" Hendrixson demanded.

"Shooting."

More feet were pattering in the halls, some bare, some shod. Excited voices whispered questions and exclamations. The butler, a solemn, solid block of a man, partly dressed and carrying a lighted five-pronged candlestick, came in.

"Very good, Brophy," Hendrixson said as the butler put the candlestick on the table beside my sandwiches. "Will you try to learn what is the matter?"

"I have tried, sir. The telephone seems to be out of order, sir. Shall I send Oliver down to the village?"

"No-o. I don't suppose it's that serious. Do you think it is anything serious?" he asked me.

I said I didn't think so, but I was paying more attention to the outside than to him. I had heard a thin screaming that could have come from a distant woman, and a volley of small-arms shots. The rocket of the storm muffled these shots, but when the heavier firing we had heard before broke out again, it was clear enough.

To have opened the window would have been to let in gallons of water without helping us to hear much clearer. I stood with an ear tilted to the pane, trying to arrive at some idea of what was happening outside.

Another sound took my attention from the window—the ringing of the bell-pull at the front door. It rang loudly and persistently.

Hendrixson looked at me. I nodded. "See who it is, Brophy," he said.

The butler went solemnly away, and came back even more solemnly. "Princess Zhukovski," he announced.

She came running into the room—the tall Russian girl I had seen at the reception. Her eyes were wide and dark with excitement. Her face was very white and wet. Water ran in streams down her blue waterproof cape, the hood of which covered her dark hair.

"Oh, Mr. Hendrixson!" She had caught one of his hands in both of hers. Her voice, with nothing foreign in its accents, was the voice of one who is excited over a delightful surprise. "The bank is being robbed, and the—what do you call him?—marshal of police has been killed!"

"What's that?" the old man exclaimed, jumping awkwardly

because water from her cape had dropped down on one of his bare feet. "Weegan killed? And the bank robbed?"

"Yes! Isn't it terrible?" She said it as if she were saying wonderful. "When the first explosion woke us, the general sent Ignati down to find out what was the matter, and he got down there just in time to see the bank blown up. Listen!"

We listened, and heard a wild outbreak of mixed gunfire.

"That will be the general arriving!" she said. "He'll enjoy himself most wonderfully. As soon as Ignati returned with the news, the general armed every male in the household from Aleksander Sergyeevich to Ivan the cook, and led them out happier than he's been since he took his division to East Prussia in 1914."

"And the duchess?" Hendrixson asked.

"He left her at home with me, of course, and I furtively crept out and away from her while she was trying for the first time in her life to put water in a samovar. This is not the night for one to stay at home!"

"H-m-m," Hendrixson said, his mind obviously not on her words. "And the bank!"

He looked at me. I said nothing. The racket of another volley came to us.

"Could you do anything down there?" he asked.

"Maybe, but—" I nodded at the presents under their covers.

"Oh, those!" the old man said. "I'm as much interested in the bank as in them; and besides, we will be here."

"All right!" I was willing enough to carry my curiosity down the hill. "I'll go down. You'd better have the butler stay in here, and plant the chauffeur inside the front door. Better give them guns if you have any. Is there a raincoat I can borrow? I brought only a light overcoat with me."

Brophy found a yellow slicker that fit me. I put it on, stowed gun and flashlight conveniently under it, and found my hat while Brophy was getting and loading an automatic pistol for himself and a rifle for Oliver, the mulatto chauffeur.

Hendrixson and the princess followed me downstairs. At the door I found she wasn't exactly following me—she was going with me.

"But, Sonya!" the old man protested.

"I'm not going to be foolish, though I'd like to," she promised him. "But I'm going back to my Irinia Androvna, who will perhaps have the samovar watered by now."

"That's a sensible girl!" Hendrixson said, and let us out into the rain and the wind.

It wasn't weather to talk in. In silence we turned downhill between two rows of hedging, with the storm driving at our backs. At the first break in the hedge I stopped, nodding toward the black blot a house made. "That is your—"

Her laugh cut me short. She caught my arm and began to urge me down the road again. "I only told Mr. Hendrixson that so he would not worry," she explained. "You do not think I am not going down to see the sights."

She was tall. I am short and thick. I had to look up to see her face—to see as much of it as the rain-gray night would let me see. "You'll be soaked to the hide, running around in this rain," I objected.

"What of that? I am dressed for it." She raised a foot to show me a heavy waterproof boot and a woolen-stockinged leg.

"There's no telling what we'll run into down there, and I've got work to do," I insisted. "I can't be looking out for you."

"I can look out for myself." She pushed her cape aside to show me a square automatic pistol in one hand.

"You'll be in my way."

"I will not," she retorted. "You'll probably find I can help you. I'm as strong as you, and quicker, and I can shoot."

The reports of scattered shooting had punctuated our argument, but now the sound of heavier firing silenced the dozen objections to her company that I could still think of. After all, I could slip away from her in the dark if she became too much of a nuisance.

"Have it your own way," I growled, "but don't expect anything from me."

"You're so kind," she murmured as we got under way again, hurrying now, with the wind at our backs speeding us along.

Occasionally dark figures moved on the road ahead of us, but too far away to be recognizable. Presently a man passed us, running uphill—a tall man whose nightshirt hung out of his trousers, down below his coat, identifying him as a resident.

"They've finished the bank and are at Medcraft's!" he yelled as he went by.

"Medcraft is the jeweler," the girl informed me.

The sloping under our feet grew less sharp. The houses—dark but with faces vaguely visible here and there at windows—came closer together. Below, the flash of a gun could be seen now and then—orange streaks in the rain.

Our road put us into the lower end of the main street just as a staccato rat-ta-tat broke out.

I pushed the girl into the nearest doorway, and jumped in after her.

Bullets ripped through walls with the sound of hail tapping on leaves.

That was the thing I had taken for an exceptionally heavy rifle—a machine gun.

The girl had fallen back in a corner, all tangled up with something. I helped her up. The something was a boy of seventeen or so, with one leg and a crutch.

"It's the boy who delivers papers," Princess Zhukovski said, "and you've hurt him with your clumsiness."

The boy shook his head, grinning as he got up. "No'm, I ain't hurt none, but you kind of scared me, jumping on me like that."

She had to stop and explain that she hadn't jumped on him, that she had been pushed into him by me, and that she was sorry and so was I.

"What's happening?" I asked the newsboy when I could get a word in.

"Everything," he boasted, as if some of the credit were his. "There must be a hundred of them, and they've blowed the bank wide open, and now some of 'em is in Medcraft's, and I guess they'll blow that up, too. And they killed Tom Weegan. They got a machine gun on a car in the middle of the street. That's it shooting now."

"Where's everybody—all the merry villagers?"

"Most of 'em are up behind the Hall. They can't do nothing, though, because the machine gun won't let 'em get near enough to see what they're shooting at, and that smart Bill Vincent told me to clear out, 'cause I've only got one leg, as if I couldn't shoot as good as the next one, if I only had something to shoot with!"

"That wasn't right of them," I sympathized. "But you can do something for me. You can stick here and keep your eye on this end of the street, so I'll know if they leave in this direction."

"You're not just saying that so I'll stay here out of the way, are you?"

"No," I lied. "I need somebody to watch. I was going to leave the princess here, but you'll do better."

"Yes," she backed me up, catching the idea. "This gentleman is a detective, and if you do what he asks you'll be helping more than if you were up with the others."

The machine gun was still firing, but not in our direction now.

"I'm going across the street," I told the girl. "If you—"

"Aren't you going to join the others?"

"No. If I can get around behind the bandits while they're busy with the others, maybe I can turn a trick."

"Watch sharp now!" I ordered the boy, and the princess and I made a dash for the opposite sidewalk.

We reached it without drawing lead, sidled along a building for a few yards, and turned into an alley. From the alley's other end came the smell and wash and the dull blackness of the bay.

While we moved down this alley I composed a scheme by which I hoped to get rid of my companion, sending her off on a safe wild-goose chase. But I didn't get a chance to try it out.

The big figure of a man loomed ahead of us.

Stepping in front of the girl, I went on toward him. Under my slicker I held my gun on the middle of him.

He stood still. He was larger than he had looked at first. A big, slope-shouldered, barrel-bodied husky. His hands were empty. I spotted the flashlight on his face for a split second. A flat-cheeked, thick-featured face, with high cheekbones and a lot of ruggedness in it.

"Ignati!" the girl exclaimed over my shoulder.

He began to talk what I suppose was Russian to the girl. She laughed and replied. He shook his big head stubbornly, insisting on something. She stamped her foot and spoke sharply. He shook his head again and addressed me. "General Pleshskev, he tell me bring Princess Sonya to home."

His English was almost as hard to understand as his Russian. His tone puzzled me. It was as if he was explaining some absolutely necessary thing that he didn't want to be blamed for, but that nevertheless he was going to do.

While the girl was speaking to him again, I guessed the answer. This big Ignati had been sent out by the general to bring the girl home, and he was going to obey his orders if he had to carry her. He was trying to avoid trouble with me by explaining the situation.

"Take her," I said, stepping aside.

The girl scowled at me, laughed. "Very well, Ignati," she said in English, "I shall go home," and she turned on her heel and went back up the alley, the big man close behind her.

Glad to be alone, I wasted no time in moving in the opposite direction until the pebbles of the beach were under my feet. The pebbles ground harshly under my heels. I moved back to more silent ground and began to work my way as swiftly as I could up the shore toward the center of action. The machine gun barked on. Smaller guns snapped. Three concussions, close together— bombs, hand grenades, my ears and my memory told me.

The stormy sky glared pink over a roof ahead of me and to the left. The boom of the blast beat my eardrums. Fragments I couldn't see fell around me. That, I thought, would be the jeweler's safe blowing apart.

I crept on up the shore line. The machine gun went silent. Lighter guns snapped, snapped. Another grenade went off. A man's voice shrieked pure terror.

Risking the crunch of pebbles, I turned down to the water's edge again. I had seen no dark shape on the water that could have been a boat. There had been boats moored along this beach in the afternoon. With my feet in the water of the bay I still saw no boat. The storm could have scattered them, but I didn't think it had. The island's western height shielded this shore. The wind was strong here, but not violent.

My feet sometimes on the edge of the pebbles, sometimes in the water, I went on up the shore line. Now I saw a boat. A gently bobbing black shape ahead. No light was on it. Nothing I could see moved on it. It was the only boat on that shore. That made it important.

Foot by foot, I approached.

A shadow moved between me and the dark rear of a building. I froze. The shadow, man-size, moved again, in the direction from which I was coming.

Waiting, I didn't know how nearly invisible, or how plain, I might be against my background. I couldn't risk giving myself away by trying to improve my position.

Twenty feet from me the shadow suddenly stopped.

I was seen. My gun was on the shadow.

"Come on," I called softly. "Keep coming. Let's see who you are."

The shadow hesitated, left the shelter of the building, drew nearer. I couldn't risk the flashlight. I made out dimly a handsome face, boyishly reckless, one cheek dark-stained.

"Oh, how d'you do?" the face's owner said in a musical baritone voice. "You were at the reception this afternoon."

"Yes."

"Have you seen Princess Zhukovski? You know her?"

"She went home with Ignati ten minutes or so ago."

"Excellent!" He wiped his stained cheek with a stained handkerchief, and turned to look at the boat. "That's Hendrixson's boat," he whispered. "They've got it and they've cast the others off."

"That would mean they are going to leave by water."

"Yes," he agreed, "unless—Shall we have a try at it?"

"You mean jump it?"

"Why not?" he asked. "There can't be very many aboard. God knows there are enough of them ashore. You're armed. I've a pistol."

"We'll size it up first," I decided, "so we'll know what we're jumping."

"That is wisdom," he said, and led the way back to the shelter of the buildings.

Hugging the rear walls of the buildings, we stole toward the boat.

The boat grew clearer in the night. A craft perhaps forty-five feet long, its stern to the shore, rising and falling beside a small pier. Across the stern something protruded. Something I couldn't quite make out. Leather soles scuffled now and then on the wooden deck. Presently a dark head and shoulders showed over the puzzling thing in the stern.

The Russian lad's eyes were better than mine.

"Masked," he breathed in my ear. "Something like a stocking over his head and face."

The masked man was motionless where he stood. We were motionless where we stood.

"Could you hit him from here?" the lad asked.

"Maybe, but night and rain aren't a good combination for sharp-shooting. Our best bet is to sneak as close as we can, and start shooting when he spots us."

"That is wisdom," he agreed.

Discovery came with our first step forward. The man in the boat grunted. The lad at my side jumped forward. I recognized the thing in the boat's stern just in time to throw out a leg and trip the young Russian. He tumbled down, all sprawled out on the pebbles. I dropped behind him.

The machine gun in the boat's stern poured metal over our heads.

"No good rushing that!" I said. "Roll out of it!"

I set the example by revolving toward the back of the building we had just left.

The man at the gun sprinkled the beach, but sprinkled it at random, his eyes no doubt spoiled for night-seeing by the flash of his gun.

Around the corner of the building, we sat up.

"You saved my life by tripping me," the lad said coolly.

"Yes. I wonder if they've moved the machine gun from the street, or if—"

The answer to that came immediately. The machine gun in the street mingled its vicious voice with the drumming of the one in the boat.

"A pair of them!" I complained. "Know anything about the layout?"

"I don't think there are more than ten or twelve of them," he said, "although it is not easy to count in the dark. The few I have seen are completely masked—like the man in the boat. They seem to have disconnected the telephone and light lines first and then to have destroyed the bridge. We attacked them while they were looting the bank, but in front they had a machine gun mounted in an automobile, and we were not equipped to combat on equal terms."

"Where are the islanders now?"

"Scattered, and most of them in hiding, I fancy, unless General Pleshskev has succeeded in rallying them again."

I frowned and beat my brains together. You can't fight machine guns and hand grenades with peaceful villagers and retired capitalists. No matter how well led and armed they are, you can't do anything with them. For that matter, how could anybody do much against a game of that toughness?

"Suppose you stick here and keep your eye on the boat," I suggested. "I'll scout around and see what's doing farther up, and if I can get a few good men together, I'll try to jump the boat again, probably from the other side. But we can't count on that. The get-away will be by boat. We can count on that, and try to block it. If you lie down you can watch the boat around the corner of the building without making much of a target of yourself. I wouldn't do anything to attract attention until the break for the boat comes. Then you can do all the shooting you want."

"Excellent!" he said. "You'll probably find most of the islanders up behind the church. You can get to it by going straight up the hill until you come to an iron fence, and then follow that to the right."

"Right."

I moved off in the direction he had indicated.

At the main street I stopped to look around before venturing across. Everything was quiet there. The only man I could see was spread out face-down on the sidewalk near me.

On hands and knees I crawled to his side. He was dead. I didn't stop to examine him further, but sprang up and streaked for the other side of the street.

Nothing tried to stop me. In a doorway, flat against a wall, I peeped out. The wind had stopped. The rain was no longer a driving deluge, but a steady down-pouring of small drops. Couffignal's main street, to my senses, was a deserted street.

I wondered if the retreat to the boat had already started. On the sidewalk, walking swiftly toward the bank, I heard the answer to that guess.

High up on the slope, almost up to the edge of the cliff, by the sound, a machine gun began to hurl out its stream of bullets.

Mixed with the racket of the machine gun were the sounds of smaller arms, and a grenade or two.

At the first crossing, I left the main street and began to run up the hill. Men were running toward me. Two of them passed, paying no attention to my shouted, "What's up now?"

The third man stopped because I grabbed him—a fat man whose breath bubbled, and whose face was fish-belly white.

"They've moved the car with the machine gun on it up behind us," he gasped when I had shouted my question into his ear again.

"What are you doing without a gun?" I asked.

"I—I dropped it."

"Where's General Pleshskev?"

"Back there somewhere. He's trying to capture the car, but he'll never do it. It's suicide! Why don't help come?"

Other men had passed us, running downhill, as we talked. I let the white-faced man go, and stopped four men who weren't running so fast as the others.

"What's happening now?" I questioned them.

"They's going through the houses up the hill," a sharp-featured man with a small mustache and a rifle said.

"Has anybody got word off the island yet?" I asked.

"Can't," another informed me. "They blew up the bridge first thing."

"Can't anybody swim?"

"Not in that wind. Young Catlan tried it and was lucky to get out again with a couple of broken ribs."

"The wind's gone down," I pointed out.

The sharp-featured man gave his rifle to one of the others and took off his coat. "I'll try it," he promised.

"Good! Wake up the whole country, and get word through to the San Francisco police boat and to the Mare Island Navy Yard. They'll lend a hand if you tell 'em the bandits have machine guns. Tell 'em the bandits have an armed boat waiting to leave in. It's Hendrixson's."

The volunteer swimmer left.

"A boat?" two of the men asked together.

"Yes. With a machine gun on it. If we're going to do anything, it'll have to be now, while we're between them and their get-away. Get every man and every gun you can find down there. Tackle the boat from the roofs if you can. When the bandits' car comes down there, pour it into it. You'll do better from the buildings than from the street."

The three men went on downhill. I went uphill, toward the crackling of firearms ahead. The machine gun was working irregularly. It would pour out its rat-tat-tat for a second or so, and then stop for a couple of seconds. The answering fire was thin, ragged.

I met more men, learned from them the general, with less than a dozen men, was still fighting the car. I repeated the advice I had given the other men. My informants went down to join them. I went on up.

A hundred yards farther along, what was left of the general's dozen broke out of the night, around and past me, flying downhill, with bullets hailing after them.

The road was no place for mortal man. I stumbled over two bodies, scratched myself in a dozen places getting over a hedge. On soft, wet sod I continued my uphill journey.

The machine gun on the hill stopped its clattering. The one in the boat was still at work.

The one ahead opened again, firing too high for anything near at hand to be its target. It was helping its fellow below, spraying the main street.

Before I could get closer it had stopped. I heard the car's motor racing. The car moved toward me.

Rolling into the hedge, I lay there, straining my eyes through the spaces between the stems. I had six bullets in a gun that hadn't yet been fired on this night that had seen tons of powder burned.

When I saw wheels on the lighter face of the road, I emptied my gun, holding it low.

The car went on.

I sprang out of my hiding-place.

The car was suddenly gone from the empty road.

There was a grinding sound. A crash. The noise of metal folding on itself. The tinkle of glass.

I raced toward those sounds.

Out of a black pile where an engine sputtered, a black figure leaped—to dash off across the soggy lawn. I cut after it, hoping that the others in the wreck were down for keeps.

I was less than fifteen feet behind the fleeing man when he cleared a hedge. I'm no sprinter, but neither was he. The wet grass made slippery going.

He stumbled while I was vaulting the hedge. When we straightened out again I was not more than ten feet behind him.

Once I clicked my gun at him, forgetting I had emptied it. Six cartridges were wrapped in a piece of paper in my vest pocket, but this was no time for loading.

I was tempted to chuck the empty gun at his head. But that was too chancy.

A building loomed ahead. My fugitive bore off to the right, to clear the corner.

To the left a heavy shotgun went off.

The running man disappeared around the house-corner.

"Sweet God!" General Pleshskev's mellow voice complained. "That with a shotgun I should miss all of a man at the distance!"

"Go round the other way!" I yelled, plunging around the corner after my quarry.

His feet thudded ahead. I could not see him. The general puffed around from the other side of the house.

"You have him?"

"No."

In front of us was a stone-faced bank, on top of which ran a path. On either side of us was a high and solid hedge.

"But, my friend," the general protested. "How could he have—?"

A pale triangle showed on the path above—a triangle that could have been a bit of shirt showing above the opening of a vest.

"Stay here and talk!" I whispered to the general, and crept forward.

"It must be that he has gone the other way," the general carried out my instructions, rambling on as if I were standing beside him, "because if he had come my way I should have seen him, and if he had raised himself over either of the hedges of the embankment, one of us would surely have seen him against . . ."

He talked on and on while I gained the shelter of the bank on which the path sat, while I found places for my toes in the rough stone facing.

The man on the road, trying to make himself small with his back in a bush, was looking at the talking general. He saw me when I had my feet on the path.

He jumped, and one hand went up.

I jumped, with both hands out.

A stone, turning under my foot, threw me sidewise, twisting my ankle, but saving my head from the bullet he sent at it.

My outflung left arm caught his legs as I spilled down. He came over on top of me. I kicked him once, caught his gun-arm, and had just decided to bite it when the general puffed up over the edge of the path and prodded the man off me with the muzzle of the shotgun.

When it came my turn to stand up, I found it not so good. My twisted ankle didn't like to support its share of my hundred-and-eighty-some pounds. Putting most of my weight on the other leg, I turned my flashlight on the prisoner.

"Hello, Flippo!" I exclaimed.

"Hello!" he said without joy in the recognition.

He was a roly-poly Italian youth of twenty-three or -four. I had helped send him to San Quentin four years ago for his part in a payroll stick-up. He had been out on parole for several months now.

"The prison board isn't going to like this," I told him.

"You got me wrong," he pleaded. "I ain't been doing a thing. I was up here to see some friends. And when this thing busted loose I had to hide, because I got a record, and if I'm picked up I'll be railroaded for it. And now you got me, and you think I'm in on it!"

"You're a mind reader," I assured him, and asked the general, "Where can we pack this bird away for a while, under lock and key?"

"In my house there is a lumber-room with a strong door and not a window."

"That'll do it. March, Flippo!"

General Pleshskev collared the youth, while I limped along behind them, examining Flippo's gun, which was loaded except for the one shot he had fired at me, and reloading my own.

We had caught our prisoner on the Russian's grounds, so we didn't have far to go.

The general knocked on the door and called out something in his language. Bolts clicked and grated, and the door was swung open by a heavily mustached Russian servant. Behind him the princess and a stalwart older woman stood.

We went in while the general was telling his household about the capture, and took the captive up to the lumber-room. I frisked him for his pocketknife and matches—he had nothing else that could help him get out—locked him in and braced the door solidly with a length of board. Then we went downstairs again.

"You are injured!" the princess cried, seeing me limp across the floor.

"Only a twisted ankle," I said. "But it does bother me some. Is there any adhesive tape around?"

"Yes," and she spoke to the mustached servant, who went out of the room and presently returned, carrying rolls of gauze and tape and a basin of steaming water.

"If you'll sit down," the princess said, taking these things from the servant.

But I shook my head and reached for the adhesive tape.

"I want cold water, because I've got to go out in the wet again. If you'll show me the bathroom, I can fix myself up in no time."

We had to argue about that, but I finally got to the bathroom, where I ran cold water on my foot and ankle, and strapped it with adhesive tape, as tight as I could without stopping the circulation altogether. Getting my wet shoe on again was a job, but when I was through I had two firm legs under me, even if one of them did hurt some.

When I rejoined the others I noticed that sounds of firing no longer came up the hill, and that the patter of rain was lighter, and a gray streak of coming daylight showed under a drawn blind.

I was buttoning my slicker when the knocker rang on the front door. Russian words came through, and the young Russian I had met on the beach came in.

"Aleksander, you're—" The stalwart older woman screamed, when she saw the blood on his cheek, and fainted.

He paid no attention to her at all, as if he was used to having her faint.

"They've gone in the boat," he told me while the girl and two men servants gathered up the woman and laid her on an ottoman.

"How many?" I asked.

"I counted ten, and I don't think I missed more than one or two, if any."

"The men I sent down there couldn't stop them?"

He shrugged. "What would you do? It takes a strong stomach to face a machine gun. Your men had been cleared out of the buildings almost before they arrived."

The woman who had fainted had revived by now and was pouring anxious questions in Russian at the lad. The princess was getting into her blue cape. The woman stopped questioning the lad and asked her something.

"It's all over," the princess said. "I am going to view the ruins."

That suggestion appealed to everybody. Five minutes later all of us, including the servants, were on our way downhill. Behind us, around us, in front of us, were other people going downhill, hurrying along in the drizzle that was very gentle now, their faces tired and excited in the bleak morning light.

Halfway down, a woman ran out of a cross-path and began to tell me something. I recognized her as one of Hendrixson's maids.

I caught some of her words.

"Presents gone. . . . Mr. Brophy murdered . . . Oliver . . ."

"I'll be down later," I told the others, and set out after the maid.

She was running back to the Hendrixson house. I couldn't run, couldn't even walk fast. She and Hendrixson and more of his servants were standing on the front porch when I arrived.

"They killed Oliver and Brophy," the old man said.

"How?"

"We were in the back of the house, the rear second story, watching the flashes of the shooting down in the village. Oliver was down here, just inside the front door, and Brophy in the room with the presents. We heard a shot in there, and immediately a man appeared in the doorway of our room, threatening us with two pistols, making us stay there for perhaps ten minutes. Then he shut and locked the door and went away. We broke the door down—and found Brophy and Oliver dead."

"Let's look at them."

The chauffeur was just inside the front door. He lay on his back, with his brown throat cut straight across the front, almost back to the vertebrae. His rifle was under him. I pulled it out and examined it. It had not been fired.

Upstairs, the butler Brophy was huddled against a leg of one of the tables on which the presents had been spread. His gun was gone. I turned him over, straightened him out, and found a bullet-hole in his chest. Around the hole his coat was charred in a large area.

Most of the presents were still there. But the most valuable pieces were gone. The others were in disorder, lying around any which way, their covers pulled off.

"What did the one you saw look like?" I asked.

"I didn't see him very well," Hendrixson said. "There was no light in our room. He was simply a dark figure against the candle burning in the hall. A large man in a black rubber raincoat, with some sort of black mask that covered his whole head and face, with small eyeholes."

"No hat?"

"No, just the mask over his entire face and head."

As we went downstairs again I gave Hendrixson a brief account of what I had seen and heard and done since I had left him. There wasn't enough of it to make a long tale.

"Do you think you can get information about the others from the one you caught?" he asked, as I prepared to go out.

"No. But I expect to bag them just the same."

Couffignal's main street was jammed with people when I limped into it again. A detachment of Marines from Mare Island was there, and men from a San Francisco police boat. Excited citizens in all degrees of partial nakedness boiled around them. A hundred voices were talking at once, recounting their personal adventures and braveries and losses and what they had seen. Such words as machine gun, bomb, bandit, car, shot, dynamite, and killed sounded again and again, in every variety of voice and tone.

The bank had been completely wrecked by the charge that had blown the vault. The jewelry store was another ruin. A grocer's across the street was serving as a field hospital. Two doctors were toiling there, patching up damaged villagers.

I recognized a familiar face under a uniform cap—Sergeant

Roche of the harbor police—and pushed through the crowd to him.

"Just get here?" he asked as we shook hands. "Or were you in on it?"

"In on it."

"What do you know?"

"Everything."

"Who ever heard of a private detective that didn't," he joshed as I led him out of the mob.

"Did you people run into an empty boat out in the bay?" I asked when we were away from audiences.

"Empty boats have been floating around the bay all night," he said.

I hadn't thought of that.

"Where's your boat now?" I asked him.

"Out trying to pick up the bandits. I stayed with a couple of men to lend a hand here."

"You're in luck," I told him. "Now sneak a look across the street. See the stout old boy with the black whiskers, standing in front of the druggist's?"

General Pleshskev stood there, with the woman who had fainted, the young Russian whose bloody cheek had made her faint, and a pale, plump man of forty-something who had been with them at the reception. A little to one side stood big Ignati, the two men-servants I had seen at the house, and another who was obviously one of them. They were chatting together and watching the excited antics of a red-faced property-owner who was telling a curt lieutenant of Marines that it was his own personal private automobile that the bandits had stolen to mount their machine gun on, and what he thought should be done about it.

"Yes," said Roche, "I see your fellow with the whiskers."

"Well, he's your meat. The woman and two men with him are also your meat. And those four Russians standing to the left are some more of it. There's another missing, but I'll take care of that one. Pass the word to the lieutenant, and you can round up those babies without giving them a chance to fight back. They think they're safe as angels."

"Sure, are you?" the sergeant asked.

"Don't be silly!" I growled, as if I had never made a mistake in my life.

I had been standing on my one good prop. When I put my weight on the other to turn away from the sergeant, it stung me all the way to the hip. I pushed my back teeth together and began to work painfully through the crowd to the other side of the street.

The princess didn't seem to be among those present. My idea was that, next to the general, she was the most important member of the push. If she was at their house, and not yet suspicious, I figured I could get close enough to yank her in without a riot.

Walking was hell. My temperature rose. Sweat rolled out on me.

"Mister, they didn't none of 'em come down that way."

The one-legged newsboy was standing at my elbow. I greeted him as if he were my pay-check.

"Come on with me," I said, taking his arm. "You did fine down there, and now I want you to do something else for me."

Half a block from the main street I led him up on the porch of a small yellow cottage. The front door stood open, left that way when the occupants ran down to welcome police and Marines, no doubt. Just inside the door, beside a hall rack, was a wicker porch chair. I committed unlawful entry to the extent of dragging that chair out on the porch.

"Sit down, son," I urged the boy.

He sat, looking up at me with puzzled freckled face. I took a firm grip on his crutch and pulled it out of his hand.

"Here's five bucks for rental," I said, "and if I lose it I'll buy you one of ivory and gold."

And I put the crutch under my arm and began to propel myself up the hill.

It was my first experience with a crutch. I didn't break any records. But it was a lot better than tottering along on an unassisted bum ankle.

The hill was longer and steeper than some mountains I've seen, but the gravel walk to the Russians' house was finally under my feet.

I was still some dozen feet from the porch when Princess Zhukovski opened the door.

"Oh!" she exclaimed, and then, recovering from her surprise, "your ankle is worse!" She ran down the steps to help me climb them. As she came I noticed that something heavy was sagging and swinging in the right-hand pocket of her gray flannel jacket.

With one hand under my elbow, the other arm across my back, she helped me up the steps and across the porch. That assured me she didn't think I had tumbled to the game. If she had, she wouldn't have trusted herself within reach of my hands. Why, I wondered, had she come back to the house after starting downhill with the others?

While I was wondering we went into the house, where she planted me in a large and soft leather chair.

"You must certainly be starving after your strenuous night," she said, "I will see if—"

"No, sit down." I nodded at a chair facing mine. "I want to talk to you."

She sat down, clasping her slender white hands in her lap. In neither face nor pose was there any sign of nervousness, not even of curiosity. And that was overdoing it.

"Where have you cached the plunder?" I asked.

The whiteness of her face was nothing to go by. It had been white marble since I had first seen her. The darkness of her eyes was as natural. Nothing happened to her other features. Her voice was smoothly cool.

"I am sorry," she said. "The question doesn't convey anything to me."

"Here's the point," I explained. "I'm charging you with complicity in the gutting of Couffignal, and in the murders that went with it. And I'm asking you where the loot has been hidden."

Slowly she stood up, raised her chin, and looked at least a mile down at me.

"How dare you? How dare you speak so to me, a Zhukovski!"

"I don't care if you're one of the Smith Brothers!" Leaning forward, I had pushed my twisted ankle against a leg of the chair, and the resulting agony didn't improve my disposition. "For the purpose of this talk you are a thief and a murderer."

Her strong slender body became the body of a lean crouching animal. Her white face became the face of an enraged animal. One hand—claw now—swept to the heavy pocket of her jacket.

Then, before I could have batted an eye—though my life seemed to depend on my not batting it—the wild animal had vanished. Out of it—and now I know where the writers of the old fairy stories got their ideas—rose the princess again, cool and straight and tall.

She sat down, crossed her ankles, put an elbow on an arm of her chair, propped her chin on the back of that hand, and looked curiously into my face.

"How ever," she murmured, "did you chance to arrive at so strange and fanciful a theory?"

"It wasn't chance, and it's neither strange nor fanciful," I said. "Maybe it'll save time and trouble if I show you part of the score against you. Then you'll know how you stand and won't waste your brains pleading innocence."

"I shall be grateful," she smiled, "very!"

I tucked my crutch in between one knee and the arm of my chair, so my hands would be free to check off my points on my fingers.

"First—whoever planned the job knew the island—not fairly well, but every inch of it. There's no need to argue about that. Second—the car on which the machine gun was mounted was local property, stolen from the owner here. So was the boat in which the bandits were supposed to have escaped. Bandits from the outside would have needed a car or a boat to bring their machine guns, explosives, and grenades here, and there doesn't seem to be any reason why they shouldn't have used that car or boat instead of stealing a fresh one. Third—there wasn't the least hint of the professional bandit touch on this job. If you ask me, it was a military job from beginning to end. And the worst safe-burglar in the world could have got into both the bank vault and the jeweler's safe without wrecking the buildings. Fourth—bandits from the outside wouldn't have destroyed the bridge. They might have blocked it, but they wouldn't have destroyed it. They'd have saved it in case they had to make their get-away in that direction. Fifth—bandits figuring on a getaway by boat would have cut the job short, wouldn't have spread it over the whole night. Enough racket was made here to wake up California all the way from Sacramento to Los Angeles. What you people did was to send one man out in the boat, shooting, and he didn't go far. As soon as he was at a safe distance, he went overboard, and swam back to the island. Big Ignati could have done it without turning a hair."

That exhausted my right hand. I switched over, counting on my left.

"Sixth—I met one of your party, the lad, down on the beach, and he was coming from the boat. He suggested that we jump it. We were shot at, but the man behind the gun was playing with us. He could have wiped us out in a second if he had been in earnest, but he shot over our heads. Seventh—that same lad is the only man on the island, so far as I know, who saw the departing bandits. Eight—all of your people that I ran into were especially nice to me, the general even spending an hour talking to me at the reception this afternoon. That's a distinctive amateur crook trait. Ninth—after the machine gun car had been wrecked I chased its occupant. I lost him around this house. The Italian boy I picked up wasn't him. He couldn't have climbed up on the path without my seeing him. But he could have run around to the general's side of the house and vanished indoors there. The general liked him, and would have helped him. I know that, because the general performed a downright miracle by missing him at some six feet with a shotgun. Tenth—you called at Hendrixson's house for no other purpose than to get me away from there."

That finished the left hand. I went back to the right.

"Eleventh—Hendrixson's two servants were killed by someone they knew and trusted. Both were killed at close quarters and without firing a shot. I'd say you got Oliver to let you into the house, and were talking to him when one of your men cut his throat from behind. Then you went upstairs and probably shot the unsuspecting Brophy yourself. He wouldn't have been on his guard against you. Twelfth—but that ought to be enough, and I'm getting a sore throat from listing them."

She took her chin off her hand, took a fat white cigarette out of a thin black case, and held it in her mouth while I put a match to the end of it. She took a long pull at it—a draw that accounted for a third of its length—and blew the smoke down at her knees.

"That would be enough," she said when all these things had been done, "if it were not that you yourself know it was impossible for us to have been so engaged. Did you not see us—did not everyone see us—time and time again?"

"That's easy!" I argued. "With a couple of machine guns, a trunkful of grenades, knowing the island from top to bottom, in the darkness and in a storm, against bewildered civilians—it was duck soup. There are nine of you that I know of, including two women. Any five of you could have carried on the work, once it was started, while the others took turns appearing here and there, establishing alibis. And that is what you did. You took turns slipping out to alibi yourselves. Everywhere I went I ran into one of you. And the general! That whiskered old joker running around leading the simple citizens to battle! I'll bet he led 'em plenty! They're lucky there are any of 'em alive this morning!"

She finished her cigarette with another inhalation, dropped the stub on the rug, ground out the light with one foot, sighed wearily, put her hands on her hips, and asked, "And now what?"

"Now I want to know where you have stowed the plunder."

The readiness of her answer surprised me.

"Under the garage, in a cellar we secretly dug there some months ago."

I didn't believe that, of course, but it turned out to be the truth.

I didn't have anything else to say. When I fumbled with my borrowed crutch, preparing to get up, she raised a hand and spoke gently. "Wait a moment, please. I have something to suggest."

Half standing, I leaned toward her, stretching out one hand until it was close to her side.

"I want the gun," I said.

She nodded, and sat still while I plucked it from her pocket, put it in one of my own, and sat down again.

"You said a little while ago that you didn't care who I was," she began immediately. "But I want you to know. There are so many of us Russians who once were somebodies and who now are nobodies that I won't bore you with the repetition of a tale the world had grown tired of hearing. But you must remember that this weary tale is real to us who are its subjects. However, we fled from Russia with what we could carry of our property, which fortunately was enough to keep us in bearable comfort for a few years.

"In London we opened a Russian restaurant, but London was suddenly full of Russian restaurants, and ours became, instead of a means of livelihood, a source of loss. We tried teaching music and languages, and so on. In short, we hit on all the means of earning our living that other Russian exiles hit upon, and so always found ourselves in overcrowded, and thus unprofitable, fields. But what else did we know—could we do?

"I promised not to bore you. Well, always our capital shrank, and always the day approached on which we should be shabby and hungry, the day when we should become familiar to readers of your Sunday papers—charwomen who had been princesses, dukes who now were butlers. There was no place for us in the world. Outcasts easily become outlaws. Why not? Could it be said that we owed the world any fealty? Had not the world sat idly by and seen us despoiled of place and property and country?

"We planned it before we had heard of Couffignal. We could find a small settlement of the wealthy, sufficiently isolated, and, after establishing ourselves there, we would plunder it. Couffignal, when we found it, seemed to be the ideal place. We leased this house for six months, having just enough capital remaining to do that and to live properly here while our plans matured. Here we spent four months establishing ourselves, collecting our arms and our explosives, mapping our offensive, waiting for a favourable night. Last night seemed to be that night, and we had provided, we thought, against every eventuality. But we had not, of course, provided against your presence and your genius. They were simply others of the unforeseen misfortunes to which we seem eternally condemned."

She stopped, and fell to studying me with mournful large eyes that made me feel like fidgeting.

"It's no good calling me a genius," I objected. "The truth is you people botched your job from beginning to end. Your general would get a big laugh out of a man without military training who tried to lead an army. But here are you people with absolutely no criminal experience trying to swing a trick that needed the highest sort of criminal skill. Look at how you all played around with me! Amateur stuff! A professional crook with any intelligence would have either let me alone or knocked me off. No wonder you flopped! As for the rest of it—your troubles—I can't do anything about them."

"Why?" very softly. "Why can't you?"

"Why should I?" I made it blunt.

"No one else knows what you know." She bent forward to put a white hand on my knee. "There is wealth in that cellar beneath the garage. You may have whatever you ask."

I shook my head.

"You aren't a fool!" she protested. "You know—"

"Let me straighten this out for you," I interrupted. "We'll disregard whatever honesty I happen to have, sense of loyalty to employers, and so on. You might doubt them, so we'll throw them out. Now I'm a detective because I happen to like the work. It pays me a fair salary, but I could find other jobs that would pay more. Even a hundred dollars more a month would be twelve hundred a year. Say twenty-five or thirty thousand dollars in the years between now and my sixtieth birthday.

"Now I pass up about twenty-five or thirty thousand of honest gain because I like being a detective, like the work. And liking work makes you want to do it as well as you can. Otherwise there'd be no sense to it. That's the fix I am in. I don't know anything else, don't enjoy anything else, don't want to know or enjoy anything else. You can't weigh that against any sum of money. Money is good stuff. I haven't anything against it. But in the past eighteen years I've been getting my fun out of chasing crooks and tackling puzzles, my satisfaction out of catching crooks and solving riddles. It's the only kind of sport I know anything about, and I can't imagine a pleasanter future than twenty-some years more of it. I'm not going to blow that up!"

She shook her head slowly, lowering it, so that now her dark eyes looked up at me under the thin arcs of her brows.

"You speak only of money," she said. "I said you may have whatever you ask."

That was out. I don't know where these women get their ideas.

"You're still all twisted up," I said brusquely, standing now and adjusting my borrowed crutch. "You think I'm a man and you're a woman. That's wrong. I'm a manhunter and you're something that has been running in front of me. There's nothing human about it. You might just as well expect a hound to play tiddly-winks with the fox he's caught. We're wasting time anyway. I've been thinking the police or Marines might come up here and save me a walk. You've been waiting for your mob to come back and grab me. I could have told you they were being arrested when I left them."

That shook her. She had stood up. Now she fell back a step, putting a hand behind her for steadiness, on her chair. An exclamation I didn't understand popped out of her mouth. Russian, I thought, but the next moment I knew it had been Italian.

"Put your hands up." It was Flippo's husky voice. Flippo stood in the doorway, holding an automatic.

I raised my hands as high as I could without dropping my supporting crutch, meanwhile cursing myself for having been too careless, or too vain, to keep a gun in my hand while I talked to the girl.

So this was why she had come back to the house. If she freed the Italian, she had thought, we would have no reason for suspecting that he hadn't been in on the robbery, and so we would look for the bandits among his friends. A prisoner, of course, he might have persuaded us of his innocence. She had given him the gun so he could either shoot his way clear, or, what would help her as much, get himself killed trying.

While I was arranging these thoughts in my head, Flippo had come up behind me. His empty hand passed over my body, taking away my own gun, his, and the one I had taken from the girl.

"A bargain, Flippo," I said when he had moved away from me, a little to one side, where he made one corner of a triangle whose other corners were the girl and I. "You're out on parole, with some years still to be served. I picked you up with a gun on you. That's plenty to send you back to the big house. I know you weren't in on this job. My idea is that you were up here on a smaller one of your own, but I can't prove that and don't want to. Walk out of here, alone and neutral, and I'll forget I saw you."

Little thoughtful lines grooved the boy's round, dark face.

The princess took a step toward him.

"You heard the offer I just now made him?" she asked. "Well, I make that offer to you, if you will kill him."

The thoughtful lines in the boy's face deepened.

"There's your choice, Flippo," I summed up for him. "All I can give you is freedom from San Quentin. The princess can give you a fat cut of the profits in a busted caper, with a good chance to get yourself hanged."

The girl, remembering her advantage over me, went at him hot and heavy in Italian, a language in which I know only four words. Two of them are profane and the other two obscene. I said all four.

The boy was weakening. If he had been ten years older, he'd have taken my offer and thanked me for it. But he was young and she—now that I thought of it—was beautiful. The answer wasn't hard to guess.

"But not to bump him off," he said to her in English, for my benefit. "We'll lock him up in there where I was at."

I suspected Flippo hadn't any great prejudice against murder. It was just that he thought this one unnecessary, unless he was kidding me to make the killing easier.

The girl wasn't satisfied with his suggestion. She poured more hot Italian at him. Her game looked surefire, but it had a flaw. She couldn't persuade him that his chances of getting any of the loot away were good. She had to depend on her charms to swing him. And that meant she had to hold his eye.

He wasn't far from me.

She came close to him. She was singing, chanting, crooning Italian syllables into his round face.

She had him.

He shrugged. His whole face said yes. He turned—

I knocked him on the noodle with my borrowed crutch.

The crutch splintered apart. Flippo's knees bent. He stretched up to his full height. He fell on his face on the floor. He lay there, deadstill, except for a thin worm of blood that crawled out of his hair to the rug.

A step, a tumble, a foot or so of hand-and-knee scrambling put me within reach of Flippo's gun.

The girl, jumping out of my path, was halfway to the door when I sat up with the gun in my hand.

"Stop!" I ordered.

"I shan't," she said, but she did, for the time at least. "I am going out."

"You are going out when I take you."

She laughed, a pleasant laugh, low and confident.

"I'm going out before that," she insisted good-naturedly. I shook my head.

"How do you propose stopping me?" she asked.

"I don't think I'll have to," I told her. "You've got too much sense to try to run while I'm holding a gun on you."

She laughed again, an amused ripple.

"I've got too much sense to stay," she corrected me. "Your crutch is broken, and you're lame. You can't catch me by running after me, then. You pretend you'll shoot me, but I don't believe you. You'd shoot me if I attacked you, of course, but I shan't do that. I shall simply walk out, and you know you won't shoot me for that. You'll wish you could, but you won't. You'll see."

Her face turned over her shoulder, her dark eyes twinkling at me, she took a step toward the door.

"Better not count on that!" I threatened.

For answer to that she gave me a cooing laugh. And took another step.

"Stop, you idiot!" I bawled at her.

Her face laughed over her shoulder at me. She walked without haste to the door, her short skirt of gray flannel shaping itself to the calf of each gray wool-stockinged leg as its mate stepped forward.

Sweat greased the gun in my hand.

When her right foot was on the doorsill, a little chuckling sound came from her throat.

"Adieu!" she said softly.

And I put a bullet in the calf of her left leg.

She sat down—plump! Utter surprise stretched her white face. It was too soon for pain.

I had never shot a woman before. I felt queer about it.

"You ought to have known I'd do it!" My voice sounded harsh and savage and like a stranger's in my ears. "Didn't I steal a crutch from a cripple?"

COMMENT AND QUESTIONS

This story does not at first appear to be a detective story but rather an adventure. There are, however, several elements of the classic detective story that this hardboiled detective story shares: unsuspected but conspicuous criminals; a variation of the sealed chamber setting (the island is cut off from the mainland); a detective who not only solves the crime and provides the evidence to the proper authorities but also physically catches one of the gang himself; and clues provided for the reader so that he can participate (the author plays fair). In fact, none of the twelve rules listed in the introduction to Part 1 is broken. However, in this story the nature of the humor, the nature of the crime (especially the fact that it is carried out by a gang, not an individual), the setting, and the language combine to produce a tone and movement very different from that of the classic detective story.

The Continental Op proves himself a keen observer and an astute judge of what he sees. Are his comments to the harbor police unexpected (when he gives the solution to the mystery)? At this point—when the culprits are revealed—the reader might lose interest in a classic detective story. How does Hammett avoid this kind of letdown in his story?

The Continental Op is committed to what he does. He likes his work. Notice that nothing he is offered (sex, money) really tempts him. What sort of security does a man have who likes his job or profession and is good at it?

What would be lost if Flippo were not in the story? Was it fortunate for Flippo that the Op "knocked him on the noodle"?

Observe how little use Hammett makes of descriptive words and phrases. On what does he rely to make his writing vivid and expressive?

The kind of wit expressed in a wisecrack is generally considered to be a distinguishing quality of American detective fiction. What use is made of this kind of humor in "The Gutting of Couffignal"?

Does the Continental Op need a name? Why or why not?

Dorothy Sayers refers to the "cheerful cynicism" of the detective story. Does that term fit this story?

RAYMOND CHANDLER

I'll Be Waiting

Raymond Chandler was the next great writer of hardboiled detective fiction following Hammett, but Chandler's talents were different. Although his novels and short stories are characterized by the same fast action and a poet's interest in description, they generally have fewer clues and less detection. His Philip Marlowe novels, especially *The Big Sleep* and *The Long Goodbye*, made excellent films because of his skill in presenting character through pointed and witty dialogue. Chandler took his writing seriously, in spite of its being a second career, begun in his mid-forties, and his accomplishments gained for American hardboiled detective fiction a new type of audience and a new respect.

Many other kinds of fiction have adopted techniques from hardboiled detective fiction. As a result, Hammett and Chandler have influenced many writers who are not in the detective-story tradition, as well as great numbers of those who are.

In "I'll Be Waiting" Raymond Chandler himself narrates the story. This narrative method enables Chandler to describe the detective, Tony Reseck, as well as the other characters in the story. (In Hammett's story, it is the Continental Op who speaks, and we must determine his appearance and nature from what he says; there is no one else to describe him for us.) Notice Chandler's interest in appearances and his way of characterizing by means of descriptive details.

At one o'clock in the morning, Carl, the night porter, turned down the last of three table lamps in the main lobby of the Windermere Hotel. The blue carpet darkened a shade or two and the walls drew back into remoteness. The chairs filled with shadowy loungers. In the corners were memories like cobwebs.

Tony Reseck yawned. He put his head on one side and listened to the frail, twittery music from the radio room beyond a dim arch at the far side of the lobby. He frowned. That should be his radio room after one A.M. Nobody should be in it. That red-haired girl was spoiling his nights.

The frown passed and a miniature of a smile quirked at the corners of his lips. He sat relaxed, a short, pale, paunchy, middle-aged man with long, delicate fingers clasped on the elk's tooth on his watch chain; the long delicate fingers of a sleight-of-hand artist, fingers with shiny, molded nails and tapering first joints, fingers a little spatulate at the ends. Handsome fingers. Tony Reseck rubbed them gently together and there was peace in his quiet sea-gray eyes.

The frown came back on his face. The music annoyed him. He got up with a curious litheness, all in one piece, without moving his clasped hands from the watch chain. At one moment he was leaning back relaxed, and the next he was standing balanced on his feet, perfectly still, so that the movement of rising seemed to be a thing perfectly perceived, an error of vision. . . .

He walked with small, polished shoes delicately across the blue carpet and under the arch. The music was louder. It contained the hot, acid blare, the frenetic, jittering runs of a jam session. It was too loud. The red-haired girl sat there and stared silently at the fretted part of the big radio cabinet as though she could see the band with its fixed professional grin and the sweat running down its back. She was curled up with her feet under her on a davenport which seemed to contain most of the cushions in the room. She was tucked among them carefully, like a corsage in the florist's tissue paper.

She didn't turn her head. She leaned there, one hand in a small fist on her peach-colored knee. She was wearing lounging pajamas of heavy ribbed silk embroidered with black lotus buds.

"You like Goodman, Miss Cressy?" Tony Reseck asked.

The girl moved her eyes slowly. The light in there was dim, but the violet of her eyes almost hurt. They were large, deep eyes without a trace of thought in them. Her face was classical and without expression.

She said nothing.

Tony smiled and moved his fingers at his sides, one by one, feeling them move. "You like Goodman, Miss Cressy?" he repeated gently.

"Not to cry over," the girl said tonelessly.

Tony rocked back on his heels and looked at her eyes. Large, deep, empty eyes. Or were they? He reached down and muted the radio.

"Don't get me wrong," the girl said. "Goodman makes money, and a lad that makes legitimate money these days is a lad you have to respect. But this jitterbug music gives me the backdrop of a beer flat. I like something with roses in it."

"Maybe you like Mozart," Tony said.

"Go on, kid me," the girl said.

"I wasn't kidding you, Miss Cressy. I think Mozart was the greatest man that ever lived—and Toscanini is his prophet."

"I thought you were the house dick." She put her head back on a pillow and stared at him through her lashes.

"Make me some of that Mozart," she added.

"It's too late," Tony sighed. "You can't get it now."

She gave him another long lucid glance. "Got the eye on me, haven't you, flatfoot?" She laughed a little, almost under her breath. "What did I do wrong?"

Tony smiled his toy smile. "Nothing, Miss Cressy. Nothing at all. But you need some fresh air. You've been five days in this hotel and you haven't been outdoors. And you have a tower room."

She laughed again. "Make me a story about it. I'm bored."

"There was a girl here once had your suite. She stayed in the hotel a whole week, like you. Without going out at all, I mean. She didn't speak to anybody hardly. What do you think she did then?"

The girl eyed him gravely. "She jumped her bill."

He put his long delicate hand out and turned it slowly, fluttering the fingers, with an effect almost like a lazy wave breaking. "Unh-uh. She sent down for her bill and paid it. Then she told the hop to be back in half an hour for her suitcases. Then she went out on her balcony."

The girl leaned forward a little, her eyes still grave, one hand capping her peach-colored knee. "What did you say your name was?"

"Tony Reseck."

"Sounds like a hunky."

"Yeah," Tony said. "Polish."

"Go on, Tony."

"All the tower suites have private balconies, Miss Cressy. The walls of them are too low for fourteen stories above the street. It was a dark night, that night, high clouds." He dropped his hand with a final gesture, a farewell gesture. "Nobody saw her jump. But when she hit, it was like a big gun going off."

"You're making it up, Tony." Her voice was a clean dry whisper of sound.

He smiled his toy smile. His quiet sea-gray eyes seemed almost to be smoothing the long waves of her hair. "Eve Cressy," he said musingly. "A name waiting for lights to be in."

"Waiting for a tall dark guy that's no good, Tony. You wouldn't care why. I was married to him once. I might be married to him again. You can make a lot of mistakes in just one lifetime." The hand on her knee opened slowly until the fingers were strained back as far as they would go. Then they closed quickly and tightly, and even in that dim light the knuckles shone like the little polished bones. "I played him a low trick once. I put him in a bad place—without meaning to. You wouldn't care about that either. It's just that I owe him something."

He leaned over softly and turned the knob on the radio. A waltz formed itself dimly on the warm air. A tinsel waltz, but a waltz. He turned the volume up. The music gushed from the loudspeaker in a swirl of shadowed melody. Since Vienna died, all waltzes are shadowed.

The girl put her hand on one side and hummed three or four

bars and stopped with a sudden tightening of her mouth.

"Eve Cressy," she said. "It was in lights once. At a bum night club. A dive. They raided it and the lights went out."

He smiled at her almost mockingly. "It was no dive while you were there, Miss Cressy . . . That's the waltz the orchestra always played when the old porter walked up and down in front of the hotel entrance, all swelled up with his medals on his chest. *The Last Laugh*.[1] Emil Jannings.[2] You wouldn't remember that one, Miss Cressy."

" 'Spring, Beautiful Spring,' " she said. "No, I never saw it."

He walked three steps away from her and turned. "I have to go upstairs and palm doorknobs. I hope I didn't bother you. You ought to go to bed now. It's pretty late."

The tinsel waltz stopped and a voice began to talk. The girl spoke through the voice. "You really thought something like that—about the balcony?"

He nodded. "I might have," he said softly. "I don't any more."

"No chance, Tony." Her smile was a dim lost leaf. "Come and talk to me some more. Redheads don't jump, Tony. They hang on—and wither."

He looked at her gravely for a moment and then moved away over the carpet. The porter was standing in the archway that led to the main lobby. Tony hadn't looked that way yet, but he knew somebody was there. He always knew if anybody was close to him. He could hear the grass grow, like the donkey in *The Blue Bird*.[3]

The porter jerked his chin at him urgently. His broad face above the uniform collar looked sweaty and excited. Tony stepped up close to him and they went together through the arch and out to the middle of the dim lobby.

"Trouble?" Tony asked wearily.

"There's a guy outside to see you, Tony. He won't come in. I'm doing a wipe-off on the plate glass of the doors and he comes up beside me, a tall guy. 'Get Tony,' he says, out of the side of his mouth."

Tony said: "Uh-huh," and looked at the porter's pale blue eyes. "Who was it?"

"Al, he said to say he was."

Tony's face became as expressionless as dough. "Okey." He started to move off.

The porter caught his sleeve. "Listen, Tony. You got any enemies?"

Tony laughed politely, his face still like dough.

"Listen, Tony." The porter held his sleeve tightly. "There's a big black car down the block, the other way from the hacks. There's a guy standing beside it with his foot on the running board. This guy that spoke to me, he wears a dark-colored, wrap-around overcoat with a high collar turned up against his ears. His hat's way low. You can't hardly see his face. He says, 'Get Tony,' out of the side of his mouth. You ain't got any enemies, have you, Tony?"

"Only the finance company," Tony said. "Beat it."

He walked slowly and a little stiffly across the blue carpet, up the three shallow steps to the entrance lobby with the three elevators on one side and the desk on the other. Only one elevator was working. Beside the open doors, his arms folded, the night operator stood silent in a neat blue uniform with silver facings. A lean, dark Mexican named Gomez. A new boy, breaking in on the night shift.

The other side was the desk, rose marble, with the night clerk leaning on it delicately. A small neat man with a wispy reddish mustache and cheeks so rosy they looked rouged. He stared at Tony and poked a nail at his mustache.

Tony pointed a stiff index finger at him, folded the other three fingers tight to his palm, and flicked his thumb up and down on the stiff finger. The clerk touched the other side of his mustache and looked bored.

Tony went on past the closed and darkened newsstand and the side entrance to the drugstore, out to the brassbound plate-glass doors. He stopped just inside them and took a deep, hard breath. He squared his shoulders, pushed the doors open and stepped out into the cold damp night air.

The street was dark, silent. The rumble of traffic on Wilshire, two blocks away, had no body, no meaning. To the left were two taxis. Their drivers leaned against a fender, side by side, smoking. Tony walked the other way. The big dark car was a third of a block from the hotel entrance. Its lights were dimmed and it was only when he was almost up to it that he heard the gentle sound of its engine turning over.

A tall figure detached itself from the body of the car and strolled toward him, both hands in the pockets of the dark overcoat with the high collar. From the man's mouth a cigarette tip glowed faintly, a rusty pearl.

They stopped two feet from each other.

The tall man said, "Hi, Tony. Long time no see."

"Hello, Al. How's it going?"

"Can't complain." The tall man started to take his right hand out of his overcoat pocket, then stopped and laughed quietly. "I forgot. Guess you don't want to shake hands."

"That don't mean anything," Tony said. "Shaking hands. Monkeys can shake hands. What's on your mind, Al?"

"Still the funny little fat guy, eh, Tony?"

"I guess." Tony winked his eyes tight. His throat felt tight.

"You like your job back there?"

"It's a job."

Al laughed his quiet laugh again. "You take it slow, Tony. I'll take it fast. So it's a job and you want to hold it. Oke. There's a girl named Eve Cressy flopping in your quiet hotel. Get her out. Fast and right now."

"What's the trouble?"

The tall man looked up and down the street. A man behind in the car coughed lightly. "She's hooked with a wrong number. Nothing against her personal, but she'll lead trouble to you. Get her out, Tony. You got maybe an hour."

"Sure," Tony said aimlessly, without meaning.

Al took his hand out of his pocket and stretched it against Tony's chest. He gave him a light, lazy push. "I wouldn't be telling you just for the hell of it, little fat brother. Get her out of there."

"Okey," Tony said, without any tone in his voice.

The tall man took back his hand and reached for the car door. He opened it and started to slip in like a lean black shadow.

Then he stopped and said something to the men in the car and got out again. He came back to where Tony stood silent, his pale eyes catching a little dim light from the street.

"Listen, Tony. You always kept your nose clean. You're a good brother, Tony."

Tony didn't speak.

Al leaned toward him, a long urgent shadow, the high collar almost touching his ears. "It's trouble business, Tony. The boys won't like it, but I'm telling you just the same. This Cressy was married to a lad named Johnny Ralls. Ralls is out of Quentin two, three days, or a week. He did a three-spot for manslaughter. The girl put him there. He ran down an old man one night when he was drunk, and she was with him. He wouldn't stop. She told him to go in and tell it, or else. He didn't go in. So the Johns come for him."

Tony said, "That's too bad."

"It's kosher, kid. It's my business to know. This Ralls flapped his mouth in stir about how the girl would be waiting for him when he got out, all set to forgive and forget, and he was going straight to her."

Tony said, "What's he to you?" His voice had a dry, stiff crackle, like thick paper.

Al laughed. "The trouble boys want to see him. He ran a table at a spot on the Strip and figured out a scheme. He and another guy took the house for fifty grand. The other lad coughed up, but we still need Johnny's twenty-five. The trouble boys don't get paid to forget."

Tony looked up and down the dark street. One of the taxi drivers flicked a cigarette stub in a long arc over the top of one of the cabs. Tony watched it fall and spark on the pavement. He listened to the quiet sound of the big car's motor.

"I don't want any part of it," he said. "I'll get her out."

Al backed away from him, nodding. "Wise kid. How's mom these days?"

"Okey," Tony said.

"Tell her I was asking for her."

"Asking for her isn't anything," Tony said.

Al turned quickly and got into the car. The car curved lazily in the middle of the block and drifted back toward the corner. Its lights went up and sprayed on a wall. It turned a corner and was gone. The lingering smell of its exhaust drifted past Tony's nose.

He turned and walked back to the hotel and into it. He went along to the radio room.

The radio still muttered, but the girl was gone from the davenport in front of it. The pressed cushions were hollowed out by her body. Tony reached down and touched them. He thought they were still warm. He turned the radio off and stood there, turning a thumb slowly in front of his body, his hand flat against his stomach. Then he went back through the lobby toward the elevator bank and stood beside a majolica jar of white sand. The clerk fussed behind a pebbled-glass screen at one end of the desk. The air was dead.

The elevator bank was dark. Tony looked at the indicator of the middle car and saw that it was at 14.

"Gone to bed," he said under his breath.

The door of the porter's room beside the elevators opened and the little Mexican night operator came out in street clothes. He looked at Tony with a quiet sidewise look out of eyes the color of dried-out chestnuts.

"Good night, boss."

"Yeah," Tony said absently.

He took a thin dappled cigar out of his vest pocket and smelled it. He examined it slowly, turning it around in his neat fingers. There was a small tear along the side. He frowned at that and put the cigar away.

There was a distant sound and the hand on the indicator began to steal around the bronze dial. Light glittered up in the shaft and the straight line of the car floor dissolved the darkness below. The car stopped and the doors opened, and Carl came out of it.

His eyes caught Tony's with a kind of jump and he walked over to him, his head on one side, a thin shine along his pink upper lip.

"Listen, Tony."

Tony took his arm in a hard swift hand and turned him. He pushed him quickly, yet somehow casually, down the steps to the dim main lobby and steered him into a corner. He let go of the arm. His throat tightened again, for no reason he could think of.

"Well?" he said darkly. "Listen to what?"

The porter reached into a pocket and hauled out a dollar bill. "He gimme this," he said loosely. His glittering eyes looked past

Tony's shoulder at nothing. They winked rapidly. "Ice and ginger ale."

"Don't stall," Tony growled.

"Guy in Fourteen-B," the porter said.

"Lemme smell your breath."

The porter leaned toward him obediently.

"Liquor," Tony said harshly.

"He gimme a drink."

Tony looked down at the dollar bill. "Nobody's in Fourteen-B. Not on my list," he said.

"Yeah. There is." The porter licked his lips and his eyes opened and shut several times. "Tall dark guy."

"All right," Tony said crossly. "All right. There's a tall dark guy in Fourteen-B and he gave you a buck and a drink. Then what?"

"Gat under his arm," Carl said, and blinked.

Tony smiled, but his eyes had taken on the lifeless glitter of thick ice. "You take Miss Cressy up to her room?"

Carl shook his head. "Gomez. I saw her go up."

"Get away from me," Tony said between his teeth. "And don't accept any more drinks from the guests."

He didn't move until Carl had gone back into his cubbyhole by the elevators and shut the door. Then he moved silently up the three steps and stood in front of the desk, looking at the veined rose marble, the onyx pen set, the fresh registration card in its leather frame. He lifted a hand and smacked it down hard on the marble. The clerk popped out from behind the glass screen like a chipmunk coming out of its hole.

Tony took a flimsy out of his breast pocket and spread it on the desk. "No Fourteen-B on this," he said in a bitter voice.

The clerk wisped politely at his mustache. "So sorry. You must have been out to supper when he checked in."

"Who?"

"Registered as James Watterson, San Diego." The clerk yawned.

"Ask for anybody?"

The clerk stopped in the middle of the yawn and looked at the top of Tony's head. "Why yes. He asked for a swing band. Why?"

"Smart, fast and funny," Tony said. "If you like 'em that way."

He wrote on his flimsy and stuffed it back into his pocket. "I'm going upstairs and palm doorknobs. There's four tower rooms you ain't rented yet. Get up on your toes, son. You're slipping."

"I made out," the clerk drawled, and completed his yawn. "Hurry back, pop. I don't know how I'll get through the time."

"You could shave that pink fuzz off your lip," Tony said, and went across to the elevators.

He opened up a dark one and lit the dome light and shot the car up to fourteen. He darkened it again, stepped out and closed the doors. This lobby was smaller than any other, except the one immediately below it. It had a single blue-paneled door in each of the walls other than the elevator wall. On each door was a gold number and letter with a gold wreath around it. Tony walked over to 14A and put his ear to the panel. He heard nothing. Eve Cressy might be in bed asleep, or in the bathroom, or out on the balcony. Or she might be sitting there in the room, a few feet from the door, looking at the wall. Well, he wouldn't expect to be able to hear her sit and look at the wall. He went over to 14B and put his ear to that panel. This was different. There was a sound in there. A man coughed. It sounded somehow like a solitary cough. There were no voices. Tony pressed the small nacre button beside the door.

Steps came without hurry. A thickened voice spoke through the panel. Tony made no answer, no sound. The thickened voice repeated the question. Lightly, maliciously, Tony pressed the bell again.

Mr. James Watterson, of San Diego, should now open the door and give forth noise. He didn't. A silence fell beyond that door that was like the silence of a glacier. Once more Tony put his ear to the wood. Silence utterly.

He got out a master key on a chain and pushed it delicately into the lock of the door. He turned it, pushed the door inward three inches and withdrew the key. Then he waited.

"All right," the voice said harshly. "Come in and get it."

Tony pushed the door wide and stood there, framed against the light from the lobby. The man was tall, black-haired, angular and white-faced. He held a gun. He held it as though he knew about guns.

"Step right in," he drawled.

Tony went in through the door and pushed it shut with his shoulder. He kept his hands a little out from his sides, the clever fingers curled and slack. He smiled his quiet little smile.

"Mr. Watterson?"

"And after that what?"

"I'm the house detective here."

"It slays me."

The tall, white-faced, somehow handsome and somehow not handsome man backed slowly into the room. It was a large room with a low balcony around two sides of it. French doors opened out on the little private open-air balcony that each of the tower rooms had. There was a grate set for a log fire behind a paneled screen in front of a cheerful davenport. A tall misted glass stood on a hotel tray beside a deep, cozy chair. The man backed toward this and stood in front of it. The large, glistening gun drooped and pointed at the floor.

"It slays me," he said. "I'm in the dump an hour and the house copper gives me the buzz. Okey, sweetheart, look in the closet and bathroom. But she just left."

"You didn't see her yet," Tony said.

The man's bleached face filled with unexpected lines. His thickened voice edged toward a snarl. "Yeah? Who didn't I see yet?"

"A girl named Eve Cressy."

The man swallowed. He put his gun down on the table beside the tray. He let himself down into the chair backwards, stiffly, like a man with a touch of lumbago. Then he leaned forward and put his hands on his kneecaps and smiled brightly between his teeth. "So she got here, huh? I didn't ask about her yet. I'm a careful guy. I didn't ask yet."

"She's been here five days," Tony said. "Waiting for you. She hasn't left the hotel a minute."

The man's mouth worked a little. His smile had a knowing tilt to it. "I got delayed a little up north," he said smoothly. "You know how it is. Visiting old friends. You seem to know a lot about my business, copper."

"That's right, Mr. Ralls."

The man lunged to his feet and his hand snapped at the gun. He stood leaning over, holding it on the table, staring. "Dames talk too much," he said with a muffled sound in his voice as though he held something soft between his teeth and talked through it.

"Not dames, Mr. Ralls."

"Huh?" The gun slithered on the hard wood of the table. "Talk it up, copper. My mind reader just quit."

"Not dames, guys. Guys with guns."

The glacier silence fell between them again. The man straightened his body out slowly. His face was washed clean of expression, but his eyes were haunted. Tony leaned in front of him, a shortish plump man with a quiet, pale, friendly face and eyes as simple as forest water.

"They never run out of gas—those boys," Johnny Ralls said, and licked at his lip. "Early and late, they work. The old firm never sleeps."

"You know who they are?" Tony said softly.

"I could maybe give nine guesses. And twelve of them would be right."

"The trouble boys," Tony said, and smiled a brittle smile.

"Where is she?" Johnny Ralls asked harshly.

"Right next door to you."

The man walked to the wall and left his gun lying on the table. He stood in front of the wall, studying it. He reached up and gripped the grillwork of the balcony railing. When he dropped his hand and turned, his face had lost some of its lines. His eyes had a quieter glint. He moved back to Tony and stood over him.

"I've got a stake," he said. "Eve sent me some dough and I built it up with a touch I made up north. Case dough, what I mean. The trouble boys talk about twenty-five grand." He smiled crookedly. "Five *C's* I can count. I'd have a lot of fun making them believe that, I would."

"What did you do with it?" Tony asked indifferently.

"I never had it, copper. Leave that lay. I'm the only guy in the world that believes it. It was a little deal that I got suckered on."

"I'll believe it," Tony said.

"They don't kill often. But they can be awful tough."

"Mugs," Tony said with a sudden bitter contempt. "Guys with guns. Just mugs."

Johnny Ralls reached for his glass and drained it empty. The ice cubes tinkled softly as he put it down. He picked his gun up, danced it on his palm, then tucked it, nose down, into an inner breast pocket. He stared at the carpet.

"How come you're telling me this, copper?"

"I thought maybe you'd give her a break."

"And if I wouldn't?"

"I kind of think you will," Tony said.

Johnny Ralls nodded quietly. "Can I get out of here?"

"You could take the service elevator to the garage. You could rent a car. I can give you a card to the garage man."

"You're a funny little guy," Johnny Ralls said.

Tony took out a worn ostrich-skin billfold and scribbled on a printed card. Johnny Ralls read it, and stood holding it, tapping it against a thumbnail.

"I could take her with me," he said, his eyes narrow.

"You could take a ride in a basket too," Tony said. "She's been here five days, I told you. She's been spotted. A guy I know called me up and told me to get her out of here. Told me what it was all about. So I'm getting you out instead."

"They'll love that," Johnny Ralls said. "They'll send you violets."

"I'll weep about it on my day off."

Johnny Ralls turned his hand over and stared at the palm. "I could see her, anyway. Before I blow. Next door to here, you said?"

Tony turned on his heel and started for the door. He said over his shoulder, "Don't waste a lot of time, handsome. I might change my mind."

The man said, almost gently: "You might be spotting me right now, for all I know."

Tony didn't turn his head. "That's a chance you have to take."

He went on to the door and passed out of the room. He shut it carefully, silently, looked once at the door of 14A and got into his dark elevator. He rode it down to the linen-room floor and got out to remove the basket that held the service elevator open at that floor. The door slid quietly shut. He held it so that it made no noise. Down the corridor, light came from the open door of the housekeeper's office. Tony got back into his elevator and went on down to the lobby.

The little clerk was out of sight behind his pebbled-glass screen, auditing accounts. Tony went through the main lobby and turned into the radio room. The radio was on again, soft. She was there, curled on the davenport again. The speaker hummed to her, a vague sound so low that what it said was as wordless as the murmur of trees. She turned her head slowly and smiled at him.

"Finished palming doorknobs? I couldn't sleep worth a nickel. So I came down again. Okey?"

He smiled and nodded. He sat down in a green chair and patted the plump brocade arms of it. "Sure, Miss Cressy."

"Waiting is the hardest kind of work, isn't it? I wish you'd talk to that radio. It sounds like a pretzel being bent."

Tony fiddled with it, got nothing he liked, set it back where it had been.

"Beer-parlor drunks are all the customers now."

She smiled at him again.

"I don't bother you being here, Miss Cressy?"

"I like it. You're a sweet little guy, Tony."

He looked stiffly at the floor and a ripple touched his spine. He waited for it to go away. It went slowly. Then he sat back, relaxed again, his neat fingers clasped on his elk's tooth. He listened. Not to the radio—to far-off, uncertain things, menacing things. And perhaps to just the safe whir of wheels going away into a strange night.

"Nobody's all bad," he said out loud.

The girl looked at him lazily. "I've met two or three I was wrong on, then."

He nodded. "Yeah," he admitted judiciously. "I guess there's some that are."

The girl yawned and her deep violet eyes half closed. She nestled back into the cushions. "Sit there for a while, Tony. Maybe I could nap."

"Sure. Not a thing for me to do. Don't know why they pay me."

She slept quickly and with complete stillness, like a child. Tony hardly breathed for ten minutes. He just watched her, his mouth a little open. There was a quiet fascination in his limpid eyes, as if he was looking at an altar.

Then he stood up with infinite care and padded away under the arch to the entrance lobby and the desk. He stood at the desk listening for a little while. He heard a pen rustling out of sight. He went around the corner to the row of house phones in little glass cubbyholes. He lifted one and asked the night operator for the garage.

It rang three or four times and then a boyish voice answered: "Windermere Hotel. Garage speaking."

"This is Tony Reseck. That guy Watterson I gave a card to. He leave?"

"Sure, Tony. Half an hour almost. Is it your charge?"

"Yeah," Tony said. "My party. Thanks. Be seein' you."

He hung up and scratched his neck. He went back to the desk and slapped a hand on it. The clerk wafted himself around the screen with his greeter's smile in place. It dropped when he saw Tony.

"Can't a guy catch up on his work?" he grumbled.

"What's the professional rate on Fourteen-B?"

The clerk stared morosely. "There's no professional rate in the tower."

"Make one. The fellow left already. Was there only an hour."

"Well, well," the clerk said airily. "So the personality didn't click tonight. We get a skip-out."

"Will five bucks satisfy you?"

"Friend of yours?"

"No. Just a drunk with delusions of grandeur and no dough."

"Guess we'll have to let it ride, Tony. How did he get out?"

"I took him down the service elevator. You was asleep. Will five bucks satisfy you?"

"Why?"

The worn ostrich-skin wallet came out and a weedy five slipped across the marble. "All I could shake him for," Tony said loosely.

The clerk took the five and looked puzzled. "You're the boss," he said, and shrugged. The phone shrilled on the desk and he reached for it. He listened and then pushed it toward Tony. "For you."

Tony took the phone and cuddled it close to his chest. He put his mouth close to the transmitter. The voice was strange to him. It had a metallic sound. Its syllables were meticulously anonymous.

"Tony? Tony Reseck?"

"Talking."

"A message from Al. Shoot?"

Tony looked at the clerk. "Be a pal," he said over the mouthpiece. The clerk flicked a narrow smile at him and went away. "Shoot," Tony said into the phone.

"We had a little business with a guy in your place. Picked him up scramming. Al had a hunch you'd run him out. Tailed him and took him to the curb. Not so good. Backfire."

Tony held the phone very tight and his temples chilled with the evaporation of moisture. "Go on," he said. "I guess there's more."

"A little. The guy stopped the big one. Cold. Al—Al said to tell you goodbye."

Tony leaned hard against the desk. His mouth made a sound that was not speech.

"Get it?" The metallic voice sounded impatient, a little bored. "This guy had him a rod. He used it. Al won't be phoning anybody any more."

Tony lurched at the phone, and the base of it shook on the rose marble. His mouth was a hard dry knot.

The voice said: "That's as far as we go, bub. G'night." The phone clicked dryly, like a pebble hitting a wall.

Tony put the phone down in its cradle very carefully, so as not to make any sound. He looked at the clenched palm of his left hand. He took a handkerchief out and rubbed the palm softly and straightened the fingers out with his other hand. Then he wiped his forehead. The clerk came around the screen again and looked at him with glinting eyes.

"I'm off Friday. How about lending me that phone number?"

Tony nodded at the clerk and smiled a minute frail smile. He put his handkerchief away and patted the pocket he had put it in. He turned and walked away from the desk, across the entrance lobby, down the three shallow steps, along the shadowy reaches of the main lobby, and so in through the arch to the radio room once more. He walked softly, like a man moving in a room where somebody is very sick. He reached the chair he had sat in before and lowered himself into it inch by inch. The girl slept on, motionless, in that curled-up looseness achieved by some women and all cats. Her breath made no slightest sound against the vague murmur of the radio.

Tony Reseck leaned back in the chair and clasped his hands on his elk's tooth and quietly closed his eyes.

COMMENT AND QUESTIONS

In most detective stories, it is the job of the detective to bring meaning or restore order to a chaotic world. He is able to fit all the pieces of a puzzle together and arrive at a final and complete solution of a crime. Does this description fit the detective in "I'll Be Waiting"? Is Tony a detective at all in the classic sense of the word?

One expects "tough" guys in hardboiled fiction. Which characters in this story are tough, and in what ways?

Eve Cressy says that Tony is "a sweet little guy." Is this an adequate evaluation of him? In what ways is he a more complex character than she can, at that time, fully appreciate?

What does Tony think of the girl? Although Chandler does not tell us what Tony is thinking, what evidence does he provide in the story?

What part does music play in the story?

Tony's hands and their movements are frequently described. Are Tony's hands expressive of his thoughts and feelings? Explain.

Of what significance is it that one of the other side, the "trouble boys," is Tony's brother?

A tendency to idealize the opposite sex is a characteristic of a kind of romanticism. Do you think that this story is "romantic"? Would you expect to find romanticism in hardboiled detective fiction? Why or why not?

If you had to write a continuation of this story, what would take place? (Remember that the final act of the tragedy has been communicated to Tony but not yet to the girl.)

NOTES

1. *The Last Laugh*. A German silent film (1924).
2. *Emil Jannings*. A distinguished German actor who starred in *The Last Laugh*.
3. *The Blue Bird*. A play by Maurice Maeterlinck (1908). The play was made into a silent movie in 1916 and was remade in 1940.

RAYMOND CHANDLER

The Simple Art of Murder

Raymond Chandler began to write detective fiction after the Depression cost him his job. He aimed for realism and truth and reacted against what he considered the artificiality of the English traditional detective story. "The Simple Art of Murder" is Chandler's justification of his kind of fiction. Although it is possibly the most famous essay on detective fiction, its appeal lies more in its splendid, provocative style than in the force of its logical arguments. In this essay Chandler's expression of his own aims and beliefs is of greater importance than his view of the practices of other writers, and the sections excerpted are those in which he states his own theories. The fascinating, moving, and much-reprinted last paragraphs of the essay suggest that there is a large element of romanticism in Chandler himself.

[In the omitted portions of the essay, Chandler criticizes golden-age writers such as A. A. Milne (*The Red House Mystery*) and E. C. Bentley (*Trent's Last Case*), whom he charges with presenting implausible and illogical materials and, more important, with writing works which do not have the authentic flavor of life in them.]

Fiction in any form has always intended to be realistic. Old-fashioned novels which now seem stilted and artificial to the point of burlesque did not appear that way to the people who first read them. Writers like Fielding and Smollett could seem realistic in the modern sense because they dealt largely with uninhibited characters, many of whom were about two jumps ahead of the police, but Jane Austen's chronicles of highly inhibited people against a background of rural gentility seem real enough psychologically. There is plenty of that kind of social and emotional hypocrisy around today. Add to it a liberal dose of intellectual pretentiousness and you get the tone of the book page in your daily paper and the earnest and fatuous atmosphere breathed by discussion groups in little clubs. These are the people who make best-sellers, which are promotional jobs based on a sort of indirect snob-appeal, carefully escorted by the trained seals of the critical fraternity, and lovingly tended and watered by certain much too powerful pressure groups whose business is selling books, although they would like you to think they are fostering culture. Just get a little behind in your payments and you will find out how idealistic they are. . . .

. . . As for literature of expression and literature of escape, this is critics' jargon, a use of abstract words as if they had absolute meanings. Everything written with vitality expresses that vitality; there are no dull subjects, only dull minds. All men who read escape from something else into what lies behind the printed page; the quality of the dream may be argued, but its release has become a functional necessity. All men must escape at times from the deadly rhythm of their private thoughts. It is part of the process of life among thinking beings. It is one of the things that distinguish them from the three-toed sloth; he apparently—one can never be quite sure—is perfectly content hanging upside down on a branch, and not even reading Walter Lippman. I hold no particular brief for the detective story as the ideal escape. I merely say that *all* reading for pleasure is escape, whether it be Greek, mathematics, astronomy, Benedetto Croce, or *The Diary of the Forgotten Man*. To say otherwise is to be an intellectual snob, and a juvenile at the art of living. . . .

How original a writer Hammett really was, it isn't easy to decide now, even if it mattered. He was one of a group, the only one who achieved critical recognition, but not the only one who wrote or tried to write realistic mystery fiction. All literary movements are like this; some one individual is picked out to represent the whole movement; he is usually the culmination of the movement. Hammett was the ace performer, but there is nothing in his work that is not implicit in the early novels and short stories of Hemingway. Yet for all I know, Hemingway may have learned something from Hammett, as well as from writers like Dreiser, Ring Lardner, Carl Sandburg, Sherwood Anderson and himself. A rather revolutionary debunking of both the language and material of fiction had been going on for some time. It probably started in poetry; almost everything does. You can take it clear back to Walt Whitman, if you like. But Hammett applied it to the detective story, and this, because of its heavy crust of English gentility and American pseudo-gentility, was pretty hard to get moving. I doubt that Hammett had any deliberate artistic aims whatever; he was trying to make a living by writing something he had first hand information about. He made some of it up; all writers do; but it had a basis in fact; it was made up out of real things. The only reality the English detection writers knew was the conversational accent of Surbiton[1] and Bognor Regis.[2] If they wrote about dukes and Venetian vases, they knew no more about them out of their own experience than the well-heeled Hollywood character knows about the French Modernists that hang in his Bel-Air château or the semi-antique Chippendale-cum-cobbler's bench that he uses for a coffee table. Hammett took murder out of the Venetian vase and dropped it into the alley; it doesn't have to stay there forever, but it was a good idea to begin by getting as far as possible from Emily Post's[3] idea of how a well-bred debutante gnaws a chicken wing. He wrote at first (and almost to the end) for people with a sharp, aggressive attitude to life. They were not afraid of the seamy side of things; they lived there. Violence did not dismay them; it was right down their street.

Hammett gave murder back to the kind of people that commit it for reasons, not just to provide a corpse; and with the means at hand, not with hand-wrought duelling pistols, curare, and tropical fish. He put these people down on paper as they are, and he made them talk and think in the language they customarily used for these purposes. He had style, but his audience didn't know it, because it was in a language not supposed to be capable of such refinements. They thought they were getting a good meaty melodrama written in the kind of lingo they imagined they spoke themselves. It was, in a sense, but it was much more. All language begins with speech, and the speech of common men at that, but when it develops to the point of becoming a literary medium it only looks like speech. Hammett's style at its worst was almost as formalized as a page of *Marius the Epicurean*;[4] at its best it could say almost anything. I believe this style, which does not belong to Hammett or to anybody, but is the American language (and not even exclusively that any more), can say things he did not know how to say or feel the need of saying. In his hands it had no overtones, left no echo, evoked no image beyond a distant hill. He is said to have lacked heart, yet the story he thought most of himself is the record of a man's devotion to a friend. He was spare, frugal, hardboiled, but he did over and over again what only the best writers can ever do at all. He wrote scenes that seemed never to have been written before.

With all this he did not wreck the formal detective story. Nobody can; production demands a form that can be produced. Realism takes too much talent, too much knowledge, too much awareness. Hammett may have loosened it up a little here, and sharpened it a little there. Certainly all but the stupidest and most meretricious writers are more conscious of their artificiality than they used to be. And he demonstrated that the detective story can be important writing. *The Maltese Falcon* may or may not be a work of genius, but an art which is capable of it is not "by hypothesis" incapable of anything. Once a detective story can be as good as this, only the pedants will deny that it *could* be even better. Hammett did something else, he made the detective story fun to write, not an exhausting concatenation of insignificant clues. . . .

The realistic style is easy to abuse: from haste, from lack of awareness, from inability to bridge the chasm that lies between what a writer would like to be able to say and what he actually knows how to say. It is easy to fake; brutality is not strength, flipness is not wit, edge-of-the-chair writing can be as boring as flat writing; dalliance with promiscuous blondes can be very dull stuff when described by goaty young men with no other purpose in mind than to describe dalliance with promiscuous blondes. There has been so much of this sort of thing that if a character in a detective story says, "Yeah," the author is automatically a Hammett imitator.

And there are still quite a few people around who say that

Hammett did not write detective stories at all, merely hard-boiled chronicles of mean streets with a perfunctory mystery element dropped in like the olive in a martini. These are the flustered old ladies—of both sexes (or no sex) and almost all ages—who like their murders scented with magnolia blossoms and do not care to be reminded that murder is an act of infinite cruelty, even if the perpetrators sometimes look like playboys or college professors or nice motherly women with softly graying hair. There are also a few badly-scarred champions of the formal or the classic mystery who think no story is a detective story which does not pose a formal and exact problem and arrange the clues around it with neat labels on them. Such would point out, for example, that in reading *The Maltese Falcon* no one concerns himself with who killed Spade's partner, Archer, (which is the only formal problem of the story) because the reader is kept thinking about something else. Yet in *The Glass Key* the reader is constantly reminded that the question is who killed Taylor Henry, and exactly the same effect is obtained; an effect of movement, intrigue, cross-purposes and the gradual elucidation of character, which is all the detective story has any right to be about anyway. The rest is spillikins[5] in the parlor.

But all this (and Hammett too) is for me not quite enough. The realist in murder writes of a world in which gangsters can rule nations and almost rule cities, in which hotels and apartment houses and celebrated restaurants are owned by men who made their money out of brothels, in which a screen star can be the fingerman for a mob, and the nice man down the hall is a boss of the numbers racket; a world where a judge with a cellar full of bootleg liquor can send a man to jail for having a pint in his pocket, where the mayor of your town may have condoned murder as an instrument of money-making, where no man can walk down a dark street in safety because law and order are things we talk about but refrain from practicing; a world where you may witness a hold-up in broad daylight and see who did it, but you will fade quickly back into the crowd rather than tell anyone, because the hold-up men may have friends with long guns, or the police may not like your testimony, and in any case the shyster for the defense will be allowed to abuse and vilify you in open court, before a jury of selected morons, without any but the most perfunctory interference from a political judge.

It is not a very fragrant world, but it is the world you live in, and certain writers with tough minds and a cool spirit of detachment can make very interesting and even amusing patterns out of it. It is not funny that a man should be killed, but it is sometimes funny that he should be killed for so little, and that his death should be the coin of what we call civilization. All this still is not quite enough.

In everything that can be called art there is a quality of redemption. It may be pure tragedy, if it is high tragedy, and it may be pity and irony, and it may be the raucous laughter of the strong man. But down these mean streets a man must go who is not himself mean, who is neither tarnished nor afraid. The detective in this kind of story must be such a man. He is the hero, he is everything. He must be a complete man and a common man and yet an unusual man. He must be, to use a rather weathered phrase, a man of honor, by instinct, by inevitability, without thought of it, and certainly without saying it. He must be the best man in his world and a good enough man for any world. I do not care much about his private life; he is neither a eunuch nor a satyr; I think he might seduce a duchess and I am quite sure he would not spoil a virgin; if he is a man of honor in one thing, he is that in all things. He is a relatively poor man, or he would not be a detective at all. He is a common man or he could not go among common people. He has a sense of character, or he would not know his job. He will take no man's money dishonestly and no man's insolence without a due and dispassionate revenge. He is a lonely man and his pride is that you will treat him as a proud man or be very sorry you ever saw him. He talks as the man of his age talks, that is, with rude wit, a lively sense of the grotesque, a disgust for sham, and a contempt for pettiness. The story is his adventure in search of a hidden truth, and it would be no adventure if it did not happen to a man fit for adventure. He has a range of awareness that startles you, but it belongs to him by right, because it belongs to the world he lives in.

If there were enough like him, I think the world would be a very safe place to live in, and yet not too dull to be worth living in.

COMMENT AND QUESTIONS

Have you ever been robbed on the streets? Do you know anyone who was an eyewitness to a robbery and didn't speak up? In what ways does Chandler's description of "not a very fragrant world" fit the world you live in? What sort of "realism" does Chandler write about here? Is there any romanticism in seeing one honorable man—the detective—facing a world of "mean streets"?

What would you say is Chandler's opinion of best sellers?

In what ways does the house dick in "I'll Be Waiting" measure up to the private detective Chandler describes in the last paragraphs of the essay?

NOTES

1. *Surbiton.* A London suburb in Surrey, in Southeast England, about twelve miles from the central part of the city.

2. *Bognor Regis.* A seaside resort in Southeast England. It acquired the "Regis" in its name from the fact that King George V, grandfather of Elizabeth II, once convalesced there.

3. *Emily Post.* An authority on good manners, whose *Etiquette* (first edition in 1922) became the standard for American social behavior.

4. *Marius the Epicurean.* A novel by the Victorian writer Walter Pater, who was noted for his precise, polished writing style.

5. *spillikins.* A game played with a pile of sticks, the object being to pull off each stick without disturbing the rest.

CARTER DICKSON

Persons or Things Unknown

This mystery is an example of a frame story—that is, a story within a story. It is, in fact, an account of a "ghost" story being told to a group of rapt listeners. This story—a spellbinding tale of violent death in Restoration England—is all the more horrifying because it took place in the very house in which the group is assembled.

Once again Carter Dickson (a pen name for John Dickson Carr) presents us with a small scene and a locked room. This time, however, it is not a hidden document but a murder weapon for which we search. When the story is concluded, no solution to the mystery is given. But the host has "solved" the crime, as he then reveals. The astute reader may also participate, for Dickson has played fair and provided all the evidence necessary for a successful armchair detective.

I

"After all," said our host, "it's Christmas. Why not let the skeleton out of the bag?"

"Or the cat out of the closet," said the historian, who likes to be precise even about *clichés*. "Are you serious?"

"Yes," said our host. "I want to know whether it's safe for anyone to sleep in that little room at the head of the stairs."

He had just bought the place. This party was in the nature of a house-warming; and I had already decided privately that the place needed one. It was a long, damp, high-windowed house, hidden behind a hill in Sussex. The drawing-room, where a group of us had gathered round the fire after dinner, was much too long and much too draughty. It had fine panelling—a rich brown where the firelight was always finding new gleams—and a hundred little reflections trembled down its length, as in so many small gloomy mirrors. But it remained draughty.

Of course, we all liked the house. It had the most modern of lighting and heating arrangements, though the plumbing sent ghostly noises and clanks far down into its interior whenever you turned on a tap. But the smell of the past was in it; and you could not get over the idea that somebody was following you about. Now, at the host's flat mention of a certain possibility, we all looked at our wives.

"But you never told us," said the historian's wife, rather shocked, "you never told us you had a ghost here!"

"I don't know that I have," replied our host quite seriously. "All I have is a bundle of evidence about something queer that once happened. It's all right; I haven't put anyone in that little room at the head of the stairs. So we can drop the discussion, if you'd rather."

"You know we can't," said the Inspector, who, as a matter of strict fact, is an Assistant Commissioner of the Metropolitan Police. He smoked a large cigar, and contemplated ghosts with satisfaction. "This is exactly the time and place to hear about it. What is it?"

"It's rather in your line," our host told him slowly. Then he looked at the historian. "And in your line, too. It's a historical story. I suppose you'd call it a historical romance."

"I probably should. What is the date?"

"The date is the year sixteen hundred and sixty."

"That's Charles the Second, isn't it, Will?" demanded the historian's wife; she annoys him sometimes by asking these questions. "I'm terribly fond of them. I hope it has lots of big names in it. You know: Charles the Second and Buckingham[1] and the rest of them. I remember, when I was a little girl, going to see"—she mentioned a great actor—"play David Garrick.[2] I was looking forward to it. I expected to see the programme and the cast of characters positively bristling with people like Dr. Johnson and Goldsmith and Burke and Gibbon and Reynolds,[3] going in and out every minute. There wasn't a single one of them in it, and I felt swindled before the play had begun."

The trouble was that she spoke without conviction. The historian looked sceptically over his pince-nez.

"I warn you," he said, "if this is something you claim to have found in a drawer, in a crabbed old handwriting and all the rest of it, I'm going to be all over you professionally. Let me hear one anachronism——"

But he spoke without conviction, too. Our host was so serious that there was a slight, uneasy silence in the group.

"No. I didn't find it in a drawer; the parson gave it to me. And the handwriting isn't particularly crabbed. I can't show it to you, because it's being typed, but it's a diary: a great, hefty mass of stuff. Most of it is rather dull, though I'm steeped in the seventeenth century, and I confess I enjoy it. The diary was begun in the summer of '60—just after the Restoration—and goes on to the end of '64. It was kept by Mr. Everard Poynter, who owned Manfred Manor (that's six or seven miles from here) when it was a farm.

"I know that fellow," he added, looking thoughtfully at the fire. "I know about him and his sciatica and his views on mutton and politics. I know why he went up to London to dance on Oliver Cromwell's grave, and I can guess who stole the two sacks of malt out of his brew-house while he was away. I see him as half a Hat; the old boy had a beaver hat he wore on his wedding day, and I'll bet he wore it to his death. It's out of all this that I got the details about people. The actual facts I got from the report of the coroner's inquest, which the parson lent me."

"Hold on!" said the Inspector, sitting up straight. "Did this fellow Poynter see the ghost and die?"

"No, no. Nothing like that. But he was one of the witnesses. He saw a man hacked to death, with thirteen stab-wounds in his body, from a hand that wasn't there and a weapon that didn't exist."

There was a silence.

"A murder?" asked the Inspector.

"A murder."

"Where?"

"In that little room at the head of the stairs. It used to be called the Ladies' Withdrawing Room."

Now, it is all very well to sit in your well-lighted flat in town and say we were hypnotized by an atmosphere. You can hear motor-cars crashing their gears, or curse somebody's wireless. You did not sit in that house, with a great wind rushing up off the downs, and a wall of darkness built up for three miles around you: knowing that at a certain hour you would have to retire to your room and put out the light, completing the wall.

"I regret to say," went on our host, "that there are no great names. These people were no more concerned with the Court of Charles the Second—with one exception—than we are concerned with the Court of George the Sixth.[4] They lived in a little, busy, possibly ignorant world. They were fierce, fire-eating Royalists, most of them, who cut the Stuart arms over their chimney-pieces again, and only made a gala trip to town to see the regicides executed in October of '60. Poynter's diary is crowded with them. Among others there is Squire Radlow, who owned this house then and was a great friend of Poynter. There was Squire Radlow's wife, Martha, and his daughter Mary.

"Mistress Mary Radlow was seventeen years old. She was not one of your fainting girls. Poynter—used to giving details—records that she was five feet tall, and thirty-two inches round the bust. 'Pretty and delicate,' Poynter says, with hazel eyes and a small mouth. But she could spin flax against any woman in the country; she once drained a pint of wine at a draught, for a wager; and she took eager pleasure in any good spectacle, like a bear-baiting or a hanging. I don't say that flippantly, but as a plain matter of fact. She was also fond of fine clothes, and danced well.

"In the summer of '60 Mistress Mary was engaged to be married to Richard Oakley of Rawndene. Nobody seems to have known much about Oakley. There are any number of references to him in the diary, but Poynter gives up trying to make him out. Oakley was older than the girl; of genial disposition, though he wore his hair like a Puritan; and a great reader of books. He had a good estate at Rawndene, which he managed well, but his candle burned late over his books; and he wandered abroad in all weathers, summer or frost, in as black a study as the Black Man.

"You might have thought that Mistress Mary would have

preferred somebody livelier. But Oakley was good enough company, by all accounts, and he suited her exactly—they tell me that wives understand this.

"And here is where the trouble enters. At the Restoration, Oakley was looking a little white. Not that his loyalty was exactly suspect; but he had bought his estate under the Commonwealth. If sales made under the Commonwealth were now declared null and void by the new Government, it meant ruin for Oakley; and also, under the business-like standards of the time, it meant the end of his prospective marriage to Mistress Mary.

"Then Gerald Vanning appeared.

"Hoy, what a blaze he must have made! He was fresh and oiled from Versailles, from Cologne, from Bruges, from Brussels, from Breda, from everywhere he had gone in the train of the formerly exiled king. Vanning was one of those 'confident young men' about whom we hear so much complaint from old-style Cavaliers in the early years of the Restoration. His family had been very powerful in Kent before the Civil Wars. Everybody knew he would be well rewarded, as he was.

"If this were a romance, I could now tell you how Mistress Mary fell in love with the handsome young Cavalier, and forgot about Oakley. But the truth seems to be that she never liked Vanning. Vanning disgusted Poynter by a habit of bowing and curvetting, with a superior smile, every time he made a remark. It is probable that Mistress Mary understood him no better than Poynter did.

"There is a description in the diary of a dinner Squire Radlow gave to welcome him here at this house. Vanning came over in a coach, despite the appalling state of the roads, with a dozen lackeys in attendance. This helped to impress the Squire, though nothing had as yet been settled on him by the new régime. Vanning already wore his hair long, whereas the others were just growing theirs. They must have looked odd and patchy, like men beginning to grow beards, and rustic enough to amuse him.

"But Mistress Mary was there. Vanning took one look at her, clapped his hand on the back of a chair, bowed, rolled up his eyes, and began to lay siege to her in the full-dress style of the French King taking a town. He slid *bons mots* on his tongue like sweetmeats; he hiccoughed; he strutted; he directed killing ogles.

Squire Radlow and his wife were enraptured. They liked Oakley of Rawndene—but it was possible that Oakley might be penniless in a month. Whereas Vanning was to be heaped with preferments, a matter of which he made no secret. Throughout this dinner Richard Oakley looked unhappy, and 'shifted his eyes.'

"When the men got drunk after dinner, Vanning spoke frankly to Squire Radlow. Oakley had staggered out to get some air under the apple trees; what between liquor and crowding misfortunes, he did not feel well. Together among the fumes, Vanning and Squire Radlow shouted friendship at each other, and wept. Vanning swore he would never wed anybody but Mistress Mary, not if his soul rotted deep in hell as Oliver's. The Squire was stern, but not too stern. 'Sir,' said the Squire, 'you abuse my hospitality; my daughter is pledged to the gentleman who has just left us; but it may be that we must speak of this presently.' Poynter, though he saw the justice of the argument, went home disturbed.

"Now, Gerald Vanning was not a fool. I have seen his portrait, painted a few years later when periwigs came into fashion. It is a shiny, shrewd, razorish kind of face. He had some genuine classical learning, and a smattering of scientific monkey-tricks, the new toy of the time. But, above all, he had foresight. In the first place, he was genuinely smitten with hazel eyes and other charms. In the second place, Mistress Mary Radlow was a catch. When awarding bounty to the faithful, doubtless the King and Sir Edward Hyde would not forget Vanning of Mallingford; on the other hand, it was just possible that they might.

"During the next three weeks it was almost taken for granted that Vanning should eventually become the Squire's son-in-law. Nothing was said or done, of course. But Vanning dined a dozen times here, drank with the Squire, and gave to the Squire's wife a brooch once owned by Charles the First. Mistress Mary spoke of it furiously to Poynter.

"Then the unexpected news came.

"Oakley was safe in his house and lands. An Act had been passed to confirm all sales and leases of property since the Civil Wars. It meant that Oakley was once more the well-to-do son-in-law; and the Squire could no longer object to his bargain.

"I have here an account of how this news was received at the manor. I did not get it from Poynter's diary. I got it from the records of the coroner's inquest. What astonishes us when we read these chronicles is the blunt directness, the violence, like a wind, or a pistol clapped to the head, with which people set about getting what they wanted. For, just two months afterwards, there was murder done."

II

Our host paused. The room was full of the reflections of firelight. He glanced at the ceiling; what we heard up there was merely the sound of a servant walking overhead.

"Vanning," he went on, "seems to have taken the fact quietly enough. He was here at the manor when Oakley arrived with the news. It was five or six o'clock in the afternoon. Mistress Mary, the Squire, the Squire's wife, and Vanning were sitting in the Ladies' Withdrawing Room. This was (and is) the room at the head of the stairs—a little square place, with two 'panel' windows that would not open. It was furnished with chairs of oak and brocade; a needlework-frame; and a sideboard chastely bearing a plate of oranges, a glass jug of water, and some glasses.

"There was only one candle burning, at some distance from Vanning, so that nobody had a good view of his face. He sat in his riding-coat, with his sword across his lap. When Oakley came in with the news, he was observed to put his hand on his sword; but afterwards he 'made a leg' and left without more words.

"The wedding had originally been set for the end of November; both Oakley and Mistress Mary still claimed this date. It was accepted with all the more cheerfulness by the Squire, since, in the intervening months, Vanning had not yet received any dazzling benefits. True, he had been awarded £500 a year by the Healing and Blessed Parliament. But he was little better off than Oakley; a bargain was a bargain, said the Squire, and Oakley was his own dear son. Nobody seems to know what Vanning did in the interim, except that he settled down quietly at Mallingford.

"But from this time curious rumours began to go about the country-side. They all centered round Richard Oakley. Poynter records some of them, at first evidently not even realizing their direction. They were as light as dandelion-clocks blown off, but they floated and settled.

"Who was Oakley? What did anybody know about him, except that he had come here and bought land under Oliver? He had vast learning, and above a hundred books in his house; what need did he have of that? What had he been? A parson? A doctor of letters or physic? Or letters of a more unnatural kind? Why did he go for long walks in the wood, particularly after dusk?

"Oakley, if questioned, said that this was his nature. But an honest man, meaning an ordinary man, could understand no such nature. A wood was thick; you could not tell what might be in it after nightfall; an honest man preferred the tavern. Such whispers were all the more rapid-moving because of the troubled times. The broken bones of a Revolution are not easily healed. Then there was the unnatural state of the weather. In winter there was no cold at all; the roads dusty; a swarm of flies; and the rose-bushes full of leaves into the following January.

"Oakley heard none of the rumours, or pretended to hear none. It was Jamy Achen, a lad of weak mind and therefore afraid of nothing, who saw something following Richard Oakley through Gallows Copse. The boy said he had not got a good look at it, since the time was after dusk. But he heard it rustle behind the trees, peering out at intervals after Mr. Oakley. He said that it seemed human, but that he was not sure it was alive.

"On the night of Friday, the 26th November, Gerald Vanning rode over to this house alone. It was seven o'clock, a late hour for the country. He was admitted to the lower hall by Kitts, the Squire's steward, and he asked for Mr. Oakley. Kitts told him that Mr. Oakley was above-stairs with Mistress Mary, and that the Squire was asleep over supper with Mr. Poynter.

"It is certain that Vanning was wearing no sword. Kitts held the candle high and looked at him narrowly, for he seemed on a wire of apprehension and kept glancing over his shoulder as he pulled off his gloves. He wore jack-boots, a riding-coat half-buttoned, a laced band at the neck, and a flat-crowned beaver hat with a gold band. Under his sharp nose there was a little edge of moustache, and he was sweating.

" 'Mr. Oakley has brought a friend with him, I think,' says Vanning.

" 'No, sir,' says Kitts, 'he is alone.'

" 'But I am sure his friend has followed him,' says Vanning, again twitching his head round and looking over his shoulder. He also jumped as though something had touched him, and kept turning round and round and looking sharply into corners as though he were playing hide-and-seek.

" 'Well!' says Mr. Vanning, with a whistle of breath through his nose. 'Take me to Mistress Mary. Stop! First fetch two or three brisk lads from the kitchen, and you shall go with me.'

"The steward was alarmed, and asked what was the matter. Vanning would not tell him, but instructed him to see that the servants carried cudgels and lights. Four of them went above-stairs. Vanning knocked at the door of the Withdrawing Room, and was bidden to enter. The servants remained outside, and both the lights and cudgels trembled in their hands: later they did not know why.

"As the door opened and closed, Kitts caught a glimpse of Mistress Mary sitting by the table in the rose-brocade dress she reserved usually for Sundays, and Oakley sitting on the edge of the table beside her. Both looked round as though surprised.

"Presently Kitts heard voices talking, but so low he could not make out what was said. The voices spoke more rapidly; then there was a sound of moving about. The next thing to which Kitts could testify was a noise as though a candlestick had been knocked over. There was a thud; a high-pitched kind of noise; muffled breathing sounds and a sort of thrashing on the floor; and Mistress Mary suddenly beginning to scream over it.

"Kitts and his three followers laid hold of the door, but someone had bolted it. They attacked the door in a way that roused the Squire in the dining-room below, but it held. Inside, after a silence, someone was heard to stumble, and grope towards the door. Squire Radlow and Mr. Poynter came running up the stairs just as the door was unbolted from inside.

"Mistress Mary was standing there, panting, with her eyes wide and staring. She was holding up one edge of her full skirt, where it was stained with blood as though someone had scoured and polished a weapon there. She cried to them to bring lights; and one of the servants held up a lantern in the doorway.

"Vanning was half-lying, half-crouching over against the far wall, with a face like oiled paper as he lifted round his head to look at them. But they were looking at Oakley, or what was left of

Oakley. He had fallen near the table, with the candle smashed beside him. They could not tell how many wounds there were in Oakley's neck and body; above a dozen, Poynter thought, and he was right. Vanning stumbled over and tried to lift him up, but, of course, it was too late. Now listen to Poynter's own words:

" 'Mr. Radlow ran to Mr. Vanning and laid hold of him, crying: "You are a murderer! You have murdered him!" Mr. Vanning cried to him: "By God and His mercy, I have not touched him! I have no sword or dagger by me!" And indeed this was true. For he was flung down on the floor by his bloody work, and ordered to be searched, but not so much as a pin was there in his clothes.

" 'I had observed by the nature of the wide, gaping wounds that some such blade as a broad knife had inflicted them, or the like. But what had done this was a puzzle, for every inch of the room did we search, high, low and turnover; and still not so much as a pin in crack or crevice.

" 'Mr. Vanning deposed that as he was speaking with Mr. Oakley, something struck out the light, and overthrew Mr. Oakley, and knelt on his chest. But who or what this was, or where it had gone when the light was brought, he could not say.' "

III

Bending close to the firelight, our host finished reading the notes from the sheet of paper in his hands. He folded up the paper, put it back in his pocket, and looked at us.

The historian's wife, who had drawn closer to her husband, shifted uneasily. "I wish you wouldn't tell us these things," she complained. "But tell us, anyway. I still don't understand. What was the man killed with, then?"

"That," said our host, lighting his pipe, "is the question. If you accept natural laws as governing this world, there wasn't anything that could have killed him. Look here a moment!"

(For we were all looking at the ceiling.)

"The Squire begged Mistress Mary to tell him what had happened. First she began to whimper a little, and for the first time in her life she fainted. The Squire wanted to throw some water over her, but Vanning carried her downstairs and they forced brandy between her teeth. When she recovered she was a trifle wandering, with no story at all.

"Something had put out the light. There had been a sound like a fall and a scuffling. Then the noise of moving about, and the smell of blood in a close, confined room. Something seemed to be plucking or pulling at her skirts. She does not appear to have remembered anything more.

"Of course, Vanning was put under restraint, and a magistrate sent for. They gathered in this room, which was a good deal bleaker and barer than it is to-day; but they pinned Vanning in the chimney corner of that fireplace. The Squire drew his sword and attempted to run Vanning through: while both of them wept, as the fashion was. But Poynter ordered two of the lads to hold the Squire back, quoting himself later as saying: 'This must be done in good order.'

"Now, what I want to impress on you is that these people were not fools. They had possibly a cruder turn of thought and speech; but they were used to dealing with realities like wool and beef and leather. Here was a reality. Oakley's wounds were six inches deep and an inch wide, from a thick, flat blade that in places had scraped the bone. But there wasn't any such blade, and they knew it.

"Four men stood in the door and held lights while they searched for that knife (if there was such a thing); and they didn't find it. They pulled the room to pieces; and they didn't find it. Nobody could have whisked it out, past the men in the door. The windows didn't open, being set into the wall like panels, so nobody could have got rid of a knife there. There was only one door, outside which the servants had been standing. Something had cut a man to pieces; yet it simply wasn't there.

"Vanning, pale but calmer, repeated his account. Questioned as to why he had come to the house that night, he answered that there had been a matter to settle with Oakley. Asked what it was, he said he had not liked the conditions in his own home for the past month: he would beg Mr. Oakley to mend them. He had done Mr. Oakley no harm, beyond trying to take a bride from him, and therefore he would ask Mr. Oakley to call off his dogs. What dogs? Vanning explained that he did not precisely mean dogs. He meant something that had got into his bedroom cupboard, but was only there at night; and he had reasons for thinking Mr. Oakley had whistled it there. It had been there only since he had been paying attentions to Mistress Mary.

"These men were only human. Poynter ordered the steward to go up and search the little room again—and the steward wouldn't go.

"That little seed of terror had begun to grow like a mango-tree under a cloth, and push up the cloth and stir out tentacles. It was easy to forget the broad, smiling face of Richard Oakley, and to remember the curious 'shifting' of his eyes. When you recalled that, after all, Oakley was twice Mistress Mary's age, you might begin to wonder just whom you had been entertaining at bread and meat.

"Even Squire Radlow did not care to go upstairs again in his own house. Vanning, sweating and squirming in the chimney corner, plucked up courage as a confident young man and volunteered to go. They let him. But no sooner had he got into the little room than the door clapped again, and he came out running. It was touch-and-go whether they would desert the house in a body."

Again our host paused. In the silence it was the Inspector who spoke, examining his cigar and speaking with some scepticism. He had a common-sense voice, which restored reasonable values.

"Look here," he said. "Are you telling us local bogey-tales, or are you seriously putting this forward as evidence?"

"As evidence given at a coroner's inquest."

"Reliable evidence?"

"I believe so."

"I don't," returned the Inspector, drawing the air through a hollow tooth. "After all, I suppose we've got to admit that a man was murdered, since there was an inquest. But if he died of being hacked or slashed with thirteen wounds, some instrument made those wounds. What happened to that weapon? You say it wasn't in the room; but how do we know that? How do we know it wasn't hidden away somewhere, and they simply couldn't find it?"

"I think I can give you my word," said our host slowly, "that no weapon was hidden there."

"Then what the devil happened to it? A knife at least six inches in the blade, and an inch broad——"

"Yes. But the fact is, nobody could see it."

"It wasn't hidden anywhere, and yet nobody could see it?"

"That's right."

"An invisible weapon?"

"Yes," answered our host, with a curious shining in his eyes. "A quite literally invisible weapon."

"How do you know?" demanded his wife abruptly.

Hitherto she had taken no part in the conversation. But she had been studying him in an odd way, sitting on a hassock; and, as he hesitated, she rose at him in a glory of accusation.

"You villain!" she cried. "Ooh, you unutterable villain! You've been making it all up! Just to make everybody afraid to go to bed, and because *I* didn't know anything about the place, you've been telling us a pack of lies——"

But he stopped her.

"No. If I had been making it up, I should have told you it was a story." Again he hesitated, almost biting his nails. "I'll admit that I may have been trying to mystify you a bit. That's reasonable, because I honestly don't know the truth myself. I can make a guess at it, that's all. I can make a guess at how those wounds came there. But that isn't the real problem. That isn't what bothers me, don't you see?"

Here the historian intervened. "A wide acquaintance with sensational fiction," he said, "gives me the line on which you're working. I submit that the victim was stabbed with an icicle, as in several tales I could mention. Afterwards the ice melted—and was, in consequence, an invisible weapon."

"No," said our host.

"I mean," he went on, "that it's not feasible. You would hardly find an icicle in such unnaturally warm weather as they were having. And icicles are brittle: you wouldn't get a flat, broad icicle of such steel-strength and sharpness that thirteen stabs could be made and the bone scraped in some of them. And an icicle isn't invisible. Under the circumstances, this knife was invisible—despite its size."

"Bosh!" said the historian's wife. "There isn't any such thing."

"There is if you come to think about it. Of course, it's only an idea of mine, and it may be all wrong. Also, as I say, it's not the real problem, though it's so closely associated with the real problem that——

"But you haven't heard the rest of the story. Shall I conclude it?"

"By all means."

"I am afraid there are no great alarms or sensations," our host went on, "though the very name of Richard Oakley became a nightmare to keep people indoors at night. 'Oakley's friend' became a local synonym for anything that might get you if you didn't look sharp. One or two people saw him walking in the woods afterwards; his head was on one side and the stab-wounds were still there.

"A grand jury of Sussex gentlemen, headed by Sir Benedict Skene, completely exonerated Gerald Vanning. The coroner's jury had already said 'persons or things unknown,' and added words of sympathy with Mistress Mary to the effect that she was luckily quit of a dangerous bargain. It may not surprise you to hear that eighteen months after Oakley's death she married Vanning.

"She was completely docile, though her old vivacity had gone. In those days young ladies did not remain spinsters through choice. She smiled, nodded, and made the proper responses, though it seems probable that she never got over what had happened.

"Matters became settled, even humdrum. Vanning waxed prosperous and respectable. His subsequent career I have had to look up in other sources, since Poynter's diary breaks off at the end of '64. But a grateful Government made him Sir Gerald Vanning, Bart.[5] He became a leading member of the Royal Society, tinkering with the toys of science. His cheeks filled out, the slyness left his eyes, a periwig adorned his head, and four Flanders mares drew his coach to Gresham House. At home he often chose this house to live in when Squire Radlow died; he moved between here and Mallingford with the soberest grace. The little room, once such a cause of terror, he seldom visited; but its door was not locked.

"His wife saw to it that these flagstones were kept scrubbed, and every stick of wood shining. She was a good wife. He for his part was a good husband: he treated her well and drank only for his thirst, though she often pressed him to drink more than he did. It is at this pitch of domesticity that we get the record of another coroner's inquest.

"Vanning's throat was cut on the night of the 5th October, '67.

"On an evening of high winds, he and his wife came here from Mallingford. He was in unusually good spirits, having just done a profitable piece of business. They had supper together, and Vanning drank a great deal. His wife kept him company at it. (Didn't I tell you she once drank off a pint of wine at a draught, for a wager?) She said it would make him sleep soundly; for it seems to be true that he sometimes talked in his sleep. At eight o'clock, she tells us, she went up to bed, leaving him still at the table. At what time he went upstairs we do not know, and neither do the servants. Kitts, the steward, thought he heard him stumbling up that staircase out there at a very late hour. Kitts also thought he heard someone crying out, but a high October gale was blowing and he could not be sure.

"On the morning of the 6th October, a cowherd named Coates was coming round the side of this house in a sodden daybreak from which the storm had just cleared. He was on his way to the west meadow, and stopped to drink at a rain-water barrel under the eaves just below the little room at the head of the stairs. As he was about to drink, he noticed a curious colour in the water. Looking up to find out how it had come there, he saw Sir Gerald Vanning's face looking down at him under the shadow of the yellow trees. Sir Gerald's head was sticking out of the window, and did not move; neither did the eyes. Some of the glass in the window was still intact, though his head had been run through it, and——"

It was at this point that the Inspector uttered an exclamation.

It was an exclamation of enlightenment. Our host looked at him with a certain grimness, and nodded.

"Yes," he said. "You know the truth now, don't you?"

"The truth?" repeated the historian's wife, almost screaming with perplexity. "The truth about what?"

"About the murder of Oakley," said our host. "About the trick Vanning used to murder Oakley seven years before.

"I'm fairly sure he did it," our host went on, nodding reflectively. "Nothing delighted the people of that time so much as tricks and gadgets of that very sort. A clock that ran by rolling bullets down an inclined plane; a diving-bell; a burglar-alarm; the Royal Society played with all of them. And Vanning (study his portrait one day) profited by the monkey-tricks he learned in exile. He invented an invisible knife."

"But see here———!" protested the historian.

"Of course he planned the whole thing against Oakley. Oakley was no more a necromancer or a consorter with devils than I am. All those rumours about him were started with a definite purpose by Vanning himself. A crop of whispers, a weak-minded lad to be bribed, the whole power of suggestion set going; and Vanning was ready for business.

"On the given night he rode over to this house, alone, with a certain kind of knife in his pocket. He made a great show of pretending he was chased by imaginary monsters, and he alarmed the steward. With the servants for witnesses, he went upstairs to see Oakley and Mistress Mary. He bolted the door. He spoke pleasantly to them. When he had managed to distract the girl's attention, he knocked out the light, tripped up Oakley, and set upon him with that certain kind of knife. There had to be many wounds and much blood, so he could later account for blood on himself. The girl was too terrified in the dark to move. He had only to clean his knife on a soft but stiff-brocaded gown, and then put down the knife in full view. Nobody noticed it."

The historian blinked. "Admirable!" he said. "Nobody noticed it, eh? Can you tell me the sort of blade that can be placed in full view without anybody noticing it?"

"Yes," said our host. "A blade made of ordinary plain glass, placed in the large glass jug full of water standing on a sideboard table."

There was a silence.

"I told you about that glass water-jug. It was a familiar fixture. Nobody examines a transparent jug of water. Vanning could have made a glass knife with the crudest of cutting tools; and glass is murderous stuff—strong, flat, sharp-edged, and as sharp-pointed as you want to make it. There was only candle-light, remember. Any minute traces of blood that might be left on the glass knife would sink as sediment in the water, while everybody looked straight at the weapon in the water and never noticed it. But Vanning (you also remember?) prevented Squire Radlow from throwing water on the girl when she fainted. Instead, he carried her downstairs. Afterwards he told an admirable series of horror-tales; he found an excuse to go back to the room again alone, slip the knife into his sleeve, and get rid of it in the confusion."

The Inspector frowned thoughtfully. "But the real problem——" he said.

"Yes. If that was the way it was done, did the wife know? Vanning talked in his sleep, remember."

We looked at each other. The historian's wife, after a glance round, asked the question that was in our minds.

"And what was the verdict of *that* inquest?"

"Oh, that was simple," said our host. "Death by misadventure, from falling through a window while drunk and cutting his throat on the glass. Somebody observed that there were marks of heels on the board floor as though he might have been dragged there; but this wasn't insisted on. Mistress Mary lived on in complete happiness, and died at the ripe age of eighty-six, full of benevolence and sleep. These are natural explanations. Everything is natural. There's nothing wrong with that little room at the head of the stairs. It's been turned into a bedroom now; I assure you it's comfortable; and anyone who cares to sleep there is free to do so. But at the same time——"

"Quite," we said.

COMMENT AND QUESTIONS

There are many examples of illegal acts by detectives and other sympathetic characters in this collection of stories. In each case we recognize that the act was justified by its circumstances and contributed to true justice when abiding strictly by the law might not have done so. There is no other case, however, where the illegal act is murder.

Consider the case of Mary Radlow Vanning in this light. Why might we condone her brutal murder of her husband? What other choices did she have? Was hers a crime of impulse? of passion?

Is Mistress Mary Radlow presented to us in the beginning of the story as a person capable of the act that concludes the story? What clues are there?

What truths does Vanning make use of in attempting to discredit Oakley with the local inhabitants?

Why are the townspeople suspicious of a man who reads and owns as many books as Oakley does?

Why is the manner of Vanning's death so "appropriate"?

Why are the guests appropriate listeners for a tale such as this?

What advantage is there in setting the story in a much earlier time in history? Would there have been a greater willingness to accept the possibility of death by supernatural means in seventeenth-century England?

NOTES

1. *Buckingham.* George Villiers, 2nd Duke of Buckingham. Writer and politician and one of the flamboyant group of courtiers surrounding Charles II.

2. *David Garrick.* Famous actor and theater manager of the eighteenth century.

3. *Dr. Johnson, Goldsmith, Burke, Gibbon, Reynolds.* A notable group of eighteenth-century men. Dr. Samuel Johnson and Oliver Goldsmith were outstanding men of letters; Edmund Burke was a parliamentarian, an orator, and a writer; Edward Gibbon wrote *The History of the Decline and Fall of the Roman Empire*; and Sir Joshua Reynolds was a prominent painter. In the latter half of the century, they and others, including David Garrick (note 2), were associated in a

well-known informal literary and social group, with Dr. Johnson at the center, simply called The Club.

4. *George the Sixth.* King of England from 1936 to 1952. Father of Elizabeth II.

5. *Bart.* Abbreviation for baronet, a British hereditary title of honor ranking below baron, held by commoners.

ROBERT BLOCH

The Cheaters

Robert Bloch is a writer of many talents. His varied kinds of mystery stories appear regularly in magazines and anthologies, and his works have been dramatized with great success. Many readers will remember the movie *Psycho*, made from a novel by Bloch, which set a trend in screen horror. The short story "The Cheaters" has plot twists and a sense of genuine horror that are very much like those that characterize the novel and film, and, in addition, it makes use of the supernatural to explore fascinating aspects of human psychology. The structure of the story is quite unusual: it contains four parts—almost four separate stories—with the final part serving as both a comment on the first three parts and a climax to the dramatic movement of the plots. This plan allows Bloch to employ a number of quite different characters and situations to express the theme of his work.

Although "The Cheaters" is primarily a horror story, in its American setting, its violence, its focus on predominantly unattractive and unusual characters, and its realistic and often slangy dialogue, it bears a definite, though limited, resemblance to hardboiled detective fiction.

1. JOE HENSHAW

The way I got those spectacles, I bought a blind lot off the City for twenty bucks.

Maggie hollered fit to raise the dead when I told her. "What you wanna load up on some more junk for? The store's full of it now. Get yourself a lot of raggedy old clothes and some busted furniture, that's what you'll get. Why, that dump's over two hunnert years old! Ain't nobody been inside it since Prohibition, it's padlocked tight shut. And you have to throw away twenty bucks for whatever you find for salvage."

And so on and so on, about what a bum I was and why had she ever married me and who wanted to be stuck away for life in the junk and second-hand business.

Well, I just walked out on her and let her keep right on jawing to Jake. He'd listen to her—listen for hours, sitting in back of the shop, drinking coffee when he should have been working.

But I knew what I was doing. Delehanty at City Hall tipped me off about this old house and told me to get in my bid, he'd take care of it.

The dump was near the wharf and it must have been class once, even though they made a speak[1] out of it back in Prohibition days and slapped a padlock on it ever since. Delehanty told me that upstairs, where nobody ever went while it was a rummy hangout, there was all kinds of old furniture from way back. So maybe Maggie was right about it being junk and maybe she was wrong. You never can tell. What I figured, there might be some real antique pieces up there. You got to take a chance once in a while, so I slapped in my bid and got the lot. City gave me three days to move the stuff out before they started razing and Delehanty slipped me a key.

I walked out on Maggie and took the truck down there. Usual thing, I have Jake drive and help me load, but this time I wanted to case the joint myself. If there really was something valuable in there—well, Jake would want a cut. So I let him stay back there and listen to Maggie. Maybe I am a dried-up old jerk like she tells it. And maybe I'm also a pretty smart guy. Just because Jake liked to dress up Saturdays and go down to the Bright Spot—

Anyway, I'm not talking about that, I'm talking about these glasses, these cheaters[2] I found.

That's all I found, too. All I could use. Downstairs was just rubbish and slats; they must have ripped out the bar when the Feds raided it. I kind of counted on finding bar stools and maybe some scrap metal, but no dice.

Upstairs was even worse. Eight big rooms, all dust and broken sticks of furniture. Busted beds, chairs with the springs sprung, nothing I could use. Old rags in some of the closets, and rotted shoes; it looked as if the people who lived here cleared out in a hurry a long time ago. Delehanty tipped me off this was supposed to be a haunted house, but in my line that's strictly a gag. I salvaged maybe two hundred haunted houses in my time—every old dump is supposed to be haunted. But I never run into anything in these places except maybe some cockroaches.

Then I came to this end room with the locked door. This looked a little better; all the other doors was open, but this one was locked tight. I had to use a crowbar on it. Got kind of excited, because you never can tell what a locked door means. Worked and sweated and finally pried it open.

Dust hits me in the face, and an awful stink. I switched on the flashlight and saw a big room with mounds of dirt all over the floor and bookshelves lining the walls. There must of been a thousand books in that room, no kidding, a regular library like.

I waded through the dust and pulled out a couple of the nearest books. The bindings were some kind of leather—that is, they used to be. Now the things just sort of crumbled in my hands, and so did the pages. All yellow and musty, which was why the stink was so bad in here.

I began to swear. I'm no *schmoe*,[3] I know there's dough in old books. But not unless they're in good condition. And this stuff was rotten.

Then I saw this here desk in the corner and so help me, right on top of it was a human skull. A human skull, all yellow and grinning up at me under the light, and for a minute I almost went for that haunted house routine.

Then I noticed how the top was bored out for one of them oldfashion goose-quill pens. The guy who collected all these books used the skull for an inkwell. Screwy, hey?

But the desk was what really interested me because it was antique all right. Solid mahogany and all kinds of fancy scrollwork on it; little goofy faces carved in the wood. There was a drawer, too, and it wasn't locked. I got excited, figuring you never can tell what you find in such places, so I didn't waste much time pulling it open.

Only it was empty. I was so mad I let out a couple of words and kicked the side of the desk.

That's how I found them. The cheaters, that is. Because I hit one of the little goofy faces and a sort of panel swung open on the left side and there was this other drawer.

I reached in and pulled out the spectacles.

Just a pair of glasses, is all, but real funny ones. Little square-shaped lenses with big ear pieces—books, I guess they call them. And a silver bridge over the middle.

I didn't get it. Sure, there was silver in the frames but not more than a couple of bucks worth. So why hide the cheaters away in a secret drawer?

I held the glasses up and wiped the dust off the lenses, which was yellow glass instead of the regular clear kind, but not very thick. I noticed little designs in the temples, like engraving. And right across the bridge for the nose was a word carved into the silver. I remember that word because I never saw it before.

"*Veritas*" was the word, in funny square letters. Could that be Greek? Maybe the old guy was Greek—the guy who had the locked library and the skull for an inkwell and the glasses in the secret drawer, I mean.

I had to squint at the lettering to see it in the gloom there because my eyes weren't so hot—and that gave me an idea.

Get to be my age, sometimes you're kind of shortsighted. I always figured on going to the eye doctor but kept putting it off. So looking at the cheaters I said to myself, why not?

I put them on.

At first my eyes hurt a little. Not hurt, exactly, but something else like hurting inside of me. Like I was being all pulled and twisted. The whole room went far away for a minute and then it came up close and I blinked fast.

After that it was all right and I could see pretty good. Everything was sharp and clear.

So I left the cheaters on and went downstairs, figuring to come back tomorrow with Jake and the truck. At least we could haul the desk and maybe sell the bed-frames for scrap. No sense in me lifting, when I had Jake for the heavy stuff.

I went on home, then.

I come in the shop and sure enough there was Jake and Maggie sitting in back having coffee.

Maggie kind of grinned at me. Then she said, "How did you make out, Joe, you lousy old baboon? I'm glad we're going to kill you."

No, she didn't *say* all that. She just said, "How did you make out, Joe?"

But she was *thinking* the rest.

I know because I *saw* it.

Don't ask me to explain. I *saw* it. Not words, or anything. And I didn't *hear*. I saw. I knew by looking at her what she was thinking and planning.

"Find a lot of stuff?" Jake asked, and I *saw*, "I hope you did because it's all mine as soon as we bump you and we're gonna bump you for sure tonight."

"What you look so funny for, Joe, you sick or something?" Maggie asked. And she said, to herself, "Who cares, he's gonna be a lot sicker soon, all right, does he suspect anything, no of course not, the old goat never got wise to us for a whole year now, just wait until Jake and I own this place together and his insurance too, it's all set."

"What you need, you need a little drink," Jake said to me, and to himself he was saying, "That's the way, get him drunk, and when he gets upstairs I'll push him down and if that don't finish him I'll clobber him with a board, it leaves the same kind of marks. Everybody knows he drinks, it'll look like an accident."

I made myself smile.

"Where'd you get the cheaters?" Maggie asked, saying also,

"God, what a homely mug on him, I get sick just looking at that face but it won't be long now."

"Picked them up over at the house," I said.

Jake got out a fifth and some water glasses. "Drink up," he said.

I sat there trying to figure it out. Why could I read their minds? I didn't know, but I could see what they were up to. I could *see* it. Could it be—the cheaters?

Yes, the cheaters. *They* were the cheaters, carrying on behind my back. Waiting now until I got drunk enough so they could kill me. Pretending to drink a lot while they got me loaded.

But I couldn't get drunk, not as long as I was *seeing* them. The thoughts going through their heads made everything turn to ice, and I was cold sober. I knew just what to do. I made them drink with me.

That helped, only their thoughts got worse. I listened to them talk but all the time I saw their thoughts.

"We'll kill him, just a little while now, why doesn't he hurry up and pass out, got to keep him from suspecting. God how I hate that puss of his. I want to see it smashed open, wait until he's out of the way and I have Maggie all to myself, he's going to die, die, die—"

I listened and I knew just what to do. After dark I said I'd put the truck in the garage for the night, and they stayed behind, thinking about how to get me upstairs now, how to keep people from suspecting them.

Me, I didn't worry about people suspecting. I put the truck away and I came back into the kitchen carrying the crowbar. I locked the door and they saw me with the crowbar, standing there.

"Hey, Joe—" said Jake.

"Joe, what's wrong?" said Maggie.

I didn't say a word.

There wasn't any time to talk, because I was smashing Jake's face with the crowbar, smashing his nose and eyes and jaw, and then I was hammering Maggie over the head and the thoughts came out but not in words, just in screams now, and then there weren't even any screams left to see.

So I sat down and took off the cheaters to polish them. I was still scrubbing at the red stains when the squad car came and the fuzz took me in.

They wouldn't let me keep the glasses and I never did see them again. It didn't matter much, anyway. I could have worn them at the trial, but who cares what the jury thought? And at the end I would have had to take them off anyway.

When they put the black hood over my head . . .

2. *MIRIAM SPENCER OLCOTT*

I distinctly remember it was on Thursday afternoon, because that's when Olive has her bridge club over, and of course she simply *must* have Miss Tooker help with the serving.

Olive is much too diplomatic to lock me in my room even when Miss Tooker isn't there, and I always wondered why I seemed to get so sleepy on Thursdays, just when I might have a chance to slip out without anyone noticing. Finally I realized she must be putting something into my tea at luncheon—more of Dr. Cramer's work, no doubt.

Well, I'm not a complete fool by any means, no matter what they think, and this Thursday I simply poured the tea down the you-know-what. So Olive was none the wiser, and when I lay down on the bed and closed my eyes she went away satisfied. I waited until her guests arrived, then tiptoed down the stairs.

Olive and her friends were in the parlor with the door closed. I had to rest a moment at the foot of the stairs because of my heart, you know, and for an instant I had the most peculiar temptation to open the parlor door and stick my tongue out at the guests.

But that wouldn't have been very ladylike. After all Olive and her husband Percy had come to live with me when Herbert died and they got Miss Tooker to help care for me after I had my first heart attack. I mustn't be rude to them.

Besides, I knew Olive would never permit me to go out alone anymore. So it would be wiser if I didn't disturb her.

I managed to leave without being seen, and took a bus at the corner. There were several people on the bus and they kept staring at me—people are so rude nowadays! I know my clothing is not in the latest style, but there is no call for vulgar curiosity. I wear highbutton shoes for the support they afford my ankles, and if I choose to be sensible regarding draughts, that is my affair. My coat is fur and very expensive; it needs relining and possibly some mending, that is true, but for all strangers know I might be quite impoverished. They need not be so rude. Even my bag attracts their attention; my fine reticule which Herbert brought back for me from abroad, in '37!

I didn't like the way they stared at my bag. It was almost as if they knew. But how could they know, or even suspect?

I sniffed and sat back, trying to decide whether to walk north or south when I got off the bus.

If I walked north, I'd need my bag.

If I walked south, like the last time—

No, I couldn't do that. The last time was frightful, I remember being in that awful place, and then the men laughing, and I had been singing, I believe, was still singing when Percy and Olive came for me in the taxicab. How they found me I'll never know; perhaps the tavern-keeper telephoned them. They got me home and I had one of my attacks and Dr. Cramer told them never to even mention it to me again. So there were no discussions. I hate discussions.

But I knew this time I must walk north. When I left the bus I began to get that tingly feeling all over. It frightened me but it felt—nice.

It felt even nicer when I went into Warram's and began to look at the cameos. The clerk was a man. I told him what I wanted and he went to look. He brought back a wide selection. I told him about my trip to Baden-Baden with Herbert and what we had seen in the jewelry stores there. He was very patient and understanding. I thanked him politely for his trouble and walked out, tingling. There was a brooch, a really lovely thing, in my reticule.

At Slade's I got a scarf. The clerk was an impertinent young snip and so I felt I really must buy a corsage to distract her attention. They were vulgar things, and cost sixty-nine cents. Not nearly worth it. But the scarf in my bag was of imported silk.

It was very exciting. I walked in and out of the shops and the bag began to fill. Then I started going into those second-hand stores near the City Hall. One never knows. My reticule was almost full, but I could still make purchases, too.

In Henshaw's I saw this lovely escritoire, obviously solid mahogany and beautifully carved. I smiled at the proprietor.

"I noticed that escritoire in your window, Mr. Henshaw," I began, but he shook his head.

"It's sold, lady. Beside, my name's Burgin. Henshaw's dead—didn't you read about it in the papers? Hanged him. I bought the place out—"

I held up my hand and sniffed. "Please spare me. But I'll glance around a bit, if I may."

"Sure, lady."

I had seen the table with the ceramics and now I approached it, but he never let his eyes stray from me. I was tingling again and very nervous. There was one piece I simply adored. I had the bag open and it only needed an instant—

He was right behind me, watching my hand move.

"How much is this?" I asked, very quickly, picking up an object at random from one of the trays on the table.

"Two bits!" he snapped.

I fumbled in my pocket and gave him a quarter, then marched out of the store and slammed the door. It was only when I reached the street that I stopped to examine the object in my hand.

It was a pair of spectacles. How in the world had I ever managed to snatch eyeglasses from that tray? Still, they were rather unusual—quite heavy, with tarnished silver frames. I held them up to the light and in the sunset I noticed a word etched across the bridge.

"*Veritas.*" Latin. *Truth.* Strange.

At the same moment I noticed the clock on the City Hall. It was past five. This would never do. I should be found out and there might be a distressing scene—

I hailed a taxicab, and as I rode I remembered that Olive and Percy were dining out tonight, and Dr. Cramer was to come over and examine me. Surely by this time they would have ascertained my absence. How could I ever explain?

Fumbling in my pocket for the fare, my hands encountered the spectacles again. And that, of course, was the solution. I placed them firmly on the bridge of my nose and adjusted the bows just as we turned into the driveway. For a moment the tingling increased and I felt I might have another attack, but then I could see clearly again and the tingling drained away.

I paid the driver and walked into the house quickly, before he had time to comment on the absence of a "tip."

Olive and Percy were waiting for me at the door. I could see them so clearly, so very clearly; Olive so tall and thin, and Percy so short and fat. Both of them had pale skins, like leeches.

Why not? They *were* leeches. Moving into my house when Herbert died, using my property, living on my income. Getting Miss Tooker to come and keep her eye on me, encouraging Dr. Cramer to make an invalid out of me. Ever since Herbert died they had been waiting for *me* to die.

"Here's the old ——— now."

I won't *repeat* the word.

For a moment I was shocked beyond all belief, to think that Percy would stand there smiling and *say* such a thing to my face! Then I realized he wasn't saying it. He was *thinking* it. Somehow, I was reading his mind.

He said, "Mother, darling, where on earth have you been?"

"Yes," said Olive. "We worried so. Why you might have been run over." Her tone was the familiar one of daughterly affection. And behind it, the thought came. "Why *wasn't* she run over, the old ———"

That word again!

I began to tremble.

"Where were you?" Olive murmured. Thinking, "Did you go off on another bat, you doddering old fool? Or were you making trouble for us, stealing from the shops again? The times Percy has had to go down and make good on merchandise—"

I caught the thought and blinked behind the spectacles. I hadn't suspected *that*. Did they *know*, in the stores, what I did? And did they permit it as long as Percy paid for what I had taken? But then I wasn't profiting at all! They were all against me. I saw it for the first time—could it be the spectacles?

"If you must know," I said, very rapidly, "I went downtown to be fitted for a pair of glasses."

And before they had time to reply, I brushed past them and went up to my room.

I was really quite upset. Not only by their thoughts but because I could tell what they were thinking. It couldn't be the spectacles. It couldn't be. Such things aren't really possible. It was only that I was so very tired and so very old—

I took off the glasses and lay down on the bed and suddenly I was crying. Perhaps I fell asleep, for when I awoke it was quite dark and Miss Tooker was coming into the room, carrying a tray. On the tray was a teapot and some biscuits. Dr. Cramer had put me on a strict diet; he knew I loved to eat and wouldn't permit it.

"Go away," I said.

Miss Tooker smiled weakly. "Mr. and Mrs. Dean have left for their dinner engagement. But I thought you might be hungry—"

"Go away," I repeated. "When Dr. Cramer comes, send him up. But you keep out of here."

Her smile faded and she started for the door. For a moment I had the queerest urge to put on the spectacles and *really* see her. But that was all an illusion, wasn't it? I watched her depart, then sat up and reached for my bag. I began to go through my souvenirs of the afternoon and was quite engrossed by the time Dr. Cramer appeared.

He knocked first, giving me time to hide the reticule and its contents, and then entered quietly. "What's all this I hear about you, young lady?" he chuckled. He always called me "young lady." It was our private joke.

"I hear you took a little trip this afternoon," he continued, sitting down next to the bed. "Mrs. Dean mentioned something about spectacles—"

I shrugged. He leaned closer. "And you haven't eaten your dinner. You were crying." He sounded so sympathetic. A wonderful personality, Dr. Cramer. One couldn't help but respond.

"I just wasn't hungry. You see, Olive and Percy just don't understand. I do so enjoy getting out into the fresh air and I hate to trouble them. I can explain about the glasses."

He smiled and winked. "First, some tea. I'd better heat it up again, eh?"

Dr. Cramer set the teapot on the little electric hotplate over on the endtable. He worked quickly, efficiently, humming under his breath. It was a pleasure to watch him, a pleasure to have him visit me. We would sit down now and have a cup of tea together and I would tell him everything. He would understand. It would be all right.

I sat up. The glasses clicked on the bed beside me. I slipped them on.

Dr. Cramer turned and winked at me again. When he winked I felt the glasses pulling on my eyes and closed them for a moment. Then I opened them again and I knew.

I knew Dr. Cramer was here to kill me.

He smiled at me and poured two cups of tea. I watched him stoop over the cup on the left side of the tray and slip the powder into the hot tea.

He brought the tray over to the bed and I said, "A napkin, please." He went back, got the napkin, sat down beside me and handed me the cup from the left side of the tray.

We drank.

My hand didn't tremble, even though he watched me. I emptied my cup. He emptied his.

He winked once more. "Well, young lady—feeling better?"

I winked right back at him. "Much better. And you?"

"First rate. Now we can talk, eh? You were going to tell me something?"

"Yes," I said. "I was going to tell you something. I was going to tell you that I know all about it. Percy and Olive had the plan and they put you up to this. They will inherit and give you one-third. The time for action was indefinite, but when I came home distraught tonight they thought it a good idea if you acted at once. Miss Tooker knew I might have an attack, anyway, and she would be convenient as a witness. Not that witnesses would be needed. You could certify as to the cause of death. My heart, you know."

Dr. Cramer was perspiring. The tea had been quite hot. He raised his hand. "Mrs. Olcott, please—"

"Don't bother to speak. You see, I can read your mind. You don't believe that, do you? You're wondering why, knowing these things, I permitted you to poison me."

His eyes bulged and he turned red as a beet.

"Yes," I whispered. "You wonder why I allowed it. And the answer is—I didn't."

He tugged at his collar and half-rose from his chair. "You—didn't?" he croaked.

"No." I smiled sweetly. "When you brought me the napkin I switched our teacups."

I do not know what poison he employed, but it was quite efficacious. Of course his excitement helped speed the process along. He managed to stand erect, but only for an instant, and then sank back into his chair.

His voice failed almost immediately. His head began to wobble. He frothed and retched and made little sounds. Then he began to bite his lips.

I wanted to read his thoughts, but there were no coherent thoughts any more, only images. Words of prayer and blasphemy commingled, and then the overpowering mastery of pain blotted out everything. It made me tingle all over.

At the end he had convulsions and tried to claw out his own throat. I stood over him and laughed. Not a very ladylike thing to do, I admit, but there was justification. Besides, it made me tingle.

Afterwards I went downstairs. Miss Tooker was sleeping and there was no one to stop me. I deserved a little celebration. So I raided the refrigerator and took up a tray loaded with turkey and dressing and truffles and kumquats—oh, they feasted well downstairs, my loving daughter and son-in-law!

I brought the brandy decanter, too.

It was enough to make me quite giddy, climbing the stairs with that load, but once I was back in my room I felt better.

I filled my teacup with brandy and toasted the figure sprawled in the chair before me. I inquired politely did he want a snack, would he care for some brandy, it was delicious and how was his heart behaving these days?

The brandy was strong. I finished all the food, every last bit of it, and drank again. The tingling was mixed with warmth. I felt like singing, shouting. I did both.

The teacup broke. I drank out of the decanter. No one to see me. I reached out and closed his eyes. Bulging eyes. My own eyes ached. I took off the spectacles. Shouldn't have worn them. But if I hadn't, I'd be dead. Now he was dead. I was alive, and tingling.

More brandy. Heartburn. Too much food. Brandy burned too. I lay back on the bed. Everything went round and round, burning. I could see him sprawled there with his mouth open, laughing at me.

Why did he laugh? He was dead. I was the one who should laugh. He had poison. I had brandy. "Liquor is poison to you, Mrs. Olcott."

Who said that? Dr. Cramer said that, the last time. But I wasn't poisoned. So why did it hurt when I laughed?

Why did it hurt my chest so and why did the room go around when I tried to sit up and fell face downwards on the floor why did I tear at the rug until my fingers bent backwards and snapped one by one like pretzel sticks but I couldn't feel them because the pain in my chest was so much stronger than anything, stronger than life itself—

Because it was death.

I died at 10:18 p.m.

3. PERCY DEAN

After the whole affair was hushed up, Olive and I went away for a while. We could afford to travel now and I made arrangements to have the whole place remodeled while we were gone.

When we returned Olive and I could really hold our heads up in the community. No more snubs, no more covert insults, no more gossip about, "Mrs. Olcott's son-in-law . . . parvenu . . . not altogether the sort of person who belongs."

We had the means now to take our rightful place in society at last. To entertain. That was the first step. The costume party was really Olive's idea, although I was the one who tied it in with our "housewarming."

It was important to invite the right people. Thorgeson, Harker, Pfluger, Hattie Rooker, the Misses Christie. I checked the list with Olive most carefully before we sent invitations.

"If we have Hattie Rooker we must invite Sebastian Grimm," she reminded me. "The writer, you know. He's visiting at her home for the summer."

We planned it all carefully, so carefully in fact that we almost forgot to select our own costumes. At the last moment Olive mentioned the fact. I asked her what she intended to wear.

"Something Spanish, with a mantilla. Then I can wear the earrings." She peered at me quizzically. "But you're going to be a problem. Frankly, Percy, you're too tubby for the usual things. Unless you choose to dress as a clown."

I almost spoke harshly to her, but it was true. I regarded my portliness in the mirror; my receding hairline, my double chin. She peered over my shoulder.

"Just the thing!" she exclaimed. "You shall be Benjamin Franklin."

Benjamin Franklin. I had to admit it wasn't a bad idea. After all, Franklin was a symbol of dignity, stability and wisdom—I am inclined to discount those absurd rumors about his mistresses—and that was the very effect I was seeking. I depended upon this evening to impress my guests. It might be an important first step.

The upshot of the matter was that I went to the costumer, told him my needs, and returned that evening with a Colonial costume, including a partial wig.

Olive was ecstatic over the results. I dressed hastily after dinner and she inspected me at the last moment. "Quite a striking likeness," she said. "But didn't Franklin always wear spectacles?"

"So he did. Unfortunately, it's too late now to procure a pair. I trust the guests will forgive the oversight."

They did.

I spent a most enjoyable evening. Everyone arrived, the liquor was good and plentiful, our catering service excellent, and the costumes added the proper note of frivolity. Although a total abstainer myself, I saw to it that old man Harker, Judge Pfluger, Thorgeson and the others imbibed freely, and their cordiality increased as the evening progressed.

It was particularly important to gain Thorgeson's friendship. Through him I could gain membership in the Gentry Club, and sooner or later I'd worm my way into Room 1200—the fabulous "poker room" where the really big deals were made; millions of dollars in contracts assigned casually as the powers-that-be dealt their cards.

The writer, Sebastian Grimm, put the next idea into my head. "Party's going nicely," he drawled. "Almost think it would be safe to leave the ladies to their own devices for an hour or so, now that the dancing has started. You haven't a poker table available, have you, Dean?"

"There's a room upstairs," I ventured. "Away from the crowd and the noise. If you gentlemen are interested—"

They were. We ascended the stairs.

I hate poker. I dislike all games of chance. But this was too perfect an opportunity to miss. Wouldn't it be natural for my guests to suggest another meeting in the future? Perhaps Thorgeson would mention the Gentry Club games, and I could remind him I was not a member. "That's easily remedied, Dean," he would boom. "Tell you what I'll do—"

Oh, it was an inspiration, and no mistake! I secured cards and chips and we gathered around the big table in the upstairs study—Thorgeson, Dr. Cassit, Judge Pfluger, Harker, Grimm and myself. I would have excluded Grimm if possible; the tall, thin sardonic writer was a disturbing element, and his presence was of no value to me. But it had been his suggestion and I couldn't very well shake him off.

Olive tapped on the door before we started to play.

"Oh here you are," she said. "I see you're in good company. Would anyone care to have buffet luncheon sent up?"

There was an awkward silence. I felt annoyance.

"Very well, then, I shan't disturb you. Oh, Percy—I found something for you just now. In—in Mother's room." She came up behind me and slipped something over my nose and ears. "Spectacles," she giggled. "You remember, we couldn't find a pair for you? But these were in Mother's bureau drawer."

She stood back and surveyed me. "Now, that does it. He really looks like Benjamin Franklin, don't you think?"

I didn't want the spectacles. They hurt my eyes. But I was too embarrassed to reprove her; merely grateful when she slipped out of the room again. The men were already intent on the distribution of chips. Thorgeson was banking. I pulled out my wallet and placed a hundred dollar bill on the table. I received ten white chips.

Obviously, they played for "blood." Very well. I smiled and placed five hundred dollars more before me. "Now for some reds." Thorgeson gave me twenty red chips.

"That's better," I commented. And it was, for I meant to lose tonight. A thousand dollars or so invested properly here would almost guarantee my acceptance by this group, if I lost graciously, like a gentleman. That was my strategy for the evening.

But it didn't work.

I have heard of clairvoyance, of telepathy, of ESP, and these phenomena I have always discounted. Yet *something* was at work tonight. For as I squinted through my spectacles at the cards, I could read the hands of the other players. Not their hands, but their *minds*.

"Pair of eights under . . . raise, I'll get another . . . two queens . . . wonder if he's going for a straight? . . . better stay in . . . never make an inside . . . raise again, bluff them out."

It came to me in a steady stream. I knew when to drop, when to stay, when to raise, when to call.

Of course I meant to lose. But when a man *knows* what to do he's a fool to abandon his advantage. That's logic, isn't it? Sound business. These men respected shrewdness, good judgment. How could I help myself?

I do not wish to dwell upon the actual incidents of the game. Sufficient to say that I won almost every hand. This psychic sense never deserted me, and I must have been over nine thousand dollars ahead when Harker cheated.

I had paid no heed to any extraneous thought or circumstance; merely concentrated on the game and the bets. And then, "I'll keep the ace until the next hand," Harker thought. I could feel it, feel the strength and the desperate avariciousness behind it. Old Harker, worth close to a million dollars, cheating over the poker table.

It stunned me. Before I could make up my mind how to react, the next hand was in play—had been played—and I was sitting there calling with a full house, queens over fours, getting ready to rake in a three-thousand-dollar pot.

Harker's monkey face creased into a grin. "Not so fast, my friend. I have"—he licked his thin lips eagerly—"four aces."

I coughed. "Sorry, Mr. Harker. But has it come to your attention that this is a seven-card stud game and you also have—eight cards?"

Everybody gasped. Gasped, then fell silent.

"An oversight, no doubt. But if you will be good enough to raise your left arm from the table—there, underneath your sleeve—"

The silence deepened. Yet suddenly it was filled with a clamor; not a clamor of words but of *thoughts*.

"The cur . . . accusing Harker, of all people . . . probably planted the card there himself . . . cheating . . . no gentleman . . . nasty little fat-faced fool . . . never should have come . . . barred from decent society . . . vulgar . . . probably drove the old lady to her grave . . .

My head hurt.

I thought if I could talk, the hurting would go away. So I told them what I knew and what I felt about them, and they only stared. So I thought if I shouted it might relieve the pressure in my head, and I shouted and ordered them out of my house and named them for what they were, but they gaped at me as if I were mad. And they kept on *thinking*.

Harker was the worst. He thought things about me which no man could endure. No man could endure such thoughts, even if his head weren't splitting and he didn't know it was all lost, they all hated him, they were mocking and sneering inside.

So I knocked over the table and I took him by the collar, and then they were all on me at once, but I had his wizened throat between my fingers and I wouldn't let go until I squeezed out all the hurting, all of it, and my glasses fell off and everything seemed to go dim. I looked up just in time to see Thorgeson aiming the water carafe at my head.

I tried to move to one side, but it was too late. The carafe came down and everything went away.

Forever.

4. *SEBASTIAN GRIMM*

This will be very brief.

When I picked up those peculiar yellow-lensed spectacles from the floor—slipping them into my pocket unobserved, in the confusion attendant upon calling the doctor and the police—I was motivated by mere curiosity.

That curiosity grew when, at the inquest, Olive Dean spoke of her mother and how she had brought a pair of glasses home with her on the night of her tragic death.

Certain aspects of that poker game had piqued my fancy, and the statements at the inquest further intrigued me.

The legend, *"Veritas,"* inscribed upon the bridge of the spectacles, was also interesting.

I shall not bore you with my researches. Amateur detection is a monotonous, albeit sometimes a rewarding procedure. It is sufficient to say that my private inquiry led me to a second-hand store and eventually to a partially-razed house near the docks. Research with the local historical society enabled me to ascertain that the spectacles had once been the property of Dirk Van Prinn; legends of his reputed interest in sorcery are common knowledge amongst antiquarians who delve into the early history of the community. I need not bother to underscore the obvious.

At any rate, my rather careful investigations bore fruit. I was able, taking certain liberties based upon circumstantial evidence, to "reconstruct" the thoughts and actions of the various persons who had inadvertently worn the spectacles since the time of their discovery in the secret drawer of old Van Prinn's escritoire. These thoughts and actions have formed the basis of this narrative, in which I have assumed the characters of Mr. Joseph Henshaw, Mrs. Miriam Spencer Olcott, and Mr. Percy Dean—all deceased.

Unfortunately, a final chapter remains to be written. I had no idea of this necessity when I started; had I suspected, I would have desisted immediately. But now I know, as Dirk Van Prinn must have known when he hid the spectacles away in that drawer, that there is danger in wisdom; that knowledge of the thoughts of others leads only to disillusion and destruction.

I mused upon the triteness of this moral, and not for anything in the world would I have emulated poor Joe Henshaw, or Mrs. Olcott, or Percy Dean, and put on the spectacles to gaze at other men and other minds.

But pride goeth before a fall, and as I wrote of the tragic fate of those poor fools whose search for wisdom ended in disaster, I could not help but reflect upon the actual purpose for which these singular spectacles had somehow been created by a long-dead savant and seer.

"*Veritas.*" The truth.

The truth about others brought evil consequences. But suppose the spectacles were meant to be employed to discover the truth about one's self?

"*Know thyself.*" Could it be that this was the secret purpose of the spectacles—to enable the wearer to look *inward?*

Surely there could be no harm in that. Not in the hands of an intelligent man.

I have always fancied that I "knew" myself in the ordinary sense of the word; was perhaps more aware, through constant introspection, of my inner nature. Thus I *fancied*, but I had to *know*.

And that is why I put them on, just now. Put them on and stared at myself in the hall mirror. Stared, and saw, and knew.

There are things about subliminal intelligence, about the so-called "subconscious," which psychiatry and psychology cannot encompass. I know these things now, and a great deal more. I know that the actual agony undergone by the victims who read the minds of others is as nothing compared to that which is born of reading one's own mind.

I stood before the mirror and looked *into* myself—seeing there the atavistic memories, the desires, the fears, the self-defeat, the seeds of madness, the lurking filth and cruelty; the slimy, crawling, secret shapes which dare not rise even in dreams. I saw the unutterable foulness beneath all the veneer of consciousness and intellect, and knew it for my true nature. Every man's nature. Perhaps it can be suppressed and controlled, if one remains unaware. But merely to realize that *it is there* is a horror which must not be permitted.

When I conclude this account I shall take the "cheaters," as Joe Henshaw so appropriately called them, and destroy them forever. I shall use a revolver for that purpose; aiming it quite steadily and deliberately at these accursed instruments, and shattering them with a single shot.

And I shall be wearing them at the time . . .

COMMENT AND QUESTIONS

Does one think in "readable" expressions—in sentences or phrases, for example? Compare your own thoughts with those that are revealed in the story.

Is the human mind able to support the weight of absolute truth? Why do we seek truth so diligently—or do we?

What details, even before Joe puts the glasses on, suggest to the reader that these are special glasses?

Why is it especially horrifying when a story about people who are ordinary and even dull or unattractive involves supernatural happenings? Explain.

Why do you think Joe doesn't try to defend himself to the police or justify what he did?

Does the last speaker, Sebastian Grimm, go too far in his expression of the "moral" of the first three parts of the story? Don't we already know what he tells us, and doesn't it seem somewhat obvious? Is the same criticism appropriate to his description of what he sees in the mirror? Would the horror be greater if we were left to imagine what he might see in himself? Discuss what you think was Bloch's purpose in including a fourth part to the story. How many "cheaters" are there in the story?

Why might Sebastian Grimm be a disturbing element to Percy Dean?

NOTES

1. *speak*. Speakeasy.
2. *cheaters*. Slang for spectacles.
3. *schmoe*. A stupid, foolish, or unconventional person.

ROSS MACDONALD

Guilt-Edged Blonde

The contemporary writer most indebted to the Hammett-Chandler tradition of hardboiled detection is Ross Macdonald, whose best-selling novels have had considerable critical acclaim.

His detective is Lew Archer, of whom Eudora Welty says:

> Archer from the start has been a distinguished creation; . . . Possessed even when young of an endless backlog of stored information, most of it sad, on human nature, he tended once, unless I'm mistaken, to be a bit cynical. Now he is something much more; he is vulnerable. As a detective and as a man he takes the human situation with full seriousness. He cares. And good and evil both are real to him.

Archer narrates this short story, as he does the Macdonald novels. In this respect, he is like the Continental Op, who narrates the stories in which he appears. But notice how different Archer's observations are from the Op's and how different the tone is from that of the Hammett story.

Hammett, Chandler, and Macdonald all write about the no-man's-land that exists between the little men who are generally law-abiding and the various types of gangsters who seem indigenous to California. This world, however, emerges with quite different qualities from the hands of each writer.

A man was waiting for me at the gate at the edge of the runway. He didn't look like the man I expected to meet. He wore a stained tan windbreaker, baggy slacks, a hat as squashed and dubious as his face. He must have been 40 years old, to judge by the gray in his hair and the lines around his eyes. His eyes were dark and evasive, moving here and there as if to avoid getting hurt. He had been hurt often and badly, I guessed.

"You Archer?"

I said I was. I offered him my hand. He didn't know what to do with it. He regarded it suspiciously, as if I was planning to try a Judo hold on him. He kept his hands in the pockets of his windbreaker.

"I'm Harry Nemo." His voice was a grudging whine. It cost him an effort to give his name away. "My brother told me to come and pick you up. You ready to go?"

"As soon as I get my luggage."

I collected my overnight bag at the counter in the empty waiting room. The bag was very heavy for its size. It contained, besides a toothbrush and spare linen, two guns and the ammunition for them. A .38 special for sudden work, and a .32 automatic as a spare.

Harry Nemo took me outside to his car. It was a new seven-passenger custom job, as long and black as death. The windshield and side windows were very thick, and they had the yellowish tinge of bullet-proof glass.

"Are you expecting to be shot at?"

"Not me." His smile was dismal. "This is Nick's car."

"Why didn't Nick come himself?"

He looked around the deserted field. The plane I had arrived on was a flashing speck in the sky above the red sun. The only human being in sight was the operator in the control tower. But Nemo leaned toward me in the seat, and spoke in a whisper:

"Nick's a scared pigeon. He's scared to leave the house. Ever since this morning."

"What happened this morning?"

"Didn't he tell you? You talked to him on the phone."

"He didn't say very much. He told me he wanted to hire a bodyguard for six days, until his boat sails. He didn't tell me why."

"They're gunning for him, that's why. He went to the beach this morning. He has a private beach along the back of his ranch, and he went down there by himself for his morning dip. Somebody took a shot at him from the top of the bluff. Five or six shots. He was in the water, see, with no gun handy. He told me the slugs were splashing around him like hailstones. He ducked and swam under water out to sea. Lucky for him he's a good swimmer, or he wouldn't of got away. It's no wonder he's scared. It means they caught up with him, see?"

"Who are 'they,' or is that a family secret?"

Nemo turned from the wheel to peer into my face. His breath was sour, his look incredulous. "Hell, don't you know who Nick is? Didn't he tell you?"

"He's a lemon-grower, isn't he?"

"He is now."

"What did he used to be?"

The bitter beaten face closed on itself. "I oughtn't to be flapping at the mouth. He can tell you himself if he wants to."

Two hundred horses yanked us away from the curb. I rode with my heavy leather bag on my knees. Nemo drove as if driving was the one thing in life he enjoyed, rapt in silent communion with the engine. It whisked us along the highway, then down a gradual incline between geometrically planted lemon groves. The sunset sea glimmered red at the foot of the slope.

Before we reached it, we turned off the blacktop into a private lane which ran like a straight hair-parting between the dark green trees. Straight for half a mile or more to a low house in a clearing.

The house was flat-roofed, made of concrete and fieldstone, with an attached garage. All its windows were blinded with heavy draperies. It was surrounded with well-kept shrubbery and lawn, the lawn with a ten-foot wire fence surmounted by barbed wire.

Nemo stopped in front of the closed and padlocked gate, and honked the horn. There was no response. He honked the horn again.

About halfway between the house and the gate a crawling thing came out of the shrubbery. It was a man, moving very slowly on hands and knees. His head hung down almost to the ground. One side of his head was bright red, as if he had fallen in paint. He left a jagged red trail in the gravel of the driveway.

Harry Nemo said, "Nick!" He scrambled out of the car. "What happened, Nick?"

The crawling man lifted his heavy head and looked at us. Cumbrously, he rose to his feet. He came forward with his legs spraddled and loose, like a huge infant learning to walk. He breathed loudly and horribly, looking at us with a dreadful hopefulness. Then he died on his feet, still walking. I saw the change in his face before it struck the gravel.

Harry Nemo went over the fence like a weary monkey, snagging his slacks on the barbed wire. He knelt beside his brother and turned him over and palmed his chest. He stood up shaking his head.

I had my bag unzipped and my hand on the revolver. I went to the gate, "Open up, Harry."

Harry was saying, "They got him," over and over. He crossed himself several times. "The dirty bastards."

"Open up," I said.

He found a key ring in the dead man's pocket and opened the padlocked gate. Our dragging footsteps crunched the gravel. I looked down at the specks of gravel in Nicky Nemo's eyes, the bullet hole in his temple.

"Who got him, Harry?"

"I dunno. Fats Jordan, or Artie Castola, or Faronese. It must have been one of them."

"The Purple Gang."

"You called it. Nicky was their treasurer back in the thirties. He was the one that didn't get into the papers. He handled the payoff, see. When the heat went on and the gang got busted up, he had some money in a safe-deposit box. He was the only one that got away."

"How much money?"

"Nicky never told me. All I know, he come out here before the war and bought a thousand acres of lemon land. It took them fifteen years to catch up with him. He always knew they were gonna, though. He knew it."

"Artie Castola got off the Rock[1] last spring."

"You're telling me. That's when Nicky bought himself the bullet-proof car and put up the fence."

"Are they gunning for you?"

He looked around at the darkening groves and the sky. The sky was streaked with running red, as if the sun had died a violent death.

"I dunno," he answered nervously. "They got no reason to. I'm as clean as soap. I never been in the rackets. Not since I was young, anyway. The wife made me go straight, see?"

I said, "We better get into the house and call the police."

The front door was standing a few inches ajar. I could see at the edge that it was sheathed with quarter-inch steel plate. Harry put my thoughts into words.

"Why in hell would he go outside? He was safe as houses as long as he stayed inside."

"Did he live alone?"

"More or less alone."

"What does that mean?"

He pretended not to hear me, but I got some kind of answer. Looking through the doorless arch into the living room, I saw a leopardskin coat folded across the back of the chesterfield. There were red-tipped cigarette butts mingled with cigar butts in the ashtrays.

"Nicky was married?"

"Not exactly."

"You know the woman?"

"Naw." But he was lying.

Somewhere behind the thick walls of the house there was a creak of springs, a crashing bump, the broken roar of a cold engine, grinding of tires in gravel. I got to the door in time to see a cerise convertible hurtling down the driveway. The top was down, and a yellow-haired girl was small and intent at the wheel. She swerved around Nick's body and got through the gate somehow, with her tires screaming.

I aimed at the right rear tire, and missed. Harry came up behind me. He pushed my gun arm down before I could fire again. The convertible disappeared in the direction of the highway.

"Let her go," he said.

"Who is she?"

He thought about it, his slow brain clicking almost audibly. "I dunno. Some pig that Nicky picked up someplace. Her name is Flossie or Florrie or something. She didn't shoot him, if that's what you're worried about."

"You know her pretty well, do you?"

"The hell I do. I don't mess with Nicky's dames." He tried to work up a rage to go with the strong words, but he didn't have the makings. The best he could produce was petulance. "Listen, mister, why should you hang around? The guy that hired you is dead."

"I haven't been paid, for one thing."

"I'll fix that."

He trotted across the lawn to the body and came back with an alligator billfold. It was thick with money.

"How much?"

"A hundred will do it."

He handed me a hundred-dollar bill. "Now how about you amscray, bud, before the law gets here?"

"I need transportation."

"Take Nicky's car. He won't be using it. You can park it at the airport and leave the key with the agent."

"I can, eh?"

"Sure. I'm telling you you can."

"Aren't you getting a little free with your brother's property?"

"It's my property now, bud." A bright thought struck him, disorganizing his face. "Incidentally, how would you like to get off of my land?"

"I'm staying, Harry. I like this place. I always say it's people that make a place."

The gun was still in my hand. He looked down at it.

"Get on the telephone, Harry. Call the police."

"Who do you think you are, ordering me around? I took my last order from anybody, see?" He glanced over his shoulder at the dark and shapeless object on the gravel, and spat venomously.

"I'm a citizen, working for Nicky. Not for you."

He changed his tune very suddenly. "How much to go to work for me?"

"Depends on the line of work."

He manipulated the alligator wallet. "Here's another hundred. If you got to hang around, keep the lip buttoned down about the dame, eh? Is it a deal?"

I didn't answer, but I took the money. I put it in a separate pocket by itself. Harry telephoned the county sheriff.

He emptied the ashtrays before the sheriff's men arrived, and stuffed the leopardskin coat into the woodbox. I sat and watched him.

We spent the next two hours with loud-mouthed deputies. They were angry with the dead man for having the kind of past that attracted bullets. They were angry with Harry for being his brother. They were secretly angry with themselves for being inexperienced and incompetent. They didn't even uncover the leopardskin coat.

Harry Nemo left the courthouse first. I waited for him to leave, and tailed him home, on foot.

Where a leaning palm tree reared its ragged head above the pavements there was a court lined with jerry-built frame cottages. Harry turned up the walk between them and entered the first cottage. Light flashed on his face from inside. I heard a woman's voice say something to him. Then light and sound were cut off by the closing door.

An old gabled house with boarded-up windows stood opposite the court. I crossed the street and settled down in the shadows of its veranda to watch Harry Nemo's cottage. Three cigarettes later a tall woman in a dark hat and a light coat came out of the cottage and walked briskly to the corner and out of sight. Two cigarettes after that she reappeared at the corner on my side of the street, still walking briskly. I noticed that she had a large straw handbag under her arm. Her face was long and stony under the streetlight.

Leaving the street, she marched up the broken sidewalk to the veranda where I was leaning against the shadowed wall. The stairs groaned under her decisive footsteps. I put my hand on the gun in my pocket, and waited. With the rigid assurance of a WAC [2] corporal marching at the head of her platoon, she crossed the veranda to me, a thin high-shouldered silhouette against the light from the corner. Her hand was in her straw bag, and the end of the bag was pointed at my stomach. Her shadowed face was a gleam of eyes, a glint of teeth.

"I wouldn't try it if I were you," she said. "I have a gun here, and the safety is off, and I know how to shoot it, mister."

"Congratulations."

"I'm not joking." Her deep contralto rose a notch. "Rapid fire used to be my specialty. So you better take your hands out of your pockets."

I showed her my hands, empty. Moving very quickly, she relieved my pocket of the weight of my gun, and frisked me for other weapons.

"Who are you, mister?" she said as she stepped back. "You can't be Arturo Castola, you're not old enough."

"Are you a policewoman?"

"I'll ask the questions. What are you doing here?"

"Waiting for a friend."

"You're a liar. You've been watching my house for an hour and a half. I tabbed you through the window."

"So you went and bought yourself a gun?"

"I did. You followed Harry home. I'm Mrs. Nemo, and I want to know why."

"Harry's the friend I'm waiting for."

"You're a double liar. Harry's afraid of you. You're no friend of his."

"That depends on Harry. I'm a detective."

She snorted. "Very likely. Where's your buzzer?"

"I'm a private detective," I said. "I have identification in my wallet."

"Show me. And don't try any tricks."

I produced my photostat. She held it up to the light from the street, and handed it back to me. "So you're a detective. You better do something about your tailing technique. It's obvious."

"I didn't know I was dealing with a cop."

"I was a cop," she said. "Not any more."

"Then give me back my .38. It cost me seventy dollars."

"First tell me, what's your interest in my husband? Who hired you?"

"Nick, your brother-in-law. He called me in Los Angeles today, said he needed a bodyguard for a week. Didn't Harry tell you?"

She didn't answer.

"By the time I got to Nick, he didn't need a bodyguard, or anything. But I thought I'd stick around and see what I could find out about his death. He was a client, after all."

"You should pick your clients more carefully."

"What about picking brothers-in-law?"

She shook her head stiffly. The hair that escaped from under her hat was almost white. "I'm not responsible for Nick or anything about him. Harry is my responsibility. I met him in line of duty and I straightened him out, understand? I tore him loose from Detroit and the rackets, and I brought him out here. I couldn't cut him off from his brother entirely. But he hasn't been in trouble since I married him. Not once."

"Until now."

"Harry isn't in trouble now."

"Not yet. Not officially."

"What do you mean?"

"Give me my gun, and put yours down. I can't talk into iron."

She hesitated, a grim and anxious woman under pressure. I wondered what quirk of fate or psychology had married her to a hood, and decided it must have been love. Only love would send a woman across a dark street to face down an unknown gunman. Mrs. Nemo was horsefaced and aging and not pretty, but she had courage.

She handed me my gun. Its butt was soothing to the palm of my hand. I dropped it into my pocket. A gang of boys at loose ends went by in the street, hooting and whistling purposelessly.

She leaned toward me, almost as tall as I was. Her voice was a low sibilance forced between her teeth:

"Harry had nothing to do with his brother's death. You're crazy if you think so."

"What makes you so sure, Mrs. Nemo?"

"Harry couldn't, that's all. I know Harry, I can read him like a book. Even if he had the guts, which he hasn't, he wouldn't dare to think of killing Nick. Nick was his older brother, understand, the successful one in the family." Her voice rasped contemptuously. "In spite of everything I could do or say, Harry worshiped Nick right up to the end."

"Those brotherly feelings sometimes cut two ways. And Harry had a lot to gain."

"Not a cent. Nothing."

"He's Nick's heir, isn't he?"

"Not as long as he stays married to me. I wouldn't let him touch a cent of Nick Nemo's filthy money. Is that clear?"

"It's clear to me. But is it clear to Harry?"

"I made it clear to him, many times. Anyway, this is ridiculous. Harry wouldn't lay a finger on that precious brother of his."

"Maybe he didn't do it himself. He could have had it done for him. I know he's covering for somebody."

"Who?"

"A blonde girl left the house after we arrived. She got away in a cherry-colored convertible. Harry recognized her."

"A cherry-colored convertible?"

"Yes. Does that mean something to you?"

"No. Nothing in particular. She must have been one of Nick's girls. He always had girls."

"Why would Harry cover for her?"

"What do you mean, cover for her?"

"She left a leopardskin coat behind. Harry hid it, and paid me not to tell the police."

"Harry did that?"

"Unless I'm having delusions."

"Maybe you are at that. If you think Harry paid that girl to shoot Nick, or had anything—"

"I know. Don't say it. I'm crazy."

Mrs. Nemo laid a thin hand on my arm. "Anyway, lay off Harry. Please. I have a hard enough time handling him as it is. He's worse than my first husband. The first one was a drunk, believe it or not." She glanced at the lighted cottage across the street, and I saw one-half of her bitter smile. "I wonder what makes a woman go for the lame ducks the way I did."

"I wouldn't know, Mrs. Nemo. Okay, I lay off Harry."

But I had no intention of laying off Harry. When she went back to her cottage, I walked around three-quarters of the block and took up a new position in the doorway of a dry-cleaning establishment. This time I didn't smoke. I didn't even move, except to look at my watch from time to time.

Around eleven o'clock the lights went out behind the blinds in the Nemo cottage. Shortly before midnight the front door opened and Harry slipped out. He looked up and down the street and began to walk. He passed within six feet of my dark doorway, hustling along in a kind of furtive shuffle.

Working very cautiously, at a distance, I tailed him downtown. He disappeared into the lighted cavern of an all-night garage. He came out of the garage a few minutes later, driving an old Chevrolet.

My money also talked to the attendant. I drew an old Buick which would still do 75. I proved that it would as soon as I hit the highway. I reached the entrance to Nick Nemo's private lane in time to see Harry's lights approaching the dark ranchhouse.

I cut my lights and parked at the roadside a hundred yards below the entrance to the lane, and facing it. The Chevrolet reappeared in a few minutes. Harry was still alone in the front seat. I followed it blind as far as the highway before I risked my lights. Then down the highway to the edge of town.

In the middle of the motel and drive-in district he turned off onto a side road and in under a neon sign which spelled out *TRAILER COURT* across the darkness. The trailers stood along the bank of a dry creek. The Chevrolet stopped in front of one of them, which had a light in the window. Harry got out with a spotted bundle under his arm. He knocked on the door of the trailer.

I U-turned at the next corner and put in more waiting time. The Chevrolet rolled out under the neon sign and turned toward the highway. I let it go.

Leaving my car, I walked along the creek bank to the lighted trailer. The windows were curtained. The cerise convertible was parked on its far side. I tapped on the aluminum door.

"Harry?" a girl's voice said. "Is that you, Harry?"

I muttered something indistinguishable. The door opened, and the yellow-haired girl looked out. She was very young, but her round blue eyes were heavy and sick with hangover, or remorse. She had on a nylon slip, nothing else.

"What is this?"

She tried to shut the door. I held it open.

"Get away from here. Leave me alone. I'll scream."

"All right. Scream."

She opened her mouth. No sound came out. She closed her mouth again. It was small and fleshy and defiant. "Who are you? Law?"

"Close enough. I'm coming in."

"Come in then, damn you. I got nothing to hide."

"I can see that."

I brushed in past her. There were dead Martinis on her breath. The little room was a jumble of feminine clothes, silk and cashmere and tweed and gossamer nylon, some of them flung on the floor, others hung up to dry. The leopardskin coat lay on the bunk bed, staring with innumerable bold eyes. She picked it up and covered her shoulders with it. Unconsciously, her nervous hands began to pick the wood chips out of the fur.

"Harry did you a favor, didn't he?" I said.

"Maybe he did."

"Have you been doing any favors for Harry?"

"Such as?"

"Such as knocking off his brother?"

"You're way off the beam, mister. I was very fond of Uncle Nick."

"Why run out on the killing then?"

"I panicked," she said. "It would happen to any girl. I was asleep when he got it, see, passed out if you want the truth. I heard the gun go off. It woke me up, but it took me quite a while to bring myself to and sober up enough to put my clothes on. By the time I made it to the bedroom window, Harry was back, with some guy." She peered into my face. "Were you the guy?"

I nodded.

"I thought so. I thought you were law at the time. I saw Nick lying there in the driveway, all bloody, and I put two and two together and got trouble. Bad trouble for me, unless I got out. So I got out. It wasn't nice to do, after what Nick meant to me, but it was the only sensible thing. I got my career to think of."

"What career is that?"

"Modeling. Acting. Uncle Nick was gonna send me to school."

"Unless you talk, you'll finish your education at Corona. Who shot Nick?"

A thin edge of terror entered her voice. "I don't know, I tell you. I was passed out in the bedroom. I didn't see nothing."

"Why did Harry bring you your coat?"

"He didn't want me to get involved. He's my father, after all."

"Harry Nemo is your father?"

"Yes."

"You'll have to do better than that. What's your name?"

"Jeannine. Jeannine Larue."

"Why isn't your name Nemo if Harry is your father? Why do you call him Harry?"

"He's my stepfather, I mean."

"Sure," I said. "And Nick was really your uncle, and you were having a family reunion with him."

"He wasn't any blood relation to me. I always called him uncle, though."

"If Harry's your father, why don't you live with him?"

"I used to. Honest. This is the truth I'm telling you. I had to get out on account of the old lady. The old lady hates my guts. She's a real creep, a square. She can't stand for a girl to have any fun. Just because my old man was a rummy—"

"What's your idea of fun, Jeannine?"

She shook her feathercut hair at me. It exhaled a heavy perfume which was worth its weight in blood. She bared one pearly shoulder and smiled an artificial hustler's smile. "What's yours? Maybe we can get together."

"You mean the way you got together with Nick?"

"You're prettier than him."

"I'm also smarter, I hope. Is Harry really your stepfather?"

"Ask him if you don't believe me. Ask him. He lives in a place on Tule Street—I don't remember the number."

"I know where he lives."

But Harry wasn't at home. I knocked on the door of the frame cottage and got no answer. I turned the knob, and found that the door was unlocked. There was a light behind it. The other cottages in the court were dark. It was long past midnight, and the street was deserted. I went into the cottage, preceded by my gun.

A ceiling bulb glared down on sparse and threadbare furniture, a time-eaten rug. Besides the living room, the house contained a cubbyhole of a bedroom and a closet kitchenette. Everything in the poverty-stricken place was pathetically clean. There were moral mottoes on the walls, and one picture. It was a photograph of a towheaded girl in a teen-age party dress. Jeannine, before she learned that a pretty face and a sleek body could buy her the things she wanted. The things she thought she wanted.

For some reason I felt sick. I went outside. Somewhere out of sight an old car engine muttered. Its muttering grew on the night. Harry Nemo's rented Chevrolet turned the corner under the streetlight. Its front wheels were weaving. One of the wheels climbed the curb in front of the cottage. The Chevrolet came to a halt at a drunken angle.

I crossed the sidewalk and opened the car door. Harry was at the wheel, clinging to it desperately as if he needed it to hold him up. His chest was bloody. His mouth was bright with blood. He spoke through it thickly:

"She got me."

"Who got you, Harry? Jeannine?"

"No. Not her. She was the reason for it, though. We had it coming."

Those were his final words. I caught his body as it fell sideways out of the seat. Laid it out on the sidewalk and left it for the cop on the beat to find.

I drove across town to the trailer court. Jeannine's trailer still had light in it, filtered through the curtains over the windows. I pushed the door open.

The girl was packing a suitcase on the bunk bed. She looked at me over her shoulder, and froze. Her blonde head was cocked like a frightened bird's, hypnotized by my gun.

"Where are you off to, kid?"

"Out of this town. I'm getting out."

"You have some talking to do first."

She straightened up. "I told you all I know. You didn't believe me. What's the matter, didn't you get to see Harry?"

"I saw him. Harry's dead. Your whole family is dying like flies."

She half turned and sat down limply on the disordered bed. "Dead? You think I did it?"

"I think you know who did. Harry said before he died that you were the reason for it all."

"Me the reason for it?" Her eyes widened in false naïveté, but there was thought behind them, quick and desperate thought. "You mean Harry got killed on account of me?"

"Harry and Nick both. It was a woman who shot them."

"God," she said. The desperate thought behind her eyes crystallized into knowledge. Which I shared.

The aching silence was broken by a big diesel rolling by on the highway. She said above its roar:

"That crazy old bat. So *she* killed Nick."

"You're talking about your mother. Mrs. Nemo."

"Yeah."

"Did you see her shoot him?"

"No. I was blotto like I told you. But I saw her out there this week, keeping an eye on the house. She's always watched me like a hawk."

"Is that why you were getting out of town? Because you knew she killed Nick?"

"Maybe it was. I don't know. I wouldn't let myself think about it."

Her blue gaze shifted from my face to something behind me. I turned. Mrs. Nemo was in the doorway. She was hugging the straw bag to her thin chest.

Her right hand dove into the bag. I shot her in the right arm. She leaned against the door frame and held her dangling arm with her left hand. Her face was granite in whose crevices her eyes were like live things caught.

The gun she dropped was a cheap .32 revolver, its nickel plating worn and corroded. I spun the cylinder. One shot had been fired from it.

"This accounts for Harry," I said. "You didn't shoot Nick with this gun, not at that distance."

"No." She was looking down at her dripping hand. "I used my old police gun on Nick Nemo. After I killed him, I threw the gun into the sea. I didn't know I'd have further use for a gun. I bought that little suicide gun tonight."

"To use on Harry?"

"To use on you. I thought you were on to me. I didn't know until you told me that Harry knew about Nick and Jeannine."

"Jeannine is your daughter by your first husband?"

"My only daughter." She said to the girl, "I did it for you, Jeannine. I've seen too much—the awful things that can happen."

The girl didn't answer.

"I can understand why you shot Nick," I said, "but why did Harry have to die?"

"Nick paid him," she said. "Nick paid him for Jeannine. I found Harry in a bar an hour ago, and he admitted it. I hope I killed him."

"You killed him, Mrs. Nemo. What brought you here? Was Jeannine the third on your list?"

"No. No. She's my own girl. I came to tell her what I did for her. I wanted her to know."

She looked at the girl on the bed. Her eyes were terrible with pain and love.

The girl said in a stunned voice, "Mother. You're hurt. I'm sorry."

"Let's go, Mrs. Nemo," I said.

COMMENT AND QUESTIONS

One of Ross Macdonald's finest achievements as a literary artist is his use of comparisons. In this story, his statement that "the sky was streaked with running red, as if the sun had died a violent death," brings together in a vivid way the bright red of bloody violence and the intense red of a California sunset. By this comparison he also suggests that to Archer, who makes the observation, the natural world is touched by the violence of the crime, which coincides with the end of the day. Such an observation tells us, too, a good deal about the detective himself and so serves as a means of characterizing him. What other examples of vivid and unusual language can you find in the story?

Why is Harry Nemo eager to persuade Archer to "keep the lip buttoned down about the dame"?

Eyes are sometimes considered to be reflectors of the soul. Notice the descriptions of eyes in this story and consider the effectiveness of these descriptions.

Harry Nemo, though a minor character in the story, is rather fully presented. His characterization is accomplished almost entirely by means of descriptive references to his physical appearance and actions. What examples do you find of this characterizing description?

What do we learn about Archer himself? Notice that in solving the crime he goes beyond the terms of his original employment; in fact, he was not actually in anyone's employ at the time. How do you interpret his putting the second hundred-dollar bill "in a separate pocket"?

Of what significance is the title?

NOTES

1. *Rock*. Alcatraz Island in San Francisco Bay, where a federal penitentiary was situated at the time of the story.
2. *WAC*. Women's Army Corps.

ROSS MACDONALD

The Writer as Detective Hero

A former college professor with a Ph.D. in English literature, Ross Macdonald is more closely connected with formal education and literary tradition than any other author of popular hardboiled fiction. Perhaps for that reason he has a special interest in the historical development of detective fiction, its position in relation to different kinds of literature, and his own kinship with other writers of detective fiction.

In this essay Macdonald places his detective, Lew Archer, in the tradition of such detectives as Poe's Dupin, Doyle's Holmes, and Chandler's Philip Marlowe, and then attempts to analyze these detective figures. Macdonald sees each author projecting himself in some way through his detective, creating a character and situation through which he can say and do things not otherwise possible. In an interview in *Esquire*, Macdonald once said, "We start out thinking we're writing about other people and end up realizing we're writing about ourselves. A private detective is just kind of an invented shadow of the novelist at work."

In addition to providing new insights into the Lew Archer story "The Guilt-Edged Blonde," this essay presents an illuminating view of the complicated nature of imaginative writing.

Aproducer who last year was toying with the idea of making a television series featuring my private detective Lew Archer asked me over lunch at Perino's if Archer was based on any actual person. "Yes," I said. "Myself." He gave me a semi-pitying Hollywood look. I tried to explain that while I had known some excellent detectives and watched them work, Archer was created from the inside out. I wasn't Archer, exactly, but Archer was me.

The conversation went downhill from there, as if I had made a damaging admission. But I believe most detective-story writers would give the same answer. A close paternal or fraternal relationship between writer and detective is a marked peculiarity of the form. Throughout its history, from Poe to Chandler and beyond, the detective hero has represented his creator and carried his values into action in society.

Poe, who invented the modern detective story, and his detective, Dupin, are good examples. Poe's was a first-rate but guilt-haunted mind painfully at odds with the realities of pre-Civil-War America. Dupin is a declassed aristocrat, as Poe's heroes tend to be, an obvious equivalent for the artist-intellectual who has lost his place in society and his foothold in tradition. Dupin has no social life, only one friend. He is set apart from other people by his superiority of mind.

In his creation of Dupin, Poe was surely compensating for his failure to become what his extraordinary mental powers seemed to fit him for. He had dreamed of an intellectual hierarchy governing the cultural life of the nation, himself at its head. Dupin's outwitting of an unscrupulous politician in "The Purloined Letter," his "solution" of an actual New York case in "Marie Roget," his repeated trumping of the cards held by the Prefect of Police, are Poe's vicarious demonstrations of superiority to an indifferent society and its officials.

Of course Poe's detective stories gave the writer, and give the reader, something deeper than such obvious satisfactions. He devised them as a means of exorcising or controlling guilt and horror. The late William Carlos Williams, in a profound essay, related Poe's sense of guilt and horror to the terrible awareness of a hyperconscious man standing naked and shivering on a new continent. The guilt was doubled by Poe's anguished insight into the unconscious. It had to be controlled by some rational pattern, and the detective story, "the tale of ratiocination," provided such a pattern.

The tale of the bloody murders in the Rue Morgue, Poe's first detective story (1841), is a very hymn to analytic reason intended, as Poe wrote later, "to depict some very remarkable features in the mental character of my friend, the Chevalier C. Auguste Dupin." Dupin clearly represents the reason, which was Poe's mainstay against the nightmare forces of the mind. These latter are acted out by the murderous ape: "Gnashing its teeth, and flashing fire from its eyes, it flew upon the body of the girl and embedded its fearful talons in her throat, retaining its grasp until she expired."

Dupin's reason masters the ape and explains the inexplicable— the wrecked apartment behind the locked door, the corpse of a young woman thrust up the chimney—but not without leaving a residue of horror. The nightmare can't quite be explained away, and persists in the teeth of reason. An unstable balance between reason and more primitive human qualities is characteristic of the detective story. For both writer and reader it is an imaginative arena where such conflicts can be worked out safely, under artistic controls.

The first detective story has other archetypal features, particularly in the way it is told. The "I" who narrates it is not the detective Dupin. The splitting of the protagonist into a narrator and a detective has certain advantages: it helps to eliminate the inessential, and to postpone the solution. More important, the author can present his self-hero, the detective, without undue embarrassment, and can handle dangerous emotional material at two or more removes from himself as Poe does in "Rue Morgue."

The disadvantages of the split protagonist emerge more clearly in the saga of Dupin's successor, Sherlock Holmes. One projection of the author, the narrator, is made to assume a posture of rather blind admiration before another projection of the author, the detective hero, and the reader is invited to share Dr. Watson's adoration of the great man. An element of narcissistic fantasy, impatient with the limits of the self, seems to be built into this traditional form of the detective story.

I'm not forgetting that Holmes' *modus operandi* was based on that of an actual man, Conan Doyle's friend and teacher, Dr. Joseph Bell. Although his "science" usually boils down to careful observation, which was Dr. Bell's forte, Holmes is very much the scientific criminologist. This hero of scientism may be in fact the dominant culture hero of our technological society.

Though Holmes is a physical scientist specializing in chemistry and anatomy, and Dupin went in for literary and psychological analysis, Holmes can easily be recognized as Dupin's direct descendent. His most conspicuous feature, his ability to read thoughts on the basis of associative clues, is a direct borrowing from Dupin. And like Dupin, he is a projection of the author, who at the time of Holmes' creation was a not very busy young doctor. According to his son Adrian, Conan Doyle admitted when he was dying: "If anyone is Sherlock Holmes, then I confess it is myself."

Holmes had other ancestors and collateral relations which reinforce the idea that he was a portrait of the artist as a great detective. His drugs, his secrecy and solitude, his moods of depression (which he shared with Dupin) are earmarks of the Romantic rebel then and now. Behind Holmes lurk the figures of nineteenth-century poets, Byron certainly, probably Baudelaire, who translated Poe and pressed Poe's guilty knowledge to new limits. I once made a case for the theory (and Anthony Boucher didn't disagree) that much of the modern development of the detective story stems from Baudelaire, his "dandyism" and his vision of the city as inferno. Conan Doyle's London, which influenced Eliot's "Wasteland," has something of this quality.

But Holmes' Romantic excesses aren't central to his character. His Baudelairean spleen and drug addiction are merely the idiosyncrasies of genius. Holmes is given the best of both worlds, and remains an English gentleman, accepted on the highest social levels. Permeating the thought and language of Conan Doyle's stories is an air of blithe satisfaction with a social system based on privilege.

This obvious characteristic is worth mentioning because it was frozen into one branch of the form. Nostalgia for a privileged society accounts for one of the prime attractions of the traditional English detective story and its innumerable American counter-parts. Neither wars nor the dissolution of governments and societies interrupt that long weekend in the country house which is often, with more or less unconscious symbolism, cut off by a failure in communications from the outside world.

The contemporary world is the special province of the Ameri-can hardboiled detective story. Dashiell Hammett, Raymond Chandler, and the other writers for *Black Mask* who developed it, were in conscious reaction against the Anglo-American school which, in the work of S. S. Van Dine for example, had lost contact with contemporary life and language. Chandler's dedication, to the editor of *Black Mask*, of a collection of his early stories (1944), describes the kind of fiction they had been trying to supplant: "For Joseph Thompson Shaw with affection and respect, and in memory of the time when we were trying to get murder away from the upper classes, the week-end house party and the vicar's rose-garden, and back to the people who are really good at it." While Chandler's novels swarm with plutocrats as well as criminals, and even with what pass in Southern California for aristocrats, the *Black Mask* revolution was a real one. From it emerged a new kind of detective hero, the classless, restless man of American democracy, who spoke the language of the street.

Hammett, who created the most powerful of these new heroes in Sam Spade, had been a private detective and knew the corrupt inner workings of American cities. But Sam Spade was a less obvious projection of Hammett than detective heroes usually are of their authors. Hammett had got his early romanticism under strict ironic control. He could see Spade from outside, without affection, perhaps with some bleak compassion. In this as in other respects Spade marks a sharp break with the Holmes tradition. He possesses the virtues and follows the code of a frontier male. Thrust for his sins into the urban inferno, he pits his courage and cunning against its denizens, plays for the highest stakes available, love and money, and loses nearly everything in the end. His lover is guilty of murder; his narrow, bitter code forces Spade to turn her over to the police. The Maltese falcon has been stripped of jewels.

Perhaps the stakes and implied losses are higher than I have suggested. The worthless falcon may symbolize a lost tradition, the great cultures of the Mediterranean past which have become inaccessible to Spade and his generation. Perhaps the bird stands for the Holy Ghost itself, or for its absence.

The ferocious intensity of the work, the rigorous spelling-out of Sam Spade's deprivation of his full human heritage, seem to me to make his story tragedy, if there is such a thing as dead-pan tragedy. Hammett was the first American writer to use the detective-story for the purposes of a major novelist, to present a vision, blazing if disenchanted, of our lives. Sam Spade was the product and reflection of a mind which was not at home in Zion, or in Zenith.

Chandler's vision is disenchanted, too, but in spite of its hallucinated brilliance of detail it lacks the tragic unity of Hammett's. In his essay on "The Simple Art of Murder," an excitingly written piece of not very illuminating criticism, Chandler offers a prescription for the detective hero which suggests a central weakness in his vision:

> In everything that can be called art there is a quality of redemption. . . . But down these mean streets a man must go who is not himself mean, who is neither tarnished nor afraid. . . . The detective in this kind of story must be such a man. He is the hero, he is everything. . . . He must be the best man in his world and a good enough man for any world.

While there may be "a quality of redemption" in a good novel, it belongs to the whole work and is not the private property of one of the characters. No hero of serious fiction could act within a moral straitjacket requiring him to be consistently virtuous and unafraid. Sam Spade was submerged and struggling in tragic life. The detective-as-redeemer is a backward step in the direction of sentimental romance, and an over-simplified world of good guys and bad guys. The people of Chandler's early novels, though they include chivalrous gangsters and gangsters' molls with hearts of gold, are divided into two groups by an angry puritanical morality. The goats are usually separated from the sheep by sexual promiscuity or perversion. Such a strong and overt moralistic bias actually interferes with the broader moral effects a novelist aims at.

Fortunately in the writing of his books Chandler toned down his Watsonian enthusiasm for his detective's moral superiority. The detective Marlowe, who tells his own stories in the first person, and sometimes admits to being afraid, has a self-deflating wit which takes the curse off his knight-errantry:

> I wasn't wearing a gun . . . I doubted if it would do me any good. The big man would probably take it away from me and eat it. (*Farewell, My Lovely*, 1940)

The Chandler-Marlowe prose is a highly charged blend of laconic wit and imagistic poetry set to breakneck rhythms. Its strong colloquial vein reaffirms the fact that the *Black Mask* revolution was a revolution in language as well as subject matter. It is worth noticing that H. L. Mencken, the great lexicographer of our vernacular, was an early editor of *Black Mask*. His protegé James M. Cain once said that his discovery of the western roughneck made it possible for him to write fiction. Marlowe and his predecessors performed a similar function for Chandler, whose English education put a special edge on his passion for our new language, and a special edge on his feelings against privilege. Socially mobile and essentially classless (he went to college but has a working-class bias), Marlowe liberated his author's imagination into an overheard democratic prose which is one of the most effective narrative instruments in our recent literature.

Under the obligatorily "tough" surface of the writing, Marlowe is interestingly different from the standard hardboiled hero who came out of *Black Mask*. Chandler's novels focus in his hero's sensibility, and could almost be described as novels of sensibility. Their constant theme is big-city loneliness, and the wry pain of a sensitive man coping with the roughest elements of a corrupt society.

It is Marlowe's doubleness that makes him interesting: the hardboiled mask half-concealing Chandler's poetic and satiric mind. Part of our pleasure derives from the interplay between the mind of Chandler and the voice of Marlowe. The recognized difference between them is part of the dynamics of the narrative, setting up bipolar tensions in the prose. The marvelous opening paragraph of *The Big Sleep* (1939) will illustrate some of this:

It was about eleven o'clock in the morning, mid October, with the sun not shining and a look of hard wet rain in the clearness of the foothills. I was wearing my powder-blue suit, with dark blue shirt, tie and display handkerchief, black brogues, black wool socks with dark blue clocks on them. I was neat, clean, shaved and sober, and I didn't care who knew it. I was everything the well-dressed private detective ought to be. I was calling on four million dollars.

Marlowe is making fun of himself, and of Chandler in the rôle of brash young detective. There is pathos, too, in the idea that a man who can write like a fallen angel should be a mere private eye; and Socratic irony. The gifted writer conceals himself behind Marlowe's cheerful mindlessness. At the same time the retiring, middle-aged, scholarly author acquires a durable mask, forever 38, which allows him to face the dangers of society high and low.

Chandler's conception of Marlowe, and his relationship with his character, deepened as his mind penetrated the romantic fantasy, and the overbright self-consciousness, that limited his vision. At the end of *The Long Goodbye* (1953) there is a significant confrontation between Marlowe and a friend who had betrayed him and apparently gone homosexual. In place of the righteous anger which Marlowe would have indulged in in one of the earlier novels he now feels grief and disquiet, as if the confrontation might be with a part of himself.

The friend, the ex-friend, tries to explain his moral breakdown: "I was in the commandos, bud. They don't take you if you're just a piece of fluff. I got badly hurt and it wasn't any fun with those Nazi doctors. It did something to me." That is all we are told. At the roaring heart of Chandler's maze there is a horror which even at the end of his least evasive novel remains unspeakable. Whatever its hidden meaning, this scene was written by a man of tender and romantic sensibility who had been injured. Chandler used Marlowe to shield while half-expressing his sensibility, and to act out the mild paranoia which often goes with this kind of sensibility and its private hurts, and which seems to be virtually endemic among contemporary writers.

I can make this judgment with some assurance because it applies with a vengeance to some of my earlier books, particularly *Blue City* (1947). A decade later, in *The Doomsters*, I made my detective Archer criticize himself as "a slightly earthbound Tarzan in a slightly paranoid jungle." This novel marked a fairly clean break with the Chandler tradition, which it had taken me some years to digest, and freed me to make my own approach to the crimes and sorrows of life.

I learned a great deal from Chandler—any writer can—but there had always been basic differences between us. One was in our attitude to plot. Chandler described a good plot as one that made for good scenes, as if the parts were greater than the whole. I see plot as a vehicle of meaning. It should be as complex as contemporary life, but balanced enough to say true things about it. The surprise with which a detective novel concludes should set up tragic vibrations which run backward through the entire structure. Which means that the structure must be single, and *intended*.

Another difference between Chandler and me is in our use of language. My narrator Archer's wider and less rigidly stylized range of expression, at least in more recent novels, is related to a central difference between him and Marlowe. Marlowe's voice is limited by his role as the hardboiled hero. He must speak within his limits as a character, and these limits are quite narrowly conceived. Chandler tried to relax them in *The Long Goodbye*, but he was old and the language failed to respond. He was trapped like the late Hemingway in an unnecessarily limiting idea of self, hero, and language.

I could never write of Archer: "He is the hero, he is everything." It is true that his actions carry the story, his comments on it reflect my attitudes (but deeper attitudes remain implicit), and Archer or a narrator like him is indispensable to the kind of books I write. But he is not their emotional center. And in spite of what I said at the beginning, Archer has developed away from his early status as a fantasy projection of myself and my personal needs. Cool, I think, is the word for our mature relationship. Archer himself has what New Englanders call "weaned affections."

An author's heavy emotional investment in a narrator-hero can get in the way of the story and blur its meanings, as some of Chandler's books demonstrate. A less encumbered narrator permits greater flexibility, and fidelity to the intricate truths of life. I don't have to celebrate Archer's physical or sexual prowess, or work at making him consistently funny and charming. He can be self-forgetful, almost transparent at times, and concentrate as good detectives (and good writers) do, on the people whose problems he is investigating. These other people are for me the main thing: they are often more intimately related to me and my life than Lew Archer is. He is the obvious self-projection which holds the eye (my eye as well as the reader's) while more secret selves creep out of the woodwork behind the locked door. Remember how the reassuring presence of Dupin permitted Poe's mind to face the nightmare of the homicidal ape and the two dead women.

Archer is a hero who sometimes verges on being an anti-hero. While he is a man of action, his actions are largely directed to putting together the stories of other people's lives and discovering their significance. He is less a doer than a questioner, a consciousness in which the meanings of other lives emerge. This gradually developed conception of the detective hero as the mind of the novel is not new, but is probably my main contribution to this special branch of fiction. Some such refinement of the conception of the detective hero was needed, to bring this kind of novel closer to the purposes and range of the mainstream novel.

It may be that internal realism, a quality of mind, is one of the most convincing attributes a character can have. Policemen and lawyers have surprised me with the opinion that Archer is quite true to life. The two best private detectives I personally know resemble him in their internal qualities: their intelligent humaneness, an interest in other people transcending their interest in themselves, and a toughness of mind which enables them to face human weaknesses, including their own, with open eyes. Both of them dearly love to tell a story.

COMMENT AND QUESTIONS

According to Macdonald, what are the advantages and disadvantages of the "split protagonist"?

What does Macdonald mean when he refers to "nostalgia for a privileged society"? Have you seen examples of this nostalgia in any of the stories you have read?

AGATHA CHRISTIE

Sanctuary

Agatha Christie's early novels helped to define and establish the detective novel; yet she was one of the first to bend its conventions (in *The Murder of Roger Ackroyd*, for example, she breaks the "rule" that the narrator must not be the murderer) and, in a series of best-selling novels, has continued to manipulate its form so as to outwit her readers. She is second only to Shakespeare as the most translated English author.

Of the several sleuths Miss Christie has created, there are two who figure in many of her works—Hercule Poirot and Jane Marple. At the farthest possible extreme from Sherlock Holmes, it might seem, stands Jane Marple. But there are similarities as well as the obvious differences. Neither can be really surprised at anything a human being may do, and neither is at a loss for an appropriate counter-measure. Similarly, Miss Marple's colleague in "Sanctuary," Bunch, is both different from Dr. Watson in some ways and like him in others. Bunch is more observant, for one thing, and she displays a more uncommon store of common sense. But both are courageous and resourceful in carrying out their share of the activities that lead in "Sanctuary," as in "The Speckled Band," to the solution of one crime and the prevention of another.

This story concerns a mysterious death in the village vicarage and an enigmatic dying "message." These are traditional detective story plot staples, but, as always, Miss Christie manages to employ them in such a way as to delight and surprise her readers.

The Vicar's wife came round the corner of the vicarage with her arms full of chrysanthemums. A good deal of rich garden soil was attached to her strong brogue shoes and a few fragments of earth were adhering to her nose, but of that fact she was perfectly unconscious.

She had a slight struggle in opening the vicarage gate which hung, rustily, half off its hinges. A puff of wind caught at her battered felt hat, causing it to sit even more rakishly than it had done before. "Bother!" said Bunch.

Christened by her optimistic parents Diana, Mrs. Harmon had become Bunch at an early age for somewhat obvious reasons and the name had stuck to her ever since. Clutching the chrysanthemums, she made her way through the gate to the churchyard and so to the church door.

The November air was mild and damp. Clouds scudded across the sky with patches of blue here and there. Inside, the church was dark and cold; it was unheated except at service times.

"Brrrrh!" said Bunch expressively. "I'd better get on with this quickly. I don't want to die of cold."

With the quickness born of practice she collected the necessary paraphernalia: vases, water, flower holders. "I wish we had lilies," thought Bunch to herself. "I get so tired of these scraggy chrysanthemums." Her nimble fingers arranged the blooms in their holders.

There was nothing particularly original or artistic about the decorations, for Bunch Harmon herself was neither original nor artistic, but it was a homely and pleasant arrangement. Carrying the vases carefully, Bunch stepped up the aisle and made her way toward the altar. As she did so the sun came out.

It shone through the east window of somewhat crude coloured glass, mostly blue and red—the gift of a wealthy Victorian churchgoer. The effect was almost startling in its sudden opulence. "Like jewels," thought Bunch. Suddenly she stopped, staring ahead of her. On the chancel steps was a huddled dark form.

Putting down the flowers carefully, Bunch went up to it and bent over it. It was a man lying there, huddled over on himself. Bunch knelt down by him and slowly, carefully, she turned him over. Her fingers went to his pulse—a pulse so feeble and fluttering that it told its own story, as did the almost greenish pallor of his face. There was no doubt, Bunch thought, that the man was dying.

He was a man of about forty-five, dressed in a dark, shabby suit. She laid down the limp hand she had picked up and looked at his other hand. This seemed clenched like a fist on his breast. Looking more closely, she saw that the fingers were closed over what seemed to be a large wad or handkerchief which he was holding tightly to his chest. All round the clenched hand there were splashes of a dry brown fluid which, Bunch guessed, was dry blood. Bunch sat back on her heels, frowning.

Up till now the man's eyes had been closed, but at this point they suddenly opened and fixed themselves on Bunch's face. They were neither dazed nor wandering. They seemed fully alive and intelligent. His lips moved, and Bunch bent forward to catch the words, or rather the word. It was only one word that he said:

"Sanctuary."

There was, she thought, just a very faint smile as he breathed out this word. There was no mistaking it, for after a moment he said it again, "Sanctuary . . ."

Then, with a faint, long-drawn-out sigh, his eyes closed again. Once more Bunch's fingers went to his pulse. It was still there, but fainter now and more intermittent. She got up with decision.

"Don't move," she said, "or try to move. I'm going for help."

The man's eyes opened again, but he seemed now to be fixing his attention on the coloured light that came through the east window. He murmured something that Bunch could not quite catch. She thought, startled, that it might have been her husband's name.

"Julian?" she said. "Did you come here to find Julian?" But there was no answer. The man lay with eyes closed, his breathing coming in slow, shallow fashion.

Bunch turned and left the church rapidly. She glanced at her watch and nodded with some satisfaction. Dr. Griffiths would still be in his surgery. It was only a couple of minutes' walk from the church. She went in, without waiting to knock or ring, passing through the waiting room and into the doctor's surgery.

"You must come at once," said Bunch. "There's a man dying in the church."

Some minutes later Dr. Griffiths rose from his knees after a brief examination.

"Can we move him from here into the vicarage? I can attend to him better there—not that it's any use."

"Of course," said Bunch. "I'll go along and get things ready. I'll get Harper and Jones, shall I? To help you carry him."

"Thanks. I can telephone from the vicarage for an ambulance, but I'm afraid—by the time it comes . . ." He left the remark unfinished.

Bunch said, "Internal bleeding?"

Dr. Griffiths nodded. He said, "How on earth did he come here?"

"I think he must have been here all night," said Bunch, considering. "Harper unlocks the church in the morning as he goes to work, but he doesn't usually come in."

It was about five minutes later when Dr. Griffiths put down the telephone receiver and came back into the morning room where the injured man was lying on quickly arranged blankets on the sofa. Bunch was moving a basin of water and clearing up after the doctor's examination.

"Well, that's that," said Griffiths. "I've sent for an ambulance and I've notified the police." He stood, frowning, looking down on the patient who lay with closed eyes. His left hand was plucking in a nervous, spasmodic way at his side.

"He was shot," said Griffiths. "Shot at fairly close quarters. He rolled his handkerchief up into a ball and plugged the wound with it so as to stop the bleeding."

"Could he have gone far after that happened?" Bunch asked.

"Oh yes, it's quite possible. A mortally wounded man has been known to pick himself up and walk along a street as though nothing had happened and then suddenly collapse five or ten minutes later. So he needn't have been shot in the church. Oh no.

He may have been shot some distance away. Of course, he may have shot himself and then dropped the revolver and staggered blindly toward the church. I don't quite know why he made for the church and not for the vicarage."

"Oh, I know that," said Bunch. "He said it: 'Sanctuary.' "

The doctor stared at her. "Sanctuary?"

"Here's Julian," said Bunch, turning her head as she heard her husband's steps in the hall. "Julian! Come here."

The Reverend Julian Harmon entered the room. His vague, scholarly manner always made him appear much older than he really was. "Dear me!" said Julian Harmon, staring in a mild, puzzled manner at the surgical appliances and the prone figure on the sofa.

Bunch explained with her usual economy of words. "He was in the church, dying. He'd been shot. Do you know him, Julian? I thought he said your name."

The vicar came up to the sofa and looked down at the dying man. "Poor fellow," he said, and shook his head. "No, I don't know him. I'm almost sure I've never seen him before."

At that moment the dying man's eyes opened once more. They went from the doctor to Julian Harmon and from him to his wife. The eyes stayed there, staring into Bunch's face. Griffiths stepped forward.

"If you could tell us," he said urgently.

But with his eyes fixed on Bunch, the man said in a weak voice, "Please—please—" And then, with a slight tremor, he died. . . .

Sergeant Hayes licked his pencil and turned the page of his notebook.

"So that's all you can tell me, Mrs. Harmon?"

"That's all," said Bunch. "These are the things out of his coat pockets."

On a table at Sergeant Hayes's elbow was a wallet, a rather battered old watch with the initials W.S., and the return half of a ticket to London. Nothing more.

"You've found out who he is?" asked Bunch.

"A Mr. and Mrs. Eccles phoned up the station. He's her brother, it seems. Name of Sandbourne. Been in a low state of health and nerves for some time. He's been getting worse lately.

The day before yesterday he walked out and didn't come back. He took a revolver with him."

"And he came out here and shot himself with it?" said Bunch. "Why?"

"Well, you see, he'd been depressed . . ."

Bunch interrupted him. "I don't mean that. I mean, why here?"

Since Sergeant Hayes obviously did not know the answer to that one he replied in an oblique fashion, "Come out here, he did, on the five-ten bus."

"Yes," said Bunch again. "But why?"

"I don't know, Mrs. Harmon," said Sergeant Hayes. "There's no accounting. If the balance of the mind is disturbed—"

Bunch finished for him. "They may do it anywhere. But it still seems to me unnecessary to take a bus out to a small country place like this. He didn't know anyone here, did he?"

"Not so far as can be ascertained," said Sergeant Hayes. He coughed in an apologetic manner and said, as he rose to his feet, "It may be as Mr. and Mrs. Eccles will come out and see you, ma'am—if you don't mind, that is."

"Of course I don't mind," said Bunch. "It's very natural. I only wish I had something to tell them."

"I'll be getting along," said Sergeant Hayes.

"I'm only so thankful," said Bunch, going with him to the front door, "that it wasn't murder."

A car had drawn up at the vicarage gate. Sergeant Hayes, glancing at it, remarked, "Looks as though that's Mr. and Mrs. Eccles come here now, ma'am, to talk with you."

Bunch braced herself to endure what, she felt, might be rather a difficult ordeal. "However," she thought, "I can always call Julian in to help me. A clergyman's a great help when people are bereaved."

Exactly what she had expected Mr. and Mrs. Eccles to be like, Bunch could not have said, but she was conscious, as she greeted them, of a feeling of surprise. Mr. Eccles was a stout and florid man whose natural manner would have been cheerful and facetious. Mrs. Eccles had a vaguely flashy look about her. She had a small, mean, pursed-up mouth. Her voice was thin and reedy.

"It's been a terrible shock, Mrs. Harmon, as you can imagine," she said.

"Oh, I know," said Bunch. "It must have been. Do sit down. Can I offer you—well, perhaps it's a little early for tea—"

Mr. Eccles waved a pudgy hand. "No, no, nothing for us," he said. "It's very kind of you, I'm sure. Just wanted to . . . well . . . what poor William said and all that, you know?"

"He's been abroad a long time," said Mrs. Eccles, "and I think he must have had some very nasty experiences. Very quiet and depressed he's been, ever since he came home. Said the world wasn't fit to live in and there was nothing to look forward to. Poor Bill, he was always moody."

Bunch stared at them both for a moment or two without speaking.

"Pinched my husband's revolver, he did," went on Mrs. Eccles. "Without our knowing. Then it seems he come out here by bus. I suppose that was nice feeling on his part. He wouldn't have liked to do it in our house."

"Poor fellow, poor fellow," said Mr. Eccles, with a sigh. "It doesn't do to judge."

There was another short pause, and Mr. Eccles said, "Did he leave a message? Any last words, nothing like that?"

His bright, rather piglike eyes watched Bunch closely. Mrs. Eccles, too, leaned forward as though anxious for the reply.

"No," said Bunch quietly. "He came into the church when he was dying, for sanctuary."

Mrs. Eccles said in a puzzled voice, "Sanctuary? I don't think I quite . . ."

Mr. Eccles interrupted. "Holy place, my dear," he said impatiently. "That's what the vicar's wife means. It's a sin—suicide, you know. I expect he wanted to make amends."

"He tried to say something just before he died," said Bunch. "He began, 'Please,' but that's as far as he got." Mrs. Eccles put her handkerchief to her eyes and sniffed.

"Oh, dear," she said. "It's terribly upsetting, isn't it?"

"There, there, Pam," said her husband. "Don't take on. These things can't be helped. Poor Willie. Still, he's at peace now. Well, thank you very much, Mrs. Harmon. I hope we haven't interrupted you. A vicar's wife is a busy lady, we know that."

They shook hands with her. Then Eccles turned back suddenly to say, "Oh yes, there's just one other thing. I think you've got his coat here, haven't you?"

"His coat?" Bunch frowned.

Mrs. Eccles said, "We'd like all his things, you know. Sentimental like."

"He had a watch and a wallet and a railway ticket in the pockets," said Bunch. "I gave them to Sergeant Hayes."

"That's all right, then," said Mr. Eccles. "He'll hand them over to us, I expect. His private papers would be in the wallet."

"There was a pound note in the wallet," said Bunch. "Nothing else."

"No letters? Nothing like that?"

Bunch shook her head.

"Well, thank you again, Mrs. Harmon. The coat he was wearing—perhaps the sergeant's got that, too, has he?"

Bunch frowned in an effort of remembrance.

"No," she said. "I don't think . . . let me see. The doctor and I took his coat off to examine his wound." She looked round the room vaguely. "I must have taken it upstairs with the towels and basin."

"I wonder now, Mrs. Harmon, if you don't mind . . . We'd like his coat, you know, the last thing he wore. Well, the wife feels rather sentimental about it."

"Of course," said Bunch. "Would you like me to have it cleaned first? I'm afraid it's rather—well—stained."

"Oh no, no, no, that doesn't matter."

Bunch frowned. "Now I wonder where . . . Excuse me a moment." She went upstairs and it was some few minutes before she returned.

"I'm so sorry," she said breathlessly. "My daily woman must have put it aside with other clothes that were going to the cleaners. It's taken me quite a long time to find it. Here it is. I'll do it up for you in brown paper."

Disclaiming their protests, she did so; then once more effusively bidding her farewell, the Eccles departed.

Bunch went slowly back across the hall and entered the study. The Reverend Julian Harmon looked up and his brow cleared. He was composing a sermon and was fearing that he'd been led astray by the interest of the political relations between Judaea and Persia, in the reign of Cyrus.

"Yes, dear?" he said hopefully.

"Julian," said Bunch, "what's *sanctuary* exactly?"

Julian Harmon gratefully put aside his sermon paper.

"Well," he said, "sanctuary in Roman and Greek temples applied to the *cella* in which stood the statue of a god. The Latin word for altar, *ara*, also means protection." He continued learnedly: "In A.D. 399 the right of sanctuary in Christian churches was finally and definitely recognized. The earliest mention of the right of sanctuary in England is in the Code of Laws issued by Ethelbert in A.D. 600 . . ."

He continued for some time with his exposition but was, as often, disconcerted by his wife's reception of his erudite pronouncement.

"Darling," she said, "you are sweet."

Bending over, she kissed him on the tip of his nose. Julian felt rather like a dog who has been congratulated on performing a clever trick.

"The Eccles have been here," said Bunch.

The vicar frowned. "The Eccles? I don't seem to remember . . ."

"You don't know them. They're the sister and her husband of the man in the church."

"My dear, you ought to have called me."

"There wasn't any need," said Bunch. "They were not in need of consolation. I wonder now." She frowned. "If I put a casserole in the oven tomorrow, can you manage, Julian? I think I shall have to go up to London for the sales."

"The sails?" Her husband looked at her blankly. "Do you mean a yacht or a boat or something?"

Bunch laughed.

"No, darling. There's a special white sale at Burrows and Portman's. You know, sheets, tablecloths and towels and glass cloths. I don't know what we do with our glass cloths, the way they wear through. Besides," she added thoughtfully, "I think I ought to go and see Aunt Jane."

That sweet old lady, Miss Jane Marple, was enjoying the delights of the metropolis for a fortnight, comfortably installed in her nephew's studio flat.

"So kind of dear Raymond," she murmured. "He and Joan have gone to America for a fortnight and they insisted I should come up here and enjoy myself. And now, dear Bunch, do tell me what it is that's worrying you."

Bunch was Miss Marple's favourite godchild, and the old lady looked at her with great affection as Bunch, thrusting her best felt hat further on the back of her head, started on her story.

Bunch's recital was concise and clear. Miss Marple nodded her head as Bunch finished. "I see," she said. "Yes, I see."

"That's why I felt I had to see you," said Bunch. "You see, not being clever—"

"But you are clever, my dear."

"No, I'm not. Not clever like Julian."

"Julian, of course, has a very solid intellect," said Miss Marple.

"That's it," said Bunch. "Julian's got the intellect, but on the other hand, I've got the sense."

"You have a lot of common sense, Bunch, and you're very intelligent."

"You see, I don't really know what I ought to do. I can't ask Julian because—well, I mean, Julian's so full of rectitude . . ."

This statement appeared to be perfectly understood by Miss Marple, who said, "I know what you mean, dear. We women— well, it's different." She went on, "You told me what happened, Bunch, but I'd like to know first exactly what you think."

"It's all wrong," said Bunch. "The man who was there in the church, dying, knew all about sanctuary. He said it just the way Julian would have said it. I mean he was a well-read, educated man. And if he'd shot himself, he wouldn't drag himself into a church afterward and say 'sanctuary.' Sanctuary means that you're pursued, and when you get into a church you're safe. Your pursuers can't touch you. At one time even the law couldn't get at you."

She looked questioningly at Miss Marple. The latter nodded. Bunch went on, "Those people, the Eccles, were quite different. Ignorant and coarse. And there's another thing. That watch—the dead man's watch. It had the initials W.S. on the back of it. But inside—I opened it—in very small lettering there was 'To Walter from his father' and a date. *Walter.* But the Eccles kept talking of him as William or Bill."

Miss Marple seemed about to speak, but Bunch rushed on, "Oh, I know you're not always called the name you're baptized by. I mean, I can understand that you might be christened William and called 'Porky' or 'Carrots' or something. But your sister wouldn't call you William or Bill if your name was Walter."

"You mean that she wasn't his sister?"

"I'm quite sure she wasn't his sister. They were horrid—both of them. They came to the vicarage to get his things and to find out if he'd said anything before he died. When I said he hadn't I saw it in their faces—relief. I think, myself," finished Bunch, "it was Eccles who shot him."

"Murder?" said Miss Marple.

"Yes," said Bunch, "murder. That's why I came to you, darling."

Bunch's remark might have seemed incongruous to an ignorant listener, but in certain spheres Miss Marple had a reputation for dealing with murder.

"He said 'please' to me before he died," said Bunch. "He wanted me to do something for him. The awful thing is I've no idea what."

Miss Marple considered for a moment or two and then pounced on the point that had already occurred to Bunch. "But why was he there at all?" she asked.

"You mean," said Bunch, "if you wanted sanctuary, you might pop into a church anywhere. There's no need to take a bus that only goes four times a day and come out to a lonely spot like ours for it."

"He must have come there for a purpose," Miss Marple thought. "He must have come to see someone. Chipping Cleghorn's not a big place, Bunch. Surely you must have some idea of who it was he came to see?"

Bunch reviewed the inhabitants of her village in her mind before rather doubtfully shaking her head. "In a way," she said, "it could be anybody."

"He never mentioned a name?"

"He said Julian, or I thought he said Julian. It might have been

Julia, I suppose. As far as I know, there isn't any Julia living in Chipping Cleghorn."

She screwed up her eyes as she thought back to the scene. The man lying there on the chancel steps, the light coming through the window with its jewels of red and blue light.

"Jewels," said Bunch suddenly. "Perhaps that's what he said. The light coming through the east window looked like jewels."

"Jewels," said Miss Marple thoughtfully.

"I'm coming now," said Bunch, "to the most important thing of all. The reason why I've really come here today. You see, the Eccles made a great fuss about having his coat. We took it off when the doctor was seeing to him. It was an old, shabby sort of coat—there was no reason they should have wanted it. They pretended it was sentimental, but that was nonsense.

"Anyway, I went up to find it, and as I was going up the stairs I remembered how he'd made a kind of picking gesture with his hand, as though he was fumbling with the coat. So when I got hold of the coat I looked at it very carefully and I saw that in one place the lining had been sewn up again with a different thread. So I unpicked it and I found a little piece of paper inside. I took it out and I sewed it up again properly with thread that matched. I was careful and I don't really think that the Eccles would know I've done it. I don't think so, but I can't be sure. And I took the coat down to them and made some excuse for the delay."

"The piece of paper?" asked Miss Marple.

Bunch opened her handbag. "I didn't show it to Julian," she said, "because he would have said that I ought to have given it to the Eccles. But I thought I'd rather bring it to you instead."

"A cloakroom ticket," said Miss Marple, looking at it. "Paddington Station."

"He had a return ticket to Paddington in his pocket," said Bunch.

The eyes of the two women met.

"This calls for action," said Miss Marple briskly. "But it would be advisable, I think, to be careful. Would you have noticed at all, Bunch dear, whether you were followed when you came to London today?"

"Followed!" exclaimed Bunch. "You don't think—"

"Well, I think it's possible," said Miss Marple. "When anything is possible, I think we ought to take precautions." She rose with a brisk movement. "You came up here ostensibly, my dear, to go to the sales. I think the right thing to do, therefore, would be for us to go to the sales. But before we set out, we might put one or two little arrangements in hand. I don't suppose," Miss Marple added obscurely, "that I shall need the old speckled tweed with the beaver collar just at present. . . ."

It was about an hour and a half later that the two ladies, rather the worse for wear and battered in appearance, and both clasping parcels of hard-won household linen, sat down at a small and sequestered hostelry called the Apple Bough to restore their forces with steak-and-kidney pudding followed by apple tart and custard.

"Really a prewar-quality face towel," gasped Miss Marple, slightly out of breath. "With a J on it too. So fortunate that Raymond's wife's name is Joan. I shall put them aside until I really need them and then they will do for her if I pass on sooner than I expect."

"I really did need the glass cloths," said Bunch. "And they were very cheap, though not as cheap as the ones that woman with the ginger hair managed to snatch from me."

A smart young woman with a lavish application of rouge and lipstick entered the Apple Bough at that moment. After looking round vaguely for a moment or two, she hurried to their table. She laid down an envelope by Miss Marple's elbow.

"There you are, miss," she said briskly.

"Oh, thank you, Gladys," said Miss Marple. "Thank you very much. So kind of you."

"Always pleased to oblige, I'm sure," said Gladys. "Ernie always says to me, 'Everything what's good you learned from that Miss Marple of yours that you were in service with,' and I'm sure I'm always glad to oblige you, miss."

"Such a dear girl," said Miss Marple as Gladys departed again. "Always so willing and so kind."

She looked inside the envelope and then passed it on to Bunch. "Now be very careful, dear," she said. "By the way, is there still that nice young inspector at Melchester that I remember?"

"I don't know," said Bunch. "I expect so."

"Well, if not," said Miss Marple thoughtfully, "I can always ring up the chief constable. I think he would remember me."

"Of course he'd remember you," said Bunch. "Everybody would remember you. You're quite unique." She rose.

Arrived at Paddington, Bunch went to the Parcels Office and produced the cloakroom ticket. A moment or two later a rather shabby old suitcase was passed across to her, and carrying this, she made her way to the platform.

The journey home was uneventful. Bunch rose as the train approached Chipping Cleghorn and picked up the old suitcase. She had just left her carriage when a man, sprinting along the platform, suddenly seized the suitcase from her hand and rushed off with it.

"Stop!" Bunch yelled. "Stop him, stop him. He's taken my suitcase."

The ticket collector who, at this rural station, was a man of somewhat slow processes had just begun to say, "Now, look here, you can't do that—" when a smart blow in the chest pushed him aside, and the man with the suitcase rushed out from the station. He made his way toward a waiting car. Tossing the suitcase in, he was about to climb after it, but before he could move a hand fell on his shoulder, and the voice of Police Constable Abel said, "Now then, what's all this?"

Bunch arrived, panting, from the station. "He snatched my suitcase," she said.

"Nonsense," said the man. "I don't know what this lady means. It's my suitcase. I just got out of the train with it."

"Now, let's get this clear," said Police Constable Abel.

He looked at Bunch with a bovine and impartial stare. Nobody would have guessed that Police Constable Abel and Mrs. Harmon spent long half hours in Police Constable Abel's off time discussing the respective merits of manure and bone meal for rose bushes.

"You say, madam, that this is your suitcase?" said Police Constable Abel.

"Yes," said Bunch. "Definitely."

"And you, sir?"

"I say this suitcase is mine."

The man was tall, dark, and well dressed, with a drawling voice and a superior manner. A feminine voice from inside the car said, "Of course it's your suitcase, Edwin. I don't know what this woman means."

"We'll have to get this clear," said Police Constable Abel. "If it's your suitcase, madam, what do you say is inside it?"

"Clothes," said Bunch. "A long speckled coat with a beaver collar, two wool jumpers, and a pair of shoes."

"Well, that's clear enough," said Police Constable Abel. He turned to the other.

"I am a theatrical costumer," said the dark man importantly. "This suitcase contains theatrical properties which I brought down here for an amateur performance."

"Right, sir," said Police Constable Abel. "Well, we'll just look inside, shall we, and see? We can go along to the police station, or if you're in a hurry, we'll take the suitcase back to the station and open it there."

"It'll suit me," said the dark man. "My name is Moss, by the way. Edwin Moss."

The police constable, holding the suitcase, went back into the station. "Just taking this into the Parcels Office, George," he said to the ticket collector.

Police Constable Abel laid the suitcase on the counter of the Parcels Office and pushed back the clasp. The case was not locked. Bunch and Mr. Edwin Moss stood on either side of him, their eyes regarding each other vengefully.

"Ah!" said Police Constable Abel, as he pushed up the lid.

Inside, neatly folded, was a long, rather shabby tweed coat with a beaver fur collar. There were also two wool jumpers and a pair of country shoes.

"Exactly as you say, madam," said Police Constable Abel, turning to Bunch.

Nobody could have said that Mr. Edwin Moss underdid things. His dismay and compunction were magnificent.

"I do apologize," he said. "I really do apologize. Please believe me, dear lady, when I tell you how very, very sorry I am. Unpardonable—quite unpardonable—my behaviour has been." He looked at his watch. "I must rush now. Probably my suitcase has gone on the train." Raising his hat once more, he said meltingly to Bunch, "Do, do forgive me," and rushed hurriedly out of the Parcels Office.

"Are you going to let him get away?" asked Bunch in a conspiratorial whisper of Police Constable Abel.

The latter slowly closed a bovine eye in a wink.

"He won't get too far, ma'am," he said. "That's to say, he won't get far unobserved, if you take my meaning."

"Oh," said Bunch, relieved.

"That old lady's been on the phone," said Police Constable Abel, "the one as was down here a few years ago. Bright she is, isn't she? But there's been a lot cooking up all today. Shouldn't wonder if the inspector or sergeant was out to see you about it tomorrow morning."

It was the inspector who came, the Inspector Craddock whom Miss Marple remembered. He greeted Bunch with a smile as an old friend.

"Crime in Chipping Cleghorn again," he said cheerfully. "You don't lack for sensation here, do you, Mrs. Harmon?"

"I could do with rather less," said Bunch. "Have you come to ask me questions or are you going to tell me things for a change?"

"I'll tell you some things first," said the inspector. "To begin with, Mr. and Mrs. Eccles have been having an eye kept on them for some time. There's reason to believe they've been connected with several robberies in this part of the world. For another thing, although Mrs. Eccles has a brother called Sandbourne who has recently come back from abroad, the man you found dying in the church yesterday was definitely not Sandbourne."

"I knew that he wasn't," said Bunch. "His name was Walter, to begin with, not William."

The inspector nodded. "His name was Walter St. John, and he escaped forty-eight hours ago from Charrington Prison."

"Of course," said Bunch softly to herself, "he was being hunted down by the law, and he took sanctuary." Then she asked, "What had he done?"

"I'll have to go back rather a long way. It's a complicated story. Several years ago there was a certain dancer doing turns at the music halls. I don't expect you'll have ever heard of her, but she specialized in an Arabian Night's turn. 'Aladdin in the Cave of Jewels,' it was called.

"She wasn't much of a dancer, I believe, but she was—well—attractive. Anyway, a certain Asiatic royalty fell for her in a big way. Among other things he gave her a very magnificent emerald necklace."

"The historic jewels of a rajah?" murmured Bunch ecstatically.

Inspector Craddock coughed. "Well, a rather more modern version, Mrs. Harmon. The affair didn't last very long, broke up when our potentate's attention was captured by a certain film star whose demands were not quite so modest.

"Zobeida, to give the dancer her stage name, hung on to the necklace, and in due course it was stolen. It disappeared from her dressing room at the theater, and there was a lingering suspicion in the minds of the authorities that she herself might have engineered its disappearance. Such things have been known as a publicity stunt, or indeed from more dishonest motives.

"The necklace was never recovered, but during the course of the investigation the attention of the police was drawn to this man, Walter St. John. He was a man of education and breeding who had come down in the world and who was employed as a working jeweler with a rather obscure firm which was suspected as acting as a fence for jewel robberies.

"There was evidence that this necklace had passed through his hands. It was, however, in connection with the theft of some other jewelry that he was finally brought to trial and convicted and sent to prison. He had not very much longer to serve, so his escape was rather a surprise."

"But why did he come here?" asked Bunch.

"We'd like to know that very much, Mrs. Harmon. Following up his trail, it seems that he went first to London. He didn't visit any of his old associates, but he visited an elderly woman, a Mrs. Jacobs who had formerly been a theatrical dresser. She won't say a word of what he came for, but according to other lodgers in the house, he left carrying a suitcase."

"I see," said Bunch. "He left it in the cloakroom at Paddington and then he came down here."

"By that time," said Inspector Craddock, "Eccles and the man who calls himself Edwin Moss were on his trail. They wanted that suitcase. They saw him get on the bus. They must have driven out in a car ahead of him and been waiting for him when he left the bus."

"And he was murdered?" said Bunch.

"Yes," said Craddock. "He was shot. It was Eccles' revolver, but I rather fancy it was Moss who did the shooting. Now, Mrs. Harmon, what we want to know is, where is the suitcase that Walter St. John actually deposited at Paddington Station?"

Bunch grinned. "I expect Aunt Jane's got it by now," she said. "Miss Marple, I mean. That was her plan. She sent a former maid of hers with a suitcase packed with her things to the cloakroom at Paddington and we exchanged tickets. I collected her suitcase and brought it down by train. She seemed to expect that an attempt would be made to get it from me."

It was Inspector Craddock's turn to grin. "So she said when she rang up. I'm driving up to London to see her. Do you want to come, too, Mrs. Harmon?"

"Wel-l," said Bunch, considering. "Wel-l, as a matter of fact, it's very fortunate. I had a toothache last night so I really ought to go to London to see the dentist, oughtn't I?"

"Definitely," said Inspector Craddock.

Miss Marple looked from Inspector Craddock's face to the eager face of Bunch Harmon. The suitcase lay on the table. "Of course, I haven't opened it," the old lady said. "I wouldn't dream of doing such a thing till somebody official arrived. Besides," she added, with a demurely mischievous Victorian smile, "it's locked."

"Like to make a guess at what's inside, Miss Marple?" asked the inspector.

"I should imagine, you know," said Miss Marple, "that it would be Zobeida's theatrical costumes. Would you like a chisel, Inspector?"

The chisel soon did its work. Both women gave a slight gasp as the lid flew up. The sunlight coming through the window lit up what seemed like an inexhaustible treasure of sparkling jewels, red, blue, green, orange.

"Aladdin's Cave," said Miss Marple. "The flashing jewels the girl wore to dance."

"Ah," said Inspector Craddock. "Now, what's so precious about it, do you think, that a man was murdered to get hold of it?"

"She was a shrewd girl, I expect," said Miss Marple thoughtfully. "She's dead, isn't she, Inspector?"

"Yes, died three years ago."

"She had this valuable emerald necklace," said Miss Marple musingly. "Had the stones taken out of their setting and fastened here and there on her theatrical costume, where everyone would take them for merely coloured rhinestones. Then she had a replica made of the real necklace, and that, of course, was what was stolen. No wonder it never came on the market. The thief soon discovered the stones were false."

"Here is an envelope," said Bunch, pulling aside some of the glittering stones.

Inspector Craddock took it from her and extracted two official-looking papers from it. He read aloud, " 'Marriage certificate between Walter Edmund St. John and Mary Moss.' That was Zobeida's real name."

"So they were married," said Miss Marple. "I see."

"What's the other?" asked Bunch.

"A birth certificate of a daughter, Jewel."

"Jewel?" cried Bunch. "Why, of course. Jewel! Jill! That's it. I see now why he came to Chipping Cleghorn. That's what he was trying to say to me. Jewel. The Mundys, you know. Laburnum Cottage. They look after a little girl for someone. They're devoted to her. She's been like their own granddaughter. Yes, I remember now, her name was Jewel, only, of course, they call her Jill.

"Mrs. Mundy had a stroke about a week ago, and the old man's been very ill with pneumonia. They were both going to go to the infirmary. I've been trying hard to find a good home for Jill somewhere. I didn't want her taken away to an institution.

"I suppose her father heard about it in prison and he managed to break away and get hold of this suitcase from the old dresser he or his wife left it with. I suppose if the jewels really belonged to her mother, they can be used for the child now."

"I should imagine so, Mrs. Harmon. If they're here."

"Oh, they'll be here all right," said Miss Marple cheerfully. . . .

"Thank goodness you're back, dear," said the Reverend Julian Harmon, greeting his wife with affection and a sigh of content. "Mrs. Burt always tries to do her best when you're away, but she really gave me some very peculiar fish cakes for lunch. I didn't want to hurt her feelings so I gave them to Tiglash Pileser, but even he wouldn't eat them, so I had to throw them out of the window."

"Tiglash Pileser," said Bunch, stroking the vicarage cat, who was purring against her knee, "is very particular about what fish he eats. I often tell him he's got a proud stomach!"

"And your tooth, dear? Did you have it seen to?"

"Yes," said Bunch. "It didn't hurt much, and I went to see Aunt Jane again, too . . ."

"Dear old thing," said Julian. "I hope she's not failing at all."

"Not in the least," said Bunch, with a grin.

The following morning Bunch took a fresh supply of chrysanthemums to the church. The sun was once more pouring through the east window, and Bunch stood in the jeweled light on the chancel steps. She said very softly under her breath, "Your little girl will be all right. I'll see that she is. I promise."

Then she tidied up the church, slipped into a pew, and knelt for a few moments to say her prayers before returning to the vicarage to attack the piled-up chores of two neglected days.

COMMENT AND QUESTIONS

This is a complex mystery. The murderer of the stranger who dies at the vicarage must be discovered, as well as the motive for the murder, so that another crime, the theft of something belonging to the dead man, may be prevented. The only clues to the murderer, the motive, and the object in question are the dying man's last words and his last feeble gestures. Enigmatic dying messages have often been employed by mystery-story writers as the main or only clues that their detectives have to the solution of a crime. This is a difficult device to use, for the message must be both inconclusive and ambiguous, yet it also must be a valid clue if rightly interpreted.

One of the most significant implications of this story is that it is not always easy to determine what is "right" and what is "wrong." Bunch Harmon lies and keeps a cloakroom ticket that does not belong to her in order to prevent a greater wrong. She—a vicar's wife—does this out of a sense of obligation to a dying man she does not even know, who appealed to her, with a single word, "please," to fulfill an unidentified task. What is Bunch's standard for behavior? Would it be harder to follow than a set of "rules"? Why doesn't the fact that Walter St. John is a criminal make any difference to her? Is it ironic that her husband is a vicar and would not understand? Is this necessarily a condemnation of him?

Why do you imagine the dying man directs his "please" to Bunch?

Why might "Julian's sense of rectitude" be a problem to Bunch in her task? Would Julian approve of what Bunch is doing?

It is a common belief that very well-educated or intelligent people are often impractical. "The absent-minded professor" stereotype reflects this attitude. How is this notion used in "Sanctuary" for mild humor?

Sherlock Holmes often makes "arrangements" to which he refers obscurely, and the reader and Watson are unenlightened until a surprising development occurs. Is there a parallel in this story?

Which attributes of the classic detective figure does Miss Marple possess? Which does she lack?

ELIZABETH BOWEN

The Demon Lover

Elizabeth Bowen is best known for her novels, such as *The Death of the Heart*, in which she sensitively explores the interior world of her characters. Many authors, however, who customarily write quite different types of fiction have felt challenged by the demands of the mystery story. Henry James and Graham Greene, among others, have evidenced great skill in their mystery stories involving the supernatural, and so has Mrs. Bowen in this chilling love story.

Toward the end of her day in London Mrs. Drover went round to her shut-up house to look for several things she wanted to take away. Some belonged to herself, some to her family, who were by now used to their country life. It was late August; it had been a steamy, showery day: at the moment the trees down the pavement glittered in an escape of humid yellow afternoon sun. Against the next batch of clouds, already piling up ink-dark, broken chimneys and parapets stood out. In her once familiar street, as in any unused channel, an unfamiliar queerness had silted up; a cat wove itself in and out of railings, but no human eye watched Mrs. Drover's return. Shifting some parcels under her arm, she slowly forced round her latchkey in an unwilling lock, then gave the door, which had warped, a push with her knee. Dead air came out to meet her as she went in.

The staircase window having been boarded up, no light came down into the hall. But one door, she could just see, stood ajar, so she went quickly through into the room and unshuttered the big window in there. Now the prosaic woman, looking about her, was more perplexed than she knew by everything that she saw, by traces of her long former habit of life—the yellow smokestain up the white marble mantelpiece, the ring left by a vase on the top of the escritoire; the bruise in the wallpaper where, on the door being thrown open widely, the china handle had always hit the wall. The piano, having gone away to be stored, had left what looked like claw-marks on its part of the parquet. Though not much dust had seeped in, each object wore a film of another kind; and, the only ventilation being the chimney, the whole drawing-room smelled of the cold hearth. Mrs. Drover put down her parcels on the escritoire and left the room to proceed upstairs; the things she wanted were in a bedroom chest.

She had been anxious to see how the house was—the part-time caretaker she shared with some neighbours was away this week on his holiday, known to be not yet back. At the best of times he did not look in often, and she was never sure that she trusted him. There were some cracks in the structure, left by the last bombing, on which she was anxious to keep an eye. Not that one could do anything—

A shaft of refracted daylight now lay across the hall. She stopped dead and stared at the hall table—on this lay a letter addressed to her.

She thought first—then the caretaker *must* be back. All the same, who, seeing the house shuttered, would have dropped a letter in at the box? It was not a circular, it was not a bill. And the post office redirected, to the address in the country, everything for her that came through the post. The caretaker (even if he *were* back) did not know she was due in London today—her call here had been planned to be a surprise—so his negligence in the manner of this letter, leaving it to wait in the dusk and the dust, annoyed her. Annoyed, she picked up the letter, which bore no stamp. But it cannot be important, or they would know . . . She took the letter rapidly upstairs with her, without a stop to look at the writing till she reached what had been her bedroom, where she let in light. The room looked over the garden and other gardens: the sun had gone in; as the clouds sharpened and lowered, the trees and rank lawns seemed already to smoke with dark. Her reluctance to look again at the letter came from the fact that she felt intruded upon—and by someone contemptuous of her ways. However, in the tenseness preceding the fall of rain she read it: it was a few lines.

Dear Kathleen,
   You will not have forgotten that today is our anniversary, and the day we said. The years have gone by at once slowly and fast. In view of the fact that nothing has changed, I shall rely upon you to keep your promise. I was sorry to see you leave London, but was satisfied that you would be back in time. You may expect me, therefore, at the hour arranged.

Until then . . .
K.

Mrs. Drover looked for the date: it was today's. She dropped the letter on to the bed-springs, then picked it up to see the writing again—her lips, beneath the remains of lipstick, beginning to go white. She felt so much the change in her own face that she went to the mirror, polishing a clear patch in it and looked at once urgently and stealthily in. She was confronted by a woman of forty-four, with eyes starting out under a hatbrim that had been rather carelessly pulled down. She had not put on any more powder since she left the shop where she ate her solitary tea. The pearls her husband had given her on their marriage hung loose round her now rather thinner throat, slipping into the V of the pink wool jumper her sister knitted last autumn as they sat round the fire. Mrs. Drover's most normal expression was one of controlled worry, but of assent. Since the birth of the third of her little boys, attended by a quite serious illness, she had had an intermittent muscular flicker to the left of her mouth, but in spite of this she could always sustain a manner that was at once energetic and calm.

   Turning from her own face as precipitately as she had gone to meet it, she went to the chest where the things were, unlocked it, threw up the lid and knelt to search. But as rain began to come crashing down she could not keep from looking over her shoulder at the stripped bed on which the letter lay. Behind the blanket of rain the clock of the church that still stood struck six—with rapidly heightening apprehension she counted each of the slow strokes. "The hour arranged . . . My God," she said, "*what* hour? How should I . . . ? After twenty-five years . . ."

The young girl talking to the soldier in the garden had not ever completely seen his face. It was dark; they were saying good-bye under a tree. Now and then—for it felt, from not seeing him at this intense moment, as though she had never seen him at all—she verified his presence for these few moments longer by putting out a hand, which he each time pressed, without very much kindness, and painfully, on to one of the breast buttons of his uniform. That cut of the button on the palm of her hand was, principally, what she was to carry away. This was so near the end of a leave from France that she could only wish him already gone. It was August 1916. Being not kissed, being drawn away from and looked at intimidated Kathleen till she imagined spectral glitters in the place of his eyes. Turning away and looking back up the lawn she saw, through branches of trees, the drawing-room window alight: she caught a breath for the moment when she could go running back there into the safe arms of her mother and sister, and cry: "What shall I do, what shall I do? He has gone."

Hearing her catch her breath, her fiancé said, without feeling: "Cold?"

"You're going away such a long way."

"Not so far as you think."

"I don't understand?"

"You don't have to," he said. "You will. You know what we said."

"But that was—suppose you—I mean, suppose."

"I shall be with you," he said, "sooner or later. You won't forget that. You need do nothing but wait."

Only a little more than a minute later she was free to run up the silent lawn. Looking in through the window at her mother and sister, who did not for the moment perceive her, she already felt that unnatural promise drive down between her and the rest of all human kind. No other way of having given herself could have made her feel so apart, lost and forsworn. She could not have plighted a more sinister troth.

Kathleen behaved well when, some months later, her fiancé was reported missing, presumed killed. Her family not only supported her but were able to praise her courage without stint because they could not regret, as a husband for her, the man they knew almost nothing about. They hoped she would, in a year or two, console herself—and had it been only a question of consolation things might have gone much straighter ahead. But her trouble, behind just a little grief, was a complete dislocation from everything. She did not reject other lovers, for these failed to appear: for years she failed to attract men—and with the approach of her thirties she became natural enough to share her family's anxiousness on this score. She began to put herself out, to wonder; and at thirty-two she was very greatly relieved to find herself being courted by William Drover. She married him, and the two of them settled down in this quiet, arboreal part of Kensington: in this house the years piled up, her children were born and they all lived till they were driven out by the bombs of the next war. Her movements as Mrs. Drover were circumscribed, and she dismissed any idea that they were still watched.

As things were—dead or living, the letter-writer sent her only a threat. Unable, for some minutes, to go on kneeling with her back exposed to the empty room, Mrs. Drover rose from the chest to sit on an upright chair whose back was firmly against the wall. The desuetude of her former bedroom, her married London home's whole air of being a cracked cup from which memory, with its reassuring power, had either evaporated or leaked away, made a crisis—and at just this crisis the letter-writer had, knowledgeably, struck. The hollowness of the house this evening cancelled years on years of voices, habits and steps. Through the shut windows she only heard rain fall on the roofs around. To rally herself, she said she was in a mood—and, for two or three seconds shutting her eyes, told herself that she had imagined the letter. But she opened them—there it lay on the bed.

On the supernatural side of the letter's entrance she was not permitting her mind to dwell. Who, in London, knew she meant to call at the house today? Evidently, however, this had been known. The caretaker, *had* he come back, had had no cause to expect her: he would have taken the letter in his pocket, to forward it, at his own time, through the post. There was no other sign that the caretaker had been in—but, if not? Letters dropped in at doors of deserted houses do not fly or walk to tables in halls. They do not sit on the dust of empty tables with the air of certainty that they will be found. There is needed some human hand—but nobody but the caretaker had a key. Under circumstances she did not care to consider, a house can be entered without a key. It was possible that she was not alone now. She might be being waited for, downstairs. Waited for—until when? Until "the hour arranged." At least that was not six o'clock: six has struck.

She rose from the chair and went over and locked the door.

The thing was, to get out. To fly? No, not that: she had to catch her train. As a woman whose utter dependability was the keystone of her family life she was not willing to return to the country, to her husband, her little boys and her sister, without the objects she had come up to fetch. Resuming work at the chest she set about making up a number of parcels in a rapid, fumbling-decisive way. These, with her shopping parcels, would be too much to carry; these meant a taxi—at the thought of the taxi her heart went up and her normal breathing resumed. I will ring up the taxi now; the taxi cannot come too soon: I shall hear the taxi out there running its engine, till I walk calmly down to it through the hall. I'll ring up—But no: the telephone is cut off . . . She tugged at a knot she had tied wrong.

The idea of flight . . . He was never kind to me, not really. I don't remember him kind at all. Mother said he never considered me. He was set on me, that was what it was—not love. Not love, not meaning a person well. What did he do, to make me promise like that? I can't remember—but she found that she could.

She remembered with such dreadful acuteness that the twenty-five years since then dissolved like smoke and she instinctively looked for the weal left by the button on the palm of her hand. She remembered not only all that he said and did but the complete suspension of *her* existence during that August week. I was not myself—they all told me so at the time. She remembered —but with one white burning blank as where acid has dropped on a photograph: *under no conditions* could she remember his face.

So, wherever he may be waiting, I shall not know him. You have no time to run from a face you do not expect.

The thing was to get to the taxi before any clock struck what could be the hour. She would slip down the street and round the side of the square to where the square gave on the main road. She would return in the taxi, safe, to her own door, and bring the solid driver into the house with her to pick up the parcels from room to room. The idea of the taxi driver made her decisive, bold: she unlocked her door, went to the top of the staircase and listened down.

She heard nothing—but while she was hearing nothing the *passé* air of the staircase was disturbed by a draft that travelled up to her face. It emanated from the basement: down there a door or window was being opened by someone who chose this moment to leave the house.

The rain had stopped; the pavements steamily shone as Mrs. Drover let herself out by inches from her own front door into the empty street. The unoccupied houses opposite continued to meet her look with their damaged stare. Making toward the thoroughfare and the taxi, she tried not to keep looking behind. Indeed, the silence was so intense—one of those creeks of London silence exaggerated this summer by the damage of war—that no tread could have gained on hers unheard. Where her street debouched on the square where people went on living she grew conscious of and checked her unnatural pace. Across the open end of the square two buses impassively passed each other; women, a perambulator, cyclists, a man wheeling a barrow signalled, once again, the ordinary flow of life. At the square's most populous corner should be—and was—the short taxi rank. This evening, only one taxi—but this, although it presented its blank rump, appeared already to be alertly waiting for her. Indeed, without looking round the driver started his engine as she panted up from behind and put her hand on the door. As she did so, the clock struck seven. The taxi faced the main road: to make the trip back to her house it would have to turn—she had settled back on the seat and the taxi *had* turned before she, surprised by its knowing movement, recollected that she had not "said where." She leaned forward to scratch at the glass panel that divided the driver's head from her own.

The driver braked to what was almost a stop, turned round and slid the glass panel back: the jolt of this flung Mrs. Drover forward till her face was almost into the glass. Through the aperture driver and passenger, not six inches between them, remained for an eternity eye to eye. Mrs. Drover's mouth hung open for some seconds before she could issue her first scream. After that she continued to scream freely and to beat with her gloved hands on the glass all round as the taxi, accelerating without mercy, made off with her into the hinterland of deserted streets.

COMMENT AND QUESTIONS

In this story detection is not involved; but, as is often true in the detective story, the reader is misled by a wrong assumption. Like Mrs. Drover, he assumes that the ghost will be found, if it is found at all, in the haunted house and that she is "home free" when she reaches the busy street, where life is going on as usual. How are the surprise and horror intensified by this combination of the supernatural with the natural and normal?

In a medieval ballad that has the same title as this story, a woman carried off under somewhat similar circumstances discovers that her lover has a cloven hoof and plans to take her to the "mountain of hell." Is such likely to be Kathleen's situation? Explain your answer.

Would anything be lost if the setting had been Mrs. Drover's house in the country rather than "her once familiar street"? Is the time of day important?

What do you find unusual about the scene in the garden on the night Kathleen's lover left to go to war?

Mrs. Drover is wearing a pink wool sweater "her sister knitted last autumn as they sat around the fire." What do details such as this contribute to the story?

Analyze the character of Mrs. Drover. Is it important that she is a prosaic woman and that her most normal facial expression is one of "assent"?

GEORGES SIMENON

Journey Backward into Time

The impressive exception to the dominance of mystery fiction
by English and American writers is the Belgian writer
Georges Simenon. His creation, Inspector Maigret of the
Paris police, has been relentlessly thinking and feeling his
way to solutions of crimes since the 1930s. Maigret uses
scientific methods, but he is not a scientific plodder. One
feels he literally takes the criminal's measure, much as Dupin
does, by putting himself into the same physical and emotional
atmosphere. Still, in this story there is enough physical
evidence, rightly interpreted by Maigret, to satisfy any court.
As you read, notice how physical details help to create
atmosphere.

I t was one of those rare cases that can be solved by studying
diagrams and documents and by applying police methods. In
fact, when Inspector Maigret left the Quai des Orfevres he
had all the facts clearly in mind—even the position of the wine
barrels.

He had expected a short jaunt into the countryside. Instead he
found himself making a long journey backward into time. The
train that took him to Vitry aux Loges, scarcely a hundred
kilometers from Paris, was a conveyance straight from the picture
books of Epinal,[1] which he had not seen since his childhood. And
when he inquired about a taxi, the people at the station thought
that he was joking. He would have to make the rest of the trip in

the baker's cart, they said. However, he persuaded the butcher to drive over in his delivery truck.

"How often do you go down there?" the inspector asked, naming the little village to which his investigation was taking him.

"Twice a week, regularly. Thanks to you, they'll have an extra meat delivery this week."

Maigret had been born only forty kilometers away, on the banks of the Loire, yet he was surprised by the somber, tragic aspect of this sector of the Forest of Orleans. The road ran through deep woods for ten kilometers without a sign of civilization. When the truck reached a tiny village in a clearing, Maigret asked, "Is this it?"

"The next hamlet."

It wasn't raining, but the woods were damp. The trees had lost most of their foliage, and the pale, raw light of the sky bore down heavily through the bare branches. The dead leaves were rotting on the ground. An occasional shot cracked in the distance.

"Is there much hunting around here?"

"That's probably Monsieur the Duke."

In another, smaller clearing some thirty one-story houses were clustered about the steeple of a church. None of the houses could be less than a century old, and their black tile roofs gave them an inhospitable air.

"You can let me off at the house of the Potru sisters."

"I guessed that was where you'd be going. It's right across from the church."

Maigret got out. The butcher drove on a little farther and opened the back of his delivery truck. A few housewives came to look but could not make up their minds to buy. It was not their regular day for meat.

Maigret had pored so long over the diagrams sent to Paris by the original investigators that he could have entered the house with his eyes shut. As it was, the rooms were so dark that he wasn't much better off with his eyes open. As he walked into the shop at the front of the house, he seemed to be stepping into a past century.

The room was as dimly lit as a canvas by an old master. The dark brown tonality of an ancient masterpiece was diffused over the walls and furniture—a monochrome in chiaroscuro broken only by a highlight here and there, on a glass jar or a copper kettle.

The elder of the Demoiselles Potru had lived in this house since her birth sixty-five years before—her younger sister was sixty-two. Their parents had spent their lives there before them. Nothing in the shop had changed in all that time—not the counter with its old-fashioned scales and its gleaming candy jars, nor shelves of notions, nor the grocery section with its stale odors of cinnamon and chicory, nor the zinc-covered slab that served as the village bar. A barrel of kerosene stood in a corner next to a smaller barrel of cooking oil. In the rear were two long tables, polished by time, flanked by backless benches.

A door opened at the left, and a woman in her early thirties came in, carrying a baby in her arms. She looked at Maigret.

"What is it you want?"

"Never mind about me. I'm here for the investigation. I suppose you are a neighbor?"

The woman, whose apron ballooned over a rounded belly, said, "I'm Marie Lacore. My husband is the blacksmith."

"I see." Maigret had just noticed the kerosene lamp hanging from the ceiling. So the hamlet had no electricity. . . .

The second room, which Maigret entered without invitation, would have been completely dark were it not for the two logs blazing on the hearth. The flickering light revealed an immense bed on which were piled several mattresses and a puffy, red eider-down quilt. An old woman lay motionless on the bed. Her haggard rigid face was lifeless except for the sharp, questioning eyes.

"She still can't speak?" Maigret asked Marie Lacore.

The blacksmith's wife shook her head in the negative. Maigret shrugged, sat down on a straw-bottomed chair, and began taking papers from his pockets.

There was nothing sensational about the actual crime, which had taken place five days earlier. The Potru sisters, who lived alone in the hovel, were believed to have accumulated a considerable nest egg. They owned three other houses in the village and had a long-established reputation as misers.

During the night of Saturday to Sunday their neighbors remembered hearing unusual noises but had thought nothing of it at the time. However, a farmer passing the house at dawn on Sunday noticed that the bedroom window was wide open, looked in, and shouted for help.

Amelie Potru, the elder sister, was lying on the floor in a pool of blood near the window, clad only in a red-stained nightgown. The younger sister, Marguerite, was lying on the bed, her face turned to the wall, dead, with three knife wounds in her chest, her cheek gashed, and one eye torn half from its socket.

Amelie was still alive. She had staggered to the window to give the alarm but, weakened from loss of blood, had fallen unconscious before she could cry out. She had no less than eleven stab wounds in her right side and shoulder, none of them serious.

The second drawer of the dresser had been pulled out and apparently ransacked. Among the linen scattered on the floor was a brief case of mildewed leather in which the sisters must have kept their business papers. It was empty, but lying near by were a savings-bank passbook, deeds to property, leases, and bills for supplies.

The Orleans authorities who made the original investigation sent Maigret detailed diagrams and photographs of the scene as well as a transcript of the questioning of witnesses.

Marguerite, the dead woman, had been buried two days after the murder. Amelie had resisted all efforts to take her to a hospital, sinking her nails into the bed sheets, fighting off neighbors who tried to move her, and demanding—with her eyes—that she be left at home. She had lost all power of speech.

The medical examiner from Orleans declared that no vital organ had been injured and that her loss of voice must be due to shock. In any case, no sound had passed her lips for five days; yet despite her bandages and her immobility she followed all proceedings with her eyes. Even now her gaze never left Maigret for a moment.

Three hours after the Orleans authorities finished their investigation, they arrested a man who from the evidence must be the murderer: Marcel, illegitimate son of the dead Potru sister. The late Marguerite had given birth to Marcel when she was twenty-three, so he must be thirty-nine years old. For a while Marcel had worked with the hounds of the Duke's hunt. More recently he had been a woodcutter in the forest and lived in an abandoned tumble-down farmhouse near the Loup Pendu pond, ten kilometers from the village.

The villagers looked upon Marcel as a brute, a miserable wretch who was little better than an animal. Several times he had disappeared, leaving his wife and five children for weeks on end. He beat his family more often than he fed them. What's more, he was a drunkard.

Maigret decided to reread at the scene of the crime the transcript of Marcel's testimony: "I came on my bicycle around seven o'clock just when the old women were sitting down to eat. I had a drink at the bar, then I went out to the courtyard and killed a rabbit. I skinned it and cleaned it and my mother cooked it. My aunt yelled her head off because I ate their rabbit, but she always yells. She can't stand me . . ."

According to the testimony of other villagers, Marcel frequently came to the Potru sisters for a private spree. His mother never refused him anything, and his aunt, who was afraid of him, did nothing more than complain.

Maigret had stopped off in Orleans to see Marcel in his cell, and got further details.

"There was more argument," Marcel said, "when I took a cheese out of the shop and cut myself a hunk. Seems I shouldn't have cut into a whole cheese . . ."

"What wine were you drinking?" Maigret asked.

"Some of the wine from the shop."

"How was the room lighted?"

"The oil lamp. Well, after dinner my mother wasn't feeling well, so she went to bed. She asked me to get her some papers out of the second drawer in the dresser. She gave me the key. I took the papers over to the bed and we went over the bills. It was the end of the month."

"You took the papers out of the brief case? What else was in there?"

"Bonds. A big bundle of bonds. A hundred francs' worth. Maybe more."

"Did you go into the storeroom?"

"No."

"You didn't light a candle to go into the storeroom?"

"Never . . . At half-past nine I put the papers back in the

drawer and then I left. I drank another slug of rotgut as I went out through the shop. . . . And anybody says I killed the old lady is a liar. Why don't you talk to the Yugo?"

To the great astonishment of Marcel's lawyer Maigret broke off his questioning.

Yarko, whom everyone called "The Yugo" because he was from Yugoslavia, was a bit of jetsam who had been washed into the village by the war and who had stayed on. He lived alone in the wing of a house near the Potru sisters and worked as a carter, hauling logs from the woods. He, too, was a confirmed drunkard, although for some time the Potru sisters had refused to serve him; he had run up too long a tab. One night they had asked Marcel to throw him out, and he had given the Yugo a bloody nose in the process.

The Potru sisters had another grievance against the Yugo. He kept his horses in a stable he had rented from them, a dilapidated outbuilding back of their courtyard, but he was always months behind in his rent. At this moment he was probably in the woods with his team.

Maigret continued to match his thoughts with the actual scene of the crime. Papers in hand, he walked to the fireplace where the Orleans men had found a kitchen knife among the ashes on the morning after the murder. The wooden handle had been completely burned, obviously to destroy fingerprints.

On the other hand, there had been plenty of fingerprints on the dresser drawer and on the brief case—and all of them had been Marcel's.

On a candlestick that stood on a table in the bedroom they had found Amelie Potru's fingerprints—and only hers. Amelie's cold eyes still followed Maigret's every move.

"I suppose your mind is still made up not to speak?" he growled as he lit his pipe.

Silence.

Maigret stooped to make a chalk mark on the floor around some bloodstains that had been indicated on the diagram.

Marie Lacore asked him, "Will you be here for a few minutes? I'd like to put my dinner on the stove."

So Maigret found himself alone with the old woman in the house he already knew by heart, although he had never seen it before. He had spent a whole day and night studying the dossier with its diagrams and sketches, and Orleans had done such a thorough job of groundwork that he was not in the least surprised, except perhaps to find the sordid reality even more shocking than he had imagined.

And yet he himself was the son of peasants. He knew that such things existed—that there were still hamlets in France where people went on living as they had lived since the thirteenth and fourteenth centuries. But to be suddenly plunged into this village in the forest, into this ancient house, into the room alone with the old woman whose alert mind seemed to be stalking Maigret—all this was like entering one of those wretched hospitals where the worst of human monstrosities are hidden away from the eyes of normal men.

When he had begun to work on the case in Paris, Maigret had jotted down a few notes on the original report:

1. Why would Marcel have burned the knife handle without worrying about his fingerprints on the dresser and the brief case?

2. If he had used the candle, why had he carried it back into the bedroom and put it out?

3. Why didn't the bloodstains on the floor follow a straight line from the bed to the window?

4. Since Marcel might well have been recognized in the street at nine-thirty in the evening, why had he left the house by the front door, instead of going through the courtyard, which led directly into open country?

But there was one bit of evidence that worried even Marcel's lawyer. One of Marcel's buttons had been found in the old women's bed, a distinctive button that definitely had come from Marcel's old corduroy hunting jacket.

"When I was cleaning the rabbit, I caught my jacket on something," had been Marcel's explanation, "and one of the buttons must have pulled loose."

Maigret finished rereading his notes. He stood up and looked at Amelie with a peculiar smile on his lips. She was going to be sorely vexed at not being able to follow him with her eyes, for he opened a door and disappeared into the storeroom.

The cubicle was dimly lit by a dirty skylight. Maigret's gaze traveled from the stacks of cordwood to the four wine barrels against the wall—the barrels he had come all the way from Paris to see. The first two barrels were full. One contained red wine, and the other white. He thumped the next two barrels. They were empty. On one of the empty barrels several tears of tallow had fallen and congealed. Technicians from Identite Judiciaire reported that the tallow on the barrel was identical with the tallow of the candle in the bedroom.

The report of the inspector in charge from Orleans had this to say about the evidence:

"The candle drippings on the barrel were probably left by Marcel when he came to drink wine. His wife admits that he was quite drunk when he got home that night, and the zigzag tire tracks of his bicycle confirm this fact."

Maigret looked about him for something he had expected to find but which apparently was not there. Puzzled, he stepped back into the bedroom, opened the window, and called to two urchins who were gaping at the house.

"Listen, boys. Will one of you run and get me a saw?"

"A wood saw?"

"Right."

Maigret could still feel the old woman's eyes boring into his back—live eyes in a dead face, eyes that moved only when his bulky figure moved.

The boys came back bringing two saws of different sizes. At the same time Marie Lacore returned from next door.

"I hope I haven't kept you waiting," she said. "I left the baby home. Now I'll have to attend to——"

"Wait just a few minutes, will you?" That was a scene that Maigret intended to skip, thank you! He'd had enough without it. He went back into the storeroom and started sawing one of the empty barrels—the one with the candle drippings on it.

He knew what he would find. He was sure of his theory. If he had had any lingering doubts about it when he arrived, they had been dispelled by the atmosphere of the old house. Amelie Potru had turned out to be exactly the sort of person he had anticipated. And the very walls of the house seemed to ooze the avarice and hate he had expected.

Another thing. When he first entered the shop, Maigret had noted a pile of newspapers on the counter. That was one important fact the Orleans reports had omitted—that the Potru sisters were also the news dealers of the village. Further, Amelie owned glasses that, since she did not wear them about the house, were obviously reading glasses. So Amelie was able to read—and thus the biggest question mark in Inspector Maigret's theory was eliminated. His theory was based on hate—a festering hate made even more purulent by long years of being shut up together within the same four walls, of sharing the same narrow interests by day, and even the same bed by night.

But there was one experience the two sisters had not shared. Marguerite, the younger, had had a child. She had known love and motherhood. Amelie had shared only the annoying aftermath. The brat had clung to her skirts, too, for ten or fifteen years. And after he had struck out for himself, he was always coming back to eat and drink and to demand money.

It was Amelie's money as much as it was Marguerite's. More, really, since Amelie was the elder and therefore had been working and earning longer.

So Amelie hated Marcel with a hate nourished by a thousand incidents of their daily life—the rabbit he had killed, the cheese he had brazenly cut into, thus spoiling its sale value. And his mother had not said a word in protest—she never did.

Yes, Amelie read the newspapers. She must have read about the scandals, the crimes, the murder trials that take up so much space in certain papers. If so, she would know the importance of fingerprints. Then, too, Amelie was afraid of her nephew. She must have been furious with her sister for showing him the hiding place of their treasure, for letting him touch the bonds he most certainly coveted.

"One of these days he'll come to murder us both."

Surely those words had been uttered in the house dozens of times, Maigret reflected as he sawed away at the wine barrel. He realized that he was perspiring and stopped sawing long enough to take off his hat and coat. He placed them on the next barrel.

The rabbit . . . the cheese . . . then suddenly the remembrance that Marcel had left his prints on the dresser drawer and the brief case. And if that was not enough, there was the readily identifiable button, which, his mother, having already gone to bed, had not yet sewed back on his jacket.

If Marcel had killed for gain, why had he emptied the brief case on the floor instead of taking it with him, bonds and all? As for Yarko the Yugoslav, Maigret had learned that he could not read.

Maigret's reasoning had begun with Amelie's wounds—eleven of them. There were too many by far and all of them were too superficial not to be extremely suspicious. Besides, they were all on the right side. She must have been clumsy, as well as afraid of pain. She wanted neither to die nor to suffer. She had expected help from the neighbors after she had opened the window to scream . . .

Would a murderer have given her time to run to the window?

And fate had laughed at her too. She had lost consciousness before her cries had awakened anyone, so she had spent the night on the floor, with nobody to stanch her bleeding.

Yes, that must have been the way it happened. It could not have been otherwise. She had killed her drowsing sister; then, her fingers wrapped in cloth of some kind to prevent leaving prints, she had opened the drawer and rifled the brief case. The bonds must disappear if Marcel were to be suspected!

Hence the candle . . .

Afterward she had sat on the edge of the bed, gashing herself timidly and awkwardly, then had gone to the fireplace (the bloodstains marked her course) to throw the knife into the embers. Finally she had walked to the window and . . .

Maigret stopped sawing. From the other room came the sound of voices raised in argument. He turned abruptly, watched the door opening slowly. The fantastic yet sinister figure of Amelie Potru stood on the threshold, swathed in bandages, wearing a curious petticoat and camisole. She stared hard at Maigret while behind her Marie Lacore protested shrilly that she had no business getting out of bed.

Maigret did not have the heart to speak to her. He finished sawing open the barrel in silence. He did not even sigh contentedly when he saw the government securities and railway bonds, still curling slightly from having been rolled up and pushed through the bung.

Had he followed his inclination, he would have beat a hasty retreat, first taking a long swig of rum straight from the bottle, the way Marcel would have done.

Amelie still spoke not a word. She stood silent, her mouth partly open. If she fainted, she would fall back into the arms of Marie Lacore, who, in her advanced state of pregnancy, might not be able to catch her.

Well, what of it? This was a scene from another world, another age. Maigret picked up the bonds and walked toward Amelie. She backed away from him.

He dropped the securities on the bedroom table and said to Marie Lacore, "Go get the mayor. I want him as a witness."

His voice rasped a little because his vocal cords were strangely tight. Then he nodded to Amelie: "You'd better get back to bed."

Despite his case-hardened professional curiosity he turned his back to her. He knew that she had obeyed him, for he heard the bedsprings creak. He stood looking out the window until the farmer who served as mayor of the hamlet made a timid, apologetic entrance.

There was no telephone in the village. A man on a bicycle carried the message to Vitry aux Loges. The gendarmes arrived at almost the same moment the butcher's delivery truck came rolling out of the woods.

The sky shone with the same pale, raw light. The trees stirred uneasily in the west wind.

"Find anything?" asked the brigadier from the gendarmerie.

Maigret's reply was evasive. He spoke haltingly, without elation, although he knew that the case of the Potru sisters would be the subject of long commentary and review by the criminologists not only of Paris but of London, Berlin, Vienna, even New York.

Listening to him now, the brigadier might well have suspected that Inspector Maigret was drunk—or, at least, a little tipsy.

COMMENT AND QUESTIONS

Often the criminal in mystery fiction is an impressive figure, one who gains the respect of his foe and of the reader by his resourcefulness and daring. He or she may be diabolical, clever, or even glamorous. Ordinarily a super-sleuth seems to require a super-villain, and the hero and the criminal in detective or spy fiction often tower over the subsidiary characters. Such larger-than-life figures lend an element of romance to certain types of mystery fiction. Simenon's Maigret stories, on the other hand, have little of this kind of appeal. They have been called naturalistic and depressing. As one reader has observed, it rains a lot, and Maigret does a lot of waiting. What is the relationship in this story between Maigret and Amelie Potru? Is it a duel of gigantic figures? How does Maigret feel about his success in solving this case?

The hatred and passion that lie behind this crime have been growing in the dark and confined rooms of the Potru sisters for years. What exactly are the causes of the crime? Could it have been prevented?

When the narrator says that this is one of those "rare cases that can be solved . . . by applying police methods," what is he implying about most crime solving?

Why will the case of the Potru sisters be the subject of commentary and review by criminologists in London, Berlin, Vienna, and even New York?

Does Maigret "solve" the case in the village or before he leaves Paris? Discuss the methods he uses that lead him to the solution of the crime.

Why does Amelie not speak?

Maigret tells us that he resisted an impulse to take a swig of rum; yet he evades the question of the brigadier whom he meets on his return journey, fearing that the man might think that he is drunk. Can you account for this?

When Maigret says that "this was a scene from another world, another age," is he referring to the backward living conditions and habits of the villagers? If not, what does he mean?

NOTES

1. *Epinal.* A French town famous for the *images d'Epinal* (popular, inexpensive colored illustrations printed there since the sixteenth century).

IAN FLEMING

Risico

James Bond may be the most famous fictional creation of the last twenty-five years. The novels about him have had vast sales, and movies made from the novels—lavish productions with a kind of self-parodying humor that the novels do not have—have played to large audiences. Even the theme music has been remarkably popular.

With James Bond, the detective hero has become a spy. The crime he fights involves the welfare of millions. Writers commenting on the thriller have observed that the spy, in his limitations and isolation, is more nearly representative of twentieth-century man than the detective. The typical spy is not a complete superman. Bond, for example, is sometimes captured and tortured, and the reader often fears that if Bond does not succeed in a mission he may forfeit his life. Like Bond in this story, the spy is frequently separated from his "team" and has to act on his own, whereas the detective nearly always has the support and help of the society in which he moves.

As you read, observe the methods of this famous spy and compare him with the detectives whose adventures you have previously followed.

"In this pizniss is much risico."

The words came softly through the thick brown mustache. The hard black eyes moved slowly over Bond's face and down to Bond's hands, which were carefully shredding a paper match on which was printed ALBERGO COLOMBA D'ORO.

James Bond felt the inspection. The same surreptitious examination had been going on since he had met the man two hours before at the rendezvous in the Excelsior bar. Bond had been told to look for a man with a heavy mustache who would be sitting by himself drinking an Alexander. Bond had been amused by this secret recognition signal. The creamy, feminine drink was so much cleverer than the folded newspaper, the flower in the buttonhole, the yellow gloves that were the hoary, slipshod call signs between agents. It had also the great merit of being able to operate alone, without its owner. And Kristatos had started off with a little test. When Bond had come into the bar and looked around there had been perhaps twenty people in the room. None of them had a mustache. But on a corner table at the far side of the tall, discreet room, flanked by a saucer of olives and another of cashew nuts, stood the tall-stemmed glass of cream and vodka. Bond went straight over to the table, pulled out a chair, and sat down.

The waiter came. "Good evening, sir. Signor Kristatos is at the telephone."

Bond nodded. "A Negroni. With Gordon's, please."

The waiter walked back to the bar. "Negroni. Uno. Gordon's."

"I am so sorry." The big hairy hand picked up the small chair as if it were as light as a matchbox and swept it under the heavy hips. "I had to have a word with Alfredo."

There had been no handshake. These were old acquaintances. In the same line of business, probably. Something like import and export. The younger one looked American. No. Not with those clothes. English.

Bond returned the fast serve. "How's his little boy?"

The black eyes of Signor Kristatos narrowed. Yes, they had said this man was a professional. He spread his hands. "Much the same. What can you expect?"

"Polio is a terrible thing."

The Negroni came. The two men sat back comfortably, each one satisfied that he had to do with a man in the same league. This was rare in "the Game." So many times, before one had even started on a tandem assignment like this, one had lost confidence in the outcome. There was so often, at least in Bond's imagination, a faint smell of burning in the air at such a rendezvous. He knew it for the sign that the fringe of his cover had already started to smolder. In due course the smoldering fabric would burst into flames and he would be *brûlé*.[1] Then the game would be up and he would have to decide whether to pull out or wait and get shot at by someone. But at this meeting there had been no fumbling.

Later that evening, at the little restaurant off the Piazza di Spagna called the Colomba d'Oro, Bond was amused to find that he was still on probation. Kristatos was still watching and weighing him, wondering if he could be trusted. This remark about the risky business was as near as Kristatos had so far got to admitting that there existed any business between the two of them. Bond was encouraged. He had not really believed Kristatos. But surely all these precautions could only mean that M's intuition had paid off—that Kristatos knew something big.

Bond dropped the last shred of match into the ashtray. He said mildly, "I was once taught that any business that pays more than ten per cent or is conducted after nine o'clock at night is a dangerous business. The business which brings us together pays up to one thousand per cent and is conducted almost exclusively at night. On both counts it is obviously a risky business." Bond lowered his voice. "Funds are available. Dollars, Swiss francs, Venezuelan bolivars—anything convenient."

"That makes me glad. I have already too much lire." Signor Kristatos picked up the folio menu. "But let us feed on something. One should not decide important pizniss on a hollow stomach."

A week earlier M had sent for Bond. M was in a bad temper. "Got anything on, 007?"

"Only paper work, sir."

"What do you mean, only paper work?" M jerked his pipe toward his loaded in-tray. "Who hasn't got paper work?"

"I meant nothing active, sir."

"Well, say so." M picked up a bundle of dark red files tied together with tape and slid them so sharply across the desk that Bond had to catch them. "And here's some more paper work. Scotland Yard stuff mostly—their narcotics people. Wads from the Home Office and the Ministry of Health, and some nice thick reports from the International Opium Control people in Geneva. Take it away and read it. You'll need today and most of tonight. Tomorrow you fly to Rome and get after the big men. Is that clear?"

Bond said that it was. The state of M's temper was also explained. There was nothing that made him more angry than having to divert his staff from their primary duty. This duty was espionage, and when necessary sabotage and subversion. Anything else was a misuse of the Service and of Secret Funds, which, God knows, were meager enough.

"Any questions?" M's jaw stuck out like the prow of a ship. The jaw seemed to tell Bond to pick up the files and get the hell out of the office and let M move on to something important.

Bond knew that a part of all this—if only a small part—was an act. M had certain bees in his bonnet. They were famous in the Service, and M knew they were. But that did not mean that he would allow them to stop buzzing. There were queen bees, like the misuse of the Service, and the search for true as distinct from wishful intelligence, and there were worker bees. These included such idiosyncrasies as not employing men with beards, or those who were completely bilingual, instantly dismissing men who tried to bring pressure to bear on him through family relationships with members of the Cabinet, mistrusting men or women who were too "dressy," and those who called him "sir" off-duty; and having an exaggerated faith in Scotsmen. But M was ironically conscious of his obsessions, as, thought Bond, a Churchill or a Montgomery[2] was about his. He never minded his bluff, as it partly was, being called on any of them. Moreover, he would never have dreamed of sending Bond out on an assignment without proper briefing.

Bond knew all this. He said mildly, "Two things, sir. Why are we taking this thing on, and what lead, if any, have Station I got towards the big people involved in it?"

M gave Bond a hard, sour look. He swiveled his chair sideways so that he could watch the high, scudding October clouds through the broad window. He reached out for his pipe, blew through it sharply, and then, as if this action had let off the small head of steam, replaced it gently on the desk. When he spoke, his voice was patient, reasonable. "As you can imagine, 007, I do not wish the Service to become involved in this drug business. Earlier this year I had to take you off other duties for a fortnight so that you could go to Mexico and chase off that Mexican grower. You nearly got yourself killed. I sent you as a favor to the Special Branch. When they asked for you again to tackle this Italian gang I refused. Ronnie Vallance went behind my back to the Home Office and Ministry of Health. The Ministers pressed me. I said that you were needed here and that I had no one else to spare. Then the two Ministers went to the PM." [3] M paused. "And that was that. I must say the PM was very persuasive. Took the line that heroin, in the quantities that have been coming in, is an instrument of psychological warfare—that it saps a country's strength. He said he wouldn't be surprised to find that this wasn't just a gang of Italians out to make big money—that subversion and not money was at the back of it." M smiled sourly. "I expect Ronnie Vallance thought up that line of argument. Apparently his narcotics people have been having the devil of a time with the traffic—trying to stop it getting a hold on the teenagers as it has in America. Seems the dance halls and the amusement arcades are full of peddlers. Vallance's Ghost Squad have managed to penetrate back up the line to one of the middlemen, and there's no doubt it's all coming from Italy, hidden in Italian tourists' cars. Vallance has done what he can through the Italian police and Interpol,[4] and got nowhere. They get so far back up the pipeline, arrest a few little people, and then, when they seem to be getting near the center, there's a blank wall. The inner ring of distributors are too frightened or too well paid."

Bond interrupted. "Perhaps there's protection somewhere, sir. That Montesi business didn't look so good."

M shrugged impatiently. "Maybe, maybe. And you'll have to

watch out for that too, but my impression is that the Montesi case resulted in a pretty extensive clean-up. Anyway, when the PM gave me the order to get on with it, it occurred to me to have a talk with Washington. CIA were very helpful. You know the Narcotics Bureau have a team in Italy. Have had ever since the war. They're nothing to do with CIA—run by the American Treasury Department, of all people. The American Treasury control a so-called Secret Service that looks after drug-smuggling and counterfeiting. Pretty crazy arrangement. Often wonder what the FBI must think of it. However." M slowly swiveled his chair away from the window. He linked his hands behind his head and leaned back, looking across the desk at Bond. "The point is that the CIA Rome Station works pretty closely with this little narcotics team. Has to, to prevent crossed lines and so on. And CIA—Allen Dulles himself, as a matter of fact—gave me the name of the top narcotics agent used by the bureau. Apparently he's a double. Does a little smuggling as cover. Chap called Kristatos. Dulles said that of course he couldn't involve his people in any way and he was pretty certain the Treasury Department wouldn't welcome their Rome Bureau playing too closely with us. But he said that, if I wished, he would get word to this Kristatos that one of our, er, best men would like to make contact with a view to doing business. I said I would much appreciate that, and yesterday I got word that the rendezvous is fixed for the day after tomorrow." M gestured toward the files in front of Bond. "You'll find all the details in there."

There was a brief silence in the room. Bond was thinking that the whole affair sounded unpleasant, probably dangerous, and certainly dirty. With the last quality in mind, Bond got to his feet and picked up the files. "All right, sir. It looks like money. How much will we pay for the traffic to stop?"

M let his chair tip forward. He put his hands flat down on the desk, side by side. He said roughly, "A hundred thousand pounds. In any currency. That's the PM's figure. But I don't want you to get hurt. Certainly not picking other people's coals out of the fire. So you can go up to another hundred thousand if there's bad trouble. Drugs are the biggest and tightest ring in crime." M reached for his in-basket and took out a file on signals. Without looking up he said, "Look after yourself."

Signor Kristatos picked up the menu. He said, "I do not beat about bushes, Mr. Bond. How much?"

"Fifty thousand pounds for one hundred per cent results."

Kristatos said indifferently, "Yes. Those are important funds. I shall have melon with prosciutto ham and a chocolate ice cream. I do not eat greatly at night. These people have their own Chianti. I commend it."

The waiter came and there was a brisk rattle of Italian. Bond ordered Tagliatelli Verdi with a Genoese sauce which Kristatos said was improbably concocted of basil, garlic, and fir cones.

When the waiter had gone, Kristatos sat and chewed silently on a wooden toothpick. His face gradually became dark and glum as if bad weather had come to his mind. The black, hard eyes, that glanced restlessly at everything in the restaurant except Bond, glittered. Bond guessed that Kristatos was wondering whether or not to betray somebody. Bond said encouragingly, "In certain circumstances, there might be more."

Kristatos seemed to make up his mind. He said, "So?" He pushed back his chair and got up. "Forgive me. I must visit the *toletta*." He turned and walked swiftly toward the back of the restaurant.

Bond was suddenly hungry and thirsty. He poured out a large glass of Chianti and swallowed half of it. He broke a roll and began eating, smothering each mouthful with deep yellow butter. He wondered why rolls and butter are delicious only in France and Italy. There was nothing else on his mind. It was just a question of waiting. He had confidence in Kristatos. He was a big, solid man who was trusted by the Americans. He was probably making some telephone call that would be decisive. Bond felt in good spirits. He watched the passers-by through the plate-glass window. A man selling one of the Party papers went by on a bicycle. Flying from the basket in front of the handlebars was a pennant. In red or white it said: PROGRESSO?—SI! AVVENTURI?—NO![5] Bond smiled. That was how it was. Let it so remain for the rest of the assignment.

On the far side of the square, rather plain room, at the corner table by the *caisse*,[6] the plump fair-haired girl with the dramatic mouth said to the jovial good-living man with the thick rope of spaghetti joining his face to his plate, "He has a rather cruel smile. But he is very handsome. Spies aren't usually so good-looking. Are you sure you are right, *mein Taubchen?*" [7]

The man's teeth cut through the rope. He wiped his mouth on a napkin already streaked with tomato sauce, belched sonorously, and said, "Santos is never wrong about these things. He has a nose for spies. That is why I chose him as the permanent tail for that bastard Kristatos. And who else but a spy would think of spending an evening with the pig? But we will make sure." The man took out of his pocket one of those cheap tin snappers that are sometimes given out, with paper hats and whistles, on carnival nights. It gave one sharp click. The maître d'hôtel, on the far side of the room, stopped whatever he was doing and hurried over.

"*Si, padrone.*" [8]

The man beckoned. The maître d'hôtel leaned over and received the whispered instructions. He nodded briefly, walked over to a door near the kitchens marked UFFICIO[9] and went in and closed the door behind him.

Phase by phase, in a series of minute moves, an exercise that had long been perfected was then smoothly put into effect. The man near the *caisse* munched his spaghetti and critically observed each step in the operation as if it were a fast game of chess.

The maître d'hôtel came out of the door marked UFFICIO, hurried across the restaurant, and said loudly to his Number 2, "An extra table for four. Immediately." The Number 2 gave him a direct look and nodded. He followed the maître d'hôtel over to a space adjoining Bond's table, clicked his fingers for help, borrowed a chair from one table, a chair from another table, and, with a bow and an apology, the spare chair from Bond's table. The fourth chair was being carried over from the direction of the door marked UFFICIO by the maître d'hôtel. He placed it square with the others, a table was lowered into the middle, and glass and cutlery were deftly laid. The maître d'hôtel frowned. "But you have laid a table for four. I said three—for three people." He casually took the chair he had himself brought to the table and switched it to Bond's table. He gave a wave of the hand to dismiss his helpers, and everyone dispersed about his business.

The innocent little flurry of restaurant movement had taken about a minute. An innocuous trio of Italians came into the restaurant. The maître d'hôtel greeted them personally and bowed them to the new table, and the gambit was completed.

Bond had hardly been conscious of it. Kristatos returned from whatever business he had been about, their food came, and they got on with the meal.

While they ate they talked about nothing—the election chances in Italy, the latest Alfa Romeo, Italian shoes compared with English. Kristatos talked well. He seemed to know the inside story of everything. He gave information so casually that it did not sound like bluff. He spoke his own kind of English with an occasional phrase borrowed from other languages. It made a lively mixture. Bond was interested and amused. Kristatos was a tough insider—a useful man. Bond was not surprised that the American Intelligence people found him good value.

Coffee came. Kristatos lit a thin black cigar and talked through it, the cigar jumping up and down between the thin, straight lips. He put both hands flat on the table in front of him. He looked at the tablecloth between them and said softly, "This pizniss. I will play with you. To now I have only played with the Americans. I have not told them what I am about to tell you. There was no requirement. This machina does not operate with America. These things are closely regulated. This machina operates only with England. Yes? *Capito?*" [10]

"I understand. Everyone has his own territory. It's the usual way in these things."

"Exact. Now, before I give you the informations, like good commercials we make the terms. Yes?"

"Of course."

Signor Kristatos examined the tablecloth more closely. "I wish for ten thousand dollars American, in paper of small sizes, by tomorrow lunchtime. When you have destroyed the machina I wish for a further twenty thousand." Signor Kristatos briefly raised his eyes and surveyed Bond's face. "I am not greedy. I do not take all your funds, isn't it?"

"The price is satisfactory."

"*Buono.* [11] Second term. There is no telling where you get these informations from. Even if you are beaten."

"Fair enough."

"Third term. The head of this machina is a bad man." Signor

Kristatos paused and looked up. The black eyes held a red glint. The clenched dry lips pulled away from the cigar to let the words out. "He is to be *destrutto*—killed."

Bond sat back. He gazed quizzically at the other man, who now leaned slightly forward over the table, waiting. So the wheels had now shown within the wheels! This was a private vendetta of some sort. Kristatos wanted to get himself a gunman. And he was not paying the gunman; the gunman was paying him for the privilege of disposing of an enemy. Not bad! The fixer was certainly working on a big fix this time—using the Secret Service to pay off his private scores. Bond said softly, "Why?"

Signor Kristatos said indifferently, "No questions catch no lies."

Bond drank down his coffee. It was the usual story of big syndicate crime. You never saw more than the tip of the iceberg. But what did that matter to him? He had been sent to do one specific job. If his success benefited others, nobody, least of all M, could care less. Bond had been told to destroy the machine. If this unnamed man was the machine, it would be merely carrying out orders to destroy the man. Bond said, "I cannot promise that. You must see that. All I can say is that if the man tries to destroy me, I will destroy him."

Signor Kristatos took a toothpick out of the holder, stripped off the paper, and set about cleaning his fingernails. When he had finished one hand he looked up. He said, "I do not often gamble on incertitudes. This time I will do so because it is you who are paying me, and not me you. Is all right? So now I will give you the informations. Then you are alone—solo. Tomorrow night I fly to Karachi. I have important pizniss there. I can only give you the informations. After that you run with the ball and"—he threw the dirty toothpick down on the table—"*che sera, sera.*"[12]

"All right."

Signor Kristatos edged his chair nearer to Bond. He spoke softly and quickly. He gave specimen dates and names to document his narrative. He never hesitated for a fact and he did not waste time on irrelevant detail. It was a short story and a pithy one. There were two thousand American gangsters in the country—Italian-Americans who had been convicted and expelled from the United States. These men were in a bad way. They were on the blackest of all police lists and, because of their records, their own people were wary of employing them. A hundred of the toughest among them had pooled their funds, and small groups from this elite had moved to Beirut, Istanbul, Tangier, and Macao, the great smuggling centers of the world. A further large section acted as couriers, and the bosses had acquired, through nominees, a small and respectable pharmaceutical business in Milan. To this center the outlying groups smuggled opium and its derivatives. They used small craft across the Mediterranean, a group of stewards in an Italian charter airline and, as a regular weekly source of supply, the through carriage of the Orient Express, in which whole sections of bogus upholstery were fitted by bribed members of the train-cleaners in Istanbul. The Milan firm—Pharmacia Colomba S.A.—acted as a clearing-house and as a convenient center for breaking down the raw opium into heroin. Thence the couriers, using innocent motorcars of various makes, ran a delivery service to the middlemen in England.

Bond interrupted. "Our Customs are pretty good at spotting that sort of traffic. There aren't many hiding places in a car they don't know about. Where do these men carry the stuff?"

"Always in the spare wheel. You can carry twenty thousand pounds' worth of heroin in one spare wheel."

"Don't they ever get caught—either bringing the stuff into Milan or taking it out?"

"Certainly. Many times. But these are well-trained men. And they are tough. They never talk. If they are convicted, they receive ten thousand dollars for each year spent in prison. If they have families, they are cared for. And when all goes well they make good money. It is a cooperative. Each man receives his *tranche*[13] of the *brutto*.[14] Only the chief gets a special *tranche*."

"All right. Well, who is this man?"

Signor Kristatos put his hand up to the cheroot in his mouth. He kept the hand there and spoke softly from behind it. "Is a man they call 'The Dove,' Enrico Colombo. Is the *padrone* of this restaurant. That is why I bring you here, so that you may see him. Is the fat man who sits with a blond woman. At the table by the *cassa*.[15] She is from Vienna. Her name is Lisl Baum. A *luxus*[16] whore."

Bond said reflectively, "She is, is she?" He did not need to look. He had noticed the girl as soon as he had sat down at the table.

Every man in the restaurant would have noticed her. She had the gay, bold, forthcoming looks the Viennese are supposed to have and seldom do. There was a vivacity and a charm about her that lit up her corner of the room. She had the wildest possible urchin cut in ash blond, a pert nose, a wide, laughing mouth, and a black ribbon around her throat. James Bond knew that her eyes had been on him at intervals throughout the evening. Her companion had seemed just the type of rich, cheerful, good-living man she would be glad to have as her lover for a while. He would give her a good time. He would be generous. There would be no regrets on either side. On the whole, Bond had vaguely approved of him. He liked cheerful, expansive people with a zest for life. Since he, Bond, could not have the girl, it was at least something that she was in good hands. But now? Bond glanced across the room. The couple were laughing about something. The man patted her cheek and got up and went to the door marked UFFICIO and went through and shut the door. So this was the man who ran the great pipeline into England. The man with M's price of a hundred thousand pounds on his head. The man Kristatos wanted Bond to kill. Well, he had better get on with the job. Bond stared rudely across the room at the girl. When she lifted her head and looked at him, he smiled at her. Her eyes swept past him, but there was a half-smile, as if for herself, on her lips, and when she took a cigarette out of her case and lit it and blew the smoke straight up toward the ceiling there was an offering of the throat and the profile that Bond knew were for him.

It was nearing the time for the after-cinema trade. The maître d'hôtel was supervising the clearing of the unoccupied tables and the setting up of new ones. There was the usual bustle and slapping of napkins across chair seats and tinkle of glass and cutlery being laid. Vaguely Bond noticed the spare chair at his table being whisked away to help build up a nearby table for six. He began asking Kristatos specific questions—the personal habits of Enrico Colombo, where he lived, the address of his firm in Milan, what other business interests he had. He did not notice the casual progress of the spare chair from its fresh table to another, and then to another, and finally through the door marked UFFICIO. There was no reason why he should.

When the chair was brought into his office, Enrico Colombo waved the maître d'hôtel away and locked the door behind him. Then he went to the chair and lifted off the squab cushion and put it on his desk. He unzipped one side of the cushion and withdrew a Grundig tape-recorder, stopped the machine, ran the tape back, took it off the recorder and put it on a playback and adjusted the speed and volume. Then he sat down at his desk and lit a cigarette and listened, occasionally making further adjustments and occasionally repeating passages. At the end, when Bond's tinny voice said, "She is, is she?" and there was a long silence interspersed with background noises from the restaurant, Enrico Colombo switched off the machine and sat looking at it. He looked at it for a full minute. His face showed nothing but acute concentration on his thoughts. Then he looked away from the machine and into nothing and said softly, out loud, "Son-a-beech." He got slowly to his feet and went to the door and unlocked it. He looked back once more at the Grundig, said, "Son-a-beech," again with more emphasis, and went out and back to his table.

Enrico Colombo spoke swiftly and urgently to the girl. She nodded and glanced across the room at Bond. He and Kristatos were getting up from the table. She said to Colombo in a low, angry voice, "You are a disgusting man. Everybody said so and warned me against you. They were right. Just because you give me dinner in your lousy restaurant you think you have the right to insult me with your filthy propositions." The girl's voice had got louder. Now she had snatched up her handbag and had got to her feet. She stood beside the table directly in the line of Bond's approach on his way to the exit.

Enrico Colombo's face was black with rage. Now he too was on his feet. "You goddam Austrian beech—"

"Don't dare insult my country, you Italian toad." She reached for a half-full glass of wine and hurled it accurately in the man's face. When he came at her it was easy for her to back the few steps into Bond, who was standing with Kristatos, politely waiting to get by.

Enrico Colombo stood panting, wiping the wine off his face with a napkin. He said furiously to the girl, "Don't ever show your face inside my restaurant again." He made the gesture of spitting

on the floor between them, turned, and strode off through the
door marked UFFICIO.

The maître d'hôtel had hurried up. Everyone in the restaurant
had stopped eating. Bond took the girl by the elbow. "May I help
you find a taxi?"

She jerked herself free. She said, still angry, "All men are pigs."
She remembered her manners. She said stiffly, "You are very
kind." She moved haughtily toward the door with the men in her
wake.

There was a buzz in the restaurant and a renewed clatter of
knives and forks. Everyone was delighted with the scene. The
maître d'hôtel, looking solemn, held open the door. He said to
Bond, "I apologize, monsieur. And you are very kind to be of
assistance." A cruising taxi slowed. He beckoned it to the
pavement and held open the door.

The girl got in. Bond firmly followed and closed the door. He
said to Kristatos through the window, "I'll telephone you in the
morning. All right?" Without waiting for the man's reply he sat
back in the seat. The girl had drawn herself away into the farthest
corner. Bond said, "Where shall I tell him?"

"Hotel Ambassadori."

They drove a short way in silence. Bond said, "Would you like
to go somewhere first for a drink?"

"No, thank you." She hesitated. "You are very kind, but tonight
I am tired."

"Perhaps another night."

"Perhaps, but I go to Venice tomorrow."

"I shall also be there. Will you have dinner with me tomorrow
night?"

The girl smiled. She said, "I thought Englishmen were supposed
to be shy. You are English, aren't you? What is your name? What
do you do?"

"Yes, I'm English. My name's Bond—James Bond. I write
books—adventure stories. I'm writing one now about drug-smuggling. It's set in Rome and Venice. The trouble is that I don't
know enough about the trade. I am going round picking up stories
about it. Do you know any?"

"So that is why you were having dinner with that Kristatos. I know of him. He has a bad reputation. No. I don't know any stories. I only know what everybody knows."

Bond said enthusiastically, "But that's exactly what I want. When I said 'stories' I didn't mean fiction. I meant the sort of high-level gossip that's probably pretty near the truth. That sort of thing's worth diamonds to a writer."

She laughed. "You mean that . . . diamonds?"

Bond said, "Well, I don't earn all that as a writer, but I've already sold an option on this story for a film, and if I can make it authentic enough I dare say they'll actually buy the film." He reached out and put his hand over hers in her lap. She did not take her hand away. "Yes, diamonds. A diamond clip from Van Cleef. Is it a deal?"

Now she took her hand away. They were arriving at the Ambassadori. She picked up her bag from the seat beside her. She turned on the seat so that she faced him. The commissionaire opened the door and the light from the street turned her eyes into stars. She examined his face with a certain seriousness. She said, "All men are pigs, but some are lesser pigs than others. All right. I will meet you. But not for dinner. What I may tell you is not for public places. I bathe every afternoon at the Lido. But not at the fashionable plage. I bathe at the Bagni Alberoni, where the English poet Byron used to ride his horse. It is at the tip of the peninsula. The *vaporetto*[17] will take you there. You will find me there the day after tomorrow—at three in the afternoon. I shall be getting my last sunburn before the winter. Among the sand dunes. You will see a pale yellow umbrella. Underneath it will be me." She smiled. "Knock on the umbrella and ask for Fraulein Lisl Baum."

She got out of the taxi. Bond followed. She held out her hand. "Thank you for coming to my rescue. Good night."

Bond said, "Three o'clock, then. I shall be there. Good night."

She turned and walked up the curved steps of the hotel. Bond looked after her thoughtfully, and then turned and got back into the taxi and told the man to take him to the Nazionale. He sat back and watched the neon signs ribbon past the window. Things, including the taxi, were going almost too fast for comfort. The only one over which he had any control was the taxi. He leaned forward and told the man to drive more slowly.

The best train from Rome to Venice is the Laguna Express that leaves every day at midday. Bond, after a morning that was chiefly occupied with difficult talks with his London Headquarters on Station I's scrambler, caught it by the skin of his teeth. The Laguna is a smart, streamlined affair that looks and sounds more luxurious than it is. The seats are made for small Italians and the restaurant-car staff suffers from the disease that afflicts its brethren in the great trains all over the world—a genuine loathing for the modern traveler and particularly for the foreigner. Bond had a gangway seat over the axle in the rear aluminum coach. If the seven heavens had been flowing by outside the window he would not have cared. He kept his eyes inside the train, read a jerking book, spilled Chianti over the tablecloth, and shifted his long, aching legs and cursed the Ferrovie Italiane dello Stato.

But at last there was Mestre and the dead straight finger of rail across the eighteenth-century aquatint into Venice. Then came the unfailing shock of the beauty that never betrays and the soft, swaying progress down the Grand Canal into a blood-red sunset, and the extreme pleasure—so it seemed—of the Gritti Palace that Bond should have ordered the best double room on the first floor.

That evening, scattering thousand-lire notes like leaves in Vallombrosa, James Bond sought, at Harry's Bar, at Florian's, and finally upstairs in the admirable Quadri, to establish to anyone who might be interested that he was what he had wished to appear to the girl—a prosperous writer who lived high and well. Then, in the temporary state of euphoria that a first night in Venice engenders, however high and serious the purpose of the visitor, James Bond walked back to the Gritti and had eight hours of dreamless sleep.

May and October are the best months in Venice. The sun is soft and the nights are cool. The glittering scene is kinder to the eyes and there is a freshness in the air that helps one to hammer out those long miles of stone and terrazza and marble that are intolerable to the feet in summer. And there are fewer people. Although Venice is the one town in the world that can swallow up a hundred thousand tourists as easily as it can a thousand—hiding them down its side streets, using them for crowd scenes on the piazzas, stuffing them into the *vaporetti*—it is still better to share

Venice with the minimum number of packaged tours and Lederhosen.

Bond spent the next morning strolling the back streets in the hope that he would be able to uncover a tail. He visited a couple of churches—not to admire their interiors but to discover if anyone came in after him through the main entrance before he left by the side door. No one was following him. Bond went to Florian's and had an Americano and listened to a couple of French culture-snobs discussing the imbalance of the containing façade of St. Mark's Square. On an impulse, he bought a postcard and sent it off to his secretary, who had once been with the Georgian Group to Italy and had never allowed Bond to forget it. He wrote, "Venice is wonderful. Have so far inspected the railway station and the Stock Exchange. Very aesthetically satisfying. To the Municipal Waterworks this afternoon and then an old Brigitte Bardot at the Scala Cinema. Do you know a wonderful tune called 'O Sole Mio'? It's v. romantic like everything here. JB."

Pleased with his inspiration, Bond had an early luncheon and went back to his hotel. He locked the door of his room and took off his coat and ran over the Walther PPK. He put up the safe and practiced one or two quick draws and put the gun back in the holster. It was time to go. He went along to the landing stage and boarded the twelve-forty *vaporetto* to Alberoni, out of sight across the mirrored lagoons. Then he settled down in a seat in the bows and wondered what was going to happen to him.

From the jetty at Alberoni, on the Venice side of the Lido peninsula, there is a half-mile dusty walk across the neck of land to the Bagni Alberoni, facing the Adriatic. It is a curiously deserted world, this tip of the famous peninsula. A mile down the thin neck of land the luxury real-estate development has petered out in a scattering of cracked stucco villas and bankrupt housing projects, and here there is nothing but the tiny fishing village of Alberoni, a sanatorium for students, a derelict experimental station belonging to the Italian Navy, and some massive weed-choked gun emplacements from the last war. In the no man's land in the center of this thin tongue of land is the Golf du Lido, whose brownish, undulating fairways meander around the ruins of ancient fortifications. Not many people come to Venice to play golf, and the project is kept alive for its snob appeal by the grand hotels of the Lido. The golf course is surrounded by a high wire fence hung at intervals, as if it protected something of great value or secrecy, with threatening "Vietatos" [18] and "Prohibitos." [19] Around this wired enclave, the scrub and sand hills have not even been cleared of mines, and amid the rusting barbed wire are signs saying MINAS, PERICOLO DI MORTE,[20] beneath a roughly stenciled skull and crossbones. The whole area is strange and melancholy and in extraordinary contrast to the gay carnival world of Venice less than an hour away across the lagoons.

Bond was sweating slightly by the time he had walked the half-mile across the peninsula to the plage, and he stood for a moment under the last of the acacia trees that had bordered the dusty road to cool off while he got his bearings. In front of him was a rickety wooden archway whose central span said BAGNI ALBERONI in faded blue paint. Beyond were the lines of equally dilapidated wooden cabins, and then a hundred yards of sand and then the quiet blue glass of the sea. There were no bathers and the place seemed to be closed, but when he walked through the archway he heard the tinny sound of a radio playing Neapolitan music. It came from a ramshackle hut that advertised Coca-Cola and various Italian soft drinks. Deck chairs were stacked against its walls and there were two pedalos and a child's half-inflated sea-horse. The whole establishment looked so derelict that Bond could not imagine it doing business even at the height of the summer season. He stepped off the narrow duckboards into the soft, burned sand and moved round behind the huts to the beach. He walked down to the edge of the sea. To the left, until it disappeared in the autumn heat haze, the wide, empty sand swept away in a slight curve toward the Lido proper. To the right was half a mile of beach, terminating in the sea wall at the tip of the peninsula. The sea wall stretched like a finger out into the silent mirrored sea, and at intervals along its top were the flimsy derricks of the octopus fishermen. Behind the beach were the sand hills and a section of the wire fence surrounding the golf course. On the edge of the sand hills, perhaps five hundred yards away, there was a speck of bright yellow.

Bond set off toward it along the tideline.

"Ahem."

The hands flew to the top scrap of bikini and pulled it up. Bond walked into her line of vision and stood looking down. The bright shadow of the umbrella covered only her face. The rest of her—a burned cream body in a black bikini on a black and white striped bathtowel—lay offered to the sun.

She looked up at him through half-closed eyelashes. "You are five minutes early and I told you to knock."

Bond sat down close to her in the shade of the big umbrella. He took out a handkerchief and wiped his face. "You happen to own the only palm tree in the whole of this desert. I had to get underneath it as soon as I could. This is a hell of a place for a rendezvous."

She laughed. "I am like Greta Garbo. I like to be alone."

"Are we alone?"

She opened her eyes wide. "Why not? You think I have brought a chaperon?"

"Since you think all men are pigs . . ."

"Ah, but you are a gentleman pig." She giggled. "A milord pig. And anyway, it is too hot for that kind of thing. And there is too much sand. And besides this is a business meeting, no? I tell you stories about drugs and you give me a diamond clip. From Van Cleef. Or have you changed your mind?"

"No. That's how it is. Where shall we begin?"

"You ask the questions. What is it you want to know?" She sat up and pulled her knees to her between her arms. Flirtation had gone out of her eyes, and they had become attentive, and perhaps a little careful.

Bond noticed the change. He said casually, watching her, "They say your friend Colombo is a big man in the game. Tell me about him. He would make a good character for my book—disguised, of course. But it's the detail I need. How does he operate, and so on? That's not the sort of thing a writer can invent."

She veiled her eyes. She said, "Enrico would be very angry if he knew that I have told any of his secrets. I don't know what he would do to me."

"He will never know."

She looked at him seriously. "*Lieber*[21] Mr. Bond, there is very little that he does not know. And he is also quite capable of acting on a guess. I would not be surprised"—Bond caught her quick glance at his watch—"if it had crossed his mind to have me followed here. He is a very suspicious man." She put her hand out and touched his sleeve. Now she looked nervous. She said urgently, "I think you had better go now. This has been a great mistake."

Bond openly looked at his watch. It was three-thirty. He moved his head so that he could look behind the umbrella and back down the beach. Far down by the bathing-huts, their outlines dancing slightly in the heat haze, were three men in dark clothes. They were walking purposefully up the beach, their feet keeping step as if they were a squad.

Bond got to his feet. He looked down at the bent head. He said dryly, "I see what you mean. Just tell Colombo that from now on I'm writing his life-story. And I'm a very persistent writer. So long." Bond started running up the sand toward the tip of the peninsula. From there he could double back down the other shore to the village and the safety of people.

Down the beach the three men broke into a fast jog-trot, elbows and legs pounding in time with one another as if they were long-distance runners out for a training spin. As they jogged past the girl, one of the men raised a hand. She raised hers in answer and then lay down on the sand and turned over—perhaps so that her back could now get its toasting, or perhaps because she did not want to watch the manhunt.

Bond took off his tie as he ran and put it in his pocket. It was very hot and he was already sweating profusely. But so would the three men be. It was a question who was in better training. At the tip of the peninsula, Bond clambered up onto the sea wall and looked back. The men had hardly gained, but now two of them were fanning out to cut round the edge of the golf-course boundary. They did not seem to mind the danger notices with the skulls and crossbones. Bond, running fast down the wide sea wall measured angles and distances. The two men were cutting across the base of the triangle. It was going to be a close call.

Bond's shirt was already soaked and his feet were beginning to hurt. He had run perhaps a mile. How much farther to safety? At intervals along the sea wall the breeches of antique cannon had been sunk in the concrete. They would be mooring posts for the fishing fleets sheltering in the protection of the lagoons before taking to the Adriatic. Bond counted his steps between two of them. Fifty yards. How many black knobs to the end of the wall—to the first houses of the village? Bond counted up to thirty before the line vanished into the heat haze. Probably another mile to go. Could he do it, and fast enough to beat the two flankers? Bond's breath was already rasping in his throat. Now even his suit was soaked with sweat, and the cloth of his trousers was chafing his legs. Behind him, three hundred yards back, was one pursuer. To his right, dodging among the sand dunes and converging fast, were the other two. To his left was a twenty-foot slope of masonry to the green tide ripping out into the Adriatic.

Bond was planning to slow down to a walk and keep enough breath to try and shoot it out with the three men, when two things happened in quick succession. First he saw through the haze ahead a group of spearfishermen. There were about half a dozen of them, some in the water and some sunning themselves on the sea wall. Then, from the sand dunes, came the deep roar of an explosion. Earth and scrub and what might have been bits of a man fountained briefly into the air, and a small shock-wave hit him. Bond slowed. The other man in the dunes had stopped. He was standing stock-still. His mouth was open and a frightened jabber came from it. Suddenly he collapsed on the ground with his arms wrapped round his head. Bond knew the signs. He would not move again until someone came and carried him away from there. Bond's heart lifted. Now he had only about two hundred yards to go to the fishermen. They were already gathering into a group, looking toward him. Bond summoned a few words of Italian and rehearsed them. *"Mi Inglese. Prego, dove il carabinieri?"* [22] Bond glanced over his shoulder. Odd, but despite the witnessing spearfishers, the man was still coming on. He had gained and was only about a hundred yards behind. There was a gun in his hand. Now, ahead, the fishermen had fanned out across Bond's path. They had harpoon guns held at the ready. In the center was a big man with a tiny red bathing-slip hanging beneath his stomach. A green mask was slipped back onto the crown of his head. He stood with his blue swim-fins pointing out and his arms akimbo. He looked like Mr. Toad of Toad Hall in Technicolor. Bond's amused thought died in him stillborn. Panting, he slowed to a walk. Automatically his sweaty hand felt under his coat for the gun and drew it out. The man in the center of the arc of pointing harpoons was Enrico Colombo.

Colombo watched him approach. When he was twenty yards away, Colombo said quietly, "Put away your toy, Mr. Bond of the Secret Service. These are CO_2 harpoon guns. And stay where you are. Unless you wish to make a copy of Mantegna's 'Saint Sebastian.'" He turned to the man on his right. He spoke in English. "At what range was that Albanian last week?"

"Twenty yards, *padrone*. And the harpoon went right through. But he was a fat man—perhaps twice as thick as this one."

Bond stopped. One of the iron bollards was beside him. He sat down and rested the gun on his knee. It pointed at the center of Colombo's big stomach. He said, "Five harpoons in me won't stop one bullet in you, Colombo."

Colombo smiled and nodded, and the man who had been coming softly up behind Bond hit him once, hard in the base of the skull, with the butt of his Luger.

When you come to from being hit on the head the first reaction is a fit of vomiting. Even in his wretchedness Bond was aware of two sensations: he was in a ship at sea, and someone, a man, was wiping his forehead with a cool wet towel and murmuring encouragement in bad English. "Is okay, amigo. Take him easy. Take him easy."

Bond fell back on his bunk, exhausted. It was a comfortable small cabin with a feminine smell and dainty curtains and colors. A sailor in a tattered undershirt and trousers—Bond thought he recognized him as one of the spearfishermen—was bending over him. He smiled when Bond opened his eyes. "Is better, yes? *Subito*[23] okay." He rubbed the back of his neck in sympathy. "It hurts for a little. Soon it will only be a black. Beneath the hair. The girls will see nothing."

Bond smiled feebly and nodded. The pain of the nod made him screw up his eyes. When he opened them the sailor shook his head in admonition. He brought his wrist watch close up to Bond's eyes. It said seven o'clock. He pointed with his little finger at the figure nine. *"Mangiare con padrone, si?"*[24]

Bond said, *"Si."*

The man put his hand to his cheek and laid his head on one side. *"Dormire."* [25]

Bond said, *"Si,"* again and the sailor went out of the cabin and closed the door without locking it.

Bond got gingerly off the bunk and went over to the washbasin and set about cleaning himself. On top of the chest of drawers was a neat pile of his personal belongings. Everything was there except his gun. Bond stowed the things away in his pockets and sat down again on the bunk and smoked and thought. His thoughts were totally inconclusive. He was being taken for a ride, or rather a sail, but from the behavior of the sailor it did not seem that he was regarded as an enemy. Yet a great deal of trouble had been taken to make him prisoner and one of Colombo's men had even, though inadvertently, died in the process. It did not seem to be just a question of killing him. Perhaps this soft treatment was the preliminary to trying to make a deal with him. What was the deal—and what was the alternative?

At nine o'clock the same sailor came for Bond and led him down a short passage to a small, blowsy saloon and left him. There were a table and two chairs in the middle of the room, and, beside the table a nickel-plated trolley laden with food and drinks. Bond tried the hatchway at the end of the saloon. It was bolted. He unlatched one of the portholes and looked out. There was just enough light to see that the ship was about two hundred tons and might once have been a large fishing vessel. The engine sounded like a single Diesel, and they were carrying sail. Bond estimated the ship's speed at six or seven knots. On the dark horizon there was a tiny cluster of yellow lights. It seemed probable that they were sailing down the Adriatic coast.

The hatchway bolt rattled back. Bond pulled in his head. Colombo came down the steps. He was dressed in a sweatshirt, dungarees, and scuffed sandals. There was a wicked, amused gleam in his eyes. He sat down in one chair and waved to the other. "Come, my friend. Food and drink and plenty of talk. We will now stop behaving like little boys and be grown up. Yes? What will you have—gin, whisky, champagne? And this is the finest sausage in the whole of Bologna. Olives from my own estate. Bread, butter, provolone—that is smoked cheese—and fresh figs.

Peasant food, but good. Come. All that running must have given you an appetite."

His laugh was infectious. Bond poured himself a stiff whisky and soda and sat down. He said, "Why did you have to go to so much trouble? We could have met without all these dramatics. As it is you have prepared a lot of grief for yourself. I warned my chief that something like this might happen—the way the girl picked me up in your restaurant was too childish for words. I said that I would walk into the trap to see what it was all about. If I am not out of it again by tomorrow midday, you'll have Interpol as well as Italian police on top of you like a load of bricks."

Colombo looked puzzled. He said, "If you were ready to walk into the trap, why did you try and escape from my men this afternoon? I had sent them to fetch you and bring you to my ship, and it would all have been much more friendly. Now I have lost a good man and you might easily have had your skull broken. I do not understand."

"I didn't like the looks of those three men. I know killers when I see them. I thought you might be thinking of doing something stupid. You should have used the girl. The men were unnecessary."

Colombo shook his head. "Lisl was willing to find out more about you, but nothing else. She will now be just as angry with me as you are. Life is very difficult. I like to be friends with everyone, and now I have made two enemies in one afternoon. It is too bad." Colombo looked genuinely sorry for himself. He cut a thick slice of sausage, impatiently tore the rind off it with his teeth, and began to eat. While his mouth was still full he took a glass of champagne and washed the sausage down with it. He said, shaking his head reproachfully at Bond, "It is always the same, when I am worried I have to eat. But the food that I eat when I am worried I cannot digest. And now you have worried me. You say that we could have met and talked things over—that I need not have taken all this trouble." He spread his hands helplessly. "How was I to know that? By saying that, you put the blood of Mario on my hands. I did not tell him to take a short cut through that place." Colombo pounded the table. Now he shouted angrily at Bond. "I do not agree that this was all my fault. It was your fault. Yours only. You had agreed to kill me. How does one arrange a friendly meeting with one's murderer? Eh? Just tell me that." Colombo snatched up a long roll of bread and stuffed it into his mouth, his eyes furious.

"What the hell are you talking about?"

Colombo threw the remains of the roll on the table and got to his feet, holding Bond's eyes locked with his. He walked sideways, still gazing fixedly at Bond, to a chest of drawers, felt for the knob of the top drawer, opened it, groped, and lifted out what Bond recognized as a tape-recorder playback machine. Still looking accusingly at Bond, he brought the machine over to the table. He sat down and pressed a switch.

When Bond heard the voice he picked up his glass of whisky and looked into it. The tinny voice said, "Exact. Now, before I give you the informations, like good commercials we make the terms. Yes?" The voice went on: "Ten thousand dollars American. . . . There is no telling where you get these informations from. Even if you are beaten. . . . The head of this machina is a bad man. He is to be *destrutto*—killed." Bond waited for his own voice to break through the restaurant noises. There had been a long pause while he thought about the last condition. What was it he had said? His voice came out of the machine, answering him. "I cannot promise that. You must see that. All I can say is that if the man tries to destroy me, I will destroy him."

Colombo switched off the machine. Bond swallowed down his whisky. Now he could look up at Colombo. He said defensively, "That doesn't make me a murderer."

Colombo looked at him sorrowfully. "To me it does. Coming from an Englishman. I worked for the English during the war. In the Resistance. I have the King's Medal." He put his hand in his pocket and threw the silver Freedom Medal with the red, white and blue striped ribbon onto the table. "You see?"

Bond obstinately held Colombo's eyes. He said, "And the rest of the stuff on that tape? You long ago stopped working for the English. Now you work against them, for money."

Colombo grunted. He tapped the machine with his forefinger. He said impassively, "I have heard it all. It is lies." He banged his fist on the table so that the glasses jumped. He bellowed furiously, "It is lies, lies. Every word of it." He jumped to his feet. His chair crashed down behind him. He slowly bent and picked it up. He reached for the whisky bottle and walked round and poured four fingers into Bond's glass. He went back to his chair and sat down and put the champagne bottle on the table in front of him. Now his face was composed, serious. He said quietly, "It is not all lies. There is a grain of truth in what that bastard told you. That is why I decided not to argue with you. You might not have believed me. You would have dragged in the police. There would have been much trouble for me and my comrades. Even if you or someone else had not found reason to kill me, there would have been scandal, ruin. Instead I decided to show you the truth—the truth you were sent to Italy to find out. Within a matter of hours, tomorrow at dawn, your mission will have been completed." Colombo clicked his fingers. "Presto—like that."

Bond said, "What part of Kristatos's story is not lies?"

Colombo's eyes looked into Bond's, calculating. Finally he said, "My friend, I am a smuggler. That part is true. I am probably the most successful smuggler in the Mediterranean. Half the American cigarettes in Italy are brought in by me from Tangier. Gold? I am the sole supplier of the black *valuta* market. Diamonds? I have my own purveyor in Beirut with direct lines to Sierra Leone and South Africa. In the old days, when these things were scarce, I also handled aureomycin and penicillin and such medicines. Bribery at the American base hospitals. And there have been many other things—even beautiful girls from Syria and Persia for the houses of Naples. I have also smuggled out escaped convicts. But"—Colombo's fist crashed on the table—"drugs—heroin, opium, hemp—no! Never! I will have nothing to do with these things. These things are evil. There is no sin in the others." Colombo held up his right hand. "My friend, this I swear to you on the head of my mother."

Bond was beginning to see daylight. He was prepared to believe Colombo. He even felt a curious liking for this greedy, boisterous pirate who had so nearly been put on the spot by Kristatos. Bond said, "But why did Kristatos put the finger on you? What's he got to gain?"

Colombo slowly shook a finger to and fro in front of his nose. He said, "My friend, Kristatos is Kristatos. He is playing the biggest double game it is possible to conceive. To keep it up—to keep the protection of American Intelligence and their Narcotics people—he must now and then throw them a victim, some small man on the fringe of the big game. But with this English problem it is different. That is a huge traffic. To protect it, a big victim was required. I was chosen—by Kristatos, or by his employers. And it is true that if you had been vigorous in your investigations and had spent enough hard currency on buying information, you might have discovered the story of my operations. But each trail towards *me* would have led you further away from the truth. In the end, for I do not underestimate your Service, I would have gone to prison. But the big fox you are after would only be laughing at the sound of the hunt dying away in the distance."

"Why did Kristatos want you killed?"

Colombo looked cunning. "My friend, I know too much. In the fraternity of smugglers, we occasionally stumble on a corner of the next man's business. Not long ago, in this ship, I had a running fight with a small gunboat from Albania. A lucky shot set fire to their fuel. There was only one survivor. He was persuaded to talk. I learned much, but like a fool I took a chance with the minefields and set him ashore on the coast north of Tirana. It was a mistake. Ever since then I have had this bastard Kristatos after me. Fortunately"—Colombo grinned wolfishly—"I have one piece of information he does not know of. And we have a rendezvous with this piece of information at first light tomorrow—at a small fishing port just north of Ancona, Santa Maria. And there"—Colombo gave a harsh, cruel laugh—"we shall see what we shall see."

Bond said mildly, "What's your price for all this? You say my mission will have been completed tomorrow morning. How much?"

Colombo shook his head. He said indifferently, "Nothing. It just happens that our interests coincide. But I shall need your promise that what I have told you this evening is between you and me and, if necessary, your chief in London. It must never come back to Italy. Is that agreed?"

"Yes. I agree to that."

Colombo got to his feet. He went to the chest of drawers and took out Bond's gun. He handed it to Bond. "In that case, my friend, you had better have this, because you are going to need it. And you had better get some sleep. There will be rum and coffee

for everyone at five in the morning." He held out his hand. Bond
took it. Suddenly the two men were friends. Bond felt the fact. He
said awkwardly, "All right, Colombo," and went out of the saloon
and along to his cabin.

The *Colombina* had a crew of twelve. They were youngish,
tough-looking men. They talked softly among themselves as the
mugs of hot coffee and rum were dished out by Colombo in the
saloon. A storm lantern was the only light—the ship had been
darkened—and Bond smiled to himself at the *Treasure Island*
atmosphere of excitement and conspiracy. Colombo went from
man to man on a weapon inspection. They all had Lugers, carried
under the jersey inside the trouser-band, and flick-knives in the
pocket. Colombo had a word of approval or criticism for each
weapon. It struck Bond that Colombo had made a good life for
himself—a life of adventure and thrill and risk. It was a criminal
life—a running fight with the currency laws, the state tobacco
monopoly, the Customs, the police—but there was a whiff of
adolescent rascality in the air which somehow changed the color
of the crime from black to white—or at least to gray.

Colombo looked at his watch. He dismissed the men to their
posts. He dowsed the lantern and, in the oyster light of dawn,
Bond followed him up to the bridge. He found the ship was close
to a black, rocky shore which they were following at reduced
speed. Colombo pointed ahead. "Around that headland is the
harbor. Our approach will not have been observed. In the harbor,
against the jetty, I expect to find a ship of about this size
unloading innocent rolls of newsprint down a ramp into a
warehouse. Around the headland, we will put on full speed and
come alongside this ship and board her. There will be resistance.
Heads will be broken. I hope it is not shooting. We shall not shoot
unless they do. But it will be an Albanian ship manned by a crew
of Albanian toughs. If there is shooting, you must shoot well with
the rest of us. These people are enemies of your country as well as
mine. If you get killed, you get killed. Okay?"

"That's all right."

As Bond said the words, there came a ting on the engine-room
telegraph and the deck began to tremble under his feet. Making
ten knots, the small ship rounded the headland into the harbor.

It was as Colombo had said. Alongside a stone jetty lay the ship, her sails flapping idly. From her stern a ramp of wooden planks sloped down toward the dark mouth of a ramshackle corrugated-iron warehouse, inside which burned feeble electric lights. The ship carried a deck cargo of what appeared to be rolls of newsprint, and these were being hoisted one by one onto the ramp, whence they rolled down under their own momentum through the mouth of the warehouse. There were about twenty men in sight. Only surprise would straighten out these odds. Now Colombo's craft was fifty yards away from the other ship, and one or two of the men had stopped working and were looking in their direction. One man ran off into the warehouse. Simultaneously Colombo issued a sharp order. The engines stopped and went into reverse. A big searchlight on the bridge came on and lit the whole scene brightly as the ship drifted up alongside the Albanian trawler. At the first hard contact, grappling irons were tossed over the Albanian's rail fore and aft, and Colombo's men swarmed over the side with Colombo in the lead.

Bond had made his own plans. As soon as his feet landed on the enemy deck, he ran straight across the ship, climbed the far rail, and jumped. It was about twelve feet to the jetty and he landed like a cat, on his hands and toes, and stayed for a moment, crouching, planning his next move. Shooting had already started on deck. An early shot killed the searchlight and now there was only the gray, luminous light of dawn. A body, one of the enemy, crunched to the stone in front of him and lay spread-eagled, motionless. At the same time, from the mouth of the warehouse, a light machine-gun started up, firing short bursts with a highly professional touch. Bond ran toward it in the dark shadow of the ship. The machine-gunner saw him and gave him a burst. The bullets zipped round Bond, clanged against the iron hull of the ship, and whined off into the night. Bond got to the cover of the sloping ramp of boards and dived forward on his stomach. The bullets crashed into the wood above his head. Bond crept forward into the narrowing space. When he had got as close as he could, he would have a choice of breaking cover to either right or left of the boards. There came a series of heavy thuds and a swift rumble above his head. One of Colombo's men must have cut the ropes and sent the whole pile of newsprint rolls down the ramp. Now was Bond's chance. He leaped out from under cover—to the left. If the machine-gunner was waiting for him, he would expect Bond to come out firing on the right. The machine-gunner was there, crouching up against the wall of the warehouse. Bond fired twice in the split second before the bright muzzle of the enemy weapon had swung through its small arc. The dead man's finger clenched on the trigger and, as he slumped, his gun made a brief Catherine wheel of flashes before it shook itself free from his hand and clattered to the ground.

Bond was running forward toward the warehouse door when he slipped and fell headlong. He lay for a moment, stunned, his face in a pool of black treacle. He cursed and got to his hands and knees and made a dash for cover behind a jumble of the big newsprint rolls that had crashed into the wall of the warehouse. One of them, sliced by a burst from the machine-gun, was leaking black treacle. Bond wiped as much of the stuff off his hands and face as he could. It had the musty sweet smell that Bond had once smelled in Mexico. It was raw opium.

A bullet whanged into the wall of the warehouse not far from his head. Bond gave his gun-hand a last wipe on the seat of his trousers and leaped for the warehouse door. He was surprised not to be shot at from the interior as soon as he was silhouetted against the entrance. It was quiet and cool inside the place. The lights had been turned out, but it was now getting brighter outside. The pale newsprint rolls were stacked in orderly ranks with a space to make a passageway down the center. At the far end of the passageway was a door. The whole arrangement leered at him, daring him. Bond smelled death. He edged back to the entrance and out into the open. The shooting had become spasmodic. Colombo came running swiftly toward him, his feet close to the ground, as fat men run. Bond said peremptorily, "Stay at this door. Don't go in or let any of your men in. I'm going round to the back." Without waiting for an answer, he sprinted around the corner of the building and down along its side.

The warehouse was about fifty feet long. Bond slowed and walked softly to the far corner. He flattened himself against the corrugated-iron wall and took a swift look around. He immediately drew back. A man was standing up against the back entrance. His eyes were at some kind of spyhole. In his hand was a plunger from which wires ran under the bottom of the door. A car, a black Lancia Granturismo convertible with the hood down, stood beside him, its engine ticking over softly. It pointed inland along a deeply tracked dust road.

The man was Kristatos.

Bond knelt. He held his gun in both hands for steadiness, inched swiftly around the corner of the building and fired one shot at the man's feet. He missed. Almost as he saw the dust kick up inches off the target, there was the rumbling crack of an explosion and the tin wall hit him and sent him flying.

Bond scrambled to his feet. The warehouse had buckled crazily out of shape. Now it started to collapse noisily like a pack of tin cards. Kristatos was in the car. It was already twenty yards away, dust fountaining up from the traction on the rear wheels. Bond stood in the classic pistol-shooting pose and took careful aim. The Walther roared and kicked three times. At the last shot, at fifty yards, the figure crouched over the wheel jerked backward. The hands flew sideways off the wheel. The head craned briefly into the air and slumped forward. The right hand remained sticking out, as if the dead man were signaling a right-hand turn. Bond started to run up the road, expecting the car to stop, but the wheels were held in the ruts and, with the weight of the dead right foot still on the accelerator, the Lancia tore onward in its screaming third gear. Bond stopped and watched it. It hurried on along the flat road across the burned-up plain, and the cloud of white dust blew gaily up behind. At any moment Bond expected it to veer off the road, but it did not, and Bond stood and saw it out of sight into the early-morning mist that promised a beautiful day.

Bond put his gun on safe and tucked it away in the belt of his trousers. He turned to find Colombo approaching him. The fat man was grinning delightedly. He came up with Bond and, to Bond's horror, threw open his arms, clutched Bond to him, and kissed him on both cheeks.

Bond said, "For God's sake, Colombo."

Colombo roared with laughter. "Ah, the quiet Englishman! He fears nothing save the emotions. But me"—he hit himself in the chest—"me, Enrico Colombo, loves this man and he is not ashamed to say so. If you had not got the machine-gunner, not one of us would have survived. As it is, I lost two of my men and others have wounds. But only half a dozen Albanians remain on their feet and they have escaped into the village. No doubt the police will round them up. And now you have sent that bastard Kristatos motoring down to hell. What a splendid finish to him! What will happen when the little racing hearse meets the main road? He is already signaling for the right-hand turn onto the Autostrada. I hope he will remember to drive on the right." Colombo clapped Bond boisterously on the shoulder. "But come, my friend. It is time we got out of here. The cocks are open in the Albanian ship and she will soon be on the bottom. There are no telephones in this little place. We will have a good start on the police. It will take them some time to get sense out of the fishermen. I have spoken to the head man. No one here has any love for Albanians. But we must be on our way. We have a stiff sail into the wind, and there is no doctor I can trust this side of Venice."

Flames were beginning to lick out of the shattered warehouse, and there was billowing smoke that smelled of sweet vegetables. Bond and Colombo walked around to windward. The Albanian ship had settled on the bottom and her decks were awash. They waded across her and climbed on board the *Colombina*, where Bond had to go through some more handshaking and backslapping. They cast off at once and made for the headland guarding the harbor. There was a small group of fishermen standing by their boats that lay drawn up on the beach below a huddle of stone cottages. They made a surly impression, but when Colombo waved and shouted something in Italian most of them raised hands in farewell, and one of them called back something that made the crew laugh. Colombo explained, "They say we were better than the cinema at Ancona and we must come again soon."

Bond suddenly felt the excitement drain out of him. He felt dirty and unshaven, and he could smell his own sweat. He went below and borrowed a razor and a clean shirt from one of the crew, and stripped in his cabin and cleaned himself. When he took out his gun and threw it on the bunk he caught a whiff of cordite from the barrel. It brought back the fear and violence and death of the gray dawn. He opened the porthole. Outside, the sea was dancing and gay, and the receding coastline, which had been black and mysterious, was now green and beautiful. A sudden delicious scent of frying bacon came downwind from the galley. Abruptly Bond pulled the porthole to and dressed and went along to the saloon.

Over a mound of fried eggs and bacon, washed down with hot sweet coffee laced with rum, Colombo dotted the i's and crossed the t's.

"This we have done, my friend," he said through crunching toast. "That was a year's supply of raw opium on its way to Kristatos's chemical works in Naples. It is true that I have such a business in Milan and that it is a convenient depot for some of my wares. But it fabricates nothing more deadly than cascara and aspirin. For all that part of Kristatos's story, read Kristatos instead of Colombo. It is he who breaks the stuff down into heroin and it is he who employs the couriers to take it to London. That huge shipment was worth perhaps a million pounds to Kristatos and his men. But do you know something, my dear James? It cost him not one solitary cent. Why? Because it is a gift from Russia. The gift of a massive and deadly projectile to be fired into the bowels of England. The Russians can supply unlimited quantities of the charge for the projectile. It comes from their poppy fields in the Caucasus, and Albania is a convenient entrepôt. But they have not the apparatus to fire this projectile. The man Kristatos created the necessary apparatus, and it is he, on behalf of his masters in Russia, who pulls the trigger. Today, between us, we have destroyed, in half an hour, the entire conspiracy. You can now go back and tell your people in England that the traffic will cease. You can also tell them the truth—that Italy was not the origin of this terrible underground weapon of war. That it is our old friends the Russians. No doubt it is some psychological-warfare section of their Intelligence apparatus. That I cannot tell you. Perhaps, my dear James"—Colombo smiled encouragingly—"they will send you to Moscow to find out. If that should happen, let us hope you will find some girl as charming as your friend Fraulein Lisl Baum to put you on the right road to the truth."

"What do you mean, my friend? She's yours."

Colombo shook his head. "My dear James, I have many friends. You will be spending a few more days in Italy writing your report, and no doubt"—he chuckled—"checking on some of the things I have told you. Perhaps you will also have an enjoyable half an hour explaining the facts of life to your colleagues in American Intelligence. In between these duties you will need companionship—someone to show you the beauties of my beloved homeland. In uncivilized countries, it is the polite custom to offer one of your wives to a man whom you love and wish to honor. I also am uncivilized. I have no wives, but I have many such friends as Lisl Baum. She will not need to receive any instructions in this matter. I have good reason to believe that she is awaiting your return this evening." Colombo fished in his trousers pocket and tossed something down with a clang on the table in front of Bond. "Here is the good reason." Colombo put his hand to his heart and looked seriously into Bond's eyes. "I give it to you from my heart. Perhaps also from hers."

Bond picked the thing up. It was a key with a heavy metal tag attached. The metal tag was inscribed: ALBERGO DANIELI. ROOM 68.

COMMENT AND QUESTIONS

Fleming describes the exchange between the professional spies in terms of a tennis match ("Bond returned the fast serve"), equating espionage with a game. Colombo says to Bond, ". . . but the big fox you are after would only be laughing at the sound of the hunt dying away in the distance." Recall that this association of spying with games is used by many writers of mystery fiction. Also, Colombo later says to Bond, "We will now stop behaving like little boys and be grown up," and his remark has the effect of putting events of the story into a half-humorous perspective for the reader.

Colombo has a man of whom he says, "Santo is never wrong about these things. He has a nose for spies." Later we are told, "Bond smelled death." Similarly, many detectives have a nose, an eye, or an instinct for clues or guilt.

As in the detective story, there is a concluding explanation. "Colombo dotted the i's and crossed the t's." In "Risico" Bond takes part in the action but doesn't fully realize what has been accomplished (he is like Watson in this ignorance), though he was responsible for the success of the raid by knocking out the machine-gun.

James Bond is like Sherlock Holmes in some of his accomplishments. He always succeeds in his mission; he thwarts international conspiracies; and he destroys personal opponents. He is more like the Continental Op in others. Like "The Gutting of Couffignal," this story seems to have more war than detection; the spy makes mistakes; and there is a spirit of adventure throughout as well as a tempting woman to distract—or try to distract—the hero.

The skillful use of recognition signals and the improvised acting that occur when Bond and Kristatos meet give the reader a sense of pleasure in watching real professionals at work. They also set up a real bond of respect between the two men. What point is Ian Fleming trying to make, within the context of the total story, about James Bond's character? About the nature of espionage work?

Is Bond at fault for letting himself be trapped and then captured? Why or why not? Suppose these men had been what they seemed at first. Could Bond have escaped? Is he saved by chance or by skill?

Is it instinct or something else that warns Bond of the warehouse booby trap? Explain.

What is Bond's first impression of Colombo (in the cafe)? Why do you suppose this is put into the story?

In what ways is Bond more vulnerable than a detective like Sherlock Holmes?

Notice the plot structure. Is the movement back and forth in space and time more effective than a straight chronological account of the events? Why or why not?

Bond's boss, M, appears only once in a brief scene with Bond. What do we know about him from this scene? Is he bad-tempered, "hard," or "sour"? How would you describe his attitude toward Bond? How does this attitude help to characterize Bond himself?

NOTES

1. *brûlé*. Flaming, as in a food served in flames.
2. *Montgomery*. Sir Bernard Law, First Viscount Montgomery of Alamein, British army officer, World War II commander in North Africa.
3. *PM*. The Prime Minister of Great Britain.
4. *Interpol*. International Police Organization.
5. *Progresso?—Si! Avventuri?—No!* Progress, yes; (taking a) risk, no.
6. *caisse*. Cashier's box or stand.
7. *mein Taubchen*. My little dove.
8. *Si, padrone*. Yes, sir (boss).
9. *Ufficio*. Office.
10. *Capito?* Do you understand?
11. *Buono*. Good.
12. *che sera, sera*. What will be, will be.
13. *tranche*. Share or "cut."
14. *brutto*. Pile, booty.
15. *cassa*. Cashier's box.
16. *luxus*. High class.
17. *vaporetto*. Motorized ferry.
18. *Vietato*. Prohibited.
19. *Prohibitio*. Prohibited.
20. *Minas, pericolo di morte*. Mines, danger of death.
21. *Lieber*. Dear.
22. *Mi Inglese. Prego, dove il carabinieri?* Me English. Please, where the police?
23. *Subito*. Soon.
24. *Mangiare con padrone, si?* Will you eat with the boss?
25. *Dormire*. Sleep.

ELLERY QUEEN

A Lump of Sugar

In this story you will match wits with an American sleuth, Ellery Queen, and have an opportunity to solve the crime by analyzing the same clues that led Ellery to identify the murderer. Ellery Queen generally plays fair with the reader, and you may enjoy trying to find solutions to the other bizarre puzzles that he unfolds in his many novels and short stories. No esoteric or highly specialized knowledge is required to figure out this one. The final part of the story appears on page 448.

I f not for the fact that Mounted Patrolman Wilkins was doing the dawn trick on the bridle path, where it goes by the Park Tavern, the Shakes Cooney murder would never have been solved. Ellery admits this cheerfully. He can afford to, since it was he who brought to that merry-go-round some much-needed horse sense.

A waiter with a hot date had neglected to strip one of his tables on the Tavern's open terrace at closing time the night before, whereupon the question was: Who had done a carving job on Cooney's so-called heart about 6 A.M. the next morning? Logic said nearly eight million people, or roughly the population of New York City, the law-abiding majority of whom might well have found Shakes Cooney's continued existence a bore. But Mounted Patrolman Wilkins was there when it counted, and it was he who collared the three gentlemen who, curiously, were in the neighborhood of the deserted Tavern and Cooney's corpse at that ungentlemanly hour.

Their collars were attached to very important necks, and when Inspector Richard Queen of police headquarters took over he handled them, as it were, with lamb's-wool knuckles. It was not every morning that Inspector Queen was called upon in a homicide to quiz a statesman, a financial titan, and an organization politician; and the little Inspector rose to the occasion.

Senator Kregg responded loftily, as to a reporter from an opposition newspaper.

Piers d'I. Millard responded remotely, as to a minority stockholder.

The Hon. Stevens responded affably, as to a precinct worker.

Lofty, remote, or affable, the three distinguished suspects in riding clothes agreed in their stories to the tittle of an iota. They had been out for an early canter on the bridle path. They had not addressed or seen any fourth person until the mounted policeman gathered them in. The life and death of Shakes Cooney were as nothing to them. Patrolman Wilkins's act in detaining them had been "totalitarian"—Senator Kregg; "ill-advised"—Financier Millard; "a sucker play"—Politician Stevens.

Delicately, Inspector Queen broached certain possibly relevant matters, viz.: In the national forest of politics, it was rumored, Senator Kregg (ex-Senator Kregg) was being measured as a great and spreading oak, of such timber as presidents are made. Financier Piers d'I. Millard was said to be the Senator's architect, already working on the blueprints with his golden stylus. And small-souled political keyholers would have it that the Hon. Stevens was down on the plans as sales manager of the development. Under the circumstances, said the Inspector with a cough, some irreverent persons might opine that Shakes Cooney—bookie, tout, gambler, underworld slug and clubhouse creep, with the instincts of a jay and the ethics of a grave robber—had learned of the burial place of some body or other, the exhumation of which would so befoul the Senator's vicinity as to wither his noble aspirations on the branch. It might even be surmised, suggested Inspector Queen apologetically, that Cooney's price for letting the body stay buried was so outrageous as to cause Someone to lose his head. Would the gentlemen care to comment?

The Senator obliged in extended remarks, fortunately off the record, then he surged away. Prepared to totter after, Financier Millard paused long enough to ask reflectively, "And how long, did you say, Inspector Queen, you have been with the New York police department?"—and it sounded like the *coup de grâce* to an empire. The Hon. Stevens lingered to ooze a few lubricating drops and then he, too, was gone.

When Ellery arrived on the scene he found his father in a good, if thoughtful, temper. The hide, remarked Inspector Queen, was pretty much cut-and-dried; the question was, To whose door had Shakes been trying to nail it? Because Shakes Cooney hadn't been a man to take murder lying down. The evidence on the Tavern terrace showed that after his assailant fled Cooney had struggled to his hands and knees, the Tavern steak knife stuck in his butchered chest, and that he had gorily crawled—kept alive by sheer meanness, protested the Inspector—to the table which the preoccupied waiter had forgotten to clear off the night before; that the dying man had then reached to the table top and groped for a certain bowl; and that from this bowl he had plucked the object which they had found in his fist, a single lump of sugar. Then, presumably with satisfaction, Shakes had expired.

"He must have been one of your readers," complained the Inspector. "Because, Ellery, that's a dying message or I'm the Senator's uncle. But which one was Shakes fingering?"

"Sugar," said Ellery absently. "In Cooney's dictionary sugar means—"

"Sure. But Millard isn't the only one of the three who's loaded with heavy sugar. The ex-Senator's well stocked, and he recently doubled his inventory by marrying that fertilizer millionaire's daughter. And Stevens has the first grand he ever grafted. So Shakes didn't mean that kind of sugar. What's sugar mean in *your* dictionary, son?"

Ellery, who had left page 87 of his latest novel in his typewriter, picked the lint off his thoughts. Finally he said, "Get me the equestrian history of Kregg, Millard, and Stevens," and he went back home to literature.

That afternoon his father phoned from Centre Street.

"What?" said Ellery, frowning over at his typewriter.

"About their horseback riding," snapped the Inspector. "The

Senator used to ride, but he had a bad fall ten years ago and now he only punishes a saddle in the gym—the electrical kind. Moneybags hasn't been on the back of a plug since he walked out on Grandpa Millard's plowhorse in '88, in Indiana. Only reason Piers d'I. allowed himself to be jockeyed into those plush-lined jodhpurs this morning, I'm pretty sure, is so he, Kregg, and Stevens could have a nice dirty skull session in the Park out of range of the newsreel cameras."

"And Stevens?"

"That bar insect?" snorted the old gentleman. "Only horse *he* knows how to ride is a dark one, with galluses. This morning's the first time Stevens ever set his suède-topped brogans into a stirrup."

"Well, well," said Ellery, sounding surprised. "Then what did Shakes mean? Sugar . . . Is one of them tied up with the sugar industry in some way? Has Kregg ever been conspicuous in sugar legislation? Is Millard a director of some sugar combine? Or maybe Stevens owns some sugar stock. Try that line, Dad."

His father said wearily, "I don't need you for that kind of fishing, my son. That's in the works."

"Then you're in," said Ellery; and without enjoyment he went back to his novel which, like Shakes Cooney, was advancing on its hands and knees.

Two days later Inspector Queen telephoned his report. "Not one of them is tied up with sugar in any way whatsoever. Only connection Kregg, Millard, and Stevens have with the stuff is what I take it they drop into their coffee." After a moment the Inspector said, "Are you there?"

"Lump of sugar," Ellery mumbled. "And Shakes evidently thought it would be clear . . ." The mumble ended in a glug.

"Yes?" said his father, brightening.

"Of course," chuckled Ellery. "Dad, get a medical report on those three. Then let me know which one of 'em had diabetes."

The Inspector's uppers clacked against his lowers. "That's my baby! That's it, son! It's as good as wrapped up!"

The following day Inspector Queen phoned again.

"Whose father?" asked Ellery, running his fingers through his hair. "Oh! Yes, Dad? What is it?"

"About the case, Ellery—"

"Case? Oh, the case. Yes? Well? Which one's diabetic?"

The Inspector said thoughtfully, "None."

"None! You mean—?"

"I mean."

"Hmm," said Ellery. "Hnh!"

For some time Inspector Queen heard nothing but little rumbles, pops, flutters, and other ruminative noises, until suddenly the line was cleared by a sound as definite as the electrocutioner's switch.

"You've got something?" said the Inspector doubtfully.

"Yes. Yes," said Ellery, with no doubt whatever, but considerable relief. "Yes, Dad, now I know whom Shakes Cooney meant!"

"Who?" demanded the Inspector.

FRANK D. McSHERRY

The Shape of Crimes to Come

Detective fiction usually deals with the violation of the legal code of a society. Obviously, the laws change as society changes: acts that were illegal during the Prohibition Era are perfectly legal today.

In this essay Frank D. McSherry surveys fiction about the future, a future in which such acts as building a wheel, marrying for love, or failing to commit suicide may be illegal. He points out that such detective science-fiction not only gives us good, fast-moving stories but makes us consider now some of the problems we may be forced to face in the near future.

A re you doing anything today that may be declared a crime tomorrow?

The detective-crime story deals with the commission and detection of criminal acts and with the circumstances surrounding such acts. A criminal act is any act that any society decides to call criminal. Under this empirical and pragmatic definition, we need not bother our heads about the fact that what may be branded a crime at one time and place may not be so labelled at another. Detective-crime stories set in the Roaring Twenties and dealing with the crime of bootlegging are still detective-crime stories despite the fact that the open sale and use of intoxicants is not now a crime and was not before Prohibition.

The category of detective-crime story therefore includes stories in which the crime involved is not a crime now, and may even be an admirable moral act now, but is a crime in the imagined future in which a given story is set. The stories which fall within this description are completely new to most mystery readers, who have tended to classify such tales (correctly) as science fiction and (incorrectly) as science fiction only. But it would be unfortunate if lovers of mystery fiction continued to overlook these works; for, quite apart from their often high qualities as fiction, they offer more food for thought than do most detective-crime stories, especially about the legal, social and philosophical problems that are marching toward us from the future with a grim inevitability. The sooner we begin thinking about some of these problems the better; and if we get a first-rate story thrown into the bargain as well, we are that much better off.

Of all the situations approaching us in the future which society may attempt to deal with by imposing criminal sanctions, first and foremost is the population explosion.

Daniel Boone left his Kentucky valley home in disgust because another family moved into the other end of the valley twenty miles away: by God, it's gitting so a feller can't sit on his own front porch no more without a whole passel of people breathing down the back of his neck! That wasn't so long ago, either, as time goes in the life of nations; but things have changed immensely in the short time since then.

Tried to cross the street—or highway—lately? It takes longer with every year that goes by. Every year there are more cars, because every year there are more people to be transported and supplied.

Have your taxes gone up lately? There are many reasons why, but one of them is the rising number of people. Twice as many people in a given area need twice as many schools, hospitals, policemen, etc.

Have prices gone up at the supermarket lately? If you have twice as many people, you need twice as many trucks to supply them with food. Twice as many trucks means so much more traffic (and traffic jams), and so many more man-hours required to deliver the food, which means that the distributor must increase his prices proportionally or go out of business.

The problems created by the population explosion seem to be

increasing all over the world. If the trend continues society may decide to deal with it by passing new criminal laws. The imposition of birth controls by law is a controversial subject as every newspaper reader knows. Does any government have the right to tell you how many children you can have? Should it be given that right? Several authors have written stories postulating that government will be given or take upon itself such a power.

In Harry Harrison's "A Criminal Act" (*Analog*, January 1967), our society takes a fairly simple and obvious course. The Criminal Birth Act of 1993 forbids married couples to have more than the legal limit of two children per couple. Though the law and the crime are new, the punishment is a secular version of an old one: excommunication. The police power of the state will no longer protect Benedict Vernall, criminal, whose wife is going to have a third child. Any public-spirited citizen who volunteers to kill Vernall will be given a license and twenty-four hours in which to do so without fear of punishment. However, since the purpose of the law is to limit the population, the charge against Vernall will be dropped if he can kill his assassin. Harrison's story tells excitingly of the twenty-four hours during which Vernall is hunted down in his own apartment by an experienced professional killer-for-thrills.

Editor John W. Campbell's introduction to the story is sharply pointed and thought-provoking, especially for those who take a blindly literal view of law-and-order. "A criminal act is, by definition, something that's against the law. George Washington was a criminal, Hitler was not . . . because he passed laws before he acted. That a thing is legal doesn't guarantee that it's good or evil." It is true that Vernall is fighting for his new baby's right to survive, but what about the right of us others to survive? There's only so much food, water and land available. Which side are you on?

Harrison's method may be accused of giving an unfair edge to any criminal who is fast with a gun. A more democratic method of solving the population problem is presented in Frederik Pohl's "The Census Takers" (*The Magazine of Fantasy and Science Fiction*, February 1956). The titular officials count the population once a year; all people over the count of 300 found in any census team's area are executed by the team on the spot. "Jumping"—

that is, packing with intent to move when a census team is in the area—is a capital crime in this society. Encountering a family of five that is guilty of this offense, the Enumerator mercifully has only the father executed.

Where the supply of food has not increased and the supply of people has, intense emotions can be generated. As Pohl's narrator recounts: ". . . I couldn't help telling him: 'I've met your kind before, mister. Five kids! If it wasn't for people like you we wouldn't *have* any Overs, did you ever think of that? Sure you didn't—you people never think of anything but yourself! Five kids, and then when the Census comes around, you think you can get smart and Jump.' I tell you, I was shaking."

Society devises a third method of dealing with the consequences of a shortage of food and a surplus of people in H. Ken Bulmer's novelette "Sunset," published in the now-deceased Scottish magazine *Nebula Science Fiction* (November 1955). In this world, not too long from now, it is a capital crime to be too ill or old to work. Society simply does not have the surplus of goods to support any person who cannot support himself. Any person who fails to pass the periodic medical checkup required of everyone is given three days' warning by the State so that he may hold and attend his own funeral, at the conclusion of which he is tastefully and painlessly put to death. Those who attempt to evade this law and practice are criminals to be executed by the police on sight and without trial.

Anton Rand, foreman at Interplanetary Shipbuilders and helping the firm to finish a new automatic rocketship for travel to settlements on Mars and Venus, has been brought up under this system and approves of it. "I don't remember the old days. . . . It must have been rather terrible to see cripples and old helpless people on the streets, and to know that somewhere in the world other people were starving for the food those useless mouths were eating. We do things decently today." He approves of the system, that is, until his father fails to pass the routine checkup and is given the customary three days' warning. Rand then turns criminal and plots to smuggle his sick father aboard the new rocket to safety on another world.

Though its writing is generally undistinguished, the story is memorable for its point of view. With grim and realistic honesty, Bulmer points out that Rand is not a hero but a villain. In the future society Bulmer postulates, Rand's attempt to save his sick father from execution is not just a technical crime but a genuinely criminal act, injurious to other human beings and to society in general. In a world so short of food that no one gets more than the bare minimum necessary to survive, the feeding of any extra person means that the amount available for the rest of us must be cut below subsistence level by just that much. Rand's act would today be admirable and moral, not criminal; but in the society of tomorrow that we are fast approaching—a society of too many people and too little food that we with our overproduction of people and our waste of natural resources are even now creating —Rand's act is, unpleasant though the fact may be to a reader of today, both illegal and immoral. Or do you prefer to defend him?

An ingenious new law that not only keeps the population down but solves the problem of the Generation Gap at the same time is shown in operation in William F. Nolan and George Clayton Johnson's novel *Logan's Run* (Dial Press, 1968). In this future world it is a capital crime to be over twenty-one.

A colored flower is indelibly imprinted on the palm of every child at birth. The color automatically changes every five years, and flickers throughout the day preceding one's twenty-first birthday. The citizen must then report promptly to the Deep Sleep factories, where he will be painlessly killed. On his twenty-first birthday the flower turns black, automatically alerting the Sandmen, or Deep Sleep police, that someone has not reported to the factories and is trying to run for his life. The police will then hunt the hated Runner down. Locating him through their many TV spy eyes throughout the city, they will kill him on sight. It is rumored, however, that some Runners have succeeded in escaping the Sandmen, that there is an underground route to safety and to the man rumored to be the oldest human now alive, almost forty years old.

Sandman Logan supports the system, hunting and killing the criminal Runners with ruthless efficiency, until the flower on his own palm begins to flicker. He fails to report to the Deep Sleep factories, telling himself he is doing so only in order to locate and destroy the underground route and die in a blaze of suicidal glory while doing his duty. Logan begins his run from the police, using his thorough knowledge of their own techniques against them.

Logan's run takes him through a world of nightmarish garishness, a world slowly breaking down and incapable of progress, since no one lives long enough to acquire the experience needed to make advances in any area of endeavor. There is time only to perform an insufficient number of repairs on the old machines. From a dying city miles under the sea, from state-owned nurseries where children are brought up entirely by machines, to the giant computer that governs the world though its parts are slowly running down and its lights slowly going out as no one comes to repair it, and to the jungle growing over the ruins of atom-bombed Washington, Logan runs into and from a nightmare world devoted entirely to the young.

Nolan and Johnson do not say that these things will happen, let alone that they ought to happen; the legal and moral problems they raise are kept in the background and implied rather than expressly dealt with. Their primary concern is to write a suspenseful chase story, filled with images of beauty and horror. *Logan's Run* is intense, almost poetic, and hard to forget. But again, whose side are you on?

Charles Beaumont provides an even more nightmarish answer to the population problem in his well-known "The Crooked Man" (*Playboy*, August 1955; *The Hunger and Other Stories*, Putnam, 1957). Here society attempts to control the phenomenon of heterosexual attraction and its resultant overabundance of babies (the story was of course written before the Pill) by structuring its legal and educational system so as to turn its citizens into sexual perverts and making heterosexual relations a crime. Adding to the grim force of this memorable and horrifying tale is the reader's feeling that, in view of what atrocities governments have committed within our lifetime, Beaumont's nightmare vision is far from impossible.

Another method of keeping the population low is adopted by the future society of Philip K. Dick's novelette "Time Pawn" (*Thrilling Wonder Stories*, Summer 1954; later revised and expanded into a novel, *Dr. Futurity*, Ace, 1960). When some strange force hurls young Dr. Parsons from his safe world of 1998 onto a night hillside, one look at the changed shapes of the stars tells him he has been thrown into the far future. But Parsons, an intelligent man, isn't especially worried. He is a trained doctor, his brain full of the race's most advanced medical knowledge, his bag full of the most advanced medical discoveries science has yet made. Surely he will be able to get along wherever he is; every society needs doctors.

Entering a city, he finds a girl dying after a vicious and unprovoked attack by a band of armed, uniformed and apparently government-supported band of juveniles. Parsons confidently goes to work, performing major surgery in a hotel lobby, removing the girl's damaged heart and replacing it with a mechanical one operated by an atomic battery. For a doctor of 1998 this is a routine and almost boring operation; the girl lives—and Parsons is promptly arrested by horrified onlookers. The charges: saving a human life and practicing medicine, both capital crimes. The next morning the girl herself signs the charges against him, then commits suicide.

Society's way of controlling the number of people is to make the teaching and practice of medicine illegal, and to authorize extra-legal killings by armed juvenile gangs. Every male is sterilized at puberty and samples of his gametes are kept in frozen form in sperm banks. The only ones allowed to reproduce are those few who win the world-wide games and tests society has devised to locate superior specimens of humanity. The death of one person automatically authorizes the birth of another from the frozen sperm of the ideal specimens, so that each newborn baby is far superior to the dead person he replaces; a man's death does not diminish mankind but advances and improves it. Naturally, therefore, a doctor, a man whose vocation is to prevent death, is a criminal.

The court mercifully takes cognizance of Parsons' unusual background and sentences him not to death but to life-long exile on Mars. But in every society there are groups that can use the services of a professional criminal. Indeed, it is one such group, armed with an imperfect knowledge of time travel, that brought Parsons to the future in the first place. For reasons of their own, they need a doctor badly; so they rescue Parsons. The plots and counterplots thus set in motion keep Parsons on the run, taking

him far forward in time to a deserted Earth where he finds a giant
stone monolith with his name carved in it; back to the past to see
Sir Francis Drake and his *Golden Hind* stop over in California on
a round-the-world trip; and back to the world he was thrust into,
where he becomes involved with a radical student society that
advocates the open teaching of medicine and is viciously hunted
by the police as a consequence.

Dr. Futurity is a fine fast-moving novel, full of action and
counterplots. It is interesting to note that in the novel one side
wins whereas in the earlier short version "Time Pawn" the other
side comes out on top. You pays your money, you takes your pick.

In our own time we have seen medical science improve to the
point where successful transplants of the heart and other vital
organs have been accomplished. As long as man can replace his
worn-out organs with brand-new ones in fine condition, he may
live virtually forever. In his short novel "The Organ-leggers"
(*Galaxy*, January 1969), Larry Niven points out some unpleasant
legal and social consequences of this new scientific advance.

Since there are many more people with damaged organs
needing to be replaced than there are people with good organs
they are willing to part with, the demand for hearts and limbs and
so on will inevitably exceed the supply. How can the supply be
increased? Niven suggests two ways. One is legal: society restores
the death penalty, applies it to more and more offenses, and finally
imposes it automatically on anyone found guilty of exceeding the
speed limit three times. A surgical team carries out the sentence,
removing the victim's vital organs and quick-freezing them for
storage in organ banks until they are called for. (Doubtless you
believe yourself to be a kindly person, but would you vote to
abolish the death penalty, even for such an offense as speeding, if
it meant that you might lose your chance for centuries of extra
life?)

The second way is illegal. New scientific advances often bring
new crimes with them. Where demand of a commodity exceeds
supply, as in Prohibition, criminal organizations arise to fill that
demand, as in Prohibition. The new criminal, the organ-legger,
supplies hearts, legs, lungs, etc., in brand-new condition to those
who are rich enough to pay his fees and desperate enough not to
care whether those organs were given up willingly and legally.

The protagonist in Niven's story is Gil Hamilton, a member of ARM, which is a branch of the UN Police Force organized expressly to track down this new breed of criminal. For some time Gil has been trying to nail a new group of organ-leggers who somewhere have found a large supply of untraceable victims. When a friend of his dies in a particularly gruesome way, Gil slowly realizes that the man was murdered and that the organ-legger group is involved.

Another problem area with which the law may attempt to deal in the future is the prevention of nuclear war. In John Wyndham's short story "The Wheel" (*Startling Stories*, January 1952), a five-year-old boy commits a capital crime: he rediscovers the wheel. In the wake of an all-out atomic war, the terrified few survivors had outlawed all discovery. They have made science the scapegoat for their own failures, and the wheel the symbol of science. Wyndham's point of course is that it is not knowledge, but what man does with his knowledge, that is good or evil.

Even in the Dark Ages some research went on, though only in narrowly circumscribed areas. In Lewis Padgett's (Henry Kuttner's) "Tomorrow and Tomorrow" (*Astounding Science Fiction*, January–February 1947; *Tomorrow and Tomorrow and The Fairy Chessmen*, Gnome Press, 1951), all scientific research is made illegal. In this future, an appalling third world war has been stopped before it has killed more than a few million people. Riots of unparalleled violence break out, for "When a man is in an ammunition dump that is on fire, he will have less hesitancy in firing a gun." No government survives the riots, and the UN's successor, the Global Peace Commission, takes over control of the world by default. Its solution to the problem of war is to make any scientific advance in any field illegal. Dedicated fanatically to the status quo, it places a murderous stranglehold on human progress for a hundred years. No one starves, no one is fired, but there is no cure for cancer or any other yet-uncured disease, nor will there be as long as that stranglehold exists.

It is not surprising that a criminal group arises that wants to restart World War III and play it through to the finish, believing that full-scale nuclear war is preferable to the slow death by strangulation that the GPC is imposing on the human race. The malcontents feel that the GPC's grip is so strong that only an atomic war can break it. They ask atomic physicist Joseph Breden, monitor of Uranium Pile One, to join them. In addition to deciding whether to join the revolutionaries, Breden has personal problems to wrestle with: lately he has been having bad dreams in which he cuts off all protective devices against sabotage on the pile, pulls out the cadmium control rods and detonates the pile, setting off an atomic explosion that will destroy not only the pile but civilization as well.

Kuttner's story, full of excitement and suspense, poses a problem not only for its protagonist but for the reader as well. Would you prefer a society where perfect safety and security is achieved for you at the price of permanent stagnation and the almost certain death of the whole race centuries later, or a society that achieves constant progress in all areas though it runs a risk of destruction in atomic holocaust?

We have seen that new advances in science may bring new crimes with them. Let us assume that psychology and genetics will have developed so far in a future time that inheritable diseases such as color-blindness, bad eyesight and rheumatic hearts can be bred out of the race entirely if its members will marry only people with the correct genes, and that one can be psychologically treated so that he will fall genuinely in love with another who possesses the proper genes. In such a world it will be a crime to marry anyone whose genes combined with yours will produce a physically or mentally defective child. Do you have the right to marry whom you please, if it can be scientifically proved that the children of that union will be defective? Should you have such a right? And when a characteristic is judged "defective," how do you judge that judgment?

The Population Control Board tells artist Aies Marlan on her twenty-first birthday whom she will marry, so that she and her chosen husband will be certain to produce children without defects. But Aies is in love with Paul, whose genes are not right for her. To escape the psychological conditioning that will destroy her love for Paul and force her to love the man the Board has chosen for her, Aies steals a plane and with Paul beside her attempts "The Escape" in John W. Campbell's short story (*Astounding Science Fiction*, May 1935; in book form, *Cloak of Aesir*, Shasta Press, 1952).

We today would tend to regard Aies and Paul as heroic revolutionaries against a vicious tyranny; but, given the advances in psycholology and genetics that Campbell postulates, the reader must consider the painful question whether they are not in reality a pair of selfish, antisocial immoralists. Behind its excellent writing and action and suspense, the story poses two basic questions. One, how much power should the government have over you? Two, may not the advance of science make the right answer to question one today a wrong answer tomorrow?

A society that has solved all its problems may well be in trouble just as deep as one with too many problems, as the British author S. Fowler Wright suggests in his novel *The Adventure of Wyndham Smith* (London: Jenkins, 1938), in which the protagonists commit the capital crime of failing to commit suicide.

A scientific experiment sends Wyndham Smith into a far distant future where the human race has solved all the problems facing us now. It is a quiet and peaceful world, without war, want or crime. And that is the ironic catch: having solved all problems, the people have nothing left to do, and are bored to death. The governing council decides that the only logical solution to the quandary is mass suicide. The people agree, and happily go off one by one to a painless death in the great suicide chambers; that is, all but Smith, the man from the past, and the beautiful girl he has fallen in love with. They become criminals, evading the mass-suicide law, and thus become the last people alive. But the dead are not fools; they have made provision for the contingency that someone, somewhere, might actually wish to go on living. They have designed and left behind them a deadly mechanical bloodhound, like a small tank, that is set to find any living thing and kill it on sight. Smith and the girl flee for their lives through an abandoned world whose superscientific devices have been permanently turned off, a world sunk in a moment to the level of the stone age.

Wright's grim, slow-moving novel asks: What is the goal of human life; and what happens after that goal is achieved? What can the human race do after all its problems are solved, all its passions spent, the Utopia it claims to want made real at last? Where can you go from the top? The novel is written in a dry, matter-of-fact pedestrian style which would kill most stories but which surprisingly makes this one immensely convincing. Incidentally, Wright used the same concept a little later for his short story "Original Sin," published in England in his collection *The Witchfinder* (Books of Today Ltd., n.d.) and in the United States in *The Throne of Saturn* (Arkham House, 1949). Again two criminals disobey the law of mass suicide. The story has a sting at the end that remains in the mind long after.

Most of the stories dealing with crimes of the future are fast-moving and full of action and suspense. Their authors are writers first, intent on telling a good story well. They do not suggest that the events, laws and solutions in their stories will happen or should happen. They are aware of the many moral, philosophical and legal problems they are raising, but they use these problems to forward the plot and make the story interesting, to provide a background for the action in the foreground. Nevertheless, they do raise the problems. Someday you and I will have to decide these problems, perhaps sooner than we wish to; and the earlier we begin to think about them the more time we will have to consider our decisions. If we are spurred to hard thinking on these topics, we will have derived more than the excitement of a rousing good story from these tales of the shape of crimes to come.

Appendix

THE CRIME BY THE RIVER

EDMUND CRISPIN

(*Conclusion*)

Presently the Chief Constable stirred, saying, "Yes, I'm glad it's over. I don't know that I ever seriously intended to try and bluff it out, but living's a habit you don't break yourself of very easily, and—well, never mind all that." He was trying hard to speak lightly. "By the way, Tom, what did I do—leave my driver's license lying on the scene of the crime?"

The Superintendent spoke carefully. "When I told you that Wregson came over to look you up at two o'clock, you assumed I said *r-o-d-e*—as, in fact, I did—when you ought to have assumed I was saying *r-o-w-e-d*."

The Chief Constable considered. "Yes. Yes, I see. If I'd really left town at lunchtime, I shouldn't have known anything about Wregson's buying a horse. And without a horse he would have sculled across the river— *r-o-w-e-d*—as he always did before. Well, well. Tom, I am not at all sure what the drill is in a situation like this, but I should imagine you'd better get into direct touch with the Home Office."

"There's no case against anyone else, sir." The Superintendent's voice was deliberately expressionless.

"Thanks very much, but no. Now that Vera's dead—"

He grimaced suddenly. "However, I'm too much of a coward to want to hang about waiting for the due processes of law. So, Tom, if you don't mind . . ."

A mile and a half beyond the house the Superintendent stopped his car to light a cigarette. But he never looked back. And even in Wregson's farmhouse, where they were starting their makeshift evening meal, no one heard the shot, no one marked, across the dark stream, the new anonymous shadow under the willow tree.

A LUMP OF SUGAR

ELLERY QUEEN

(Conclusion)

"We ruled out all the reasonable interpretations of sugar," said Ellery, "leaving us where we started—with a lump of sugar in Cooney's clutch as a clue to his killer. Since the fancy stuff is out, suppose we take a lump of sugar in a man's hand to mean just that: a lump of sugar in a man's hand. Why does a man carry a lump of sugar with him?"

"I give up," said the Inspector promptly. "Why?"

"Why?" said Ellery. "Why, to feed it to a horse."

"Feed it to a—" The old gentleman was silent. Then he said, "So that's why you wanted to know their riding history. But Ellery, that theory fizzled. None of the three is what you'd call a horseman, so none of the three would be likely to have a lump of sugar on him."

"Absolutely correct," said Ellery. "So Shakes was indicating a fourth suspect, only I didn't see it then. Cooney was a bookie and a gambler. You'll probably find that this fellow was over his noggin in Cooney's book, couldn't pay off, and took the impulsive way out—"

"Wait, hold it!" howled his father. "*Fourth* suspect? What fourth suspect?"

"Why, the fourth man on the bridle path that morning. And he *would* be likely to carry a lump of sugar for his horse."

"*Mounted Patrolman Wilkins!*"

448

FOR FURTHER READING

Many detectives who figure in a series of works are, of course, not represented in this anthology. The first list below presents some of these characters, along with titles of recommended works in which they appear.

There are also excellent works of mystery, including espionage and detection, that have a hero who appears in no other story. The second list gives several especially readable works of this sort.

A third list supplies a brief bibliography of works about mystery fiction (appreciations, histories, studies).

I. OTHER DETECTIVES

Inspector Roderick Alleyn
> Handsome, upper class, well-educated, quiet but keen, atypical of fictional Scotland Yard men; married to a famous painter

AUTHOR: Ngaio Marsh

TITLES: *Overture to Death, Dead Water, Death in Ecstasy, Death of a Peer, Killer Dolphin*

OBSERVATIONS: The Roderick Alleyn works are consistent in quality, are traditional, often have persuasive details about the theater world, and usually contain interesting characters.

Sir John Appleby
> Well-educated and scholarly Scotland Yard inspector, followed in the series of novels from early in his career through his retirement

AUTHOR: Michael Innes

TITLES: *Death by Water, The Bloody Wood*

OBSERVATIONS: There are many books in the series; they possess a high quality of general style, are often pleasantly bookish, and vary from book to book in strength of plot and construction.

Martin Beck
> An official in the national Swedish police force; a realist (if not a cynic), often bored and further disillusioned by his work and

his colleagues; one of the few widely-selling detectives created by non-English-speaking authors

AUTHORS: Maj Sjowall and Per Wahloo

TITLES: *Murder at the Savoy, The Laughing Policeman, The Fire Engine That Disappeared*

OBSERVATIONS: In these somewhat naturalistic novels, police procedures and investigations of crimes provide a vehicle for quite direct social comment.

Father Brown

Unprepossessing in appearance and deceptively shortsighted, but exasperatedly blunt toward the pretentious and the superstitious.

AUTHOR: G. K. Chesterton

TITLES: "The Oracle of the Dog," "The Invisible Man," "The Miracle of Moon Crescent," "The Secret Garden," "The Dagger with Wings," and many others in five collections of Father Brown stories.

OBSERVATIONS: The Father Brown stories are full of wit and startling things. They bear the mark of a master stylist on every page and a moral in every conclusion.

Albert Campion

British, deceptively fatuous-looking, an aristocrat whose title is not known, said by Jacques Barzun to be heir to the throne of England

AUTHOR: Margery Allingham

TITLES: *The Fashion in Shrouds, The Tiger in the Smoke, Flowers for the Judge,* many short stories (see *Mr. Campion and Others*)

OBSERVATIONS: This is one of the very best series, having a varied and suggestive style that often makes a good use of slang, colorful plots and scenes, and excellent humor.

Kate Fansler

American literature professor in a city university, observant and intelligent, no eccentricities

AUTHOR: Amanda Cross

TITLES: *Poetic Justice, The Theban Murders*

OBSERVATIONS: These novels are well-paced and convincing, with little emphasis on action and violence.

Dr. Gideon Fell

Forceful and impressive in appearance and personality; notable for his large size, his black cape and shovel hat, and his eyeglasses on a ribbon; a student of the history of beer-drinking as well as of criminal behavior; modeled on G. K. Chesterton

AUTHOR: John Dickson Carr

TITLES: *The Mad Hatter Mystery, The Arabian Nights Murder, Hag's Nook, The Case of the Constant Suicides*

OBSERVATIONS: Carr is an imaginative and consistent writer of locked-room mysteries; his plots are outstanding, but the dialogue sometimes seems forced.

Commander George Gideon

Another Scotland Yard man; forceful and energetic, a juggler of many simultaneous investigations; a feeling as well as a thinking man.

AUTHOR: J. J. Marric

TITLES: *Gideon's Fire, Gideon's River, Gideon's Vote*

OBSERVATIONS: Marric's virtues are not those of the poet or scholar, and style is rarely an attraction in his works, but plot and complication and sheer movement are quite good.

Inspector Alan Grant

A Scotsman; in the tradition of the thoughtful, observant, and quietly competent Scotland Yard official

AUTHOR: Josephine Tey

TITLES: *The Daughter of Time* (a classic), *A Shilling for Candles, To Love and Be Wise*

OBSERVATIONS: The novels generally contain apt psychological observations, well-drawn characters, and sound and unusual plot; in *The Daughter of Time* Inspector Grant even investigates from his hospital bed a case nearly 500 years old.

Inspector Hannasyde

Undistinguished by manner or eccentricities, a methodical and observant Scotland Yard sleuth

AUTHOR: Georgette Heyer

TITLES: *A Blunt Instrument, Death in the Stocks*

OBSERVATIONS: In most of the novels there are clever uses of the conventions of the form as well as continuing development and interest throughout the plots; some memorable characters generally loom larger in the books than Hannasyde.

Henry

    A waiter at the dinner meetings of the Black Widowers' club and a solver of the problems brought up at these meetings; an unprejudiced possessor of common sense, but the owner of no specialized knowledge

AUTHOR: Isaac Asimov

TITLES: "The Pointing Finger," "The Obvious Factor," and other stories

OBSERVATIONS: These short stories are well told and neatly concluded, make good uses of supporting characters, and are imaginatively varied in their choice of plot.

Travis Magee

    A Florida adventurer, inhabitant of the houseboat "The Busted Flush"; a helper of clients who have been swindled but who have no grounds for legal action

AUTHOR: John D. MacDonald

TITLES: *The Scarlet Ruse, The Deep Blue Goodbye, A Tan and Sandy Silence*

OBSERVATIONS: John MacDonald examines Florida fauna with a clear-sighted view similar to that with which Ross Macdonald has looked on California inhabitants; the stories are somewhat violent, and the detection is liberally mixed with adventure.

Philip Marlowe

    American private eye in the Hammett tradition, tough but sentimental, a champion of women and an especial foe of the decadent wealthy

AUTHOR: Raymond Chandler

TITLES: *Farewell, My Lovely; The Lady in the Lake; The Little Sister*

OBSERVATIONS: Chandler displays a conscious care in word choice and description, and he produces novels with somewhat episodic plots, a poetic style, and wry observations.

Perry Mason

    A detecting lawyer; moderately tough, occasionally illegal in tactics; an energetic and wisecracking defender of the underdog

AUTHOR: Erle Stanley Gardner

TITLES: *The Case of the Perjured Parrot, The Case of the Negligent Nymph, The Case of the Curious Bride, The Case of the Vagabond Virgin*

OBSERVATIONS: The early books are probably best; in later ones the somewhat rigid formula produces plots that have a great consistency of outline and stereotyped minor characters.

Sir Henry Merrivale

"The Old Man"; a baseball fan and cricket star; corpulent, ebullient, hot-tempered, and outspoken; modeled on Winston Churchill

AUTHOR: Carter Dickson

TITLES: *Nine—and Death Makes Ten, He Wouldn't Kill Patience, The Skeleton in the Clock*

OBSERVATIONS: The Henry Merrivale novels are entertaining and clever and have meticulously constructed plots, but the emotional scenes in mid-story are sometimes strained.

Miss Marian Phipps

A spinster, author, and strictly amateur detective to whom mysteries just happen

AUTHOR: Phyllis Bentley

TITLES: "Miss Phipps and the Siamese Cat," "Miss Phipps Is Too Modest," and other stories

OBSERVATIONS: These stories emphasize pleasant and straightforward narrative with small, curious problems being successfully solved by imaginative but not complicated investigations.

Hercule Poirot

Belgian living in England, retired from police work; user of psychology and mind ("little gray cells") more than leg-work; a lover of symmetry and neatness

AUTHOR: Agatha Christie

TITLES: *Death in the Air, Peril at End House, The Clocks, Mrs. McGinty's Dead, The Murder of Roger Ackroyd* (a classic)

OBSERVATIONS: In all the Agatha Christie novels, the main interest is in plots; in addition there are usually appropriate economy of presentation, the charm of the traditional detective story, and some particularly deft touches of characterization.

Inspector Purbright

Best known for the company he keeps—a foil for other characters, sensible but not inspired

AUTHOR: Colin Watson

TITLES: *Bump in the Night; Coffin, Scarcely Used*

OBSERVATIONS: Watson seems to take special care with two aspects of his novels: the wit, which is frequently fine, and the satire, which is often effective; the crime and its investigations are not often his chief concern.

Rabbi David Small

A slight and frail-appearing New England rabbi; a highly intellectual scholar, possessor of few illusions about human nature

AUTHOR: Harry Kemelman

TITLES: *Friday the Rabbi Slept Late, Saturday the Rabbi Went Hungry*

OBSERVATIONS: In these novels the interest in the politics of a synagogue congregation and aspects of Jewish custom and thought are effectively balanced by logical analyses of seemingly ordinary crimes that the police have not yet solved.

George Smiley

A scholar-spy-detective, described by his one-time wife's friend as "a toad in a sou'wester," a fine reflector of the pain and horror produced by the cold world of Le Carré's creation

AUTHOR: John Le Carré

TITLES: *Call for the Dead, A Murder of Quality*

OBSERVATIONS: These two titles may suit the general reader of mysteries more than Le Carré's *The Spy Who Came in from the Cold*, though Le Carré sees the world in them, too, from the view of the cynical critic; there are very fine movement and plot development and some good characterization in each novel.

Sam Spade

American private detective, hard and competent, very much a loner, described as a "blond Satan"

AUTHOR: Dashiell Hammett

TITLES: *The Maltese Falcon* (a classic)

OBSERVATIONS: A fascinating and carefully crafted work, this novel shows the main qualities of the hardboiled school of writers but also retains some important features of the traditional detective story.

Nigel Strangeways

Convincingly literary, "modern" or advanced in many of his

views, not consciously eccentric, partly modeled on W. H. Auden

AUTHOR: Nicholas Blake (C. Day-Lewis)

TITLES: *End of Chapter, The Beast Must Die, Malice in Wonderland*

OBSERVATIONS: These novels are allusive and literate, though the plots are only good (not great). The novels succeed because of Strangeways and the sensitive and thought-provoking treatment of the investigation.

Inspector Henry Tibbett

Seemingly just a competent and intelligent Scotland Yard man, but also highly adaptable, versatile, and sometimes even emotionally vulnerable

AUTHOR: Patricia Moyes

TITLES: *Death on the Agenda, Down Among the Dead Men, Murder Fantastical*

OBSERVATIONS: Tibbett's wife and marriage add interest to some novels, since many of the Inspector's cases come up while he is vacationing. *Murder Fantastical* is detective-story humor at its most exuberant; the characters, much more than stock eccentrics, are irresistible.

Philip Trent

Painter-journalist who reports on and investigates certain cases for a newspaper

AUTHOR: E. C. Bentley

TITLES: *Trent's Last Case* (a classic), *Trent's Own Case*

OBSERVATIONS: *Trent's Last Case* seems only slightly dated despite its age (1912); like Wilkie Collins' *The Moonstone*, it is a fascinating story of detection and love.

Nero Wolfe

Most appropriately named, a great tun of a man who raises orchids, reads, and plans elaborate and exotic feasts; legwork done by Archie Goodwin, who always has a wisecrack and an observant and critical eye for women.

AUTHOR: Rex Stout

TITLES: *Some Buried Caesar, Too Many Cooks, The Doorbell Rang, The Golden Spiders, The Mother Hunt*

OBSERVATIONS: Stout is steadily interesting; the plots are usually resolved in a gathering of suspects in Wolfe's study; and there is always a fine stock of witticism from the irascible Wolfe.

II. OTHER MYSTERIES

Mostly Murder by Frederick Brown (stories)
The Thirty-Nine Steps by John Buchan
Death Comes as the End by Agatha Christie
The Moonstone by Wilkie Collins
Rebecca and *My Cousin Rachel* by Daphne Du Maurier
The Blessington Method by Stanley Ellin
The Turn of the Screw by Henry James
Above Suspicion, The Venetian Affair, and other works by Helen
    MacInnes
The Red House Mystery by A. A. Milne
Frankenstein by Mary Shelley

III. STUDIES AND APPRECIATIONS OF MYSTERY FICTION

The Annotated Sherlock Holmes by W. S. Baring-Gould
    This two-volume work is a good source for a great deal of
    information, supposition, and comment. It is a must for the
    Holmes follower.

Nero Wolfe of West Thirty-Fifth Street by W. S. Baring-Gould
    This work will be of particular interest to the fan of Rex Stout.
    It constitutes a summary of what such a reader will have
    observed, but perhaps forgotten, about Wolfe's cases, eccentri-
    cities, and pithy comments.

A *Catalogue of Crime* by Jacques Barzun and Wendell Hertig
    Taylor
    Barzun and Taylor prefer the traditional detective story, and
    there is little about other types of mystery in this useful
    catalogue. However one might disagree with the orientation
    toward a particular type of detective story or with various
    comments made by the authors, the book, as a list of works, is
    invaluable.

Who Done It? by Ordean Hagen
    This "guide to detective, mystery, and suspense fiction" is
    useful as a catalogue of titles, but there are few notes. The list
    of awards winners in the field and the lists of movie versions of
    works of mystery fiction may be helpful.

The Art of the Mystery Story edited by Howard Haycraft
> This vast collection of essays, published in 1946, is the great classic in the field, and it remains unsurpassed in its area of coverage.

Murder for Pleasure by Howard Haycraft
> This is a good-natured, light, and appreciative study, notable for its tolerant and affectionate observations. It contains much useful information on the development of the detective story up to 1941.

The Armchair Detective edited by Allen J. Hubin (a quarterly journal)
> This journal is "devoted to the appreciation of mystery, detective and suspense fiction" and is full of interesting information, much of it bibliographic.

The Mystery Writer's Art edited by Francis M. Nevins
> This is a collection of essays on writers from Poe to Ross Macdonald, many of which explore provocative topics and all of which are quite readable.

In the Queens' Parlor by Ellery Queen
> In this work are collected fascinating anecdotes and comments from the most indefatigable worker in promoting detective fiction in the United States and one of the country's most successful and consistent writers of detective fiction.

Agatha Christie, Mistress of Mystery by G. C. Ramsey
> This work is mostly an appreciation, but it is a good survey and summary with useful lists of works, alternate titles, and dates.

The Puritan Pleasures of the Detective Story by Erik Routley
> This is a well-written book that has an interesting thesis and many sound observations concerning things read in a "misspent middle age."

Mortal Consequences, A History from the Detective Story to the Crime Novel by Julian Symons
> Despite some dubious assessments, this is the best history and

general study of detective and crime fiction. Mr. Symons is very widely read in the area of his study, skillful in his generalizations, and articulate in his presentation. In addition, and equally important, he is genuinely interested in crime fiction and is himself a successful writer of it.

"Detective Fiction," a special number of the (London) *Times Literary Supplement* (February 25, 1955)

Several of these articles are especially good, and even the advertisements contribute to an understanding of the state of detective fiction twenty years ago.